DO THEY KNOW I'M RUNNING?

ALSO BY DAVID CORBETT

BLOOD OF PARADISE

DONE FOR A DIME

THE DEVIL'S REDHEAD

DO THEY KNOW I'M RUNNING?

A NOVEL

DAVID CORBETT

BALLANTINE BOOKS NEW YORK

Do They Know I'm Running is a work of fiction. Names, characters, places, and incidents are the products of the author's imagination or are used fictitiously. Any resemblance to actual events, locales, or persons, living or dead, is entirely coincidental.

A Ballantine Books Trade Paperback Original

Published in the United States by Ballantine Books, an imprint of The Random House Publishing Group, a division of Random House, Inc., New York.

BALLANTINE and colophon are registered trademarks of Random House, Inc.
MORTALIS and colophon are trademarks of Random House, Inc.

Library of Congress Cataloging-in-Publication Data

Corbett, David
Do they know I'm running? : a novel / David Corbett.
p. cm.
ISBN 978-0-8129-7755-4 (pbk.)
eBook ISBN 978-0-345-51515-5
1. Salvadorans—United States—Fiction. 2. Immigrants—Fiction.
3. Human trafficking—Fiction. 4. Border crossing—Fiction. I. Title.
PS3603.O732D6 2010
813'.6—dc22 2009043930

Printed in the United States of America

www.mortalis-books.com

2 4 6 8 9 7 5 3

Design by R. Bull

For Ms. TumbleMutt DishFish

Sin ti

No hay clemencia en mi dolor

AUTHOR'S NOTE

The characters within these pages are entirely the product of the author's imagination and should not be confused with real individuals living or dead. Although many of the locales depicted in this book exist, some—such as Rio Mirada and San Pedro Lempa—are the author's inventions. Even existing cities and places have been changed and shaped to suit various dramatic purposes, and thus the narrative should be seen as taking place entirely within a fictive world.

Being a man doesn't mean not being a child anymore
but beginning to be a criminal.

—Carlos Fuentes, "The Mariachi's Mother"

Will they see me coming?
Do they know I'm running?

—Los Lobos, "The Road to Gila Bend"

DO THEY KNOW I'M RUNNING?

IT WAS DAYBREAK AND THE RANCHER, STANDING AT HIS KITCHEN window, watched two silhouettes stagger forward through the desert scrub. One clutched the other but they both seemed hurt. The porch light, the rancher thought, that's the thing they been walking toward all night. See it for miles. All the way from the footpaths snaking through the mountains out of Mexico.

Rooster lurched at the end of his chain, hackles up, that snarl in his bark, trying to warn the strangers off. They just kept coming. All right then, he thought. Not like you wanted this. He set his coffee in the sink and went to the door leading out to the porch and collected the shotgun kept there, racked a shell into the chamber, stepped outside.

Streamers of winter cloud laced the sky, pale to the east, purplish dark to the west. A cold parched wind keened in the telephone wires. The landscape bristled with nopal, saguaro, cholla. Black ancient ironwood cropped up here and there among the mesquite and Joshua trees.

Before he could close the door behind him, his wife called his name. She eased forward unsteadily out of the hallway shadow, robe cinched tight. The gaunt face, once framed with steel-gray hair pulled back and braided into a rope, now seemed all the more stark with her pallor and the stubbled baldness. The treatments were savaging her bone marrow too. He wondered sometimes whether the cure wasn't worse than the disease—wondered as well whether he'd be anywhere near as brave when his time came.

Where does the promise go when it leaves you, he wondered. He wished the years had made them calm and strong and wise, but here they were, her sick, him afraid, trying to protect each other—their stake owned free and clear but now little more than a borderland throughway, shadows scurrying past the house at night, sometimes trying the door, shattering a window, hoping for shelter or water or food. Same problem everywhere: the Stanhope girl—raped last spring. Old woman Hobbes—robbed at knifepoint, truck stolen, the fridge ransacked and the house turned upside down for cash before the culprits scurried off, leaving her tied up in her garage. Enough, everybody said. Things're only getting worse across the border. We'll form patrols. We'll make an example out of every goddamn tonk we catch.

But there's more to "enough" than the saying of it, too much terrain to patrol and too many who still slip through to make an example mean anything. Ask the two lurching forward. The promise hadn't left them just yet. It was as simple as a steady light glowing at the foot of a mountain pass with the black desert floor beyond. He felt the pump gun's weight in his hands, a commensurate weight on his soul. It was that second burden that haunted him.

"They don't look too good," she told him, feeling her way forward, hand to the wall.

He met her eyes. "They do that sometimes."

"Is that how we think now?"

"Not because we want to. Remember that part."

He turned away and marched across the porch onto the hardpan, telling the dog to be still. The two figures—the one being dragged, on closer inspection, appeared to be female—staggered past a line of cholla with their huge bulbs of barbed spikes. God only knows what they suffered in the night, he thought: sidewinders, rattlers, scorpions. Thieves. But pity won't help. Pity's the problem.

As they came within twenty yards he saw it, stuffed into the man's pants. A pistol. It happened of its own accord then—shotgun raised, tight to the shoulder, barrel aimed straight at the armed man's midriff.

"*¡Alto! Tengo una escopeta. Esta es propiedad privada*."

It was half the Spanish he knew—Stop, I have a shotgun. This is private property—but he might as well have shouted it to the wind. The man just kept coming, one of the woman's arms hooked across his shoulder. The other hung limp at her side. Her steps were ragged, she looked barely conscious. The rancher felt his finger coil tight around the trigger.

"I said stop! *Alto*, damn it. Won't say it again. Next thing I do is shoot."

As though rousted from a terrible dream, the stranger glanced up, still shuffling his feet, dragging the woman.

From behind: "He's barely more than a boy."

"Stay in the house!" The guilt and fear, knowing she was right—knowing too that he was all that stood between them and her—it quickened into rage and the impulse quivered down his arm into his hand.

Then the young half-dead stranger with the pistol called out in a dust-dry voice, his words a challenge and a plea and a cry of recognition all in one. "Don't shoot! Help us . . . please . . . I'm an American . . ."

The rancher tucked the gun butt tighter into the clenched muscle and aching bone of his shoulder. Don't believe him, he told himself. Don't believe one damn word.

PART I

(THREE MONTHS EARLIER)

ONE

ROQUE SAT UP IN THE PREDAWN STILLNESS, STARTLED AWAKE BY a wicked dream: menacing dog, desolate twilight, the sticky dampness of blood and a sense he was carrying some kind of treasure, something he'd have to fight to keep. Rising on one elbow, he glanced past Mariko toward the bedside clock. Three-thirty, the hour of ghosts. Rubbing the sleep from his eyes, he told himself it was time to go.

Gently, he tugged the sheet from her sleep-warm shoulder. She'd want to be wakened before he gathered his clothes and slipped out. "This kind of thing isn't known for its shelf life," she'd told him once. "I want to make the most of my chances."

Twenty years separated them—practically a crime, given he was eighteen. He realized there were probably clinical terms to explain the thing, especially since he was motherless. In his own heart, though, it felt simple—they both were lonely, he liked her a lot, she seemed to like him back and he enjoyed getting his ashes hauled, an inclination she happily, at times rabidly indulged. The sex was always instructive, seldom routine, often kinky, especially once she cracked open that second bottle of wine. If any of that's a problem, he thought, let somebody else worry about it. Every important connection he'd ever had was with someone older than he was—musicians, librarians, a cop here and there—why should this be any different?

She had her back to him, sleeping on her side, pillow balled tight beneath her chin as she snored. The dim glow of the clock reddened her shoulder, and he traced the back of his fingers across her arm, caressed her hip, the skin tight and smooth, then guided his thumb along the little trough of muscle in the small of her back, moving on from there to cup one plump cheek of her *culo* with his palm. She stirred finally, burrowing her face into the pillow to stifle a yawn. Lifting her head, she whispered over her shoulder, eyes glistening with sleep: "It's you."

He took a moment to study her profile in the dim light, the distinctive shape of her eye, the girlish lashes, the pudgy nose. "You were expecting . . . ?"

She blinked herself awake, moaned and barked a raspy cough into her fist. "Hope springs eternal."

Roque waited. "Oh yeah?"

"Tell you what—do me a favor, before you go?" She wiggled her can.

The musk from their earlier lovemaking still lingered, mixed with the vaguely floral tang of cold wax from a dozen tea candles scattered across the hardwood floor, their flames spent. "Just go back to sleep," he said, recalling the scene from earlier, tiny tongues of fire all around as they thrashed and rocked and cried out, shadows quivering high up the bare white walls. Mariko, a Buddhist, had a flair for the ceremonial.

"No, I mean it." Her voice was fogged with drowsiness and she writhed luxuriously in a kind of half stretch, burying another yawn in the pillow. "It's okay."

"It feels, I dunno, wrong. You half asleep, I mean."

"For God's sake, Roque, it's all *wrong*. That's what makes it so delicious."

Sure, of course, that's what this is. Wrong. He shook it off. "You know what I'm saying."

She flipped over, finger-parting the tousled black hair framing her boxy face. "There. Awake. Better?"

"Don't be mad."

"Who says I'm mad?"

"I just—"

"Shush. Kiss me."

He leaned down, instantly hard at the touch of her mouth, even with her breath sour and hot from the wine. It scared him sometimes, the intensity, the need. She wasn't what any of the guys he knew would call a *cosota linda*, a looker, and with that a song lyric ghosted up:

So make your mark for your friends to see
But when you need more than company . . .

They'd met back in May during Carnaval, San Francisco's biggest Latino celebration outside El Día de los Muertos, with samba dancers shimmying through the Mission in feathered headdresses and Bahía skirts while drum brigades hammered out a nonstop *batucada*. Bands of all kinds and every level of smack played hour-long sets throughout the weekend: *ranchera*, *salsa*, *bachata*, *calypso*, *charanga*, *cumbia*, *reggaetón*. It was Roque's maiden gig with Los Patojos, a salsa-funk outfit in the Azteca/Malo/Santana mold but with a jazzier edge, and when Lalo called him onto the stage near the end of the set he introduced him as "The best young guitarist I've heard in a long, long time—Roque Montalvo!" They ran through three numbers to wrap up the hour, a reggae-inflected tune-up of Tito Puente's "Mambo Gallego," a *timba* reworking of War's "Ballero," and the finale, a double-time *cumbia* vamp on an old Byrds tune:

Don't forget what you are
You're a rock 'n' roll star

"Hey!" Her rough hands locked at his nape and she tugged at his shoulder-length hair. "Where'd you go?"

He shook off the memory, busted. "Sorry, I—"

"You'll make an old lady self-conscious."

"Don't talk like that."

"Oh please."

"I mean it. Really—"

She cut him off with another kiss, lingering, a nibble here and there, a swipe with her tongue. Refocused, he reached down, probed gently with his fingers, parting the feathery lips to get at the warmth inside, already moist. She moaned, a deep soft purr from the back of her throat, encouraging him, guiding him. He'd been such a wack lover when they'd met, all the usual young slob faults—the selfishness, the fumbling, the rush. Except for two girls he'd met at gigs, his pre-Mariko love life had been limited to pumping the muscle and wishful thinking, and the two exceptions had been disasters of opposite kind, the one girl just lying there in sweet-natured panic, the other thrashing around in such unconvincing bliss he'd almost stopped mid-fuck to ask if she was having a seizure. Mariko had taught him to relax, focus, think of it as dancing. Not the best analogy, perhaps, musicians being such clueless dancers, but he'd come around.

She said, "I want you inside."

"So quick?"

"I didn't say quick. I said inside."

She guided him in. As always, he shuddered—so perfect, that feeling, like finding home.

"Just that," she whispered. "Don't move. Okay?"

She hooked her legs around his, locking their bodies tight, nuzzling her hips against his before returning to her kisses, deeper now. Another moan, this one longer, rose in the pit of her throat, followed by a tremor quivering up her spine.

Despite himself, Roque's eye strayed toward the bedside clock. Three forty-five now. Soon Tío Faustino would be out of bed, getting ready to leave for the Port of Oakland where he worked hauling drayage. Tía Lucha would be preparing breakfast and getting ready for her shift at Food 4 Less. Godo would be stirring too, if he'd slept at all.

Drawing back his glance, his eyes met hers. She broke off the kiss, unwrapped her legs. "I know you have to go."

"It's just, you know—"

She cupped his face in her palm. "It's all right."

Godo was his half brother, back from the war. He spent his nights lurching around in bed, popping painkillers and antidepressants, chasing them with beer, unable to muster more than a few minutes' sleep at a time. Better the insomnia, though, than the nightmares. It was why Roque couldn't share the room anymore. No telling who or what Godo might mistake him for when he bolted awake, screaming.

"Sorry," he said, thinking: You're saying that a lot.

"Don't be." She brushed his face with her fingers. "It's been lovely. It always is, Rocky."

It was one way she teased him, mispronouncing his name.

"Roque," he corrected, his part of the bit. "Rhymes with O.J."

"Yes. How sad for you."

He lowered his head, touched his brow to hers. "I love you."

She turned her face away. "I told you—"

"I mean it."

"What difference does it make what you *mean*?" Like that, the mood turned, as it did on occasion. Too often, actually, and more and more of late. "How many times—"

"Fine. Okay."

He pulled away and gathered his clothes from the floor, threw on his sweatshirt, stood up to tug on his jeans, sat back down to lace his high-tops. You're acting your age, he thought, unable to stop himself, at the same time wondering if he really did mean it: I love you. Maybe he was just raising the stakes, he wasn't sure.

To his back, a whisper: "Roque?"

He wanted her to reach out, touch him, say it: I love you too.

Or just: I'm sorry. But neither the caress nor the words came. He launched up and crossed the room, kicking several tea candles across the floor like little tin pucks.

Wood-plank shelves faced each other down the dark hallway, stacked with unfired pots, bowls, vases: Mariko Detwiler, Fine Ceramics. The clay smelled cold and damp and it made him think of fresh graves and with that another song lyric teased its way up from memory: *The house is dark and my thoughts are cold.*

He thumped down the porch steps, the fog cool on his skin, the air dank from the nearby wetlands. Lingering beneath the chinaberry tree in the dark front yard, he watched as the hall light came on and her silhouette materialized in the doorway. Timidly he ventured a farewell wave. She did not wave back.

CINCHING THE HOOD OF HIS SWEATSHIRT TIGHT, HE BEGAN TO RUN. Craftsman bungalows lined the block, some tricked out like minor museums, others sagging with neglect. At the bottom of the hill he skirted a thicket of blood-red madrone and turned onto the river road where he had the gravel berm to himself, dodging waist-high thistle. The solitude gave him space to think.

He knew what the *chambrosos* would say, it was all because he was an orphan—the sloppy lust for cougar poon, the pissy sulk upon leaving, even the musical gunslinger ego bit to soothe his pride. And sure, from as early as he could remember he'd sensed an absence at the center of things. Her name was Graciela, she came to the States a Salvadoran refugee, pregnant with her first child, a boy. Three years later she was dead, a massive hemorrhage within hours of delivering her second son. And so there they were, Godofredo and Roque, two American brothers, a toddler and an infant—different fathers, both absent; same mother, now dead.

They got taken in by their spinster aunt, Lucha, also a refugee. Roque knew zip about his old man and what he knew of his mother came from a handful of faded snapshots and Tía Lucha's tales, not all of them kind. He came to think of his mother the way some people regard an obscure and troubling saint. *Mi madre descabellada*, the unholy martyr.

As for Godo, he'd never forgotten what it was like: three years old, slow to English, wary of strangers, possessive of his mother who one day went to the hospital and never came back—and for what? Some little shit weasel of a brother.

THE SIGN AT THE STREET READ "HUNTINGTON VILLAGE," THOUGH NO one could tell you who Huntington was: a trailer park, home to several dozen Salvadoran families, as well as Hondurans, Guatemaltecos, the inescapable Mexicans, even a few Pacific Islanders. The streets were gravel and the shade sparse, no laundry hut, no playground, no management on the premises. Here and there, a brave patch of grass. He lived in a single-wide with Godo and Tía Lucha and Tío Faustino, his aunt's *marido*. She was no longer a spinster.

It was temporary, their living here, so Tía said, just until she and Tío Faustino could reestablish some credit. It wasn't really their fault, of course, losing the house—a crooked mortgage broker, a Mexican no less, had slipped an extra loan into escrow, more than a hundred Latino victims in the scam. It would take years and lawyers and more money thrown to the wind before any of that resolved. Meanwhile they lived as best they could, crammed into six hundred square feet, Tía and Tío, Roque and Godo.

Passing the gravel bed near the gate that served as parking, Roque noticed that Tío Faustino's rig was gone. That meant it was already four—Tío had left for the Port of Oakland, to get in the queue for container pickup. Roque redoubled his pace until he could make out the random tinny carillon of Tía Lucha's wind chime swinging from the doorstep awning.

Pulling up outside the trailer, he tugged his key from his jean pocket and slipped it in the lock, opening the door as quietly as he could, only to find his aunt waiting in the kitchenette, sitting at the table in her plaid robe, sipping Nescafé.

"You're up already," he said clumsily.

She responded using Spanish, peering over the edge of her cup.—*Is it your turn to be the problem around here?* Her eyes were sad and proud and blasted from exhaustion, her hair lying tangled across her birdlike shoulders. Her face was narrow and dark, weathered, an *indígena* face; shortly she would slather on pancake to lighten its complexion in preparation for a day at the cash register.

Roque went to the fridge, saw a can of guava nectar and another of 7UP, his weakness, picked the latter and popped the lid, all to avoid an answer.

—*I don't expect you to be a virgin. Your mother named you for a poet, it's your privilege to act like an idiot. You're using protection, yes? Please tell me that much.*

"It's not your problem," he replied in English, a way to assert his distance. It was one of those ironies, how the older ones praised the new country but stuck to the old country's tongue.

—*Not today, but when the baby arrives and you have no clue if it's really yours?*

"It's not an issue, okay?"

She cocked her head, studying him.—*You're telling me she's a boy?*

He rolled his eyes, put down his can and ambled over to the table. Agony aunt, he thought. He'd read the phrase in a book recently and thought instantly of Tía Lucha. Leaning down, he kissed her graying black hair, the texture of stitching thread, a smell like almonds, some dollar-a-bottle shampoo.

He switched to Spanish.—*We'll pretend you never said that.*

On the shelf behind her, Salvadoran *sorpresas*, little clay tableaus made in Ilobasco, shared space with skeletal Day of the

Dead figurines. He'd often celebrated El Día de los Muertos with her, it was why he'd never felt singled out for misery despite his mother's death. He learned not to take it personally. Sorrow was inescapable, a condition, not a punishment.

—We'll pretend because it's not true, or because you're ashamed?

—Don't make me angry, Tía.

—So it's a girl.

—A woman.

—And she's not pregnant.

—She can't get pregnant.

Tía Lucha studied him like he was suggesting something impossible, or infernal.*—She told you that?*

—Can we change the subject?

—Oh Roque, don't be a fool, women lie, especially about that.

—Tía . . .

—And then they come and tell you, "I can't believe it, it's a miracle, a blessing from God." How old is this woman?

Roque turned to head back toward his brother's bedroom. *—I'll check in on Godo.*

She closed her eyes and rubbed the lids.*—Don't wake him, please.*

Acidly, Roque thought: Godo asleep? Now that would be a miracle.

He sometimes wondered if being parentless wasn't a blessing in disguise. It gave him a kind of freedom from the usual attachments that seemed to hold others back. Life would be more fluid for him because love and desire and ambition would be a question of choice, not obligation. And yet, if that were true, how would he keep from merely drifting? Wasn't that what love and respect were about, providing gravity? Otherwise there was just loneliness.

The oven door stood slightly ajar; an aromatic warmth greeted him as he bent down to peer inside. Two plates covered with napkins rested on the middle rack.

—*One of these for me?*

—*You know it is*.

Using a dish towel, he pulled out one plate. Beneath the napkin, he found his breakfast: pureed black beans with cream, fried plantains and yucca, corn tortillas.

He joined her at the table with his plate, wondering how angry she would get if he added some peanut butter. He'd been known to plow through an entire jar in a single sitting, until she told him that if he didn't stop he'd end up in emergency with a bowel blockage. Even as he stole a glance at the open oven door, secretly craving the other plate, Godo's share, he pictured the jar of crunchy in the fridge. He was ravenous. Sex did that to him.

Tía Lucha glanced back toward the bedrooms to the rear. —*Your brother. No matter what I do, no matter what I say . . .* Hand to her mouth, eyes spent.—*Nothing gets better. Another miserable night*.

Not glancing up from his plate, Roque said:—*Don't worry, Tía. I'll take care of it from here*.

TWO

WHAT THE WHOLE THING GETS DOWN TO, GODO THOUGHT, HEAD tilted back, draining the last few drips from the can—the trick to it, as it were, the pissy little secret no one wants you to know? He crushed the empty and tossed it onto the floor where it clattered among the others, then belched, backhanding his scarred lips to wipe them dry. Figure it out, *cabrón*: The whole thing gets down to knowing which guilt you can live with.

He sat propped on pillows in the mangled bed, his altar to insomnia, the bedside lamp still burning. Soon daybreak would smear the curtains with its buttery gray light. He shuddered. Strange, fearing the night, lying awake with the room all lit up like you're some sniveling bed wetter, only to dread the dawn.

Across the room the rabbit-eared TV flickered. Nothing to watch at this hour, of course, just news any idiot could see through, no-name reruns. He'd squelched the sound, only to conjure not silence but the usual holocaust zoo tramping through his brain.

Focus on the physical, he reminded himself—the moment, as they say. The doughy mattress sighed beneath his weight. Armpit stench and foot funk added a manly tang. The rest of him was a wreck. He'd been hard and sleek after basic, plenty of PT, then hulking around the scalding desert with seventy pounds of gear, buffed and brutal. Now? A hundred and eighty pounds of discharge, a mess in the bed, a hash of scars weepy with some nagging infection.

As for his face, well. It was all still there, basically, and that was no small matter. He'd met another jarhead in the ward at Landstuhl who'd been trapped in a burning truck, an IED attack, all the flesh of his face melting from the heat. The doctors tried to put something back but there's only so much magic in the bag. The guy came away hairless, beardless, his face a kind of mask—no chin, no ears, no nose—his remolded skin this mottled waxy pink. Sent home like that to Parkersburg and his hillbilly bride-to-be.

So, Godo thought, things could be worse. Nice mantra. Next time you're in the moment.

He licked his rough lips, already parched again, but resisted the urge for another brew. Two six-packs down, plus Percocet for the pain, a Lexapro chaser for the depression, erythromycin for the nagging infection in his leg—so it went, every night, flirting with sleep, chasing off the sickness, the ghosts.

He'd made it through the night okay, though. Mostly. Nothing too stark, thank God. Just the Al Gharraf firefight in scattershot flashback, strobing through memory, blending with Diwaniyah, Fallujah . . . The jittery images stitched back around through memory on endless rewind—the crippling light of an RPG, deafening chaos, tracers vanishing into shadow, the shadows firing back, and the staggering upchuck stench of blood and shit everywhere, men he knew. Himself.

He pinched the bridge of his nose until polarized geometries flared and whirled on the backs of his eyelids, then his hand moved on, gently fingering the pitted scars on his face. Little ugly cousins to the ones on his legs, his arms, dozens of them, jagged red clots of seared flesh. Shrapnel so hot it cauterized its own scalding wounds. Not Al Gharraf or Diwaniyah or Fallujah. That other thing. But don't go there. You held it at bay all night, don't give in now. Be strong. Down that rathole lies the guilt. And, you know, screw that.

A tear threaded down his cheek. He made no move to wipe it

away, preferring to pretend it wasn't there. Instead, he reached up and gripped his head, as though to keep it whole. An invisible hatchet cleaved his skull and he fought back a scream, begging for time to pass, so he could take another Perc, the pain a banshee inside his skull. Breathe, he told himself. Pain is just there to betray you. Pain is illusion.

Time passed . . . two minutes . . . five . . . Gradually the banshee's wail subsided, leaving a backwash of dread and leaden numbness. But that was okay. That was pretty good, actually.

He dropped his hands from his head and rose onto one elbow to liberate a hissing fart, then the next thing he knew a dog appeared in his mind's eye, scavenging at dawn. Christ no, he thought, why now? He noticed it then—first light, the curtains—and everything coalesced. There they were, his squaddies, geared up in full battle-rattle, high on Rip It or ephedra or coffee crystals swallowed dry, Chavous in the Humvee turret manning the Mark 19, the rest lugging their M16s, throwing down the checkpoint . . . a crunching hardpack underfoot, the sky a whirl of grit, ominous flares of dawnlight in the east . . . the family of four, dad in his rumpled suit, mom in her *hijāb*, the bug-eyed boy, the swaddled infant, crammed into their rust-bucket Cressida with the single headlight . . . the horn-honking American *pistoleros* in their black Chevy Blazer, drunk on their own swagger behind the tinted glass . . . a shouting match with the Blazer's driver, a dare, Godo's big macho fuckup . . . the emaciated dog, arch-backed and trembling, lingering in the corner of his eye . . . noticed too late, the *haji* in the full-length *abaya*, garb of a woman, walk of a man, strolling up to the checkpoint . . . Godo preoccupied, Gunnery Sergeant Benedict stepping forward to cut off the cross-dressing *haji* . . . then the sheering blast of scalding light, ripping good Gunny Benedict into blood and wind.

Cutting the world in two, before and after.

His hand lurched toward the nightstand, reaching for the pill bottle, but he caught himself, drew back the hand. No. No more Perc, not yet. Not that kind of pain. Unless you down them all.

Better yet, a weapon. He had a Beretta 9mm in the drawer, two loaded clips, a .357 Smithy with speed loaders under the bed, keeping company with a Remington pump. Name one man who returned from war, he thought, and didn't weapon up, if only to cut short the weirdness.

He closed his eyes. In time the dread and self-pity drifted back into the toxic beery Percocet fog. He forgot what he'd been thinking.

A timid knock at the door. "Godo?"

Roque peered in. His eyes were bloodshot, his cheeks flushed. He'd run home from somewhere. The big mystery—where?

Roque said, "You awake?"

"Take a wild guess."

Roque ventured in, profile dappled with color as he snuck a glance at the TV. Godo had to admit it stung, knowing his hotshot musician faggot little brother wouldn't share the room anymore. Neither of them could be quite sure what might happen when Godo shot up in bed in a howling sweat. But Roque wasn't camped out on the front-room couch, either. He was sneaking out at night, getting some action, some poon, some *pashpa*. It was one more thing to hate him for—they were brothers, after all.

"It's time to check your leg." Roque turned away from the TV. "The dressing, I mean."

"It's fine."

"You always say that."

Godo cocked a smile, clasping his hands behind his head. "Really? Hey, here's a thought." He belched.

"When's the last time you looked?"

"Oh, blow me."

Somewhere outside a car door slammed. A dog started to bark. Like that, the thing materialized in the corner of his eye again: starving, child-eyed, razor thin, slinking in the rubble, waiting for a corpse to feed on. Benedict's corpse, what was left of it.

Roque pointed to the leg. "You want to go back to the ER?"

Godo snapped to. "What?"

"You want to go back to the ER, have them drain off another six ounces of pus?"

"I want six ounces of pus, I'll drain your dick. Where you sleeping these nights?"

Roque blushed. Godo wagged a knowing finger.

"Roquito's got himself a *mamasota*."

"Shut up."

"Got himself a scraggle, a gack. A little *bicha*."

Outside, another car door slammed. The dog's barking grew more crazed. Godo felt a prickling of sweat on his neck. Hard to explain to people, this thing he had with dogs now.

"Godo, please, I need—"

"*Que vergón, cabroncito*."

"I need to check the dressing on your leg."

"Come on, humor me—who's the lucky squirrel?"

For the merest second, a defiant gleam enlivened Roque's eyes. He was pissed. Here it comes, Godo thought. Gonna tell me how hot his *mamita* is, maybe even spit out her name. But before that could happen Roque's expression regained its put-upon blankness.

"I'm not playing, Godo, you always—"

"Hey, *hembrito*, I'm not playing neither. Gotta make sure you're taking the proper precautions. Like, you know, you putting one bag or two over her head before you fuck her?"

The kid flinched like recoil from a slap and Godo almost dared him: Come on. Say it. Have some balls and *say it*. But by degrees the hate drained from Roque's eyes, replaced by a sad superiority. Go ahead and mock, he seemed to be saying. Then look at yourself, check out your face. From now until the day you die, the best you can hope for is a pity fuck. Even if you pay for it.

Suddenly, from the front of the trailer, the muffled crash of shattered glass. Tía Lucha screamed. Roque froze.

Godo scrambled to the edge of the bed, reached underneath, pulled out the Remington pump-loader, weapon of choice for close quarters, and chambered a round of nine-pellet buckshot. He rose to his feet, swaying.

Outside, the dog fell silent.

Roque reached out his hand, whispered, "Godo, wait, let me check—"

Godo cracked back hard with his elbow, slamming Roque's jaw. To his credit, the kid didn't cry out, just a breathy grunt as he spun down and away with the blow. We'll save our sorrys for later, Godo thought. Gotta know which guilt you can live with. The impact clarified everything. Inside, the mental fog lifted, his thoughts turned solid and simple and whole. Outside, the visible shimmered. His skin pricked with sweat, his breathing slowed and steadied. He was in the moment. Crouching to lower his center of gravity, gunstock nudged tight to his shoulder, he flattened himself against the wall and inched out into the hallway.

THREE

ROQUE STAGGERED FROM THE BEDROOM IN A BLUR OF PAIN, JAW seizing up as he tried to peer past Godo. Bit by bit, like working a puzzle, he made out two men in black raid jackets, hovering over Tía Lucha in the low squat living room at the trailer's far end. They held pistols. Laminated shards from the door window lay scattered across the drab carpet. The acronym ICE in white letters flared across the backs of their jackets. They were immigration agents, *la migra*. Then why break in?

Planted on the couch, hands flat against the tattered cushion, his aunt gazed up at the two strangers, eyes flaring. In the corner, Roque's guitars, a white Telecaster and an Ovation Legend acoustic, rested upright in their chrome stands. He felt a sudden, embarrassing urge to rescue them.

Godo inched forward, strangely calm. Where the hall opened onto the kitchen, a joining crease in the trailer's flooring gave way beneath his weight, emitting a pealing moan. Both agents spun their heads around.

Godo shouted, "Hands in the air!"

The one on the left was bodybuilder thick but short with a buzz cut tapering into a widow's peak. The other was willowy, red-haired, skin dusted with coppery freckles. They pivoted apart, raising their weapons. "Federal agents!"

"Like hell!"

Godo had the drop on them both, the freckled one exposed,

the kitchen counter shielding the one with the widow's peak, at least from the waist down.

"Put the weapon—"

"You broke in!"

"Your weapon! Drop it! Now!"

Outside, someone charged down the narrow gravel passage between trailers, his body thudding against the aluminum walls as he got chased, caught from behind, wrestled to the ground amid curses in both Spanish and English, then a helpless yowl of pain.

"I'm not saying it again!"

"Put *your* weapons down!"

"*¡Godofredo, no, escúchame!*" Tía Lucha, pleading: Listen to me.

The one with the widow's peak edged farther left and a little forward, crouching low behind the counter. Freckles stayed put, barking, "Put the goddamn weapon *down*!"

"Look at me," Godo said, that same offbeat calm. "Look at my goddamn face. Go on, shoot, think I give a fuck?"

From behind, Roque, a whisper: "Godo—"

Mistaking the plea for a warning, Godo swung the shotgun toward the counter. "Back the *fuck* up."

Widow's Peak froze. His trigger finger fluttered. Freckles brayed, "Last chance!"

"You're fucking intruders!"

"Put the mother . . . fucking . . . weapon . . . *down*!"

"You, not me!"

"*¡Ellos te matarán!*" They'll kill you. Tía Lucha's voice, all pity and terror, it froze the men where they stood. For a second—five? ten?—no one moved. Outside, the pursuers rustled their prey to his feet, thudding against the trailer wall once more, then crunching back along the gravel the way they'd come. The ensuing silence felt like a sign. Roque dared to hope that no one would die, common sense would win, everyone would step back from the lunatic edge and—what? Laugh? Shake hands? Exchange *abrazos*?

Widow's Peak spoke up for the first time. "I can place a slug through your brain, crater face, before you get off round one. Not to mention, you shoot, the woman gets hit. Who you think you're fooling?"

Godo, shotgun already trained that direction, tsked mockingly. "*Perro bravo*." Mean dog.

"Won't say it twice."

"You've mistaken me for someone else, *puto*." Godo tightened the coil of his finger around the shotgun's trigger. "I'm a pill-crazed killer. And I don't know who that woman is."

The trailer door flew back. All heads turned—except for Godo and Widow's Peak, their eyes locked in mirrored stares, weapons up.

Another agent peeked in at the doorway, shielding himself. Beyond him, Roque spotted more men, dozens of them, dogs too, flashlights crisscrossing the fog-shrouded maze of trailers. The one at the door had his pistol drawn, but after a quick glance first at Godo, then the glass shards on the floor, he made a show of setting his gun down just inside the doorway. Calmly, to the other two agents: "Holster your weapons."

Freckles rucked up his shoulders. "He's got a shotgun—"

"Holster your weapons!" Still using the doorway for shelter, he said to Godo, "It's okay. Let's all calm down."

Godo kept the Remington shouldered. "Who says I'm not calm?"

"You're back from OIF, am I right?"

Godo cocked his head a little, to ease the stress in his neck. "Thundering Third."

The agent in the doorway nodded, eyes fixed on the shotgun barrel. "Okay, then. Excellent. I'm not saying this to yank your chain, okay? But I've got you beat by a decade or so. I deployed with the First Battalion, Third Marines during Desert Storm. Spent most of my tour in Kaneohe Bay, though."

"Lucky you."

"What say we all take a deep breath—"

"Get the two cowboys the fuck outta my house."

Freckles: "We've come here for Pablo Orantes."

Godo, incredulous: "Happy?"

"Pablo Orantes, where is he?"

"He's in fucking El Salvador. You should know—you're the ones who deported him." Godo gestured with the Remington. "Now get the fuck out of this trailer."

Widow's Peak hadn't budged. Freckles said, "Is Pablo Orantes on these premises?"

The third agent, taking all this in, finally eased through the doorway into the trailer, eyes still fixed on Godo, a way to make sure there were no misunderstandings. His hair brushed the ceiling, even with a slight forward lean. He looked older than the other two, crow's-feet, brush of gray at the temple, necktie beneath the raid jacket lending an odd formality. The jacket was blue, not black. Snapping his fingers to make sure he got the other two agents' attention, he then gestured subtly for them to stand down. "I'll handle this."

"We're here for a fugitive alien named—"

"I said I'll handle it."

Only then did Roque notice how woozy he was; unconsciously, he'd been holding his breath. Sucking in a mouthful of air, he let his body slump heavily against the wall.

Freckles, focusing on Roque for the first time: "Is that Pablo Orantes?"

"I fucking told you, ass wipe, Happy's in El Salvador." Godo turned to the older agent. "Get them to leave."

"I'll do that. Meanwhile, be wise to lower the shotgun, don't you think?"

"They leave first. I'm not getting queered by these two."

"Nobody's doing anything to anybody. These two agents are going to step outside, right here in the carport. You and I will talk through what needs to be talked through. We square?"

"They broke in."

"I hear what you're saying."

"I was in my rights."

"We'll discuss that." He gestured for the two agents to pass in front of him, out the door. They did, unhappily—Freckles first, then Widow's Peak, who exchanged one last eye fuck with Godo. The two agents perched at the foot of the doorstep, at which point the older one said, "Okay now. I've asked politely. Lower your weapon."

Slowly, Godo let the barrel of the shotgun drop, his shoulders unclenched. For the first time, Roque noticed the pungent stench of sweat, not just the others, himself too, then another odor, fouler still—infection. Godo's dressing, still unchanged.

On the sofa, Tía Lucha shuddered and put her face in her hands. The agent extended a gentling hand and said, "Everything's okay, *señora*."

Godo, swaying a little, steadied himself with the wall, then raised himself up again with a shoulder roll, like a boxer manning his corner. Loud, so the pair outside could hear: "I grease those two shitbirds inside my own home? Not a jury in America would convict me."

"Let's both be grateful you don't have to test that theory." The agent picked up his pistol from the floor and holstered it. "Shall we sit?"

"I'm good where I am."

The older man's glance tripped toward Roque, as though wondering if he weren't, in fact, Pablo "Happy" Orantes. Tío Faustino's son. Roque and Godo's cousin, in a manner of speaking. Turning back to Godo, he again looked hard at the ruined face. "You've been stateside since when?"

Godo wiped at some sweat and uttered a small, ugly, disbelieving laugh. "My turn to ask you something." His pitted skin shimmered in the kitchen light. "Tonight, when you plant your ass on the couch, front of the TV, you and those two glorified rednecks outside—when you're watching yourselves, watching all the people in these shitbag trailers get rounded up, ask yourself why. They do what you want. They do it cheap. But you watch all that. And when the next bit comes on, the one about the war, when the names of the dead scroll by: Rodriguez, Acevedo, Castellanos, Hernandez . . ." He counted them off, each name a finger. "Hear what I'm saying? Come on, look me in the eye, tell me honest, two jarheads, goddamn Thundering Third, right? Tell me to my face that doesn't fuck with you."

FOUR

PERCHED HIGH BEHIND THE WHEEL OF HIS FREIGHTLINER CAB, Faustino impatiently raided his lunch of cheese and beef tongue *pasteles*, prepared by Lucha, glancing up now and then through the wiper arc on his grime-caked windshield, watching the vast threadwork of lights grow dim along the crane booms and catwalks, daybreak sapping the dark from the sky. A San Cristóbal medallion hung from the rearview mirror, its pale blue ribbon entwined with a rosary.

He was waiting in his queue at the Port of Oakland, the complex as vast as a city itself. At every berth, longshoremen in hard hats scurried beyond the fences like dug-up termites, forklifts growling to and fro and belching smoke amid cursing shouts and horn blasts and siren shrieks. Jumbo cranes hoisted freight containers from the cavernous holds of cargo ships, the vessels so huge they dwarfed the piers to which they were moored.

Hundreds of truckers like Faustino—out of bed by three, down here by four-thirty to snag a place in line—sat idly in their rigs, waiting hours for a single load. And while they sat, they sweated the constant back and forth of cops and overeager port security flacks who hoped to pop them for a bum taillight, bare tread on a tire, excessive exhaust, anything. Most of the trucks were old—Faustino drove a '94 day cab—and offers by the Port Commission to help finance new ones were laughable. Who could afford the monthlies, the interest, let alone the hike in insurance? Even the anti-exhaust systems they were hawking, ten to fourteen thousand a pop, were out of reach for most guys.

It sounded like a lot to outsiders—hundred dollars a load for just a drayage run, from the port over to the warehouse in Alameda, a matter of minutes—but the way they made you sit, wasting away the hours, you were lucky to get two runs a day.

And the nickel-and-dime stuff ate you alive. Faustino did his own repairs, juggled his accident coverage with his registration payment month by month, part of the constant trade-off, short-changing one thing to make good on another. Near impossible to meet costs, let alone get ahead. Desperation became a kind of genius, making you sharp and clever and tight with a dollar, but it was their hole card too. The shippers had you by the throat and they knew it.

With his forefinger, he scooped up a smear of cheesy *pastele* filling from the crumpled tinfoil, unable to remember the last time he'd sat at the table and shared breakfast with Lucha or eaten one of her lunches without the stench of diesel souring the back of his throat.

Meanwhile, outside his window: "Check this out—I'm moonlighting last weekend, hauling rock? Heavy load, incline. Boost gauge hovers around nine psi. Been a while since I drove a boost, but ain't that high?"

A circle of drivers, arms crossed, gathered on the pavement, biding time till the line budged. Risky, Faustino thought, gabbing away in the open like that. The shippers will say you're organizing. Then watch your life turn to hell.

"With a loaded trailer? Twelve psi, easy. Nine's fine. What's your speed?"

"There's the thing. I can barely break forty on an incline if I'm towing."

Faustino cocked an ear halfheartedly, like it was a game between teams he had no stake in. Even if he'd thought the coast was clear, he wouldn't have climbed down, joined in. He didn't feel much like camaraderie these days.

What he felt was ashamed—losing the house, cheated out of it, all because the mortgage broker, a Mexican, all smiles and small talk, said he was dying to give them the Latino dream. They'd found the house, fourteen hundred square feet, three bedrooms, one-and-a-half baths, nothing extravagant, and the broker had the loan, low interest going in, adjustable three years out. They signed the papers, wrote the check, moved in, no mean trick since Faustino was *sin documentos*. Two months later? Some guy they've never heard of shows up, demands an extra fifteen hundred a month, they're already behind, says it's to repay the short-term loan for the down payment. He had all the paperwork, Faustino's and Lucha's signatures right there, part of the ungodly stack the escrow officer had slid past them at the title company. That was bad enough but when the rate adjusted and the new monthly kicked in, it became too much. They'd trusted people. They'd trusted a Mexican. They'd been fools.

They lived in that humiliating trailer now, trying to get their legs beneath them again, except Godo was back from the war, body in shreds, brain not right. And Roque, who should be working, helping out. He's gifted, Faustino reminded himself. "That boy could be the next Carlos Santana"—he was ten when they started saying that. Teachers agonizing over him at school, saying he had the mind but not the will, reading *novelas policíacas* during class, tapping out rhythms with his pen or just lost in the clouds. Then he met old Antonio, the retired bandmaster who played boleros at parties. That was it, like the guitar descended from heaven and spoke. Roque learned classical and flamenco from the old man, pieces from Spain and Argentina, Cuba, Brazil, and it was magical, watching him turn calm and mindful, cradling the guitar. Then, boom, he's a teenager and it's pickup offers, garage bands, jam sessions, sometimes with real musicians, guys who got paid, which was how he met his latest teacher, Lalo, a professor at San Francisco State. He took Roque on as a special protégé, introducing him to jazz. Lucha bought him the electric so he could stand on his own among the others, prove himself. What else was there to do, let him turn out like Godo? Or worse—Pablo?

Outside, the men continued: "Motor got rebuilt with a new pump maybe ten thousand miles ago, idles and runs like a champ, just weak on towing." Faustino resisted a smile, not just at their rough-edged English, which to his ear, even after all this time in *Gringolandia*, could sound like rocks tumbling inside a bucket. The way *norteños* go on about their trucks, he thought, it was the same way they talked about family, sickness, politics. All you needed were the right tools, a good manual, everything would be fine. They listened to these people on the radio, Dr. Laura, Dr. Phil, hoping to fix their problems. They're like children up here, Lucha said, they want to be told what to do, get punished but not too bad. Things are too easy, they get bored, which is why they spend so much time thinking about how to improve themselves. The divine, the invisible, death, it scares the living crap out of them, which is why they're so noisy, so devoted to money and war and machines. Faustino knew what it meant to rely on his truck, he was no stranger to an obsession with its workings, but it was different. He knew there was no such thing as a diesel that could change his life.

He wondered what the loads would be today. Hopefully not avocados. Or bottled beer or boxes of slate tile, especially if they were packed high inside a twenty-footer. The shippers were notorious for over-packing those, so the cans were too heavy. And they knew which were which, the vessel planner had to balance the weight onboard the ship, but that kind of info never got passed on to the terminal operators or the stevedores, let alone the drivers. You could get a tri-axle chassis from the yard if you knew you'd be heavy ahead of time, but that never happened. Instead you found out only after you got your load and who could afford to wait another few hours to change a chassis at that point?

You took your chances.

Tickets for weight could cost you ten grand. Worse, if the load wasn't just heavy but stacked too high? Might not even clear the truck yard before the thing went over on you, spend the rest of the day dealing with cops and the port people, all that paperwork. Or worse.

Trucker in Florida pulling a reefer load crushed a young model when his rig flipped, trying to dodge a wreck. Another guy right here in Oakland found out the chassis the yard crew gave him had shot brakes—same deal, swerved to miss a pileup, the thing went over on him, pancaked a Saturn wagon, whole family inside. And of course they always blamed the drivers, never the shippers. Everybody had a story like that or knew someone who did.

Faustino's involved a load of goats.

He was carrying them to Guerneville where they were going to be used to clear brush—four hundred animals in all, stacked tight on tiered shelving in the trailer, to keep them from moving around, hurting themselves en route. None of them was more than two years old, babies almost. Faustino petted a few before closing up the back, heading out.

Right outside Sonoma, he blew out a tire on a tight turn—the rig belonged to the company, not him, he'd pointed out the wear but they'd said it was fine, go, drive. The cab nosed down with the blowout, the load shifted, the trailer went with it. Some of the goats got crushed by the shelving. Others scrambled free through the back door that busted open in the crash, dozens of them, roaming around wine country, chewing up anything they could find.

When the cops arrived they closed the trailer up again. Faustino tried to tell them no, don't, the animals will suffocate, but they ignored him. The rest of the goats died, the ones on top smothering the ones below. Their screaming was terrible to hear.

The woman who ran the company, called to the scene, watched animal rescue pulling out one carcass after the other, bodies twisted, bloody, limp. They were stacked five deep along the roadbed like cordwood. She came to the patrol car where Faustino sat in the backseat and just stared for a moment, then broke down, cursing him.

Eight years ago that happened, Faustino thought. He still winced at the memory.

Someone started banging on his driver-side door. Glancing down, Faustino recognized one of the men from the circle who'd been yabbering all this time. McBee, that was his name.

"Better run, *amigo*." He pointed back toward Maritime Street.

Checking his rearview, Faustino saw the swirling lights, the unmarked sedans speeding forward. They'd blocked the end of the cul-de-sac as well—there was no way out, except on foot.

A low-rising green lay between him and the inlet, with sapling elms and small tussocks of beach grass lining the walkway, but it offered nothing like a hiding place. Could he swim across the channel to the next berth over? Would he be any safer if he did?

The rosary and San Cristóbal medallion hung there from his mirror, helpless.

"Forget the truck, Faustino. We'll get it to you somehow. Leave the keys. Run!"

FIVE

GODO SAT ON THE SOFA BESIDE TÍA LUCHA, BEFOGGED BY a follow-up Percocet, a Lexapro for good measure, his leg wound clean and re-dressed, courtesy of Roque, who sat across the room, patting his hands together nervously. He was eyeing his guitars as though afraid they too might somehow get dragged off this morning. Such a punk, Godo thought, no particular ill will.

The medication conjured a numb remove. Leaning forward to see past his aunt, he peered out the window, watching the *muchachos* line up outside the black ICE bus, surrounded by dogs and armed men. "*Pobrecitos*," his aunt whispered. Poor things. Godo nodded to acknowledge the sentiment but found it hard to muster much feeling one way or the other. The meds, he thought, they drop you into this strange place, this room you know but don't know. You get stuck.

Meanwhile, just outside the trailer, the three agents were arguing among themselves. Listening in, Godo felt certain he heard one of them say, "They want to be taken prisoner," but that was before, the invasion, the Kuwaiti terp talking about the deserters the regiment intercepted. Ragged silhouettes scuttling along the raised earthworks running west to Nasiriyah, lit from behind by distant oil fires, some in uniform, others wearing civilian clothes or traditional robes, choking on dust from the shamal winds, rags on their feet, gear discarded behind, littering the desert for miles. "They say if they go back the way they came, they'll be killed by fedayeen." Akbar, the terp's name was. Everybody called him Snackbar. He had to tell the Iraqis they wouldn't be taken prisoner, the Americans had barely enough water for themselves. The deserters shambled to their feet, a few crying out against the faithless marines, clutching handbills the Americans had dropped from drones promising humane treatment to prisoners. The rest just turned away, staggering east. You're here to hunt, Godo thought, remembering what Gunny Benedict had told his squad the night before as they'd set out for battle. Think like a killer, not a friend. Be bold, trust no one, fear nothing. Act like you're already dead—it just might save you.

He glanced again past the curtains at the captured *muchachos*, hands tied behind their backs with plastic come-alongs, some of them shirtless or shoeless despite the cold morning mist. They didn't look like they'd wanted to surrender.

The raid had netted two dozen or so, "illegals" they'd get called that night on the news. Godo knew a few by name, knew the roofers and landscapers and body shops they worked for, even the dirt-poor villages to which they'd get sent and from which they'd inevitably return.

Meanwhile the two ICE agents continued going at it with the older one, who turned out to be FBI—Lattimore his card read, Special Agent James Lattimore. The dispute, from what Godo could pick out, concerned the need for a warrant to search the trailer. They'd checked everyone's papers, confirmed that Tía Lucha's temporary protected status was valid, Godo and Roque were both citizens by birth, every handgun in the house was registered. But none of that mattered to the ICE men. They were, they said, with all the scorn for Lattimore they could muster, in the course of a legitimate operation targeting known alien felons, meaning they could search wherever they damn well pleased.

"I'm not getting a Bivens claim slammed down my throat because of you two," Lattimore said. "Call in, have the shift supervisor draft a warrant, walk it over to the magistrate and have somebody hike it over here."

Sound reasoning, Godo supposed, but the tiff had nothing to do with law or procedure or good sense. It had to do with who could swing the biggest dick. The ICE guys felt humiliated, called on the carpet in front of a family of nacho niggers. No red-blooded American male over the age of nine could be expected to take that. Funny, he wanted to tell them, how sometimes that big dick just gets in the way. Take it from me.

The phone rang. Roque got up from the table and answered, holding the receiver in the crook of his shoulder as he tucked in his shirttail, conducting this mindless bit of business with such hip artlessness Godo felt an instant flash of jealousy, like he was being forced to watch his shit-for-brains *hermanito* turn into a rock star right there before his very eyes. And maybe he was. God help me, Godo thought, then Roque shot a wary glance out the screen door toward the agents, who were listening in. He turned his back to them, lowering his voice.

The door opened. Lattimore stepped in, the other two humping along behind. Roque cut short the call—"Okay, thank you, I have to go"—then returned the receiver to its cradle and turned back toward the room, tucking his hands in his pockets. It was odd, he still had that same lax grace about him, except the eyes.

"Let me guess, *señores*. You want to know who that was."

The Spanish was meant as ridicule. Godo felt impressed. Meanwhile, to his credit, Lattimore said nothing, just waited. The man had the patience of a wall.

Roque added, "But you already know what I just found out, I'll bet. *¿Verdad?*"

Lattimore held pat for another beat, then: "Faustino Orantes."

Tía Lucha stiffened, eyes bugging with fright. Godo, snapping his head toward Roque: "What's he talking about?"

Using Spanish, to be sure his aunt didn't misunderstand, Roque said:—*They picked up Tío at the port, some kind of raid. Nobody's sure where they took him.*

Tía Lucha lifted her hands from her lap and, folding them as though for prayer, covered her nose and mouth and closed her eyes. She took three shallow breaths, trembling.

Lattimore said, "And yes, I'd like to know who that was on the phone just now."

Roque ignored him, instead kneeling down in front of his aunt, stroking her arm. Finally: "I don't have to answer that."

Weeks later, Godo would look back on this moment as the point in time when Roque found his backbone. Either that or his terrible angel had come, whispering in his ear: Hey *cabrón*, take heart—you're already dead.

IT WAS AFTER NINE BEFORE ROQUE COULD BREAK AWAY. TÍA LUCHA begged off work to spend the day searching for Tío Faustino; Roque sat by the phone in case she called. Come nightfall he put some dinner together from leftovers, made sure Godo got his medicine, watched a little TV with him in his room. Finally, when the first six-pack was history and Godo dropped off, Roque pulled on his sweatshirt, turned off the ringer on the phone, slipped out for Mariko's. He'll wake up at some point and find himself alone, Roque thought, and that could go a dozen different ways. But he's not the only one with needs.

Jogging up Mariko's block, he noticed a strange car parked out front, lights on in her living room. He waited outside for the man to leave—graying blond hair, yuppie rugged, North Face vest, Timberland boots, a mere peck on the cheek as he said goodbye—waited ten minutes longer, then walked up and rang the bell.

"You had company," he said when the door opened.

Wineglasses lingered on the living room floor near the futon, one empty, the other half so. The bottle sat uncorked off to the side. Given the sparse furnishings, the bare walls and hardwood floor, the arrangement resembled sculpture.

She stared, those dark almond eyes. "You're not going to turn jealous, are you?"

There was no smell of sex. And she was dressed in a bedraggled pullover and drawstring pants, everything bulky and shapeless, not the stuff of come-hither.

"Who says I'm jealous?"

"Because it would be dreadful form, given the age difference."

He warned himself: Steady. Don't get sucked in. "You know, it's hard to keep up. One minute, I'm so damn mature. The next, when you want to put me in my place—"

"I have friends, I have clients. Sometimes we meet here. You can't be part of that world."

Roque's chest clenched; the knot felt cold. "I said I wasn't jealous."

Mariko studied him—not without a hint of longing, he thought. "In my experience, it's always the ones who tell you they're not jealous who are."

"Maybe that says more about your experience than it does about me."

He went to kiss her. She turned her head, offering her cheek.

"It's been a long day." She crossed her arms over her breasts, smothering them beneath the nubbly sweater. "I have a client consult early tomorrow."

"They took my uncle away." It was smarmy and manipulative, he realized that. But he had to get her to drop the put-upon snit she was hiding behind. He deserved better.

The almond eyes turned glassy. "What are you saying?"

"ICE. *La migra*. They nabbed him at the port and we don't know where he is. My aunt and some of the other women from the trailer park have gone down to the federal jail in San Bruno, see if they can find anything out."

"Who's looking after your brother?"

"Godo's fine. He won't really need me till morning." There, he thought, that puts things plain.

"I can't let you stay."

Roque forced a smile. Can't? "I didn't ask to."

"Not in so many words."

"Not in any words."

"You're angry."

"You're talking to me like I'm a problem."

Just outside, a neighborhood cat in heat emitted that distinctive guttural howl.

"Look, I'm sorry about your uncle."

"Yeah. It's fucked. But you can't let me stay."

"You said you didn't want to."

"I said I didn't ask."

"My God." She pushed her hands into her wild black hair. "What are we fighting about?"

"I'll go." He turned for the door.

"Roque, I don't have what it takes for this."

He glanced over his shoulder. "For what?"

"For what's happening, right now, between us."

"And what's that?"

"Stop it!"

"Stop what? I'm serious."

"This game you're playing. This *thing* that you're *doing*."

"Huh." He struck a pose. "This thing."

"If you want to talk about what happened with your uncle, we'll talk. But there's something else going on and I just don't have what it takes to deal with it right now."

"Maybe I should come back when you do."

"And what the hell is that supposed to mean?"

She was shouting. But he'd become invested in seeing her cry. Somebody, somewhere was supposed to cry.

"I'm just saying, maybe I should come back. Tonight's, you know, not good."

The rutting cat cried out from the dark again. Mariko said, "No. Please don't."

"Excuse me?"

"I want you to leave and not come back."

The cold knot in his chest dropped like a stone into his stomach. "What are you saying?"

"We both knew this couldn't go on forever."

"I didn't know that." He wondered if that was true. "The guy who left—"

"Here it comes. I knew it."

"I love you."

She brought herself up short in the middle of an unpleasant laugh. "No, you don't. You just like the way it sounds."

"Why are you insulting me?"

"I'm telling you the truth. If that's insulting—"

"The truth? Agents busted into our trailer today, looking for my cousin. They almost got into a shootout with Godo, I mean they were *this close*, okay? Then, way I hear it, my uncle got chased from his truck at the port, run down like a crook. He's been hauling loads there five years, suddenly he's a security risk, the fascist fucks."

"Things are different now. You know that."

"My uncle's in a cell someplace. At least, that's the best I can hope for. But in a few weeks, maybe less, he'll be on a plane to El Salvador, not much me or my aunt or anyone else can do about it. And we kinda need Tío's cash input at the moment. Money's kinda tight."

"Maybe it's time you thought about a job."

The tone, he thought, so snide, so bogus. "Okay. You're right. I should go."

"And not come back."

"You don't mean that."

"I don't? I said it—I can't take this, okay?" A tear scrolled down her cheek. He reached out to hold her but she tore herself away. "Get out!"

"Why are you—"

"Get! *Out!*"

She looked around, saw the empty wineglass on the floor and stooped to pick it up. Cocking her arm, she readied herself to hurl it.

"Put it down." He turned and without looking back walked out the front door. She slammed it behind him but didn't turn the lock. He wondered at that, lingering on the porch. Shortly he heard it, coming from inside, not the sound of weeping, something else, something much different, a sudden thick crashing, the splintering hollow thud of earthenware smashing against wood. By the time he snuck back in, came up behind her in the long narrow hallway, she was ankle deep in clay shards, face in her hands, shoulders heaving. And then the shelves were bare, he thought, the words sounding like a line from a fairy tale.

He picked his way through the debris, noticing how the fresh-grave smell was even more pronounced now, wrapped his arms around her, whispering her name as he nuzzled her hair. Listening to her shallow sobs, he thought: But this was what you wanted, right? Someone somewhere crying.

Hours later, when he rose from her bed to head back home, he asked himself what it meant, to bed this woman he cared for so much when she wouldn't look at him, when even during sex the tears didn't stop—unable or unwilling to climax, turning away from him as he pulled out short of climax himself, burying her fist in her mouth and her face in the pillow, steeled to his presence but no longer demanding he go.

SIX

ROQUE SLOWED TO A JOG AS HE NEARED HUNTINGTON VILLAGE. Fog drifted off the wetlands, hazing the streetlamps. The screech of a blue jay answered a distant car horn.

He wondered if the agents had come back hoping to wrap up the prior day's business, snatch the few stragglers who'd eluded them—like Happy, who hadn't been seen anywhere around here since, Christ, when, two years ago? The prospect of a confrontation, ordered to show ID, forced splay-legged against the chain-link fence with its thorny bougainvillea, it momentarily distracted him from what had just happened with Mariko.

He'd meant to comfort her; she'd remained inconsolable. The woman who made him feel smart, capable, a lover, a man, she'd peeled back the layers of his ego to reveal a whole new level of fuckup. He felt out to lunch, dishonest, guilty. He felt eighteen.

His chest heaved from the run as he peered through the fogged-in darkness, edging toward the trailer-park entrance, checking for sedans, clean-cut cops in bulky raid jackets. The maze of trailers sat quiet and mostly dark. The air smelled of pine and sewer muck. You go back soon, he told himself, you make sure she's okay. You stay until she talks to you.

The tinny clamor of wind chimes grew louder as he neared the trailer; he saw lights up front. Tía's awake, he thought, one more thing to tweak his guilt. Godo would be too, of course. I'm gonna catch hell, he thought, for leaving him alone. Okay. Fine. Unlocking the door with his key, he eased it open, stepped inside. Glancing at the breakfast nook, he stopped short.

"Close the door," Happy said.

He was sitting next to Tía Lucha at the kitchenette table, his face bearded and stern, looking like a saint from some old Dominican prayer card. The beard was new. Always lean, he seemed gaunt now, eyes bulging from their sockets like small black plums. The rest of his face composed itself into a wary, tight-lipped scowl and his body seemed coiled, ready to bolt or lash out. He wore jeans, work boots, a plaid flannel shirt. His black hair was cropped short.

"Where the hell did you come from?"

Happy's long-fingered hands clutched a mug of Tía Lucha's Nescafé, which he raised halfway to his lips before answering. "That's a long story."

"When did you get here?"

Tía Lucha piped in:—*He's been back almost a week*.

Roque was stunned. "You knew?"

—*Of course not. Why would I keep something like that from you if I knew?*

She seemed dazed, even fearful, an effect enhanced by the day's first smears of thick white makeup, which gave her face a clownish unreality. Her glance darted between Roque and Happy, her gifted if irksome nephew, her *marido*'s fugitive son.

Roque said, "I meant no offense, Tía."

She rolled her eyes. Happy downed the last of his coffee.

Roque said, "Does Godo know you're here?"

Happy turned in his seat to get out. "We had our chat." He rose and offered a grateful nod to Tía Lucha. To Roque, he said, "Walk with me."

"I need to check the dressing on Godo's leg."

Happy glanced back down the hall toward Godo's room. "It can wait."

—

OUTSIDE, THE FOG LINGERED. HAPPY HIKED UP THE COLLAR OF HIS shirt. "You forget how cold it gets here," he said, walking briskly toward the gate, hunched forward. He cast an impatient glance over his shoulder, urging Roque to keep pace.

Once they were out on the river road he turned north, one wash of headlights after the other spraying his back as the morning's first traffic made its way toward Napa. He ignored the cars or trucks as they rushed by but Roque could tell from the dock of his head as each one passed that he was noting who was inside.

Several hundred yards on he turned off the gravel roadbed into the parking lot for a small weatherworn strip mall—a cash-only car repair, a discount mattress outlet, a combination *panadería/tienda/envío de dinero*. If not for the raid the day before, clusters of bleary men would already be gathered in the parking lot, trying to stay warm as they waited for contractors to swing by, collect them for a day's work. Happy headed for a battered Ford pickup scalloped with rust, bearing Arizona plates. Climbing behind the wheel, he said, "Get in."

As Roque closed the door behind him, Happy lit up a cigarette, the rubbery match flame hollowing his features. After shaking out the match and exhaling a long plume of smoke, he turned to stare across the pickup's cab with a strangely menacing sadness.

"Been spending your nights boning some broad twice your age. How'd that happen?"

Roque felt the blood drain from his face. "Who told you that?"

"Who says I needed to be told?" Happy tapped his ash through the window vent. "Tell me, Roque, your *vieja*, when she takes you into her bed . . ." He affected a throaty purr.

"Fuck you."

"Watch your mouth."

"You been spying on me?"

"I know things," Happy said. "Get used to it."

"Yeah? What else do you know?"

"That's my business. What's with Godo?"

"Tía Lucha didn't tell you?"

"Never mind what she told me, I wanna hear it from you."

"Hear what?"

"He's fucked up."

"Ya think?"

Happy reached across and swatted the back of Roque's head. "Don't be such a punk."

"Don't touch me."

Happy, in whiny nasal mimicry: "*Don't touch me.*" Then: "His dick still work?"

Roque had to process that. "There's some things we don't share."

"I mean has he gotten it wet since he got back? Given how he looks, I was thinking maybe . . ." Happy rubbed his thumb and index finger together, suggesting cash.

"Who am I, his pimp?"

Happy chuckled at that, then took another long drag, blowing the smoke out, watching it billow against the windshield. "Face the way it is? He looks like a fucking dartboard."

"Tell him that. I dare you."

Happy let that go, except to say, "You got a point. Nothing wrong with his temper. Spent maybe two minutes with him, he wants to mix it up."

"You want Godo mellow, you'll have to kill him."

"There's a thought."

"What's that supposed to mean?"

"Fuck's sake, Roque, chill out. By the way, not everybody who was over there came back fucked up. You get that, right?"

"How would you know?"

Happy picked a fleck of tobacco off his tongue. "That's another long story." He turned to gaze out at his window at the mold-freckled storefronts. A crow perched on the rain gutter, framed by fog. "How come you're not pitching in with money?"

"Who says I'm not?"

"You're really starting to piss me off with this."

"I've got a line on a band gig. Maybe."

"Maybe?"

Roque shrugged. "Hard to say."

"Really? Hard to say what, your family needs the bread? Hard to say they're fucked, my old man deported?"

An eighteen-wheeler thundered past, rattling the pickup's windows. The crow on the gutter fluttered its wings. "Maybe we can get a lawyer."

"Fucking hell—you stupid? What's a lawyer gonna do except take our money? You think—" Happy stopped short, glancing in his rearview mirror. A patrol car pulled into the strip-mall lot. Murmuring, "What's this asshole want," he stubbed out his cigarette, dropped the butt between his feet. "Keep talking," he told Roque.

"About what?"

"About anything. So we don't look like we're casing this dump."

Roque let his glance dart once out the cab's back window, then started babbling, launching into the first thing that came to mind. Happy, eyes glued to the mirror, spoke to the reflection: "Come on, fuckwad. You run the plates, we're gonna do this." With painful slowness, the patrol car eased along the storefronts, shining a flashlight through the window glass.

"Open the glove box," Happy said.

Roque obeyed. The butt of a pistol lay exposed within a folded newspaper. "Jesus—"

Happy turned toward him, their eyes met. The menacing sorrow was gone, replaced by emptiness. "Tell me another story."

"You're not gonna shoot a cop."

"I'll shoot you, you don't calm down. Tell me another story."

The black-and-white, having finished its check of the stores, eased toward the end of the parking lot, only to circle back and come abreast of the pickup, so the driver sides matched up. The cruiser's tires were muddy, the windshield caked with rainy grime. The cop lowered his window and gestured for Happy to do the same. The glove box remained open.

The officer said, "Mind telling me your business here?"

Happy turned so his body blocked whatever view the cop might have through the window. "I'm just sitting here talking with my cousin, officer. He's getting married next month and he's worried about money."

The cop studied Happy at length, an occasional attempt to glance past him toward Roque. The man had a thick putty-colored face with baggy eyes, more bored clerk than cop. "Kinda early, don't you think?"

"Only time we had. We both gotta head off for work soon."

"What say you do that now."

"Yes, sir. You wanna see my license and registration?"

Happy reached for the glove box. Roque's throat closed up, he couldn't get his breath.

The cop glanced away, dipping his head toward his radio, deciphering a sudden shock of words ensnarled in static. "Just get to where you need to be."

"Okay, sure." Happy toggled his keys, cranking the engine. "Thank you, officer."

He pulled out and the cop stayed put, the two of them watching each other in their rearviews. Happy turned south, heading back toward the trailer park. He dug another smoke from the pack in his shirt pocket, set it between his lips, then rummaged in his pants pocket for his matches. "I'm gonna drive a ways," he said, "not pull in, understand?"

Roque nodded. He could finally breathe. "You're the one driving."

Happy lit a match one-handed, held it to the tip of his cigarette, tilted his head back as he waved out the flame, then tossed the matchbook onto the dash. "Let's get back to what we were talking about."

Unable to stop himself, Roque glanced over his shoulder out the back window. Like a nagging itch, the cop was there, trailing several car lengths behind.

Happy said, "I see him. Relax, will you?" He glanced toward the glove box, which Roque had yet to close. "With Godo fucked up the way he is, it's gonna be up to you. No excuses."

Roque went cold. He glanced at the weapon, then back at the cop, then Happy. "What do you mean? Up for what?"

"I said relax. I'm talking about my old man."

Roque wiped his palms on his jeans, trying to picture Tío Faustino in a crowded cell, unable to sleep, scared. "What about him?"

For the first time that morning, Happy smiled—an acid grin, vanishing almost instantly—as he glanced in his mirror. Behind them, the patrol car slowed, then turned off into another strip mall. A clerk not a cop, Roque thought.

Happy said, "Shut up and I'll tell you."

SEVEN

GODO WASN'T SURE AT FIRST IF WHAT HE HEARD WAS REALLY A knock at the door—the sound seemed timid, maybe just a tree branch brushing the roof. He muted the TV. It came again.

He swung his legs to the floor and leaned down, reaching under the bed, not for the shotgun this time but the Smithy .357. Be cool, he told himself, no reruns of yesterday. Could just be one of the neighbors, wanting to beg some favor off Tía Lucha. That happened a lot—patron saint of mooches, that woman. But then he glanced at the clock and thought, My God, has it really been an hour since she left for work? Can't be. He blinked, shook off the watery drift of things, checked again. Sure enough, not just an hour, a little more.

His leg felt leaden and balance was iffy but he made his way down the hallway and into the kitchen just as a third knock sounded. Pausing beside the door, he stared at the square of cardboard taped up where the window used to be.

He called out, "Yeah?"

No answer at first. Then: "Hello?" It was a man's voice, unfamiliar.

Godo tensed. "Who's there?"

A preliminary bout of throat-clearing. "I'm a friend of Faustino's. Drove his rig up from the port. Parked it out front. Got his keys here."

Godo stepped past the door toward the window, edged back the curtain. He was a knobby squint of a man with large hands, a reddish mustache too big for his face, ears poking out from under a graying mop of windblown hair. He wore a mechanic's one-piece coverall, stained at the knees from oil, other smeary markings here and there.

Godo reached around to the small of his back, tucked the .357 into his pants, covered it with his shirt and opened the door. The man seemed taken aback by the sight of his face.

Extending one of his outsize hands. "Name's McBee. You Faustino's son?"

The question reminded Godo that Happy of all people had appeared out of the blue that morning. Or was he making that up? A drugged-up dream, a figment of his bleak mind—no, he thought, it happened, we fought. But Christ, we always fought. Suddenly he remembered his hand and glancing down he saw it, same pitted red scars as on his face, locked in the fierce pumping grip of this stranger. McBee. Chafing calluses coarsened the man's palm.

Godo said, "Not son. Nephew, sort of."

McBee seemed content with this information, delayed though it was. He took his hand back, dug around in what appeared to be a bottomless pocket, then produced Tío Faustino's key chain. "I can leave these with you?"

"Sure." Godo shook his head to clear away the Percocet muck. McBee dropped the keys into his hand. From somewhere in the trailer park, a woman's voice could be heard: "*¡Oye, nalgón, no me jodas!*" Listen, fat ass, don't fuck with me.

McBee broke the spell. "Any way I could bum a ride to the bus station? Gotta get back to Oakland. Can't waste the whole day, losing money as it is."

Godo caught a hint of dutiful poor-me in his tone, the only snag in the man's act so far. "I don't have a car, sorry. My aunt took it to work."

The news seemed to baffle McBee. He dog-scratched his ear. "Point me the right direction at least?"

Godo snapped out of his stupor. "Sorry. I'll walk you, how's that?" He thumbed the door lock plunger, searched for Tío Faustino's keys, found them in his hand, reminded himself not to forget about the pistol nudging his ass crack, then stepped out onto the doorstep. "Follow me."

McBee blanched, stepping back to make way. "You sure?"

"I'm positive. Get the blood moving. You coming?"

He shortly regretted not donning a jacket but then shook off the cold, faulting himself for wanting snivel gear. During the invasion he'd slept shivering in shallow ranger graves, wet from rain or choking from windblown dust, hoping not to get run over by a tank in the night, clutching his weapon, happy as a drunk come payday. Jesus, he thought, how soft you get and so fast. He fought against the hobbling pain breaking through the Percocet, willing himself forward. McBee kept pace behind, patient despite the crippled speed and mercifully short on conversation.

Near the trailer-park gate Godo spotted Tío Faustino's Freightliner cab and felt a misty want, picturing his uncle, wondering when he might see him again. Strange, how girlish the moods sometimes. The truck's engine was ticking from its cooldown and he caught a whiff of diesel, the scent sending him back instantly to the cramped confines of his Humvee, packed into the backseat with the rations and water cans, the ammo and thermite grenades, C-4, claymore mines, the bale of concertina wire and cammie nets, bolt cutters, map books, chemlites, a pickax and sledgehammer—Chavous in the opposite seat; Mobley in the turret manning the Mark 19, his ass a fart's breadth away from Godo's face; Gunny Benedict in front with his maps; Pimentel at the wheel, bitch-slapping the radio, screaming at the static. They were pealing toward Al Gharraf, preparing to take fire.

"You all right?"

Godo snapped his head toward the sound.

"You stopped walking," the man said. McBee. He sounded concerned. Maybe frightened.

Godo said, "Sorry."

"Listen, if this is too much, I'm serious, just point me in the right—"

"I'm fine. Come on."

At the gate Godo swung south and they marched along the gravel roadbed toward the center of town where the transit center was located. The wind was sharper here, keening off the mudflats and the grass-lined river, but now Godo embraced it, letting the cold meld with the throbbing ache in his leg. His gooseflesh cheered him and his pitted skin blushed from the stinging air. Beyond the wetlands the Mayacamas range lurked in the drizzle. Stunning, he thought, miraculous, resisting an urge to cry out: Get some!

With the engaging monotony of one step begging the next, time fell into its crazy hole again. He lost all track. Ten minutes? Twenty? Maybe this means I'm finally in the moment, he thought merrily, buoyed on pheromones, but then he noticed, just up the roadbed, near the edge of the commercial district, an arch-backed dog rummaging in some Dumpster overfill. He stopped, feeling his lungs constrict. Shortly, the frame confused him, a line of towering dusty palms, a sagging concrete wall, a roadside bag of trash, then impulse threw him to the ground, locked up in a fetal curl, burying his head in his arms. Seconds warped around his brain as he waited out the blast. Rather than the dust-scattering concussion he was expecting, though, he felt instead a gentle prodding kick to the sole of his shoe.

"Listen, I don't mean to keep bringing this up—"

Godo's eyes shot open. The light was gray, not ocher, the air wet and cold, not parched.

"—but if you need help, or I should get you to a doctor—"

Godo scrambled to his knees in a panic, combed the grass

with his hands, searching out the spider device—two batteries, the curving wires, the unspent shell.

"—you gotta let me know, okay? Otherwise I'd just as soon—"

Jerking his head up, Godo fixed the man in his eye. McBee. Hillbilly stock, grip like a pipe wrench.

"—not impose on you. I'll just head on downtown here, if this is the way."

A station wagon had pulled to the curb a little ways on. A broad-faced man in a ball cap stared back over his shoulder at them.

To McBee, Godo said, "Don't look at me that way."

McBee took a clumsy step backward. "I didn't mean—"

"Who the fuck are you, look at me like that? I served for you, asshole."

McBee put up his hands, another step back, quicker. "Look—"

"Fuck you, white trash."

McBee dropped his hands, now clenched into fists. His crabbed eyes turned fiery. "You go ahead and wallow around on the ground there, piggy. Go on. I did your uncle a favor, I lost half a day's pay for the privilege. I'm done being nice." He spat, then stormed off.

Godo struggled to his feet, bellowing, "I don't owe you, honk. I paid. I paid big." Turning toward the man in the station wagon, he reached to the small of his back, gripped the gun, and held it up above his head. "You feelin' me here, Elmer?" The fat-faced man jumped in his seat, threw his car in gear and sped away, tailpipe belching smoke. A Latina dragging a pigtailed child on the far side of the street stopped to stare until her eyes met Godo's, at which point she scooped up the toddler and hightailed off. Godo glanced over his shoulder, trying to get a better look at the skulking dog. But there was none. The palms remained, the listing wall, the Dumpster dripping trash bags. No dog.

God help me, he thought.

He put the gun away, then began plodding home. Within twenty steps the fluidity of time failed him, the seconds like daggers, every footfall an ordeal. The pain in his leg shot down into his heel and up into his spine and he gritted his teeth, clenched his fists, closed his eyes, walked.

As traffic passed, he tried to let the whisking hum of the tires against pavement lull him into a trance. Every now and then, though, peeking up, he saw drivers staring, passengers too, gazing at the pock-faced stumbling madman and he wondered: Who are these creatures? What world do they come from? He laughed. That was it—they came from Mars or the moon or MySpace, instructed by their overlords to annoy the fuck out of anything that moved. He could hear their voices tripping away inside his brain, beamed in by radio wave, echoing things he'd heard before, things other creatures, all heartfelt eyes and misty smiles, had said when he'd ventured out.

Things like: "Welcome home."

Things like: "Thank you."

Things like: "Support the troops!"

Except the troops don't need or want your support, thank you very much. They don't want the bumper-sticker bravado, the teary moms sporting Yankee Doodle ribbons on their watermelon tits, the brainwashed kids with the scrubbed little grins and roadkill eyes. The mascara wives bearing heart-attack casseroles and lukewarm beer or shag-assing off to bed for a little marital poon that can only go screamingly haywire. One trip to the VA, listening to the other guys rotating back, taught you that much. The troops respectfully request that you and your gung-ho support kindly fuck off. The troops do not recognize you as human.

Better yet: "Bring the troops home!" Yeah? Permission requested to saw off your head, the better to shit down your neck. What the fuck do you know about it? You know nothing—because you don't want to, you want to wax indignant, you want to blame the same old crew, the greedy preening stuffed suits you blame for everything. You want to say the magic word: peace. Well fuck you. Fuck peace. Fuck a home that has to be shared with the prissy likes of you.

Someone called his name.

He turned toward the sound. A vintage Impala, tricked out like a showpiece, had pulled to the curb, passenger-side window rolled down. A pair of *chavos* in the car, both watching, waiting. The faces, yes, he knew these two.

"*Hola, chero*. The fuck you been?"

The voice conjured a name: Chato. The other one, behind the wheel, was Puchi.

"Need a lift?"

The next thing he knew he was in the backseat, the black vinyl upholstery cool and tight. A whiff of reefer, sweat disguised with Brut. He could make out Puchi's eyes in the rearview. He wore an A's cap with the brim cocked up in front, a gray hoodie. He seemed bigger, bulkier than Godo remembered. Weights, maybe. Prison?

Chato, a few years younger and riding shotgun, turned around in his seat so he and Godo were face-to-face. An angry whitehead wept pus just beneath one heavy-lidded eye. He wore a hairnet, his coif meticulous, black and sleek and combed straight back, while on his neck three tattooed letters appeared: BTL. Brown Town Locos. It was the name of the *clica* he and Puchi belonged to, the one Godo had danced around the edges of before enlisting. The name seemed a relic from an ancient time.

Chato held out his fist till Godo bumped it with his own. "My brother from another mother. Long time."

True, Godo thought. Two years at least. An eternity, given what happened in between. Chato had been a mere *mocoso*, a little snot, back then.

"Iraqistan. Musta seen some serious shit. Bet you waxed your share of raghead motherfuckers, am I right?"

The kid was wired and his breath smelled and Godo had to resist an impulse to reach out and rip the hairnet off.

Puchi chimed in, "Wondered when we'd see you around, man. Heard some things, didn't know what was true, figured we'd wait till we caught you out and about."

Godo waved his hand idly toward his face, as though to conjure its pitted ugliness in a gesture. "*Malacara*," he said, figuring that explained it all.

"Yeah, but you're not all *picoteado* from squeezing your zits," Puchi said, slapping Chato's shoulder. The kid glared back venomously. "And it's not like we're gonna mock you, homes. Not the way it is."

Godo tried to picture what that meant—The Way It Is—wondering if it bore any resemblance to Some Serious Shit. The effort to make more sense of it foundered as they passed the fenced confines of a vast construction site, rising in tiers up a broad bare hill. Baymont, the neighborhood was called, that or Hoodrat Heights, depending on who you talked to. Boon-Coon-a-Luma. Ho Hill. At least, those were the names thrown around before Godo left for basic.

He'd heard the story in bits and pieces after that, following the hometown news from afar, how some developers had wanted the whole hill condemned, war-era federal housing never meant to be permanent but grandfathered in, city council deadlocked on eminent domain. So a local fixer, former honcho with the firefighters union, hired some bent ex-cop to torch the whole neighborhood, burn every home to the ground. The plan was to blame it on some arson freak, this patsy they let die in the fire, and for all practical purposes it succeeded, though the players turned on one another when the bent cop got exposed. Not that that stopped anything. What was left of the neighborhood wasn't worth rebuilding. The condemnation vote finally passed and the developers lined up like trick-or-treaters. Then some of the local stakeholders, good old boys whose families ran things here, they began wrangling over secondary spoils; the construction unions demanded a local-labor rider in any contracts; the town's greenies hired a lawyer and challenged the EIR; the Building Department red-flagged every plan submitted, slowing things to a crawl; then the bottom fell out of the housing market and the mortgage crisis hit, financing dried up. So here it was, a vast plot of nothing, stalled in its tracks before the first shovel bit dirt. Two years now and counting, old houses torn down, nothing new built back up. As for all the families who'd lived here? Don't ask.

Across the side of a panel truck parked just inside the project perimeter, some tagger had written: *Rio Mirada—Where your hopes come to die*.

"You heard about the big bad clusterfuck, huh?" It was Chato, following Godo's eyes.

Godo snapped to. "Some. Here and there. You know, the news." He didn't remember coming this way during his trek with McBee from the trailer. Were they driving back a different route? "I watch a lot of TV," he added sheepishly.

Puchi said, "We were hoping for work, man. Whole town was. Lay some brick, pound some nails, whatever. Then the buzzards showed up. Everybody gotta have their slice of the pie. And if they don't? Nobody gets nothing."

"Nobody," Chato chimed in solemnly.

Godo, still staring out the window, said, "So what is it you two do? For work I mean."

Puchi said, "Happy didn't tell you?"

"Happy?"

"You seen him, right?"

"This morning, yeah. First time, actually. Why?"

Puchi and Chato traded glances up front.

Godo said, "What's the big secret?"

"We're in the moving business," Puchi said.

Chato laughed, a snide little wheeze.

"Great punch line." Godo felt his temper inching toward red. "Guess I missed the joke."

"It's a trip, man," Chato said, unaware. "Check this out: We got no license, the trucking company, I mean. It's so fucked up, it's like, backwards, you know? Like permission to steal. Yuppies never see it coming."

"See what coming?"

"Here we are, man." Puchi slowed to a stop and dropped the tranny into park, the Impala's 427 throbbing in neutral. They were out in front of the trailer park. How, Godo wondered, did we get here so quick?

Puchi turned around in his seat. "Good to see you, my man. Maybe now, with Happy back, we'll see a little more of you."

Chato added, "He talk to you about that?" He seemed eager, too much so. The kid was *pasmado*, all tics and quirks.

Puchi cut him off with a glare. "Come on, let the man out. Got someplace I need to be."

Just as suddenly as he'd found himself inside the car, Godo now found himself standing on the gravel roadbed. A gust of wind off the river blew grit in his eyes. Chato cocked his hand into a pistol and winked. "Later, masturbator."

The black Impala rumbled off. Godo watched the six tail-lights recede, remembering another car, another time, another two *vatos* up front. Him and Happy.

The car was Tía Lucha's, the weed under the seat Godo's. They were coming back from a house party in Vallejo, this girl he had a moon-howl crush on, name of Ramona Sánchez. A fly *morena*, long straight hair, heartbreaker eyes, smart but not stuck up, little cue-ball titties but an ass that said Step Right Up. Godo stood there in the kitchen, nursing the same beer for almost an hour, slick but not too, cracking jokes, teasing, asking about her people. If she was bored she hid it well, leaning back against the wall, smile to knock you over.

Meanwhile, Happy sulked, too bashful to chat up a girl of his own, too angry to just hang, enjoy himself. He stood there chain-smoking, clutching the neck on a fifth of Jack, scaring the lipstick off the pigs, never mind any girl worth looking at. Finally he went out back to chill with Puchi and the boys. Godo checked in on him now and again, made sure he didn't get into it with anybody he couldn't handle.

As the night idled away, Godo drifted in and out of the house, keeping track of Ramona, see if anyone else was hitting on her, not too obvious, slipping into the bathroom for a rail with Enrique, Cap'n Crank, catching a bump later on, just enough to keep the edge on his cool.

When he caught her gathering her things off the couch, he strolled on up, helped her with her jacket, asked if he could walk her out. Her girlfriend was there but that was fine, Godo had a knack with chaperones. At the curb he asked for her number, wrote it on his palm with her eyebrow pencil. She shot him that knock-down smile as they drove away, and he told himself: Wait a couple days, then call her.

No more romance on the agenda, he got tanked. Tequila shots, chased with beer, a few more bumps of crank. Sprawled on the couch, he rocked out to the music in hammered bliss: Zurdok, "Abre los Ojos." Molotov, "Karmara." Control Machete, "Sí Señor." The music made him think of Roque, Tía Lucha's precious, her favorite, the mother killer. Hand him his due, the kid had chops. But what a truly perfect day it would be, he mused, when that gifted little twerp woke up and had to look life in the eye: *fuego, sonrisas, realidad y dolor*.

Fire, smiles, reality and pain.

Sí señor . . .

A little after midnight, Happy appeared. All he said was, "Gimme your keys, *manudo*."

Godo scored the pot on the way out, an ounce to mellow his drift, copped from Puchi, the crowd's preferred *mariguanero*.

That was what the Brown Town Locos were good for, crank and weed, that and stealing shit. Bumming papers off him too, Godo rolled a number, toking away as Happy drove. The night was cold and still. No moon. The bud turned him philosophical.

He said, "You know, *cabrón*, way you act, women gonna think you're a *mariquita*." A faggot. "Gonna think you learned to fuck in jail."

Happy's hand sailed across the car, snatching the doob away. "Who are you now, the prince of pussy?"

Godo reached over to grab back his blunt. "Don't be dissing my girl, *cabrón*."

Happy fended him off. "*Zorra flaca*." Skinny slut.

"I mean it, fuckface."

Godo tried again to snag back the joint, Happy dodged the grab. Godo persisted. A blur of hands, then Happy launched a crackback elbow, landing the blow square and hard. A clap of searing white, Godo reached for his nose. A dollop of blood stained his pants. His eyes watered from the pain.

"*Hijueputa* . . ." Son of a whore.

He threw a punch. Happy dodged the blow, pivoting away. The wheel went with him. The car veered across the double line, then whipped into a spin as Happy overcorrected. An oncoming pickup veered to miss them, screech of tires, angry honk. They stalled out straddling the center divide—lucky, for a few seconds anyway. A cop, lurking on a side street maybe three hundred yards down, saw the whole thing. Not that the two of them noticed. They were back at it, wild drunken haymakers landing once in every five tries but coming fast and hard regardless, only stopping when the cop hit his strobe.

They froze. The red light swirled. Happy whispered, "*Estoy chingado*." I'm screwed.

He bolted, throwing open the door, leaping from the car, charging down the gravel roadside berm through weeds to the riverbank, hunting a way to cross. The cop spotted him, a voice calling through the squad car's loudspeaker for him to stop and the headlights now square on Godo, sitting there, too stupid from liquor and weed to toss the ounce stashed under the seat.

It would all play out like a tedious movie from there, the backup units blocking off the road, the chopper with its searchlight, the dogs. Godo would remember the back and forth at the window, the officer with his steel-gray crew cut, very professional, very polite.

"I'd like to know if you'll agree to a search of the vehicle."

By that point Godo was a fatalist. What would happen would happen.

"I can get a warrant, just a matter of time. I detect a distinct odor of marijuana, your pupils are dilated, your companion fled the scene. You were observed driving erratically—"

"I wasn't driving."

"You have gang tattoos."

That made Godo laugh. He looked at the backs of his hands: a dragon, a bat. "These?"

The cop leaned closer. "Let me explain something to you, son. Here's how it will go: I'm a decorated officer with twelve years' experience working this city, with expertise of particular relevance to the matter at hand, numerous multiagency task forces, narcotics unit, youth gang outreach. Am I getting through?" The two cops behind him grinned like jackals. "I say those are gang tats. Think any judge in this county is going to second-guess me?"

Godo's eyes burned. Fearing he might cry, he bit his lip, telling himself, Don't be a bitch. "I don't care," he whispered.

The cop accepted this remark with an oddly warm smile. "Thank you. That's consent. Please step outside the vehicle."

Godo watched as they tossed the car, thinking: sly motherfucker. They found the pot but nothing else worth bagging and tagging, no open containers, no crank, no weapons. Half an hour later the dogs cornered Happy out among the sloughs on the river's far side, hiding in a patch of oleander. He and Godo were taken to lockup in separate cars. I'll never see him again, Godo realized. The weed was a California misdemeanor, no more than a fine for him, his bigger problem would be public intoxication and even that was just another minor beef—a lecture from the bench, community service, counseling. But for Happy, the pot was an aggravated felony. No matter what any lawyer tried to do, no matter what Godo said under penalty of perjury—the pot was his, no one else's, he'd paid for it, hidden it under the seat—none of it mattered. Happy wasn't a citizen. His case was heard in immigration court and he drew a hanging judge. Not only did he get deported; he was barred from reentry for the rest of his life. Exile, for an ounce bag of Godo's bud.

It took only one time, looking into Tío Faustino's eyes, for Godo to realize there was no other option. He had to go away, someplace strange and terrible. If he came back, he had to come back changed. And so he headed to the small featureless office downtown, where the man in the olive-green pants, the khaki shirt and tie, the famous high-and-tight buzz cut, sat behind his simple desk, Stars and Stripes on one side, Marine Corps colors on the other.

"I just got popped on a weed charge," Godo said. "That gonna be a problem?"

EIGHT

THE DULL CHIME SOUNDED BEYOND THE THICK DOOR. ROQUE cupped his hands, a gust of breath, hoping for warmth. A ten count, longer, then she appeared, dressed in paint-stained sweats, wiping her clay-muddied hands with a towel. Her eyes looked scalded.

"You're working," he said, remembering the debris from last night.

She forced him to endure an unnerving silence.

"I thought I'd check in on you. Make sure you're okay."

"I'm fine." Her voice barely a whisper.

Something in her reticence suggested shame. Given his own, Roque found this encouraging. "I was hoping we could talk. I hated leaving this morning, the way things stood."

Her eyes seemed focused on a spot several feet beyond him. "And how," she said, "would you say things stood?"

A sudden wind sent a shudder through the chinaberry tree, rattling loose a few pale leaves. "Can I come in?"

Her eyes blinked slowly, just once, like a cat's. She stepped back and he followed her to the kitchen, grateful for the warmth.

She poured them both tea in the breakfast nook. A wooden statuette of a bodhisattva named Jizo—typically portrayed as a child monk, she'd once explained, guardian of women and travelers, enemy of fear, champion of optimism—rested on a teakwood platform at the center of the table. Steam frosted the windows looking out on her terraced backyard. In the sink, a drip from the faucet made a soft drumbeat against the blade of a carving knife perched across a bowl.

"Something strange has come up," he said. "I kinda wanted someone to talk to."

She sat with her elbows propped on the tabletop, cup lifted, as though to hide behind it. "I thought you wanted to discuss what happened between us."

"I do. Yes. I'm just saying . . ." The thumping drip from the sink unnerved him. "Last night, why couldn't you stop crying?"

She regarded him with sad disbelief, then chuckled. "What a treat it would have been to get asked that at the time."

"I'm sorry."

"I gathered that. Or I wouldn't have let you in." She brushed a stray lock of hair from her eyes. "What will it take to get you to pay attention to what I'm feeling, Roque?"

"I thought I did pay attention."

A rueful snort. "We had sex."

He felt his stomach pitch. The woody scent of the tea didn't help. "It wasn't like that."

"I know it wasn't. But it wasn't all loving kindness, either."

"I'm sorry."

"Stop saying that, please. You're being sorry isn't much help, frankly." She sat back, glancing out at her dormant garden. "I haven't much wanted to get into this, but things haven't been so great for me the past year or so. The drinking tells you that much. That's new, trust me. I never used to drink, not like now, not till after my divorce."

She'd been married to an air force captain. "Your husband didn't love you."

She made a face, like he'd missed the point entirely. "Yes, he did, Roque. Just badly."

"Talk like that, anything passes for love."

"Oh please, just once, try to realize that things are going to look very different to you in a few years, all right?"

He blanched from the scolding. Gradually, anger brought his color back.

She said, "I can tell you're taking that the wrong way."

"There's a right way?"

"Yes, actually." Beyond the steam-fogged window a crow rustled the branches of the tangerine tree. "I'm trying to make you understand what middle age is like."

He slumped in his chair. "That's all you ever talk about."

"Please, listen. You get to where I am, see all the things you wanted that never showed up and realize, finally, they never will. This time of year just makes it worse. I'm feeling all bitter and Brahmsian and bored with myself." She shivered. "God, that sounds like the line from a song. What I mean is, this thing, here, between you and me? It's just an attempt to pretend I'm not really getting older. There. That simple, that stupid, that sad. As for you—"

This part wasn't new. "You think I'm needy."

"I think you need, yes, a kind of love I can't promise or provide."

"And what about the love I can provide?"

"I'm more concerned about what you can't promise, actually."

"Which is?"

"Please, stop being so angry, so—"

"You think you know how I feel. So why do you get so scared when I try to tell you what I'm actually feeling?"

"I was your age once, remember. I had passion and confidence and exuberance, all that lovely stuff. I envy you. But I can't recover what I've lost through you."

Roque was floored. You think I don't understand despair, he thought. You think I don't know what it means to be lonely and desperate for something to justify the hassle of getting through the day. You think I don't see what Tía Lucha and Tío Faustino and you and everybody else your age goes through, that I don't get it, I don't care.

"I can give you back your hope."

She looked chastened. Then: "No, you can't."

"I can make you happy."

"You do make me happy. You infuriate me and, I'm sorry, bore me sometimes, but yes, I'm mostly happy when we're together. But—here again, the age factor comes in—happiness isn't as important as I once thought. It's a pretty slim commodity, actually."

"You'd rather be unhappy?"

"Happiness comes and goes, is what I'm saying. A little sunlight on a gray day, poof, my spirits lift. A melody in my head. On the street, a dog wags its tail—"

"That's not happiness," he said. In fact, what it sounded like was boredom.

"Yes, it is. That's the sneaky truth about happiness. It's pretty ho-hum stuff. As for hope, it's just a way to trick yourself into thinking the future can't go wrong."

"What I mean by happiness is how we feel when we're together."

"That will change."

"Yeah. It'll get better."

"You can't know that. Trust me."

"If you really believe that, why live?"

Her eyes met his. "The question I ask myself several times a day."

"Don't talk like that."

" 'Death is like the falling of a petal from a rose. No more. No less.' " She turned her cup in its saucer, as though it were a sort of compass. "In case you're interested in the Zen view."

"You're not seriously—"

"I know, how thoroughly *seppuku* of me."

"Stop joking about it."

"Don't worry, I'm not contemplating suicide. But do I think about death more and more? Why yes I do. And you shouldn't.

It would be wrong and selfish and cowardly of me to inflict all that on you. Besides, there are worse things than loneliness. I let myself forget that."

"You'd rather be alone than with me."

"You make me want to drink, Roque. You make me want to drink and fuck and laugh and forget."

"And that's so terrible?"

"It's cowardice. It's unfair. To us both." She said this with a sort of guilty kindness, fiddling with her cup. "You mentioned that something had come up, right? And you needed to talk about it."

"Yeah. My uncle. The one they arrested yesterday."

"He's not really your uncle, though, if I remember."

"Close enough. I owe him. Big-time. His son, Happy, he's come back. He got deported, couple years ago. Showed up out of the blue. I met with him this morning."

She looked at him askance. "What are you saying?"

"Tía Lucha has to stay here to earn enough to look after Godo. Godo's too messed up to travel anywhere, that's not gonna change. Happy's not supposed to be here in the first place, no way he can just come and go."

"Go where?"

"El Salvador."

Her eyebrows arched. "Why—"

"I have to go down and make sure the money we send gets into the right hands, make sure Tío Faustino doesn't get screwed by the *mareros*."

"The who?"

"Gang members. They're the ones who can get him through Guatemala and Mexico. The borders have tightened up down there. It's not as easy as it used to be to come north. Money's not enough, you'll just get ripped off. Or worse. And Tío Faustino's no spring chicken."

"And you'll be doing what in all this?"

"We get close to the border, the *mareros* take Tío, hike him overland, I drive through the checkpoint. I've got an American passport, it's like magic down there. I pick up Tío on the other side, some designated spot. Guatemala, then Mexico, then the U.S."

"That's insane. How can you trust these people?"

"Like we've got a choice? The drug cartels took over the smuggling routes. You can't just go it alone, too easy to get killed or betrayed. Happy already has some angle worked, he hooked up with these people when he came across this last time. All we need's the money."

"I can't believe you're even thinking—"

"I can't let the family down."

"Your family shouldn't ask you to do something so stupid."

"Please, don't talk about my family like that."

"You've got too much promise."

"It's not about me."

"You're just trying to prove yourself. To this cousin."

His hand ventured across the table, searching for hers. "It's nice, by the way, to hear you say I've got promise."

"I've always said that. When does all this happen?"

"Happy's got a line on a job for me, some moving company, guys he knows." He drew back the neglected hand. "Like I said, we need money, more so now. It'll take anywhere from six weeks to six months for them to deport Tío Faustino. They've got laws on the books, from the civil war, making it harder to send Salvadorans back home. It creates a lot of red tape. But he's got no case, no lawyer can help him, he's screwed. So it's just a matter of time."

She rose from the table, walked to the sink, staring out past the muslin curtains. "I'm not going to save you from yourself, Roque, if that's what you came here for."

He felt stunned. "That's what you think?"

She opened the spigot, ending finally the thudding drip, and rinsed her cup. "I care about you. What you're thinking of doing, I wish I could stop you, talk you out of it. But I also get the feeling that's precisely what you want me to do. It feels manipulative. It feels wrong."

"It is wrong. Everything you just said."

"That's not what I meant."

"I know what you meant." He glanced again at the bodhisattva Jizo, guardian of travelers. What she meant was goodbye, she'd been saying it all along. Maybe it was time he listened.

PART II

NINE

"HAVE I TOLD YOU LATELY THAT I HATE THIS?"

Roque sat slumped back in his seat, watch cap and work gloves in his lap, as he studied the images in the mirror outside his window: Puchi and Chato standing at the back of the truck, shaking down the couple whose furniture the crew had just hauled to their new home in Pinole. The man taught high-school history. His wife, flamboyantly pregnant, worked for a florist.

Happy sat behind the wheel. He was smoking, waiting for the word: Unload or take off. In time, he said, "You got some better idea how to pay for Godo's meds, cover the nut on getting my old man back here, I'm all ears." Cocked head, reflective smile. "Into each life, *mi mosca muerta*"—my little innocent, literally my dead fly—"some fucking rain must fall."

Roque turned his gaze toward the sky. The winter sun hovered beyond a filmy mass of noonday cloud. "Thanks for the update."

"Life's full of things you gotta do, not wanna do."

"No shit? Try practicing scales six hours a day."

Happy stubbed out his smoke. "Scales, yeah. I bet it's a bitch."

Let it go, Roque told himself. He regarded Happy differently now, admiration too lofty, respect too blasé, but that was the emotional territory.

He'd asked Roque's help writing a letter to his father, asking forgiveness for being such a crap son, explaining what the last two years had been like since being deported. Roque could hardly believe some of the things Happy told him to write down: the cops with dogs at the airport in Comalapa, who led him to a dank basement room, called him a faggot, told him to strip, just to check for gang tats; the hunchback priest who played harmonica and let him stay at his shelter for three days in the capital, then kicked him loose; old Tripudo the truck driver, a friend of the humpback priest, who took him on, teaching him how to handle a rig, only to betray him, turn him over to some rogue cops who handcuffed him, hooded him, drove him to the prison in Mariona, the one they call La Esperanza: Hope; the *marero* inmates who rat-packed him, beat him, raped him, almost drowned him in a cistern stewing with unspeakable filth, mocking him as he lay there on the floor, hands bound, gasping for breath, gazing up at the towers of mayonnaise jars in the disgusting cell—that was how they smuggled in cell phones, knives, drugs, inside jars of mayo; the plump balding warden who saw him the next morning, dressed in his pristine uniform, a parrot perched on his chair back, explaining how it would be: Happy was given a cellphone number, he'd be driven into San Salvador, he was to call the number, tell whoever answered he was sent by Falcón, then do as directed; the restaurant in San Salvador with more than a hundred restless men waiting in line outside, ex-soldiers, ex-guerrillas, answering an ad for contractors in Iraq; the call from a nearby phone booth to a raspy voice that told him to come around the back of the restaurant; the beefy *guanaco* at the table in the empty dining room, with his dyed hair and crisp white guayabera, brandishing an unlit cigar, telling Happy he'd been hired as a driver hauling freight between Abu Ghraib and Najaf—the coalition liked Salvadorans, the man said, they didn't crap their pants when a bomb went off—for which he'd be paid $2,500 a week, all but $250 of which he'd kick back to a numbered account. That was the deal, go to Iraq and get shaken down or go back to that cell with the *mareros* and get punked to death, which was how Happy wound up in the same hell as

Godo, except fate denied them the privilege of knowing that or ever getting in touch.

Roque didn't know how he'd survived it, not that Happy had come back unscathed. The sullen moods he'd always been known for now seemed not just more severe but even a little sinister—but who could fault him for that? And yet he never complained, not about what happened in El Salvador or Iraq or anything else. Roque sometimes marveled at that, how Happy stared life down, standing there at the edge of every moment, unrushed, unworried, as though, by expecting nothing anymore, not from life, not from people, he'd somehow been set free.

At the same time, within the family, he was kind. He spoke to Godo like an equal, not a rival, not that they didn't get into it now and then. Like a pair of dogs in a pit sometimes, those two, but not near as bad as before he went away. And he showed Tía Lucha a level of deference even she found unsettling. The only person he treated the same as before was Roque. He was the one person Happy still expected something from.

Meanwhile, at the back of the truck, Puchi was explaining to the parents-to-be how it would go. The couple could pay an extra three grand to get their stuff unloaded or everything stayed in the truck, the crew would drive away and put everything they owned in storage until they came up with the money. It was their own fault, he'd tell them, not quite those words, their failure to realize that the initial low bid was just an estimate (a lie—the lowball quote was presented as final), and that only once their belongings were loaded could a full and fair price for the move be calculated (another lie—the setup was in play from the start).

Insinuated but left unsaid was a hint of accusation. The couple had been greedy, hoping to score off a bunch of wetbacks, rather than pay the going rate. Well, they deserved what they got and it would only get worse if they didn't play smart. American Amigos Moving wasn't licensed, so the couple had no real recourse. There was no agency to complain to, no cops to call; this was a civil matter, the officers would say, not a criminal one. That was the mind-bending irony at the heart of the scam, your only shot at justice was with a company that was straight to begin with. Basically, the lovely couple could cough up or get screwed. Puchi was explaining all this with Chato sulking nearby in his hairnet and hoodie and work gloves, chewing on a toothpick, smirking at the lady, eye-fucking the man.

"When I was in Iraq," Happy said, "sometimes the foreman would tell us to drive the route even if there was nothing to carry. Several times a week we did this, one direction or both. This one time, I hauled a single bag of mail, nothing else, on a fucking flatbed. Know why? Because the company was getting paid by the trip, not the load." He glanced at Roque, smiling as though the things he knew could cripple the mind. "This is a war zone I'm talking about. You never knew what was out there. But hey, shut up, it's money. You die, tough luck. It was insane, the arrogant dumbfucks you had to deal with, the I-don't-give-a-shit attitude, the rip-offs, but the geniuses who run things, they're all, Hey, don't ask questions, you're fucking with the war. So you think this couple here's getting screwed by us? Trust me, they've already been fucked so bad by Uncle Sam we're practically the good guys."

Even given all Happy had been through, there were limits to what Roque would swallow. "That's messed-up thinking."

Happy nodded and said, "Maybe so." Lighting another smoke—he'd developed an incredible habit during his years away—he added, "I was just trying to make you feel better."

Roque glanced toward his mirror again, just in time to see the history teacher shove Puchi in the chest. "Ah nuts," he said, reaching for the door handle.

"What?"

"We got a scrapper."

Roque hustled to the back of the truck and was shortly joined by Happy. The history teacher, who was lanky but muscular, had

Puchi in a headlock now, the two of them thrashing around on the ground. Puchi wasn't fighting back very hard. In fact, unless Roque was mistaken, Puchi was laughing.

Meanwhile Chato hovered nearby, the same nervy smile on his face he wore no matter what was happening. In the driveway, the woman with the basketball belly stood there aghast, hands in the air, watching her husband try to claim back some manhood. She was dressed in a shapeless smock, a stretched-out cardigan, kneesocks with worn heels, scuffed clogs. Roque wondered what they intended to name the baby.

The neighborhood was one of those forgettable developments shooting up everywhere now, the houses all basically the same, neat but slapdash, too close together, bottom rung on the American dream. No one was looking out their windows at the wrestling match. Why bother? The new neighbors would be gone, or you would, before any favor could be returned.

Finally Puchi broke free, stood up, brushed himself off. Sure enough, he was chuckling. The teacher scrambled to his feet, scavenged around for his glasses. "You're not getting away with this!" Tufts of hair stood out from his head, his face shiny and red.

Puchi signaled to the crew: Back in the truck. "Let's go," he said.

The teacher found his glasses. "You're not going anywhere."

"I have to call the office," Puchi said. "You attacked me."

"You're cheating us!"

"May be an extra thousand on top of the three you already owe. Have to call, find out."

That was when the woman spoke up. "For God's sake just pay them, Peter." Her eyes were dull with disappointment but her voice had an odd allure. Throaty, an alto, it reminded Roque of a young Celia Cruz. The man's head snapped toward her. Something between them suggested a bitter history and Roque guessed the baby played a part in that. He sensed as well that the woman had reached a truce with her life in a way the man resented.

"How am I supposed to—"

"Peter, please," she cut him off. "Don't make things worse than they already are."

Listen to her, Roque thought, but the guy just seemed more pissed. Turning back, he said, "This is why people want to send you all back where you came from. For Christ's sake, we're on your side."

Of course you are, Roque thought. Who else would be chump enough to hire a company with a name like American Amigos Moving? But that was when the guy did the strangest thing. Spinning toward Chato, he lashed out with a wayward backhand. "What the hell are you grinning at—eh, *pendejo*?"

The guy wants to get pounded, Roque thought, so he can hold it against his wife, but then Happy stepped in. With one arm outstretched to keep Chato at bay, he met the man's eye, not threatening, almost sad. "Let us unload your things," he said quietly. "We'll get you into your new home, then we'll be gone."

"Listen to him, Peter."

"Whose side are you on, Belinda?"

"Let me help you," Happy said. "Let's get this thing done."

Smooth, Roque thought, like he was daring the guy: Raise your game. Trust me. Strange coming from Happy, who expected nothing from people anymore. Stranger still, it worked.

Happy and Puchi and the history teacher drove off to wire an extra three grand through Western Union. Roque and Chato waited on the sidewalk while the pregnant wife locked herself inside the house, nothing but her and the bare rooms and all that fresh paint. Roque chased chord progressions around in his head, visualizing the various fingerings for the inversions, wishing he were someplace else. Chato patted his hairnet, murmured insults, did a couple dozen push-ups, shadowboxed, cracked his knuckles, the whole time wearing that same wiggy smile.

When Happy and Puchi came back in the truck, the teacher parked across the street, slammed his car door and told the crew to unload everything on the driveway, he didn't want them inside his house. That seemed to work for all concerned. The guy could either lug it all in himself in a pique of sucker's pride or call whatever old friends wouldn't hold his cheap *tacaño* stupidity against him.

"Don't think this is the end of things," the guy said when Puchi and Chato climbed up into the back of the now empty truck. "I'm calling the Better Business Bureau. I'll post notice on the Web. I'll make it my daily business to see nobody gets screwed by you fuckers again."

Too late, Roque thought as he slammed the door to the cab. They had jobs lined up through next month, same scam as for these two birds, if not through American Amigos Moving then Nuevo California Shipping and Transport or Marko's Movers or half a dozen other names, each with its own ad on the Internet, each with its own sham address. It was part and parcel of the American way of life, cheap Latino labor. Who with his head on straight could act surprised if once in a while the tables got turned?

And yet, Roque told himself, that was just another kind of messed-up thinking, like *tigueraje*, the peculiarly Latino answer to conscience. If something was there for the taking, only a fool wouldn't grab it. It explained a lot of things south of the border, like how a subcontinent filled with basically decent, generous, hardworking people, millions upon millions of them, could be enslaved for generations by a handful of smug, prissy, sadistic thieves. Sooner or later, you bought in. You learned: Gotta go along to get along, every man has his price, greed is the grease on the wheel. You recognized the *tigueraje* in your own soul.

Happy's cell phone rang. He plucked it from his coat pocket, listened briefly, and said first "Okay," then "*Cuídate*" before snapping it shut and stuffing it back in his pocket. To Roque, he said, "I'll drop you off at home. Start packing. You're on the red-eye to Comalapa."

HAPPY SEEMED UNUSUALLY SOLEMN ON THE DRIVE TO THE AIRPORT, even by his standards, but that didn't keep him from repeating the same instructions over and over. Roque nodded absently, occasionally adding a "Sure" or "I get it" just to convince Happy he was listening. As they pulled up to the curb outside the international terminal, Happy put the truck in park, clicked on his flashers and reached across the seat for Roque's arm.

"One last thing. This is important." Happy licked his lips, an odd show of nerves. "You're not gonna just be bringing my dad back. Okay? There's another guy coming."

Roque felt like a hundred pounds of deadweight just got lashed to his back. "How long you known this?"

"He's Iraqi, I met him over there. His name's Samir."

Something wasn't getting said. "Iraq?"

A woman cop pacing a nearby crosswalk let out an earsplitting whistle shriek, trying to get traffic to move. The crowded terminal glowed and hummed, a temple of chrome and glass.

"He was our terp, for the company I worked for. He went out on convoys with us."

"How am I supposed to find him?"

"It's taken care of." Then: "He's a good guy. If things get tricky, you can trust him. He's smart, he knows his way around. He can help you."

The roar of an airliner in takeoff drowned out everything else for a moment, the honking horns, the cop and her whistle, the cries of the skycaps, the loudspeaker announcements. But Roque felt it even stronger than before, a charge in the air, something left hanging.

Finally, Happy said, "Samir saved my life."

It came out like a guilty secret. Roque couldn't help feeling he'd just been enlisted in an impossible promise. "This another one of those long stories you're always coming up with?"

"Yeah." Happy seemed to drift back from somewhere far away. "You better go. But ask him about it. Samir. He'll tell you."

Roque murmured, "Whatever," and reached for the door handle, but Happy reached across the cab again, gripping Roque's shoulder and turning him back. Their eyes met. Happy's were hard and grave as he said, "I'm proud of you—know that? We all are."

TEN

EVEN THE STUFFED PANDA ON THE SOFA REEKED OF CIGARETTE smoke. Happy nudged it aside to sit, conceding he wasn't really one to judge, given his own habit of late.

The bear belonged to Vasco's daughter, Lucía, who often got stranded here for hours. "Time to myself," the mother called it, which struck a more suitably parental tone, Happy supposed, than "heading out to tweak with the bitch patrol." *El otro equipo. Las marimachas*. The other team. Lesbos. That's what Vasco called them, at least when Chula, his wife, wasn't in earshot.

Vasco ran Puchi and Chato's crew, a mishmash of rough-edged and luckless Salvadorans, most of them present or former Brown Town Locos who'd outgrown street dealing. They had big-heist pretensions now, with hopes of being regarded as bona fide *salvatruchos*: members of Mara Salvatrucha, MS-13. The gang had become to Salvadorans what La Eme, the Mexican Mafia, was to *mejicanos*, bigger even, because their territory covered all of Central America south to Nicaragua, and cities as distant as Boston, Washington, Houston, Chicago, San Francisco and the hub: Los Angeles. But as yet it was a sprawling, hydra-headed mess. No one had established the kind of command and control that could confer on any of its would-be *clicas* status as bona fide or bogus. There were too many wannabes, even out-and-out phonies.

But that was Happy's in. He had a message from the emperor. He had status to confer.

Vasco's office sat perched atop the garage for the truck yard where they parked and maintained the three long beds used for American Amigos and the other strong-arm movers. Downstairs, Chato and Puchi and a few other *vatos* were working late, sharing a blunt as they lazily swept out the bays and hosed down the trucks.

Lucía wasn't there, for which Happy felt grateful. The child was a homely rag of a girl, both needy and remote. More to the point, she was mean. Not that Happy blamed her. She always seemed to be suffering from pink eye, a phlegmy cough, some kind of rash, and who wouldn't get a bitch on with Vasco and Chula for parents.

Coils of copper wire lay stacked in the corner, stolen from empty houses and office buildings and even the pull boxes for streetlights, from which the wire had been dragged out by force after sawing through the bundled cable, latching it to the hitch on the back of a pickup. Quite an operation, as Happy knew firsthand; he'd been part of the crew that ripped out this particular batch. It was big news in Rio Mirada, the number of public buildings vandalized, the intersections where the streetlights merely flashed because the conduits had been gutted. No sooner would the repairs be complete than Vasco's *malandrines* would strike again.

"This is a cash-strapped city," the police chief had intoned on TV the other night. "We really could use the public's help on this."

In the opposite corner, handbills for mortgage assistance lay scattered in haphazard piles: *In Foreclosure? Save Your Home! We Buy Houses for Cash!* Vasco was the local ghetto hump for the company that worked the scam, tricking people into refinancing plans that stripped out all their equity through cash-back-at-closing schemes, disguising the payouts as costs and fees. Sometimes they snatched title outright, leaving the homeowners with nothing. Happy wondered if they were in league with the crooks who'd screwed his father and Lucha.

Vasco was yammering away on the phone, dressed in a black cowboy shirt with white piping, black jeans, white sharkskin boots with a matching belt, rocking in his chair and clutching his cigarette like a dart. He'd wrapped up the conversation minutes ago but was dragging it out, trying to show Happy who was boss, who could be made to wait.

Finally Vasco signed off and tossed the phone onto his desk, after which he rubbed his eyes, scratched his paunch, gazed out the window. His neck bore a patch of shiny flesh, the ghost of a tattoo he'd had removed. "Pinole was a problem?"

Happy didn't answer right away. Two could play this game. "That a surprise?"

Vasco waved the question away while exhaling a final plume of smoke, stubbing out his butt. "You said there was something to discuss."

Happy could feel, like a thumb flick, the pulse in his throat. "I've got a proposal. Not just me. Me and some people back in El Salvador." The words sounded odd inside his skull, bats fluttering out of a cave.

Vasco mustered a yawn but his eyes betrayed his interest. "What people?"

"The guys who helped me get across."

"I never heard this."

"Heard what?"

"That you were involved with any, you know, people. Crossing over."

"How the hell else was I gonna do it?"

"Beats me." Vasco was already lighting up another smoke. "You still in contact?"

"Would I be pitching this if I wasn't?"

"I dunno, you tell me."

Happy resisted an urge to get up, cross the room, tip Vasco out of his chair like a pumpkin from a wheelbarrow. "You don't want the offer, I'll take it to Sancho."

Emilio "Sancho" Perata was the shot caller for the 23rd Street Locos Salvatruchos, out of Richmond, as yet the only quasi-legitimate northern MS-13 *clica* outside San Francisco.

Vasco said, "Sancho would laugh in your face. Then he'd string you up by the balls."

"Not for three million a year."

For a moment, it felt as though gravity had loosened its hold on things. The whole room seemed to float.

Vasco said, "Get outta town."

"Things've been loose up till now, right? No *el mero mero* calling the shots for everybody. That's gonna change. And the *clicas* that get in first, make the connection to the chiefs below the border—"

"You mean L.A."

"L.A. answers to El Salvador now. That's something you should know. Fuck, El Salvador *is* Los Angeles now. All the deportees."

"How the fuck you know these people?"

"Prison. After I got sent down myself."

Vasco tipped back and pondered that, rocking. His face was pockmarked and sagging from all the abuse, the crank and the liquor, the pills and the smoke, plus the stress of his petty empire. The purplish fluorescence of the overhead light didn't help. "Why should I trust some *mensos* in lockup? Especially when they're thousands of miles away?"

"Because if you don't, somebody else will. Sancho, for one. You wanna end up answering to him?"

"Won't happen. Not me."

"Oh yeah. You."

"Bullshit. What is this, some kind of threat? You come in here, try to shake me down?"

"I'm offering you a shot at one and a half mil a year."

"I thought you said three."

"Three tops, one and a half guaranteed. That sound like a shakedown to you?"

In the window behind Vasco the moon peeked beneath a vast ledge of cloud. Downstairs, one of the *vatos* cackled, "*Te lo dije, él es un malapaga*." I told you, he's a deadbeat.

Vasco met Happy's eyes and let the stare linger. "Smuggling what, exactly?"

"First thing, you help me get my uncle and another guy across the border."

"That's not my problem."

"You wanna get to phase two it is. My people are in with the Valle Norte cartel. They're gonna move the product by boat, it'll sail out of Turbo, Colombia, hidden on pallets under loads of tropical fruit—bananas, plantains, mangoes. After a layover in Acajutla it'll come into the Oakland port, my dad and I will know which shipments, he'll work it so he gets the load. He'll truck it to a warehouse in Richmond owned by an importer who's already on board. You'll divide up the shipment, send it to the various wholesalers around the bay. They pay you, you skim your share, the rest goes back south through the channel."

"These people have names?"

"You buy in, then you'll know what you need to know."

"This is bullshit. You're winding me up. *Buy in*?"

Happy reminded himself this was all for his father. "How else you think this happens?"

"How much?"

"Thirty grand."

"You're out of your fucking mind."

"That's five jobs like the couple in Pinole today. For one and a half mil a year on the back end. Guaranteed."

"Nothing's guaranteed."

"You're not paying attention to what I'm telling you."

"You think I'm handing thirty large to you with nothing but—"

"You're not handing it to me."

"Who then?"

"You're wiring it to El Salvador. Once it gets there, my father and this other guy I mentioned? They get brought up across the border. Once that's done, you're in on the franchise."

"Okay, that's twice now you've mentioned this other guy. Who is he?"

Happy paused for the proper effect. "He's from the Middle East."

Vasco blanched. "You saying what I think you're saying?"

"Once he's here, he vanishes, you have no more connection to him."

"And when he does whatever he's gonna do, and they connect all the dots and find out how he got across?"

"There's no way to tie you to it."

"You said I'm wiring money."

"From somewhere here in the Bay Area to San Salvador, happens a thousand times every day. You smurf it down in smaller amounts, use a fake name, or have everybody on the crew send a piece, fake names again, and we bribe the guy at the *envío de dinero* window. It gets picked up by someone on the other end, again a fake name, he vanishes on that end. Who knows where he goes, who he meets or what he does with the money? You got ghosts on both ends and they can't track one guy sneaking across the border regardless. Can't be done, no matter what they say. Meanwhile, once he's across and forgotten, you get rich."

Vasco seemed puzzled by it all and angry he had to work so hard figuring out the downsides. "You say this guy, this Arab, he's coming across with your old man? He does, they get caught, that ties the Arab to you. You're tied to me. I'm fucked."

"They'll split up before they cross. Christ, use your head." Happy decided not to mention Roque's involvement and made a mental note to keep it a secret from here on out. "You think everybody's stupid but you?"

Vasco wasn't backing off. "You got somebody on the border, somebody you're bribing to get everybody across."

Happy shook his head. "Vasco, listen to me, it's not your problem."

"Like hell it's not my problem. Some bent fed gets caught helping a terrorist across, you think they're not gonna fuck his ass bloody till he coughs up every goddamn name he knows?"

"He won't know yours."

"Prove it."

"The guy who takes the money in San Salvador is like twenty links removed from anybody taking a cut at the border, and that's all cash, hand to hand."

Vasco's gaze drifted toward the window again, met his reflection in the glass. "How long you been sitting on this?"

"What do you mean?"

"How long you known about it?"

"You think I been shopping it around?"

"How *long*?"

"The coke thing's been in the works for a while. Since I've been back I get texted every few days, progress reports, questions. Then my old man got popped and I said, Let's do it. Started putting a plan together, to bring him back and get this other thing rolling, the franchise. They added the curve, the Arab. Said the one depended on the other. I've got no say."

"And you chose me." Vasco didn't sound pleased or privileged. "Why?"

"You want me to go someplace else?"

"Answer the fucking question."

Happy told himself: Let him rant. It would make the prospect of getting the last laugh that much sweeter. "Just seemed wise, start with somebody I know."

"Not like we've ever been exactly tight, though. Am I right?"

"No, which is why I won't have a problem taking this someplace else, you turn it down."

"You're setting me up." Vasco cracked a sick smile, pointing his finger. "You're setting me up, cocksucker."

Happy unbuttoned his flannel, opened it. "Pat me down, you feel that way."

"I want nothing to do with no ragheads blowing up buildings."

"You're not seeing the whole picture. I take this elsewhere, you don't just lose the Colombian franchise. You gonna find yourself on the bottom looking up at whoever grabs it. Don't say I didn't warn you. Guy who steps forward gets to play kingpin this end of the bay. *El mero mero*. Could be you. If so, you're the one who gets to collect taxes. Nobody moves nothing without giving you a piece. You walk into any *salvadoreño* business you want, you tell them what they pay, you'll protect them from anybody else tries to move in, shake them down. You'll have the muscle to kick the *norteños* back into Sonoma, you'll run things up here. This anoints you. You turn your back on this, though, all that shit rains down on you. You can ride or get ridden. Just the way it is. Meanwhile, you're already set up to launder the money through the business here, all the other shit you got in play. That's one more advantage you've got over the competition. They're just street hustlers. They can't take it to the next level."

Vasco's black eyes jittered back and forth as he thought it through. He was sick of being dictated to by the men working the mortgage scam, you could tell by the way he talked about it. They were no smarter than he was but there were angles to the thing he hadn't mastered yet, a degree of finesse he lacked. Sooner or later the moving racket would tap out and there was only so much copper wiring to steal and there were rumors the price was about to tank. Everybody was trying to get into identity theft, computer scams, low risk, high reward, but that wasn't Vasco's realm. He'd come up through street dealing and takeovers, spent a few years inside himself, Santa Rita on a possession beef, Folsom for the armed robbery. He'd emerged from prison pledged to a cagier tack, conning the dupes, but he wasn't a natural. Basically, he was stuck, edging thirty, chasing around for his next good idea, tied to a crank-whore shrew and her demon child. If he didn't make a bold move soon he'd get eaten alive from above or betrayed from below.

"You say you and your old man, you work the port angle."

"Vasco, stop worrying and thank your luck."

"How much a piece you want for that? You haven't brought that up."

"I figure twenty points."

"*Twenty fucking points?*"

"The port's where the risk is. That's where they look the hardest."

"You just shaved three hundred grand off my one-point-five mil."

"Stop looking at the floor, look at the ceiling. Three mil's easy you work it right, first year alone, and that's just the coke run."

"Meaning what, six hundred grand for you, that right?"

"Add in the protection money, the taxes, the other rackets you got going? You can be in the shit, you want. But you gotta step up."

Vasco turned away, glancing down into the truck yard. Puchi was hurling rocks at the crows perched on the telephone wires. Chato shadowboxed, the others looking on, cheering, mocking. "I say yes to this, Godo comes in."

Happy cocked his head, as though he hadn't heard right. "Sorry?"

"Godo. He helps pay off this outrageous nut you're asking for."

"You seen him since he's been back?"

"I've heard."

"He's not good. I'm serious."

"Listen to me. I start seeing money like you're talking about moving through here? Gonna need to weapon up. Godo knows more about that than the rest of us put together. At least, if he doesn't, fucking jarheads aren't what they're cracked up to be."

"Vasco—"

"He can teach us things. Things we'll need to know, in case the *norteños* don't pack off to Sonoma all peaceful."

"Vasco, listen. I mean it, Godo's damaged, way more than you know. He can't remember dick one moment to the next, his mind wanders, he makes shit up—"

"Okay," Vasco cut in, leaning forward, his voice a whisper, "now it's time you listen to me, *chero*. Godo comes in, gives the boys some weapons training, some tactics for protection, you hear where I'm going. Or be my guest, shop this can of worms around. Because you know and I know that anybody who bites is going to bitch you down to five points at best, or just push you aside altogether, maybe worse, when the thing is up and running. Here, you got a history. Nobody's gonna turn you out. But there's a price to that, right? Godo comes on board. This is not negotiable. I'm not so stupid I don't know you brought this here first because this is where you wanna be. I don't blame you. I'm grateful, matter of fact. And I'm not saying Godo steps up and pitches in somehow, helps us lean on anybody. Unless, of course, he's okay with that. But the guys respect him, he knows things we don't. So that's the way it is, or yeah, I'm gonna pass. And I'm not handing thirty grand to nobody till I meet a real live human being, not just you, who can vouch that this isn't a jar of smoke. The guy who owns this warehouse you talked about, maybe."

Happy suddenly found himself wondering what Vasco's stint in Folsom had been like, how many nights he'd suffered through the kind of thing the *mareros* had inflicted amid the mayonnaise jars in the cell at Mariona. "I can try to arrange a meet. Probably not with the warehouse guy, not until you're in. But somebody."

"If this thing is real, you can make it happen."

"As for Godo—"

"You can make that happen too."

"I need some time to think about it."

Vasco lit another smoke with the end of his last. He was smiling. The smile said: Now who gets to ride, who gets ridden?

Happy said, "Problem is, we don't *have* time."

"Your problem. Not mine. Not yet, anyway."

"If anything happens, to Godo I mean—"

"Like what?"

"He has a meltdown. He freaks out. He almost shot two agents during a raid at the trailer park."

"I heard." Vasco chuckled. "I like that, actually."

"You weren't there. Way it got told to me, it was fucking spooky."

"Godo scares people. I don't see the problem. Now what's it going to be?"

"Like I said, I need time."

Again, that smile. Stop worrying, it said. Thank your luck. "But, *chero*, you said it yourself. You don't *have* time."

Happy pictured it then, Vasco face flat on the concrete floor, held down by the others, a rag stuffed in his mouth as one by one they took him, shamed him, made him their punk. "If anything happens to Godo, I hold you to account."

Vasco waved him off. He propped his boots on his desk, ankles crossed. "Since when are you two so close? Don't remember you guys having one good thing to say about each other."

Happy got up to go. Glancing back at the foul-smelling panda, he said, "Ever think of washing that thing? Can't be good for the girl, way it is."

Vasco looked at him like he'd just proposed the absurd. "What, you get your ass deported to El Salvador, you come back an expert on kids?"

ELEVEN

ROQUE HAD TO TELL HIMSELF: STOP STARING. IT WASN'T JUST the bruise—strange how, even with the plum-colored swelling and the gash across her cheek, the girl somehow remained stunning—or the fact that, from time to time, her uneasy eyes met his. She was a prisoner. Pity wouldn't free her.

He'd been in El Salvador a total of four hours, arriving at the airport in Comalapa before dawn. He'd skated through customs, not so much as a glance inside his knapsack, then ventured out into the soft green heat of daybreak outside the terminal—the sidewalk jammed with well-wishers greeting friends and relatives back from *Gringolandia*, cabbies hawking fares to the capital, touts with bullhorns steering *grenchos* to the psychedelic chicken buses headed for the smaller provincial towns.

He stopped milling and chose a spot to wait against the terminal's dark wall of glass. In time, a droop-lidded *cholo*, thin as a tomcat, edged his way through the crowd. He wore a T-shirt three sizes too large emblazoned with the Arizona Cardinals logo and the words "World Champions, Super Bowl XLIII."

The *cholo* snagged Roque's arm. "You're the musician." His lips curled in a slack smile, as though both offering a compliment and slapping down a challenge. "Call me Sisco."

He led the way out to a parking lot shaded by eucalyptus trees where a battered Volkswagen Golf waited, tapping out a drumbeat against his thighs as he sang under his breath, "Money for nothin' and your chicks for free." The singing brought on a coughing jag and when he went to cover his mouth Roque noticed the gang tats on his hands, a sinewy art nouveau X on one, three simple dots the other, the telltale thirteen.

"Met your uncle, by the way," he said once the cough was under control. "Nice old dude. Kinda quiet."

As though in tribute, he said little himself all the way to San Salvador, preferring instead to play the radio, a weak-signal pirate station featuring radical tracks the mainstream outlets wouldn't touch, hiking the volume when a favorite tune came on: Pescozada's "Anarquía," Mecate's "El Directo," a punk number by an outfit named Metamorffosis, a dark-wave track by a band called Wired.

Sprawling tracts of sugarcane and bananas vanished into the sunbaked distance. Here and there, women in long skirts and tight black braids pinned laundry up on the barbed wire surrounding their topple-down houses of wood and tin, packs of bone-thin children looking on. Dogs roamed freely, their roadkill quickly set upon by buzzards called *zopilotes*. Meanwhile, bilingual billboards touting everything from Nine West fashion to the inescapable Whopper popped up over and over along the highway, to the point Roque sometimes wondered if he'd really left *Gringolandia* at all.

Coming on noon, they arrived at a crabbed and decrepit *barrio popular* named La Chacra on the ass end of the capital. A grayish soup of dust and car exhaust fouled the air, along with the stench of fermenting trash. The Río Acelhuate, which ran sluggishly through the barrio, was so thick with excrement and toxic waste its mud-brown surface had a purplish glaze.

Sisco slowed to pass a barefoot urchin toddling down the broken pavement, trailing a brood of chickens. A three-story monolith of cinder block rose up at the end of the street, slathered with garish paint, tagged with Mara Salvatrucha graffiti. Scraps of laundry hung limp from rope clotheslines strung along the walkways while *salvatruchos* clustered on every stair, leaning over the railings, smoking blunts or Marlboros and staring down with suspicion, curiosity, indifference, hate.

Roque tried to picture his mother living in a place like this. Maybe she had before fleeing the war, not that anything would be accomplished if he found out one way or the other. He felt an odd lack of curiosity, being in the land of her birth. No matter what, the absence would remain. There was no secret charm or trick that would cure him. Besides, life wasn't something you cured. You lived it. Mariko taught him that much, before kicking him to the curb.

He grabbed his knapsack, shouldered it, patted his pockets for what seemed the thousandth time, checking to be sure he had his passport, then followed Sisco across the street to a squat tin-roof house. At the door Sisco knocked twice, waited until the plate at the judas hole slid back, then presented himself to the disembodied eye peering out. "C'mon, Slobnoxious, *abierto*." A clatter of bolts and chains, then the door edged open, revealing a short broad shovel-nosed *guanaco* Roque's age, maybe a year younger, wearing no shirt, baggy Dickies tugged down below his boxers, a Yankees cap kicked left atop his head.

The kid eyed Roque up and down, then stepped aside, gesturing them into a low-ceilinged room, empty except for two wood chairs and a haphazard array of car-seat cushions. A smell of stale grease and cheap weed lingered. A spray-paint roll call of the local *clica*, Los Putos Bravos, covered one whole wall: Bug, Chega, Lonely . . . Pepón, Snorky, Budú . . . Timo, Malote, Slick . . .

Suddenly Sisco's eyes lit up. "Wait—your last name's Montalvo, right?" He cast a quick glance at Roque, then the doorman's Yankee's cap. "Roque *Montalvo*."

It sounded like a trick question. Roque nodded uneasily.

"Come on, you know what I'm talking about. Salvadoran dude. Same name. Plays center field for the Red Sox?"

He waited, checking Roque's face, then the doorman's, like the coincidence wasn't just curious, it was meaningful—he expected the two strangers to square off, share a little heat, some New York–Boston bullshit. Then Roque realized it was the colors: blue, red. A gang thing. Seconds passed. Everybody gaped at everybody else.

Finally Sisco broke the spell, slapping Roque's arm. "Just messing with you, homes. Ain't no Roque Montalvo plays for the Red Sox."

Turning away, he chested his thumbs, tenting his Cardinals T-shirt. "And the Steelers won the Super Bowl. Welcome to fucking El Salvador."

AT THE END OF THE LONG HALL AN OPEN DOORWAY LED INTO WHAT appeared to be a makeshift recording studio, the walls of the room stapled with cheap acoustic foam. That was when Roque saw her for the first time.

She was seated on a milk crate in the far corner, knees clenched tight, fists tucked beneath her arms. She had the slinky build of a dancer, a graceful neck, two dark moles dotting the hollow of her throat. Her lips were ripe and womanly but real, not plumped by a needle. She wore a white cotton top, jeans, sandals, her long black hair parted on one side and tied into a ponytail—a simple look, Roque thought, but this was no simple girl. She was a *pichona*, a stone beauty, and yet beneath the cocky edge he sensed damage, her face almost feral in its blankness, the mark of some thug's backhand darkening her cheek.

Roque guessed the thug in question was one of the two sitting at the desk backed up against the wall, the pair of them watching a video track on a twenty-four-inch wide-screen iMac G5.

It wasn't the only big-ticket toy in the room. He noticed as well a Sony camcorder, a Butterscotch Blonde Stratocaster with a Vibrolux Reverb amp, a Martin Marquis acoustic, a Korg Triton keyboard, a Digidesign 003 control surface, JBL monitors, Bluebird microphones. He realized now why so much had been made of his being musical. He was here to work.

Sisco caught a glance at what the other two were watching and drifted in behind, leaning toward the monitor. A snarling vocal track—just voices, the usual gassy blustering bullshit, half-assed hip-hop—droned from the JBLs. Roque let his knapsack slip from his shoulder and traded a quick glance with the girl, who regarded him with the same cold fear and barely disguised hate she directed toward the others. I'm not one of them, he wanted to tell her. Given what he'd come to El Salvador to do, though, and who he'd have to deal with to get it done, he wasn't quite sure how true that was.

Finally, one of the two *mareros* at the table cocked his head around to take in Roque. He was somewhere in his twenties, wearing a pale blue polo shirt with tan slacks, as though on break from the sales floor at Circuit City. His face told another story, though: narrow, almost Jesuitical, a pampered goatee, intelligent eyes.

The other cat was huge, shaved head, weight-lifter pop to his muscles, shirtless like the doorman, all that skin ribboned with freak-show ink from his skull down to his waist. To his credit, it wasn't the usual garish chaos. The designs seemed to cohere, with a theme involving dark towers, billowing flames, redemptive lilies.

Glancing at the monitor, Roque realized much of the video had been shot in the front room and featured the tattooed giant, with Sisco and the doorman and the Jesuit popping up here and there among nameless others, all of them vamping in poses of clichéd menace, posturing wildly, throwing *placas*—inverting the devil's horn hand sign to form an *M* for Mara Salvatrucha—brandishing chrome .45s and ivory-handled nunchuks, a wicked collection of knives, a sawed-off pistol-grip shotgun, assault rifles, even a shoulder-mounted rocket launcher. Roque glanced around the room for the weapons, saw none. He had no clue what to make of that.

As for the video, he'd seen dozens like it, the Web was crawling with them. Surprising, he thought, given what he knew of guys like this, that they hadn't added a shot of the girl's jacked-up face. Maybe they were saving that for a later take.

The Jesuit offered a nod in greeting but did not extend a hand. "Ever hear of a guy named Piocha?" His English lacked accent, the voice raspy and deep.

"Yeah," Roque said. Piocha was the stage name of Jorge Manuel, El Salvador's most famous guitarist.

"We got him slotted to do the music track for this video. But Sisco here, he talked to your uncle. He says you know your way around a studio."

Bullshit, Roque thought, Piocha wouldn't come near these guys. "Not sure how my uncle would know that," he said, not wanting to seem overly agreeable. He knew this sort, not so different from Godo or Happy, really. Avoid confrontation, they saw you as weak. "But yeah, I've spent some time at a board."

It wasn't a total lie. He'd sat with Lalo during his recording sessions, paid decent enough attention. He could muddle his way through. The Jesuit invited him to sit and Roque called up the program, noticing a lack of manuals, at which point it dawned on him the stuff was stolen.

It took him ten minutes to figure out their settings, plug everything into the right ports, check to be sure their version of Pro Tools and their Mac OS were compatible, test the Digi 003 for gremlins. Beyond that, without a MIDI to complicate things, it was basically just a digital tape deck.

"Okay, before I start—I'm Roque, by the way?"

The tattooed hulk and the Jesuit traded glances. "Chiqui," the big one said. Short for Chiquitín, Roque guessed: Tiny. The Jesuit followed, "You call me Lonely," said with a pinpoint stare. Roque remembered the name from the wall. Assuming it answered to the same reverse logic as Tiny, he figured it meant the guy was never at a loss for company, female company in particular, clarifying finally who the girl in the corner belonged to.

"Okay," he began again, "I guess I need some idea of what it is you guys are after."

Chiqui began to say something but Lonely cut him short. "How about you show us what you got, put something together for us to judge, then we'll see who needs what."

Roque got that it wasn't a suggestion. "Right."

He replayed the vocal track, got a feel for the beat, a standard rap rhythm, apparently kept with nothing but an inner metronome. The good news, they could hold a beat. That permitted him to lay down a click track for reference.

"Okay," he said to no one in particular, "I'm gonna add a drum bit on the Korg. See what you think." He trolled through the samples on the keyboard, chose one heavy on the backbeat with a Bo Diddley shuffle, fashioned a four-minute loop and played it through the monitor. The wave patterns jagged hypnotically on the computer screen and the Digi dials self-adjusted like a ghost was working the panel. A little theater, he thought, amp my cred. With just the drum track the video instantly seemed bolder, more polished. He glanced around the room. "Sounds like money to me, what you guys think?" The answer was in their faces.

Lonely pointed to the corner. "What about the *zorra*, man?"

Up until that moment, Roque had no inkling the girl was anything but window dressing. "What about her?"

"The bitch is here to sing." Lonely gestured for her to get up, come over. "She knows it."

Roque hadn't felt truly dirty until that moment. He reminded himself this was all for Tío Faustino. He had no choice who to rely on, who to deal with, but the girl's eyes made no distinctions. She rose, arms crossed, and edged up to the pop filter on the microphone.

Roque asked, "What, exactly, is she singing?"

"You figure it out, *culero*. 'Take Me Out to the Fucking Ball Game' for all I care."

If these two are lovers, Roque thought, it was one of those fucked-up death-do-we-part situations, where you can't tell the love from the hate, the pain you suffer—or inflict—only deepens what you feel. But the girl's body told him different: no catty arched spine, no cocked hip, no pout. And the light in her eyes was cold with fright.

"Let me get a few instrumental tracks down first," he said, hoping to buy some time. "And I have to move a few things around, get situated." He turned to her then. Hoping to sound kind but not arouse any jealousy, he said, "You can sit down for now."

"She don't speak English," Lonely said. Accusing. Mocking.

Roque, trying again: "*Puedes sentarte por ahora*."

For the merest instant, her glance settled on him with something other than hate. Please, he thought, don't. Almost instantly the fear returned and she pivoted around, walked back to the milk carton, sat.

He tuned the Stratocaster and the Martin using the keyboard, adjusted the tone and volume dials for the cobalt pickups on the Strat, striving for the spooky hollowed-out bite the guitar was known for, then fiddled briefly with the Digi's volume levels, making sure the waveforms were full and set as high as possible without peaking into distortion. He could feel his heart pounding and once or twice snuck a chance to wipe his damp palms on his jeans. He ran the video twice more to make sure the rhythm track was properly synched, then dubbed in a bass track, again using the Korg, choosing a fat round punchy tone. On top of that he laid down an organ effect, a churchy thrum, with a Hammond B-3 sample.

As he worked, he felt the mood turn in the room. Everyone got quiet, calm, almost reverential. Then a boy appeared in the doorway.

Roque pegged him at ten years old, but kids grow up small down here, he thought. The boy had a cloth bag in one hand, a bottle of Champán in the other, the local variety of cream soda. Lonely gestured him forward. The kid stole a glance at Roque first, then did as he was told.

Lonely snatched the bag from him, peered inside. "*¿Cuánto?*" How much?

The kid, tottering foot to foot, reached behind to scratch his back beneath his shirt. "*Dos cientos, más o menos.*" Two hundred, more or less.

Lonely glanced up, met the boy's eyes. "*¿Más o menos?*" He lashed out, slapped the kid's face, then launched into what felt like a full five minutes of insulting venom, accusing the boy of stealing, skimming off the protection take that had been collected by other *mareros* in shakedowns of the city's bus drivers. The boy stood there and took it, valiant in his way, verging on tears but never giving in. Lonely made to slap him twice more, but settled for just watching him cringe. He asked three times, shouting finally, how much did he steal? The boy answered, "*Goma*," nothing, his voice a little weaker, a little less convincing, each time.

Finally, Lonely ended with: "*Te gusta hacerte el suizo. Consigo mi dinero, lelito.*" You like to play dumb. I get my money, you little fool.

He waved the boy out with disgust. Once he was gone, Lonely turned back to Roque. "What the fuck you looking at?"

Roque collected the Martin, switched to an open D tuning, adjusted the mike down to chair level. His hands were shaking. Get it together, he told himself as he recued the video. Figuring Lonely and his boys for secret sentimentalists, like most punks, he laid on the schmaltzy rubato as he strummed a flamenco-style rhythm track, complete with backhand flourishes and syncopated thumb slaps on the guitar's spruce top. Gradually, the pulse in his neck stopped throbbing.

He followed up with a muted arpeggio pattern on the Strat,

echoing the bass line but elaborating on it too, giving it an edge, a little extra momentum. When it came time to solo he built it in Dorian mode like Santana in "Evil Ways," the off-kilter minor jarring at first then jelling, almost medieval in its eerie drift, but full of bite and heat. After one particularly aching lick he could sense it, the gravitational turn, every eye and ear in the room drawn to him and him alone, and he finished with a series of slowly ascending arpeggios ending in a scream.

Finally, he gestured the girl over again and readjusted the mike-stand height. He wanted to ask her name but knew better. Using the Strat, he played the vocal line he wanted her to follow, no words, just nonsense syllables or open vowels. The thing had enough verbiage as is. He let the girl know it would be okay if she improvised a little, even though he'd be echoing her on the guitar. Using the effects pedal, he bought himself a little distortion, a touch of phase delay, some sustain, then recued the track and said, "*¿Listo?*"

She nodded. He counted it off.

By now the track seemed full and solid, all that was lacking was the haunting high notes, the skin-tingling wail of the *bruja*. The girl obliged, getting it instinctively, her voice throaty but pure. He was impressed. The only problem was, at the high end of her range, she trended flat. He tried to get her pitch to lift by echoing her notes on the guitar, a howling whisper tracking her vocal line, but either she'd never had to blend before, meaning she'd never sung harmony, or she was too scared to hear him.

Once the track was over she glanced at him shyly, fingers twined. He bit back a grin at her girlishness and again caught himself staring at her face, the two punctuating moles on her throat. He told her how much he liked her voice, how rich the tone was, how gutty the timbre, but he wanted to run through the thing again.

—*This time*, he said, *visualize the notes in the air, like balloons, aim for the top, let your voice skim along the upper surface. Understand?*

She swallowed nervously. Nodded.

He recued the track, met her eye, counted off.

They ended up doing four more takes before she nailed it, pitch and all, at which point Roque couldn't hold back his smile anymore, if only from relief. It had been fear after all, tightening her voice. Each time, he followed her improvisations, the same harsh keening whisper in echo, riding the sustain, occasionally jumping a fifth or an octave, then settling back in, note for note. The melody spoke of longing, heartbreak, cold regret, which brought a wistful gravitas to the cocksure gangster bullshit. It made the *mareros* look like men, something they'd botched ridiculously on their own.

But the really marvelous thing was watching her face change as she sang. She winced on anything above an A, clearly still limited by the bruise and gash on her cheek, maybe other wounds he couldn't see, but her voice turned that pain into something clean and nameless. She knew what it meant to suffer, and not just a crack across the jaw. Her face surrendered to it.

When the last take was over, Sisco let go with an almost lovelorn sigh: "*Qué vergón*." Fucking great. Chiqui's rubbery tattooed face twisted into a garish smile. Only Lonely held back. He got up, tugged his Dickies straight, adjusted the sag. "Let's take a break, light up a blunt. Maybe a couple more run-throughs after that."

Roque set the Strat back gently in its chrome stand. "I've come a long way. I'd like to see my uncle."

The room went still. Lonely offered a scornful smile. "Yeah, we'll get to that."

Roque thought about the boy, the beating he had coming. "Look, you do another take, it'll just be different, not better. Right now, it's the best it's gonna get. Trust me." He knew not to come on too strong, naysay the guy with his boys right there, not to mention the girl. But he couldn't afford to let himself get conned into wasting more time. He tried to sound obliging but not cowed. Let the sadistic prick be the good guy, he told himself, a trick perfected growing up with Godo. He picked up his knapsack, making a point not to glance toward the girl.

"Believe me, I've been there when it got to be take after take, till everybody's beat and confused and bored. Once in a while, maybe, you can make decent music that way. You're so exhausted you're almost dreaming your way through it. But, you know, it's luck if that happens. As it stands? You're gonna blow people away, no joke. Now—I know my uncle's gonna be worried, okay?"

THEY REACHED SUCHITOTO AT TWILIGHT. AFTER THE SQUALOR OF LA Chacra, Roque was unprepared for the cobblestone streets, the sleepy architecture, the colonial-era buildings with their eye-slamming colors, a shock of red here, a soothing turquoise there, warm fat yellows in between. A statue of Don Quixote fashioned from scrap metal jousted with a chalk-white cathedral. Plump *sirvientas* in pale blue livery, their hair pinned up, cradled infants and glanced down from wrought-iron balconies.

In the distance, Roque could see Lago de Suchitlán, the lake nestled among rolling hills bronzed by sunset. At the edge of the city they took a ferry—in truth, little more than a small tented barge—crossing to a village called San Pedro Lempa.

Sisco drove down a street of tidy but nondescript shops and houses, past a high foundry wall of arched red brick, then turned left onto a dirt lane that curved up a wooded hill, stopping in front of a yard surrounded by a tall thorny hedge, shaded by mango trees. Beyond the passageway into the yard, the house resembled virtually every other Roque had seen, cinder-block walls, tin roof, but it seemed larger than most, almost palatial, even though the guttering light beyond the curtains suggested kerosene lamps or candle flame.

As Roque prepared to get out, Sisco made his first remark of the trip. "In case you're curious—the *mamita*? Her name's Lupe. Girl is fucking fly, no?"

It couldn't be a good thing, Roque thought, knowing any more about her. He forced a shrug. "Pop the trunk, I'll get my bag."

As he grabbed his knapsack Sisco sidled alongside. A flip smile played across his face, made all the more unnerving by the red glow of the taillights. "*Mejor un bombón para dos*," he said, "*que una mierda para uno*."

It was the first time he'd spoken more than a word or two of Spanish: Better a candy for two than a piece of shit for one. Roque felt his mouth go dry. No matter what he responded, it would get back and that could only harm the girl. Lupe.

"It's not my concern," he said finally. "I've got enough on my hands as is."

Sisco drove off in a spume of exhaust and Roque stood there, watching the taillights disappear beyond the first hill. Rewinding the whole miserable situation in his head, he wondered how badly he'd misjudged things.

Turning back toward the fenced-in yard, he called out, "Tío?"

The stillness didn't feel threatening, just empty. He wondered if he hadn't been stranded, no one around, a little revenge, courtesy of Lonely, who'd seen right through his feigned indifference for the girl. Then a rustling stirred from deep within the house. Shortly a tiny woman appeared in the doorway, Indian braids, a simple white blouse that matched her apron, a long dark skirt. She carried a flickering kerosene lamp.

Roque had no idea what to say to her.

Thankfully, Tío Faustino appeared, edging his way past with a murmured word, then hurrying across the packed dirt yard.

Roque dropped his knapsack and prepared for the embrace, a fierce homesick hug, and soon he felt the trickle of dampness on his uncle's rough cheek.

"Roque, Roque, Roque. *Mi hijo. Al fin. Estás aquí.*"

My son. Finally. You're here.

TWELVE

HAPPY SHOOK OFF THE COLD RAIN AND CHOSE A TABLE NEAR THE back, a midweek lunch crowd, banter and body heat and the raucous aromas of a Vietnamese kitchen. Almost instantly the waiter appeared—three chins, ratty sweater, Asian comb-over. Happy, picking a number at random, ordered a bowl of pho, a ginger-laced soup with noodles and grilled meat, served with mung-bean sprouts, sliced hot chilies, sprigs of fresh cilantro. What he found himself craving, though, was a cigarette. As always his stomach roiled. The diarrhea was back.

He'd never know, he supposed, the cause, whether it was what happened in the Salvadoran prison that night or the skunky untreated water he and all the other foreign workers got for bathing and laundry in Iraq, day in, day out, seeping in through the eyes, the skin, the mouth, courtesy of a private company awarded the contract for on-base services by the Pentagon, a no-bid deal worth billions. If the latter, he could count himself lucky in some regards, all he'd lost was his appetite. He knew other men with incurable rashes, seeping abscesses, whole limbs flaring red with infection. He could conjure a bad itch just thinking about them.

He turned the card over in his hands, obtained from Tía Lucha: Special Agent James Lattimore, Federal Bureau of Investigation. The embossing on the card felt oddly reassuring. A straight cop, according to Roque, not that the kid knew just how bent cops could get. Regardless, Happy didn't have much choice;

he couldn't just walk in to the FBI vestibule, ask for the most honest guy they had.

He studied the restaurant's clientele: government workers, library patrons, museum day-trippers, law students, tattooed punks, flaming gays, Tenderloin trannies, even a few Vietnamese. He tried to imagine who the spy might be. The freckled plump brunette two tables over, picking at her split ends and reading a paperback titled *Dead Ex*? Or the buff preppy in the Men's Wearhouse suit, thumbing away on his BlackBerry. Maybe the throwback Italian with his shameless gut and the Philly hair, racing form spread across his table as he jawed into his cell. Don't rule out the scruffier sorts, he thought. One in particular caught his eye, a pierced waif in tasseled leathers with goth eye shadow and a stubbled head, hunched over her food like she was still in juvie, a snitch maybe, recruited, bribed, coerced by Lattimore to serve as his scout. And don't ignore the couples, either, though by and large they seemed far too preoccupied with each other to eavesdrop on anybody else.

Suddenly, there he was, standing in the restaurant doorway, impossible to miss, ducking a little so as not to smack his head. He made eye contact with no one and no one with him, then his gaze found the back of the room.

Happy felt his throat clench shut, thinking: He wants, he can slip the cuffs on right here, reentry after deportation, anywhere from two to twenty years in federal stir. Everything crumbles into dust then. But he'd felt the man out, half a dozen phone calls already, letting him know who he was, reminding him of the standoff at the trailer, his cousin the crazy jarhead with the fucked-up face, all as prelude to a discussion of what he, Pablo "Happy" Orantes, had to offer.

He recognized the type from Iraq, the square but savvy American, lanky build, steady gaze, easy gait, smile of a troop master, heart of a killer. He wore a trench coat over a sport jacket and tie, and his hair had wisps of gray at the temple. Shaking out his umbrella first, he ambled over to Happy's table, pulled out the available chair, extended his hand.

"Pablo? Jim Lattimore."

The offered palm was cold from the walk outdoors, the handshake firm and quick, the voice like whiskey. He draped his coat on the back of his chair and sat.

"You can call me Happy."

An impassive smile. "Okay." The waiter approached with a menu, Lattimore waved him off, ordering from memory, round steak and brisket, plus hot green tea. Nodding toward Happy's soup, he said, "That's going to get cold."

Happy couldn't help himself, he chuckled—nerves, suspicion, relief—glancing down at the rainbow skim of cooling fat, then back up at the scarily smart face. "You could play yourself in a movie, know that?"

It took a second for Lattimore to process the observation. "The opportunity's never arisen." He paused, leaning back in his chair as the waiter set down his tea. "That could probably be said about a lot of people. You, for instance. Not to say I pictured you perfectly from your voice on the phone, but even if you hadn't been the only Hispanic in here, I think I would have figured you for my guy."

Happy's craving for a cigarette intensified. My guy? "What you see, what you get." Shivering from a sudden brisk chill, he glanced around for the source of the draft, found none.

"Few people can really hide who they are. I get lied to every day, every cop does. A mask is harder to come by than most people think."

Okay, Happy thought. Got to that quick. "I'm not lying."

"I hope not."

In their previous phone connections, Happy had laid out the basic parameters of what he had to offer: Vasco Ramírez was ready to bankroll the movement of a terrorist into the country on behalf of Mara Salvatrucha, in exchange for sole control of a cocaine smuggling operation through the Port of Oakland. Happy had explained the involvement of his family, who he was, what baggage he brought to the table, probed a little of where Lattimore stood, what he could reciprocate, what he couldn't, all discussed cat and mouse, no cards shown, bluff and counter-bluff.

Strangely, Lattimore was less than thrilled with the case, at least from what Happy could tell given his reaction so far. He'd said, "You have any idea how many desks I'm going to have to clear this with?" From that and a few other remarks, Happy'd gathered that the thing was a clusterfuck of such grotesque proportion any agent in his right mind would say "Not me" and walk. But Lattimore wasn't backing away, he was just peeling the onion. Truth be told, Happy found his reaction encouraging.

The balding waiter showed up with Lattimore's pho, then held out an inquiring hand toward Happy's, wearing a vaguely offended frown.

Happy said to Lattimore, "You want it? Take it back to the office, have it for lunch tomorrow. I dunno, whatever your hours are, maybe dinner tonight."

Lattimore glanced up and held Happy's eyes with his own. He was looking for something, reading.

Happy added, "I didn't put anything in it."

Lattimore chuckled, then glanced toward the waiter, shook his head no. As the waiter carried it away—a perk for the dishwasher, maybe, or something to reheat for another customer—Lattimore unwrapped his chopsticks. "I'm going to have to 302 this meeting. Write it up, I mean. I'll also have to log my receipt. I know this sounds stupid, but it's just tidier, at this stage, if I don't buy you lunch."

With that small admission, said with embarrassment at the pettiness of the great bureaucratic wheel ready to crush them both, Happy sensed the exact measure of his folly. He could finally calculate the full faith and credit of the damage this might do not just to him but to everyone in the family, everyone he meant to protect. It felt like the whole of his life, clutched in a stranger's fist. It felt like the weight of the world plopped onto his back but not before it had been calculated down to the micro-ounce by faceless nobodies in a million identical cubicles buried underground in some bunker near Quantico. But what other options did he have? Every time he tried to think of another way out, whatever ideas came to bear soon drifted off like mist. Wishful thinking wouldn't cut it. It was up to sheer will now, that and luck.

"I trust your judgment on the paperwork," his voice so quiet he barely heard it himself.

Lattimore picked a strip of lean steak from his bowl. In the background, the Italian with the throwback bouffant struggled from his chair and lumbered out into the rain, no coat, racing sheet held aloft for an umbrella. "Who else knows about the terrorist angle to this thing?"

Happy drifted back. "Vasco's the only one I've mentioned it to. I don't know who he might have talked to about it. My guess is nobody."

"Your cousins?"

"There's no connection there. Not yet."

Lattimore raised an eyebrow. "Yet?"

"Vasco put down a condition for laying out the money. Godo, my cousin, he comes on board, teaches the guys a thing or two about weapons, stuff he learned in the marines."

Lattimore paused. "And that would be useful to him, this Vasco character, why exactly?"

"He figures this thing goes through, the money's real, he's gonna need heat."

Lattimore trolled through his bowl for another strip of meat, fished it out, let the broth drip off, brisket this time. "What about the other cousin? The younger one."

"Roque?"

"Pretty soon he's going to find out he's got a very interesting passenger for this trip he's about to make."

"I told him about it, before I put him on the plane."

"Told him what, exactly?"

"You're right." Happy scratched his ear. "I didn't tell him he was a terrorist."

"Because . . . ?"

"Because he's not. And because that would just freak Roque out."

"What about the people down there?"

"They think he's some guy I brought back from Iraq. Which is the truth, by the way."

"Okay, we'll get to that. I'm just trying to feel my way through this conspiracy you've created, figure out the reach."

"Right now," Happy said, "far as I know, just me and Vasco. But once he gets his guys in gear, they become part of it, right? They pull jobs to make the money so things move ahead, they're in, even if they don't know exactly what the money's for."

"Basically. Yes."

"Okay. It's just—"

"But as of now, this minute, as best you can tell me, there's no one in El Salvador who thinks they're doing anything but helping ship your father and some essentially harmless Arab dude up the pipeline. Have I got that right?"

Happy felt a trickle of sweat winnow down his back. He wished he knew what the correct answer was. "Yeah. That's right."

"If the guys on the Salvadoran end found that out—"

"They'd make me pay."

"You sure they haven't guessed?"

"If they had, I'd have the bill already, believe me."

Somewhere in the room, someone sneezed, somebody else laughed. From the kitchen, the sudden bright sizzle of meat hitting hot oil. "Remind me," Lattimore said, "what are we talking about here, per head."

"Twelve grand. Twenty-four total."

"They're not making you pay for your cousin Roque too?"

"He doesn't need a coyote. He's got a passport."

"But they're offering protection along the way, right?"

"Look, I let them shake me down for more, I look like a stooge. Guys like that, they think you're over a barrel, they'll ass fuck you just because they can."

The plump brunette paid her tab, down to quarters and dimes, wrapped her frayed hair in a scarf, tucked her paperback into a purse the size of a saddlebag, then got up to leave.

"Okay," Lattimore said. "But twelve grand per, that's still on the high end, don't you think? I've heard nine, coming all the way from El Salvador, unless you're talking about a boat."

"What's your point?"

"No point. Just thinking out loud. Could be they've already factored in a terrorist surcharge."

"Reason the amount's as high as it is, I'm paying for a car. No way I'm making my old man jump trains to get here like I had to. Fucking brutal. He's tough and all but he's not young, know what I'm saying? And Samir, if they thought he was really a terrorist, believe me, I'd be paying fifty, maybe a hundred grand to get him here. No, I told them the story—"

"What story?"

Happy bristled, then reminded himself: Chill. "The truth."

Lattimore cocked his head a little to one side, the merest of smiles. "Well, if you don't mind, how about giving me a dose."

"You saying I ain't been straight with you?"

"It's a little too soon in the process for me to know one way or the other. I'm hopeful."

"I haven't lied to you."

"That's nice to hear. Now, about Samir."

The craving for a smoke became overwhelming, he almost

asked if he could duck outside for just a quick drag or two, but Lattimore, he'd read delay as deceit.

"Where should I start?"

"A full name would be nice."

"Samir Khalid Sadiq."

Licking his teeth, Lattimore took out a notepad, jotted it down. "And you met him . . . ?"

"He was a terp, the company I worked for. He studied English and Spanish at Baghdad University, was pretty fluent in both. He always hoped to travel someday, Spain, the States, maybe Latin America."

"Pretty ambitious dream for the average Iraqi."

"He's Palestinian, actually."

Lattimore stopped writing, cocked an eyebrow. "Really?"

"They're no small minority in Iraq. Saddam liked having them around, to show some kind of support for the cause but he was, like, this paranoid motherfucker. Palestinians got certain work privileges but were watched real close. Samir told me all this, I didn't know squat about Iraq or Palestine or anything over there till I was dropped down into the middle of it.

"Samir was happy as hell the Americans showed up. He figured he could get a job working for the military, the press, State Department, whatever, and that would be his ticket out, you know? So he begged around, got the brush-off from you guys, no answer as to why, but kept on looking and ended up with us. Rode in my cab a couple times, when we convoyed between Najaf and the Isle of Abu—that's what we called the warehouse compound at Abu Ghraib, that or Rocket City. The Salvadoran troops were stationed in Najaf, we handled their resupply and the redevelopment projects there."

"How did he end up in El Salvador? Samir, I mean."

"I'm getting to that. The Shiites hated the Palestinians, the grief started almost as soon as the Americans showed up. But once the 2005 elections were over, and the Shia parties took power? Palestinians are Sunni and without Saddam around they no longer meant shit to nobody. Regular Sunnis could give a fuck. Shiite militias came around, making threats, nailing up handbills telling people that any Palestinians better leave their homes now or they'd get the boot, maybe the torch. That was before the mosque in Samarra got hit. Once that happened, all bets were off. The militias, especially Sadr's thugs, the Jaish al Mahdi? They just began picking people off. Samir lived in the al-Baladiyat neighborhood of Baghdad and the cocksuckers just lobbed in mortars. No joke. Next came the death squads, house-to-house dragnets, roadblocks. Guys got whacked right there on the spot, bullet to the head, and their families were told to leave or face the same. Samir was, like, especially vulnerable, because he was working with the coalition. So his wife's brothers, they say enough is enough, they take their sister—Samir's wife, her name's Fatima—and his daughter away, wind up at the refugee camp near Al Tanf."

"That's in, what, Syria?"

"Along the border. Syria won't let the Palestinians in. Neither will Jordan. They don't want Palestinians to get the idea that they can resettle permanently anywhere, except, you know, Palestine." Happy watched as the buff preppy in the everything-must-go suit walked out and the goth girl tried to poach what he'd left behind on his plate, only to have the waiter swoop in like a bat, clear it away. "Samir was left in his house all alone, which was just an invitation. You never knew when the Mahdi motherfuckers were gonna throw up a checkpoint or come prowling around and his national ID card says right there he's Palestinian. So he walked away from everything he owned, began sleeping at the Isle of Abu. He tried to get the Americans to listen to him, give him some sort of asylum, so he could bring his family over here? Like talking to a wall, if he was even lucky enough to get some low-level desk jockey to hear him out. That's when he began to think he'd have an easier time getting to El Salvador.

People don't realize, but there's a lot of Palestinians in El Salvador, over a hundred thousand. Last presidential election, both candidates came from Palestinian families, one an old guerrilla, the other some right-wing radio talk-show guy. They first came over right before World War I—again, I knew none of this shit before I met Samir. The Turks were recruiting young men to be soldiers in the army, they controlled most of the Middle East. So families in Syria, Lebanon, Palestine, all over, they shipped their sons to Latin America, sometimes the whole family."

"He have any connections in El Salvador? Samir, I mean."

"Just me. But I told you about how I wound up in Iraq, the warden I was kicking back to? By this time I'd wised up a little, figured I had more leverage than I'd thought, especially after the ambush my convoy was in and the press it got. I could go to a reporter, expose them all. He'd never suffer as bad as he should, but the company would likely lose its contract and the warden would lose his cushy little niche at the prison. I told him to find a sponsor for Samir, so he could get a visa to El Salvador. He fought it, you know, bitch that he is, but I'd made him a fucking bucket of money, I asked for none of it back. It was the best deal he was gonna get. So Samir was on the same flight as me."

"What about his family?"

"Last I heard? Still in Al Tanf."

"Why doesn't he petition the Salvadoran government to bring them over?"

"What kind of future they got there? No jobs, no family or friends, wife and kid don't know the language. Just another refugee camp, this one full of strangers. Who speak Spanish. The game is all about getting *here*. He gets across the border, tries for asylum, then asks for his family. Only option that makes sense from his point of view."

"You two had this in mind all along?"

"He was going to come with me when I made the trip north, but we couldn't get enough money together for the two of us. So the deal was I'd come, see if I could work up some bread, then pay for him to follow. I didn't know at the time my old man and Lucha'd been swindled out of their house. And then almost as soon as I get here, boom, Pops is snagged in an ICE raid, sent packing. So here I sit."

Lattimore, having done as much damage to his pho as he was going to, gestured for the waiter to take it away. He sat back, appraising Happy. "I can't guarantee anything regarding Samir's amnesty."

"You can put in a word?"

"That I can do. But that's not all you want."

"I want citizenship for my old man," Happy said. "Me too. No more worrying when somebody's gonna show up at the door, drag me or him away. I want immunity for my cousins. They're both in this thing now and they've got no clue what's going on behind their backs."

"They know they're conspiring to bring a deported alien back into the country."

You motherfucker, Happy thought. "Hey, I'm giving you gang members who, as far as they know, are helping bring a terrorist into the country. I read the papers. I know what that means to you guys. You can wire me up. I'll testify, the whole bit. You look at the big picture, I'm not asking for so much. You throw in the fact my cousin fought in Iraq, got his face chewed to shit, his brain fried, his leg messed up. I'd say my family's done its share."

Lattimore's face assumed an impressive blankness. "I'll have to run it by my supe, but I don't think he'll be the problem. The AUSA—the prosecutor in the U.S. attorney's office—that's where we'll hit a snag. And what you're asking for? All I can do is make a recommendation. I can't promise any of it. Period. We get that straight right now or this conversation's over."

Happy nodded. By now only a couple other tables remained occupied, the lunch crowd having thinned out. Using a hand towel, the waiter wiped away the glaze of moisture from the window, then stared pensively at the midday drizzle, the windswept street, as though he hoped to see his future out there. This was, after all, America.

"If everything goes well," Lattimore said, "you come in, have what's known as a free talk. We can get you somebody from the Federal Public Defender if you don't have your own lawyer. Then we make a proffer. After that and about two hours of paperwork, we wire you up, send you out for what, if this were a drug sting, we'd call a reliability buy. Get a chance to see you in action, hear what you can actually get these mutts to agree to on tape."

"This all happens how soon?"

"You're dealing with the federal government here. We're a hippo, not a gazelle."

"Yeah, well," Happy said, feeling in his pocket for his lighter, his smokes, "my cousin Roque's down in El Salvador, hanging around, cooling his jets. Nothing goes forward till Vasco puts some money on the table. And he's not gonna do that till he meets the guy who owns the warehouse where all this Colombian cocaine is supposed to wind up."

"Interesting." Lattimore signaled the waiter, two fingers lifted—separate checks. "And how exactly is that going to happen?"

A fly looped down onto the tablecloth, landing next to Happy's unused spoon. "Funny," he said, shooing it away. "I was about to ask you the same thing."

THIRTEEN

THE SECOND DAY ROQUE WAS IN SAN PEDRO LEMPA THE GUITAR arrived, a gift. Rumor had spread through the village that he was a musician, a guitarist from California. Someone collected the old forgotten thing from some dusty corner or perch, and it arrived with a bag of green *jocotes* and a jar of pickled cabbage called *curtido*, delivered by three giggling sisters in blue school jumpers, the oldest of whom looked no older than twelve.

The instrument was hopeless, scuffed pine with tired nylon strings, tin pegs that couldn't hold a tuning for more than five minutes, but at one time it must have represented a considerable expense on someone's part, a month's pay at least. Without a word about cost, though, they had given it to him, the sisters said, so he could play for Carmela, the tiny *indígena* woman with the ropelike braid in whose home he and Tío Faustino were staying. Carmela showed little interest in being serenaded, though—she spent all day in her garden, tending to the flowers she sold at market—and so Roque was free to practice his fingerings and scales and passing chords, plugging away for hours on end to the breathless amazement of the three sisters, as well as the flock of pals who straggled along after school each day as that first week bled into the next.

They were waiting on the money. Roque had no idea what the holdup was, Happy refused to discuss it over the phone and so there was nothing to do but settle in. Time passed differently here. With so few distractions, every minute seemed to swell like a breath, full of silence except for the continuous pizzicato of his guitar, the crunch of Carmela's spade, the large black *pijuyos* cawing in the mango trees. Roque could only imagine that, given the curious distension of time, the incessant repetition of his scales became maddening to anyone in earshot—major, minor, pentatonic, heptatonic, Dorian, Phrygian, Lydian, aeolian, mixolydian, ascending, descending, chord fingering, arpeggio fingering. No one ever said as much, though; everyone here was cursed with an excess of humility and patience. And the children, they plopped down in the dusty yard and gripped their knees in rapt attention as though this stranger had come all those hundreds of miles just to play for them.

Come dusk, the adults gathered at the outside table for the evening meal: *pupusas*, *curtido*, *casamiento*, the last a kind of leftover casserole, beans and rice, fried with onion and an aromatic flower called *loroco*. Roque set aside the practice grind and played a few of the traditional songs he knew: "Sin Ti," "Hay Unos Ojos," "Pena de los Amores," even El Chicano's "Sabor a Mí," more a sentimental favorite than a classic. The others were Cuban boleros, Mexican *rancheras*, nothing especially Salvadoran. From what he'd learned listening to the older ones, given the annihilation of everything indigenous over the past century—culture, crafts, people—there wasn't anything like a uniquely native repertoire except maybe *chanchona*, a cheesy kind of dance music, full of spicy jokes and a thumping *cumbia* two-beat, big with hicks and lounge acts. Regardless, the old songs obliged him to slow down, concentrate not on technique but feeling. And the key to feeling, he'd learned, was simplicity.

At times someone or other would sing along, if only under his or her breath, then chuckle soulfully when the song concluded, perhaps leaning over to squeeze Roque's shoulder and thank him. Tío Faustino seemed particularly fond of "Sin Ti"—Without You—and Roque found himself increasingly moved by the deep whispery tone-deaf voice. He couldn't recall, not once in the years since Tío Faustino had entered his life, hearing the older man sing. And in the pauses between songs, as he retuned the peevish guitar, he'd glance up and catch his uncle gazing at nothing, seated in one of the scrap-wood chairs they called *trastos* here, head propped on his hand, fingers lost in his graying hair as he nursed a glass of beer.

One night, the older man remained outside later than usual, staring across the lake toward Guazapa, the gentle slopes of the volcano luminous, a dark silvery green in the moonlight. Roque was about to say good night when his uncle gestured for him to sit.

—See that mountain, Roque? Celestina and I were living there when Pablo was born. We were part of the frente, *and the volcano was a staging area for raids into the capital. I've never told you about all that. People your age know so little. It isn't your fault. Hard to talk about. And what good does rehashing the bad do?*

He fussed with his shirt, waved away a nagging fly. Every little gesture, transformed by moonlight, seemed cinematic, even with the clumsiness of drink.

—I was a mechanic, changing tires, this little shop not far from Chinameca, where I grew up. I knew nothing of Marx, Lenin, that was all lofty nonsense as far as I was concerned. I just wanted a better job. I wanted my girlfriend to be a little less sad, you know? I wanted a country where I wasn't scared all the time, where I didn't have to go to work and listen to one of my buddies whisper, "Hey, Faustino, somebody heard you moping and groaning the other day and a couple guys came asking for you this morning."

Roque followed his uncle's gaze across the lake.*—What was it you said that pissed them off?*

—Roque, I could have complained about the weather, okay? If some government snitch wanted to make points with the local jefe, *he'd say I was bad-mouthing the army or the regime or some colonel's homely wife. Though, I admit, in this one case I'd shot off my mouth stupidly.*

There was this dentist named Regalado in Santiago de María, had connections with some colonels. Tight as turds in a frog's ass, these people. He started what everyone thought was a boy scout troop, but these guys didn't go hiking in the hills, learning knots and birdcalls. They killed people—teachers, union members, anybody Regalado considered a Communist. Bodies showed up at the edge of town, maybe just a severed head in a ditch. One time two hands were nailed to the door of a church where the priests were sympathetic to the campesinos.

Celestina was a teacher in Las Marías, doing Bible-study groups, teaching people their poverty wasn't a punishment from God, they had dignity. Regalado's scouts came looking for her one day. She got word just in time, slipped out a window in the schoolhouse, one shoe in each hand, running barefoot through the coffee groves.

I heard about it that night, no idea where she was, crazy with worry. At work the next day I was fuming, I wanted to butcher the little creeps who'd come to get her. There was a guy in the shop getting a flat fixed, some phone-company minion from Santiago. He heard me going on. We called them orejas, *guys like that. Ears. They were everywhere, government informants, a hundred thousand of them, all across the country. Next day, it's my turn for a visit. And like Celestina, I was lucky—never forget that, Roque. Call it what you want: the hand of God, the Virgin Mother, your guardian angel or just dumb luck. All of us who survived the war, we know some unseen force got us out. The ones who didn't make it out, well, they weren't so lucky.*

He reached suddenly for his glass of beer and, aiming badly, knocked it over. He cursed, his voice catching in his throat.

—Maybe it's time for bed, Tío.

—Don't treat me like an old fool. I haven't finished my story.

—I'm sorry, I—

—Be patient, Roque. Listen. I'm telling you this for a reason. A few weeks later, I met up with Celestina again at the stronghold on Volcán Guazapa. The comandantes *discouraged men and women*

getting together. Marry yourself to the struggle, they said. Trust me, people were screwing right and left. Not that we were atheist sex fiends, having orgies and black masses, all that government propaganda crap. There was a very brotherly, sisterly feeling among us. The compas *would bathe in the river wearing just their scanties, the men too, and nothing would happen. But we paired up when we could, if only for comfort. Nothing makes you feel more alone than knowing how easily you can die. And so Pablito came along right before the government launched its huge offensive to get us off the mountain.*

We'd been staging raids from there against the army for a couple years by then. And we had radio broadcasts on Radio Venceremos telling people about the massacres, the atrocities in El Mozote, Copapayo, Mirandilla, Zacamil. The army officers, they hated that radio, hated anyone who dared tell the truth. Finally they started bombing us with white phosphorus to burn away the trees, because we hid in the forests up the side of the volcano.

There was this American, a doctor who came to help us, his name was Charlie Christian. We called him Camilo. He'd been a helicopter pilot in Vietnam, then became a doctor just to help people like us. Celestina worked with him as a nurse. That's what most of the compas *did, they worked medical, or food, or explosives. No joke, the women were very good at making and planting land mines, they had smaller hands, better control.*

Celestina saw a boy who was burned all over his body being treated by Camilo and that was when she said we had to get out. The boy had been burned in a bombing raid. There was this kind of plane we called a push-and-pull, it circled once, saw a campfire, and came back, lower this time, so we knew it was on a bombing run. Everyone ran to their shelters—we called them tatús*—but this boy's mother didn't get the door closed in time. The bomb was a direct hit. The explosion cut her in two, she was burned to cinders. The boy, he was maybe two years old, his skin hissed and steamed as they pulled him out. But he was still alive. His mother, shielding him with her body, saved him.*

They took him to Camilo and he did what he could. When Celestina saw that little boy caked in mud and clay to cool his skin, only his eyes and nostrils visible . . . She couldn't bear the thought of seeing Pablo like that. She began secretly making plans to desert. But it was too late. The cuilios, *the government troops, they were coming up the mountain. They sent their three toughest battalions—Atlacatl, Belloso, Bracamonte—plus the First Brigade. Ten thousand men. Only way out was to go by way of Copapayo to Chalatenango, cross the Río Lempa up there. We called it a* guinda, *a forced retreat, and even the villagers were coming with us, because they knew the troops would kill them regardless. That was just how it was.*

He fell quiet for a moment, staring off as though at a ghost, or the hope of one. Roque brought him back with:—*You had to leave the mountain . . .*

—*Right. We were struggling through the forest, dragging our mules, carrying the wounded on our backs or in hammocks strung up to a pole so two men could carry them. Nothing to eat but tortillas and sugarloaf. Some of the children died of malnutrition. I saw one boy vomit up worms from his mouth, his nose, right before he died. His mother carried his corpse with her because there was no time to bury him.*

The villagers were lagging behind because they had so many children. Celestina gave me Pablo, told me to go ahead, she would stay behind and round up the others, get them to pick up the pace. I argued, but there was something in her eye, something that scared me. I felt like I could see all the way down into her soul. And there was nothing there. She was already gone. How do you explain things like that? Anyway, it was the last time I ever saw her alive.

Roque reached out for his shoulder, thinking: *Sin ti*. Without you.—*You don't need to tell me any more, Tío.*

—*Please, Roque, let me finish*. He smeared the heels of his hands across his face.—*The government caught up with them near Tenango. The soldiers used guns and machetes. Twenty-eight people, mostly women and kids, butchered. By the time I made it back there, vultures were picking the flesh from the dead. Dogs were carrying bones away. Some of the women had been sliced open like iguanas when you harvest the eggs. You saw shoes, clothes, schoolbooks scattered all around, some of it charred black, because the cowards tried to hide the evidence by burning it. A few mules were still alive, torn up by gunfire or shrapnel, some with their guts hanging out. The braying, it was hideous. We shot them just for the silence. I found Celestina facedown in a clump of* chichipince. *You're not a boy anymore, I don't need to spell out what they did to her.*

Roque felt paralyzed.—*Tío*—

—*I was such a loser compared to her. I fell apart, became worthless as a soldier, a father, a man. I knew that if I didn't get Pablo out of the country, he might get captured when I did, then he'd get sold to some family abroad. There was quite a racket in that back then. My superiors knew that too, finally they just told me to go, leave, head for the States, I was no good to the* frente *anymore. I was no good to anyone.*

There was a group of people, a few nurses, a professor, a couple reporters, all marked for death and they were heading north, with plans to end up in Los Angeles. I went with them, bringing Pablo. But I couldn't stay, too many people around MacArthur Park just reminded me of what had happened. I had a friend working in the Napa vineyards, he said I should come stay with him, his wife could help with Pablo. And so I ended up in Rio Mirada. A few years later I met Lucha—and you, your brother.

Roque wished for something to say, anything to ease his uncle's heart, if only for a moment. But all he could come up with was:—*I'm sorry.*

Tío Faustino looked up, eyes glassy and vacant.—*No, Roque. I didn't tell you all that to make you feel guilty.*

—*I meant*—

—*You were kind to listen.*

—*Tío*—

—*I'm a silly, sad old man.* He hefted himself from his chair.—

The moonlight, it makes me morose. And with that, yes, we should head off to bed. He turned to go in but then stopped, gazing one last time across the glimmering lake.—"*We are the artificers of our own history,*" *they said*. A morbid chuckle.—*Whatever the hell that means*. He wiped his face again, then gripped Roque's arm, squeezed.—*I am so proud of you, you know? So gifted. So thoughtful. Everyone says so.*

ROQUE STAYED UP LATE THAT NIGHT, UNABLE TO GET HIS UNCLE'S story out of his head, wondering how people survive such things. He sat beneath the mango trees, strumming gently as Carmela's exotic flowers filled the warm night air with their fruitlike scents: Arrayn Silvestre smelling like limes, *sapuyulo* like oranges. The full moon had waned, the yard was dark.

About midnight he heard a car slow and stop at the bottom of the hill, the motor died, a door opened and closed. He listened for footsteps, heard none, went back to playing. Then he sensed it, someone nearby, before hearing the twig snap. Turning toward the sound, he watched as Sisco ventured slowly forward, hands plunged into the pockets of his baggy pants.

"*Hola, chero.*" The kid rocked on his heels, a kind of mocking uneasiness.

Roque thought he smelled drink, but something else too, vaguely chemical, like ether or ammonia. "Why did you park down the hill?"

"What the fuck is that supposed to mean?"

"Is something wrong?"

"Fuck yes something's wrong, *puto*. It's been, like, almost three weeks."

Roque put the guitar down, for fear Sisco might try to grab it from him, smash it against a tree, just to make some senseless point. "I don't have anything to do with that."

"Fuck you don't."

"My cousin won't even talk to me about it. The money, it's in his hands."

Sisco pivoted a little in place, like he was trying to find something to kick. He began to cough, couldn't stop himself for several seconds, his chest rattling with phlegm.

Roque wondered at Sisco's life here. He'd heard stories about other DPs—deportees from the States—thinking in American slang, living in Spanish, the culture a fading reactionary echo of some fictive golden past, with a chafing revolutionary undertone. The DPs were the hip outsiders, the hopelessly lost but strangely successful: *reggaetón* deejays, concert promoters, hair stylists, tattoo impresarios in a country that put you in prison for flashing your ink. The DPs had cache, if no real rank. They were, hey, Americans. Roque couldn't imagine Sisco in such company. What was his gift? Sulking, back talk, hanging around. He'd soon be on the way back north to some street corner. Or else get shot dead right here.

The kid finally collected himself, got control of his cough, and the words uncoiled from within him as though off a spool. "Okay, fuck me, what I'm saying—hear me out, *chero*—what I'm saying? Next time, it won't be me standing here. Am I getting through? It's gonna be Lonely. And he don't like you. He thinks you wanted to snag his bitch. Look, look, just listen, a'ight? Lupe? She's fine and all but she ain't like his *chorba* or nothin'—not even, not close. But you put pussy in the room, the smell gets on everybody, know what I'm saying? So he's got this thing for you now, he don't like you. He don't respect you. You're fool material. So get this shit together. It's finance, man. Plans been made, the money's supposed to be, like, in hand, in place, what-the-fuck-ever, we ain't seen shit, and it's a fucking problem. Get it done. Make a call. Or you can kiss that sorry old man you call your *tío* goodbye, 'cuz he ain't goin' no place."

FOURTEEN

HAPPY SQUINTED AGAINST THE SUNLIGHT, NURSING HIS LAST cigarette of the pack. Forklifts roared forward and beeped backing up, bearing pallets of shrink-wrapped bananas, plantains, mangoes and melons from long-bed containers, delivering them to the panel trucks abutting the loading dock. Hard hats—blue, white, yellow—bobbed everywhere like gumballs; the workday hustle kicked into gear. With the concrete floor still wet from its morning hose-down, every footfall slapped or screeched.

Secretly he envied these men, honest work, honest pay, if there was such a thing. At a glance he could pick out at least half a dozen he suspected of being illegal, drivers especially, like his old man. Ironic, since at that very moment there were enough feds nearby to arrest half of Richmond.

"Your guy's in love with his fucking phone," Vasco said, glancing for the thousandth time at his watch. "Feels like all I've done since you talked me into this is wait."

"If I've already talked you into this," Happy said, "what the fuck are we doing here?"

In truth, everybody was getting itchy, unless he had a badge. Happy'd heard that morning from his father in San Pedro Lempa that the *mareros* were suddenly jacked with impatience, leaning hard now, popping up in the middle of the night, wanting their money, ready to pull the plug if it didn't get wired down yesterday. And Vasco just got greedier the longer Happy stalled, the greed made him edgy, his edge made him an impossible pain in the ass. But Lattimore worked on government time, which seemed to have only three gears: Stalled. Stuck. Backwards.

It wasn't like they had to wire up the warehouse. The feds had used it before, their favorite snare, home field, hidden video everywhere. When stings weren't in play, the company that actually owned the place used the cameras to guard against employee theft—"shrinkage," they called it. Even the office was miked, everything go. It was the paperwork jamming the gears.

Two days after that first face-to-face at the Vietnamese restaurant, Happy went in for his free talk, as Lattimore called it, or "off-the-record proffer," per the assistant U.S. attorney. Happy laid out everything he'd done, no threat of prosecution: sneaking back into the country with the help of his ganged-up *polleros*, planning to do the same for his dad, lending some muscle to Vasco's pathetic moving-van shakedowns, stripping copper wire for him. But it wasn't Happy's past that brought them all together. They wanted to hear about the future.

The conference room had a flag in the corner, a tray of coffee and ice water anchoring a long shiny table, a portrait of FBI director Robert Mueller III—Bobby Three Sticks, Lattimore called him. His supervisor, a reedy and taller-than-average Filipino named Orpilla, passed a consent form in front of Happy that asserted he willingly agreed "to assist in the making of undercover recordings at the sole direction of law enforcement officials." The form promised Happy the federal government wouldn't prosecute him for anything that popped up in those recordings; all bets were off, though, if state or county prosecutors went ahead. He'd have to work that out on his own. Happy read the form, waived his right to have someone from the public defender's office advise him. Prior experience convinced him public defenders existed simply to slow things down, not change their direction or, God forbid, improve their odds. He signed where he saw his name. Orpilla took the executed form and tucked it into a folder.

It was the AUSA, though, who was driving the bus. The guy's name was Jon Pitcavage—overachiever eyes etched with crow's-feet, a tight scrub of graying black curls, the build of a serious gym rat. He wore a snappy pinstripe suit and leaned into his words. If Happy read Lattimore's body language right, he had little use for Pitcavage, except he was the one AUSA in San Francisco, supposedly, who knew where the gas pedal was, not just the brake. He got points among the agents for that—though, apparently, only that.

Happy repeated for Pitcavage what he'd already laid out for Lattimore. The attorney listened with elbows on the table, hands clasped, thumbs bobbing against his chin. Once Happy wrapped up, the guy leaned back in his swivel chair, crossed his legs, rocked pensively back and forth. Guy likes being watched, Happy thought, while over the man's shoulder, far beyond the conference-room window, an airliner razored a vapor trail across an otherwise perfect sky.

"This scenario," Pitcavage said finally, "the quid pro quo—this Vasco character gets sole control of the narcotics operation involving the Valle Norte cartel and shot-caller status with Mara Salvatrucha, in exchange for funding the smuggling of this Arab alien, this would-be terrorist, into the country—as I understand it, this was all your idea?"

Happy felt the familiar bilge of nausea rising from below. "Yeah."

"But there is no smuggling operation, correct? And the Arab, as far as you know, owes no allegiance to any known terrorist organization."

"Samir—he's Palestinian—he actually helped the coalition forces in Iraq."

Pitcavage glanced toward Lattimore. "An interpreter."

Happy said, "That's right."

"And this coconspirator in Richmond, the warehouse owner, the person who is supposed to receive these fictitious shipments of cocaine from, where was it?" He leafed through his notes. "Turbo, Colombia—you just made that up."

"Read about it on the Web, actually. Sounded good. Thought it'd get Vasco to bite."

"But he didn't bite, did he?"

Happy cleared his throat. "Not exactly."

"He wanted verification. He wanted to see an honest-to-God warehouse, a real live owner. Golly, I'm stunned. Just like he'll probably want to see a cocaine shipment before too long, don't you think? Where do you suppose that might come from?"

Happy felt like he had a living thing thrashing around in his gut. "I figured I'd be in touch with you people by then. That was something we'd have to work out."

"We." Pitcavage's eyes looked scorched. "How I always love the sound of 'we.' "

"Look," Happy said, "if you think I just made this crap up so I could shake Vasco down, get him to pay for my old man's trip back, you weren't paying attention. Get serious, I do that, and Vasco finds out everything else, the coke, the Colombians, the terrorist, it's all just crap? He'd lean hard. Me and my family, we'd pay and just keep paying. Like I told you, I want citizenship, me and my dad both. Can't get that from Vasco. I want that, I gotta come here. Way I see it, my cousin Godo already earned it, earned it for me, my dad, both. But I'm ready to go the extra mile, make sure you get what you want, 'cause yeah, I surf the Net, I read the articles about how you guys are trying to link up gangs and the ragheads. Dream bust, those two tied together. And I know how to make that happen, who to put with who. I give you your shot. And I know this doesn't just stop here. I know this opens doors for you. People gonna read about this case and they're gonna say: We gotta stop these *maras*, these gangs. We gotta let the cops off the leash. So instead of treating me like I'm the shit on your shoe, maybe you should see I'm not the problem here. I won't ask for thanks but I won't sit here and beg, neither. Just want what me and my family deserve. And what I deserve, this minute? Is to be taken a little more serious."

Pitcavage ran his tongue inside his lower lip, as though scouring out a speck of food. "You honestly believe that this bag of snakes you came in here with is a dream bust?"

"I *deserve* to be taken more *serious*."

The lawyer turned to Lattimore and Orpilla and, as though Happy had just vanished, launched off on a new tack. "I'll sign off on the recording, it's reasonable and legal. As for the setup, the way I understand it there's been no Barraza harassment, no pressure, no cajoling. Admittedly, your genius here has devised the crime but we're clear there, that's established law. If there's no prior disposition to terrorist activity there certainly is to the smuggling. No special feel-good motive's been contrived, nobody's gone all buddy-buddy. It's about greed, period.

"The one weak spot, beyond the obvious tactical headaches, is the unusual attractiveness of the crime. What is it, anywhere from one and a half to three mil this Vasco clown thinks he'll be clearing per annum? But there's been no promise it's a sure thing, he hasn't been told they can't get caught. He knows the risk. And one discussion, boom, he's in. You get him and these other idiots on video, you get them on tape, plenty of it, you know the drill. And it's all got to happen quick, before somebody catches on there aren't any shipments coming from Turbo and never will be. I figure we've got a month, tops. Any longer, the thing will unravel. And unless I'm mistaken, this interpreter and the source's father should be back in the States by then. So that's your time line."

Pitcavage rose from his chair, stole a glance out the window. The vapor trail resembled a line of coke on a blue mirror.

"Get these guys expressing full knowledge and consent. I don't need a pledge to al-Qaeda, like those buffoons in Liberty City, though that would be sweet. But they make it clear they know what's going on: quid pro quo, a cocaine franchise for a terrorist across the border. You get me that, I don't see a jury backing off a verdict. You've heard me say it before: We don't have to wait until buildings come down to prove somebody's a terrorist. And your genius is right, the MS-13 angle makes it particularly attractive. These guys want to claim they weren't predisposed, they can walk away any time they want. Make sure everybody on the joint task force stays in the loop. I'll be surprised if we don't see plea deals all the way down the table. Defense will cry entrapment but they always do. And they always lose. Entrapment's just what they tell their clients so the bills get paid."

He tamped down his tie and turned to leave, stopping himself only to address Happy one last time. "You're absolutely certain this interpreter's name is Samir Khalid Sadiq?" He posed the question as though to imply there were varieties of deceit, especially in the Muslim world, that were not just hard to discern, they were impenetrable.

"Yes." Happy swallowed. "At least, you know, that's the name he always used around me. Always."

The lawyer shot a warning glance across Lattimore's bow, then left like time was money and the money was down the hall. And that was pretty much the last Happy saw of Assistant U.S. Attorney Jon Pitcavage.

LATTIMORE GUIDED HAPPY TO THE ELEVATOR AND DOWN TO A LOWER floor where his own cubicle was buried. Happy felt a little shocked to see what a rat's nest it was, binders stacked helter-skelter on every surface, copies of *National Gang Threat Assessment*, *National Intelligence Assessment: The Terrorist Threat in the U.S. Homeland*, *A Parent's Guide to Internet Safety* and a dozen others scattered everywhere to the point you had to wonder if something might collapse if it was all hauled away. The only personal items he could see were a gym bag stuffed with ripe sweats and three framed photographs on the shelf, one of a sprawling colonial-style house in the country somewhere; another of an older couple, parents maybe; the third of a tricked-out Harley with gold and crimson flames on the gas tank. Happy supposed the mess made sense. For all the sharp, battened-down attitude the man possessed, it wasn't too much of a stretch to imagine a daredevil slob lurking just beneath the skin. He wore no wedding band, never spoke of kids. Maybe the whole of his life was contained, one way or another, in this clutter.

Removing a clump of files from the chair beside his desk, Lattimore waited for Happy to sit, then commenced to unpack his memory, searching out every possible detail he could bring to bear about Samir: schooling, family, wife, in-laws, best guess on dates he stayed in Abu Ghraib, dates he traveled with the convoy to Najaf, everything and anything so it could be passed along to field agents in Baghdad. "If your story doesn't pan out on that front," Lattimore said, "the plug gets yanked quick, understand? We can't have a Trojan horse rolling toward the border. Everything shifts gears then and we focus on making sure he gets nowhere close."

Happy glanced again at the pictures in their dime-store frames. "You live with a man day in and day out," he said, "you go through hell with him—I told you, he saved my life—you get a sense of when he's making crap up. You know, tell a good story. You figure out too, when he's speaking for real."

From there it was farther still into the bowels of the federal building, to the lair of a tech named Merriwether. Curiously, given the cutting-edge nature of his job, he was the oldest guy Happy met that day—mudslide of chins, wispy hair swirling around a freckled bald spot. Happy found it easier to picture him selling vacuum cleaners to housewives than miking up snitches.

It turned out there wouldn't be a body wire. "Very old school," Merriwether explained. Instead they had a flannel shirt with a microphone in the collar, a tiny video camera in one of the buttons. Happy felt like 007 as he shouldered into it.

"We used to have an on/off switch right here in the cuff," Merriwether said, "but defense lawyers complained that if the CI could switch the tape on or off himself, how did anyone know when he might have been making a threat, offering a bribe?"

The backup recorder turned out to be the battery for a cell phone. It sent out a continuous signal to the nearest relay tower, no need for a booster transmitter.

As they walked back to the elevator together, Merriwether put his hand on Happy's shoulder. "Don't worry about anything except getting these people to say what they're supposed to say." A few brisk pats. "You'll be frightened. That's understandable. If you find yourself at a loss for what to say, ask a question, any question. You'd be surprised how often that works."

"THIS YOUR GUY?" VASCO POINTED WITH HIS CHIN ACROSS THE TRUCK yard at the figure striding toward them. He was lithe but short, a boxer's gait, decked out in a black suit, a silver silk shirt buttoned tight to the collar.

"He'll call himself Zipicana," Lattimore had said, "the name of some underworld spirit, Mayan Quiché lore. And don't wear your flannels or bring the cell-phone battery to the meet. You'll see why."

As the man named Zipicana came nearer, Happy could make out the smeary reddish blotches on his face and neck, the faint outlines ghosting the skin, and wondered at the missing tattoos, assuming laser treatment. The guy skipped up the concrete steps onto the loading dock but ignored both Happy and Vasco, continuing on instead toward the office across the warehouse floor. Vasco and Happy exchanged baffled glances, then fell in behind.

Zipicana gestured for them to wait outside as he climbed the wood-plank steps to the office, which resembled a work-site trailer. He knocked, entered, spoke briefly with the owner, who was still yammering away on his phone. Happy was beginning to wonder just how long this charade was going to last when the balletic Zipicana turned back, opened the office door and snapped his fingers for them to step inside.

Before anyone could say boo, the warehouse owner rose from his desk and approached Happy and Vasco, bearing a black wand-like instrument. He waved it up and down both their bodies, like he wanted to remove some lint, and Happy realized why he'd been told to leave the spy gear behind, not just because it was redundant. The guy was checking for RF frequencies, to be sure neither of them was wired. It was all pure theater, of course; the guy was undercover FBI. He knew better than anyone he'd find nothing, unless Vasco had secrets of his own.

A murmured apology, the magic wand returned to its drawer, introductions ensued. The owner-agent identified himself simply as Nico. Happy resisted the impulse to glance around the room, search out the cameras, the microphones.

"You're here," Nico told Vasco, plopping back down in his chair, "because Happy put your name forward. Otherwise we could just as easily turn to Sancho Perata."

Like that, Vasco flushed bright red. "Listen, Sancho's got no trucks. I do. I'm watching your dock here all morning, thinking this is perfect. I'm your guy."

Happy could only marvel at Vasco's predictability. Make it a competition, make it with Sancho, he'd throw all qualms overboard and fight to win.

Nico just stared across the desk, unfazed. "My point, you're here because you've been vouched for."

Vasco bit back his pride, let it drop. The talk turned to the operation, Nico explaining the code they'd use over the phones: "produce" for cocaine—the particular fruit would change day to day, the meaning wouldn't—and Vasco would refer to his wholesalers as "grocers," not customers. "Other than that, a shipment's a shipment. I'm the consignee on all bills of lading, you place orders through me. I mention a number and an invoice, that's what you owe. Keep it simple. You get shorted on your end, it's not my problem."

"What kind of loads are we talking?"

"Five hundred kilos."

Vasco looked like he'd just swallowed an egg. "Okay. But you break it down here in the warehouse, right? Separate my product out from, you know, the fruit."

"Why would I do that?"

Vasco's shoulders buckled together. "What the fuck am I gonna do with a couple dozen pallets of bananas?"

It was like he'd farted.

"You don't take the whole shipment," Nico said, "who needs your goddamn trucks? You drive in here, leave the pallets behind, I mean, you nuts? Blows the whole scheme. I want the whole load out of here. Otherwise why am I doing business with you? And this way we can both plead ignorant, some cop stops you on the street, checks the load, finds—"

"But *what* the *fuck* am I gonna—"

"Sell it to your local bodega, cluckhead. Give it to a homeless shelter, throw it in the goddamn bay, what the fuck do I care?"

Happy cringed at the false note—*cluckhead*, something only a cop would say—as Vasco lashed back with some abuse of his own, too hot to let his ears cue him in. Meanwhile, Zipicana sat there watching the back and forth with solemn eyes. Finally, he lifted his hand, as though stepping in to referee.

"There's something else we need to discuss." His scrutiny shuttled face to face, then settled on Vasco. "You have the thirty?"

Vasco, still fuming over the bananas, "I have some questions first."

"I give a fuck about your questions. You don't have the money, we're done."

"Yeah." Vasco glanced at Happy, the gaze poisoned with blame. "I've got the money."

Zipicana pulled a slip of paper from his pocket and handed it to Vasco. Happy recognized it, the list of Banco de Cuscutlan account numbers passed along from Lonely in San Salvador for wire transfer of the thirty thousand. "Divvy it up any way you want," Zipicana said, "not all the same amount, though. Don't be stupid. And make sure it gets done today."

Vasco tucked the paper into his breast pocket. "How soon till we get a shipment?"

"A month. Maybe six weeks."

Vasco's eyebrows levitated. "Six weeks? Why the fuck—"

"That's nothing you need to know."

"Like hell it ain't. I'm out thirty grand till then."

Zipicana grinned, his eyes more cold than mocking. "What, you want interest?"

"I'm putting my ass out in the wind here. Happy vouches for me. Who vouches for you?"

"Listen to you." It was Nico, leaning back in his chair while Zipicana rose to his feet with a stagy air of menace. He doffed his suit jacket, then began unbuttoning the silver shirt, cuffs first, then the collar, then on down. "Who vouches for me?" He stripped the shirt off with a flourish, then lifted his welterweight arms, turning slowly to display the tattoos no laser had touched, his torso a billboard. A spiderweb covered his left shoulder, a black widow dangling on a thread, the number 13 on its back in a red hourglass, while from below a devil's claw emerged from flames to clutch his heart. Two masks appeared on his right shoulder, one happy, one sad—Smile Now, Cry Later—with fist-size letters and numerals in chainwork down that side of his chest: M—S—1—3. The name Mara Salvatrucha scrolled in a vine down one arm, while down the other you could read amid florid decoration: Sleep with the maggots, *norputos*. On his back, across his shoulders, in finely detailed Gothic lettering: *13 por vida, 18 son putas*. A black billiard ball with a 13 in the white circle bore the added inscription: Rest in Piss, *Jotos*. Then, in the small of his back, a graveyard of headstones, each bearing the name of a dead *chamaco*: Skyny, Gato, Slayer, Pincho, Dreamer, El Culiche, Vampi, Pingüe, Zorro . . .

Happy glanced over at Vasco and gauged from his expression that he was thinking: Who vouches for this guy? The madhouse. The street. The devil.

"Let me tell you something," Zipicana said, reaching for his shirt. "We don't need you, am I right? What we got to sell, we can find a buyer. No problem. And whoever steps up, he gets more than five hundred kilos and a bunch of fucking bananas. He gets the crown, understand? So what you want to ask yourself"—he slipped on the shimmery silk shirt, fussed the collar into place—"is this: Do I want to rule or be ruled? Who do I want for partners? Who do I want for enemies? Because the storm is coming, *chero*. You want to be ahead of it, not behind it."

Out in the warehouse, a pallet crashed to the floor, followed by echoing curses. Vasco sat there fuming. "I ask for some sort of proof this is more than just wind," he said, "you make threats. I'm supposed to sit here and take that. It's a lot to ask, especially considering the other angle to this we still haven't discussed."

Zipicana, tucking in his shirttail: "You're talking about the extra cargo coming up by separate carrier."

"I'm talking about the fucking Osama you guys are bringing across the border."

There, Happy thought, feeling both a flash of dread and a wave of relief. Please God, he thought, no foul-ups, no tech glitches. Meanwhile, Vasco ragged on. "You want me to front thirty grand, stick out my neck on something I want no part of, and in return you offer me take-it-or-leave-it, with a threat for good measure. I'm getting screwed three ways here with nothing but a promise for my trouble."

Zipicana made a face like he understood. But. "Remember, we don't know you."

"You said I was vouched for."

"We're talking terms here. You want the plum job, you gotta

go the extra mile. You don't want to, don't bitch about what you missed. Don't come to me begging for your chance back."

With his thumbs Vasco tapped out a furious rat-a-tat on the arms of his chair. One of the workers came up to the office window, pushed back his blue hard hat and knocked softly on the glass to get Nico's attention. Nico held up five fingers. The guy shook his head, ambled off. Happy wondered if he was undercover too. Or the real owner, wanting his office back.

Zipicana sat down on the edge of Nico's desk. "You say you want no part of this other thing, our lonesome friend who's coming up to visit. What's that about? You got some feeling for this shitbag country? You know what happened to Happy's family here. I won't bore you with my story. I'll bet, though, your own family has a tale or two, am I right?"

Vasco met Zipicana's eyes and, after a moment, nodded.

"Like they give a rat's ass about us. Fuck us in a heartbeat and play to the cameras. You seen what I seen. You hear what I hear. To hell with this country. Nothing but fat fucks and loudmouths. Somebody wants to bring down Disneyland, Dodger Stadium, Golden Gate Bridge, Candlestick Park—*who the fuck cares*? And the more cops have to waste time focusing on that shit? Better for guys like you and me. Better for *business*. No matter how bad things get, people gonna want their high. Especially then. You think about that. Meantime, you just wire the money to the numbers I gave you, you'll see, you got no problems being linked to the Arab, me, anything. That's a promise. You're like a silent partner, okay? You can't ask for better than that, not with what we're offering you a piece of."

HOURS LATER, DURING DEBRIEFING, HAPPY ASKED LATTIMORE ABOUT Zipicana: Where did he come from? How did he know how to pinball Vasco so well?

"Liked his shtick, did you?" Lattimore sat at his cluttered desk, slogging through paper. Short-tempered from the monotony, he slammed his desk drawers, glared at the phone if it interrupted. "Yeah, Ol' Zippy-hana, as we like to call him, sure knows how to put on a show."

Happy could sense the shortness of temper cycling his direction. "I don't get it. He pretty much said the same thing I—"

"Correct. And I ran through all that with Zippy, told him the weak spots in your improv, so to speak. Thought we had ourselves a meaningful chat. Turns out I should've saved my goddamn breath."

"I don't—"

"The point is to persuade him, Mr. Orantes, seduce him into the scheme, not box him in so bad he's got no way out. Christ, Vasco, the dumb cluck, he doesn't go along, what's he looking at? Slavery, basically. Looking up at a woeful dipshit like Sancho Perata running his life. I'd call that hell on earth." He began peeking under files, looking for his pen. "His real name is Chimo, by the way. Chimo Trujillo. Used to be a shot caller for the Normandie Locos till we got him on a carjacking beef."

Happy wanted to get away from Lattimore's resentment, but where would he go? They were all trapped now, caged together in the same machine, this lie.

"And of course Vasco sits there, ready for his close-up, and basically says, 'You're threatening me. What else can I do but agree to whatever you say?' Lawyer's gotta be brain-dead not to make hay with that."

Happy's stomach was roiling again. He would've popped out for a quick smoke if he hadn't already ripped through his pack. "But Pitcavage said they always say that." The weakness in his voice, the wishful thinking, even he could hear it. "And they always lose."

"Yeah, and I've heard a lot of other things he's said, right around the time things turn real." Lattimore found his pen, opened a folder, fingered through the 305 reports already filed, searching out some forgotten detail like it was the most thankless chore of his life. "But ol' Chimo, yeah. Guy could sell eggs to a goddamn chicken, I'll grant him that."

FIFTEEN

THEY GOT OUT OF THE CAR AND SMELLED THE POND FIRST, THE water foamy with scum. Chato made an ignorant crack, something about farmers and pigs, secrets of the barnyard. He'd been holding court the whole drive, a barky crank-fueled mania that only got worse when he fired up a blunt, sailing off into high bake: I'll put in a good turd for you. Let me give you a turd of advice. Honest, dude, I give you my turd of honor. On and on and on—he must've said "turd of honor" a hundred times—to the point Godo had to resist the urge as the trunk popped open to grab the first gun he saw, shoot the little fucker right there, put him out of everyone else's misery.

Luckily, the other two had grown sick of him too—Puchi, who'd driven, and a third guy Godo hadn't met before, Efraim. They jumped on the kid and he shut up finally, at least as long as it took to unload the weapons: a Mossberg shotgun, a Glock with the ungainly eighteen-round mag, a more manageable Sig Sauer 9mm and three M16s, bought in pieces over the Internet and at gun shows, assembled by Efraim, who had quickly become Godo's favorite of the bunch: quiet, capable and just a little haunted. By what, Godo wasn't sure, but it made him feel a kinship.

Happy had pushed him into this. It's for the family, he'd said, think of Tío Faustino. Vasco was a dick but they were all dicks. He was paying the freight, end of story. This is how the devil hands back your soul, Godo thought. It's not a gift.

He'd mustered the foresight to push for an outdoor venue, not an indoor shooting range. Secretly, he'd feared the extra compression, the echo, all those weapons firing at once. He gave himself credit for not losing it on the way over, cringing under every overpass, fearing an IED lay stuffed inside every roadkill pelt.

Beneath streaming clouds, the fetid pond gave way to a meadow of knee-high grass and silvery thistle crowned with seedpods. A windbreak of walnut trees rimmed one end of the property, the other three guarded by a broken fence, all helter-skelter rails and tottering posts. Behind the house sat a buckle-roofed barn that once, he was told, held a cockfighting pen. All deserted now, snatched away from Efraim's family by the county for back taxes. The nearest neighbors lived a mile away beyond a range of low hills.

Efraim led the way to the front door, tore away the county notice and the sagging yellow ribbon, then shouldered the door open. The wood splintered with a gratifying crack. Kicking aside some debris, he gestured everyone in.

Dusty emptiness, footfalls echoing on scuffed wood. The sun-bleached walls bore the rectangular ghosts of pictures and mirrors now gone. Efraim led them to what had once been the dining room and they sat near a southern window, enjoying the intermittent warmth whenever the sun peeked through the clouds as they lunched on *tortas* bought from a taco wagon along the way, chasing their mouthfuls with swigs of orange soda.

The food kept Chato from yapping. Godo, his appetite iffy, appreciated the meal for the silence alone. It also gave him a chance to regard Efraim more mindfully. The guy was sleek and dark with soulful eyes but there was a bitter streak running through him. To Godo that spoke of depth. This is the guy who'll pay attention, he thought, who'll remember what he learned when the time comes to use it, who won't freak or improvise crazily if everything goes to hell.

After lunch, Efraim produced the three M16s. They were patchwork, different years' models hashed together, one with an M4 upper assembly, another an AR-15 stock, a lot of soldering to hold them together, serviceable all the same. Chato picked one up, that imbecile grin, strumming the thing. "This the ax you used over in Iraqistan, right?"

Godo flashed on a story he'd heard, about a jarhead in Al Anbar who was goofing off, playing air guitar with his piece, when he accidentally discharged a round and killed another marine the next tent over.

"Full auto," Chato vamped, "spray the fuck out of anything you see."

Godo reached over, lifted the weapon from his hands. "Not these," he said. "Three-shot burst is the best you'll get. And that's a waste of ammo because muzzle lift after the first shot makes the next two sail high. Now clam the fuck up and pay attention."

He showed them how to release the magazine, jack back the charging handle and eye the chamber for live rounds. Once it was clear none of the rifles was loaded, he demonstrated the proper way to hold the weapon, cheek flush against the comb of the stock, butt plate tucked tight to the shoulder. He made each of them thumb off the safety twenty times, so it was something they'd associate with habit, not fumbling need.

Chato complained about the repetition. Godo pinned him with a look. "One more fucking word, you go up in the hayloft and spy for cops. I'm not telling you again."

Godo collected one of the rolled-up targets he'd brought, purchased from a gun shop in Rio Mirada. They had man-shaped silhouettes on them, so everyone remembered they were here to learn how to shoot people, not big red dots. He taught them how to blade the V notch, rest the target's center atop the sighting post. He made them do this over and over, bringing the weapon up to the shoulder, aiming, sighting, letting the weapon drop again—sitting, kneeling, standing, prone. After half an hour of this, the complaints were universal, even Efraim looked bored.

"I'm trying to train your muscle memory," Godo said. "You think this is rough? They did this to me for a whole damn week at Pendleton, called it 'snapping in.' "

"Ain't no 'snap' about it." Chato again.

Godo, turning: "I said one more word."

"This is bullshit."

"Fine." Godo jerked the rifle out of his hands. "You can use the shotgun. Even a girl can hit a target with buckshot."

"*Chucha de tu madre*."

Godo stepped forward, pressed his face close to Chato's. "My mother's what?"

A weaselly shrug, glancing away. "You heard me."

It was galling to realize the guy was Roque's age. And while Roque was stepping up, this loudmouth *lelo*, this fool, thought he already knew everything his ignorant ass would never comprehend if you planted it in his brain with a trowel. "Get the fuck outta my sight."

Puchi, stepping in: "Godo, come on. He was just letting off steam, man."

"Let me hear him say it. C'mon, runt, apologize."

"*Picoteado*." Pock face.

Godo actually found that funny. "Little ranker bitch."

"*Vete a la chingada*." Go to hell.

"Shut the fuck up!" It was Efraim now, chiming in. Despite the raised voice, he held his rifle down, like the thing was loaded. Right mind, right habits. "You're wasting my time."

"And who the fuck are you?" Chato, mocking. "You own this place? Not no more, *puto*."

For some reason, that was the thing that pushed Godo over. He reached out, gripped the shoulder of Chato's hoodie, started dragging him toward the door. Chato dug in, sneakers squealing against the hardwood, arms windmilling, then Godo finally dropped the M16, let it clatter on the floor and landed one solid shoulder-driven fist into the center of the kid's face, feeling the nose turn to slop. Chato staggered, dropped to one knee. Godo, letting go of the sweatshirt finally, turned to Puchi. "Take care of him."

As they headed off to the kitchen sink, Chato yelped over his shoulder, "Fuck you up, man." Godo picked up the rifle, let the fury subside. As he did, he saw the lone donkey wandering the street, braying in distress, while looters rampaged through the nearby buildings, stacking their booty onto trucks, pushcarts, wheelbarrows, all of Baghdad convulsed in a kind of mass kleptomania. And if the looters spotted the marines staring at them, they just waved, smiled. Laughed.

After a moment, Efraim said, "*Tato*?"

Godo shook himself out of it. "C'mon. We haven't even practiced trigger pulls yet."

Half an hour later they were outside, Chato with his busted nose and raccoon eyes posted in the hayloft by majority vote, the other three tacking up targets against the barn wall. Knowing the sound of the M16s blazing away would mess with his head in ways he couldn't predict, Godo told Puchi and Efraim to let him demonstrate first a proper firing stance for the four standard positions. As he did, he squeezed off a round in each position. A froth of sweat beaded up instantly, his neck, his face, a sudden impulse to hit the deck. He commanded himself to hold it together. Strange memories or just hallucinatory bullshit slashed through his mind and he flinched more than once, jarring his aim. No one seemed to notice, though, or if they did they had the tact to stow it. Gradually the shock of it wore off. He began to feel not just okay but comfortable. With the comfort came a curious kind of acceptance.

He let the other two take a crack at it then, firing off three-shot clusters. He showed them how to compensate for muzzle lift, gauge for wind, zero their sights. When an hour's worth of shooting brought no squad cars or any other outside interest, they let Chato come down and try a few rounds, hopeless though he was. Godo let him wield the Mossberg and the kid took to the shotgun like pie. No point bothering to show him how to shoulder it, the various assault-and-carry positions, Rhodesian ready, Taylor assault, the kid wouldn't listen anyway. Shrugging off his sulk, he pranced about like he'd stepped off a movie screen, blasting at the barn wall, crying out "Boo-yah" while Puchi and Efraim tried out the pistols, getting a little Hollywood themselves, the spirit of the thing, and all Godo could think about were those *hajis* in the rubble-strewn street, thieving their way to freedom, staring back at the helpless marines, shooting them the thumbs-up, here and there a peace sign, cackling. Mocking.

BACK AT THE TRAILER THAT NIGHT, HE FELT SPENT IN A WAY THAT echoed the exhaustion he'd known nowhere but combat. Why he should feel this way now, after a day doing nothing but coaching three hopeless mutts, escaped him.

He dropped his gun-filled duffel onto the floor and his body onto the bed, unable even to muster the will to kick off his shoes or kill the light, suddenly aware he'd not given his gimp leg so much as a moment's thought the past few hours as he tumbled down into a soft heavy sleep without alcohol, without pills, first time in weeks. Then an earthquake, a furious shaking, and he felt the hand first and knew it was real and stirred himself, leaping back from the touch, terrified, forgetting where he left his weapons.

"Hey, it's me. Godo, relax. It's me."

Godo placed the tone, reassuring and yet a little put out, before he recognized the voice. His eyes felt like someone had dripped syrup into them. Gradually, Happy took form, craning over the bed. He was dressed in a black work jacket, T-shirt, jeans, looking like a second-story man. Tía Lucha stood behind him in the doorway, her face stripped of the moon mask. She looked sad, human, like herself, not the person she became out there, in *Gringolandia*.

"You were making this sound, man." Happy sat down on the edge of the bed, gestured to Tía Lucha that everything was okay. "Thought I needed to flip you over or something."

Godo swept a damp palm across his face. Why was he sweating?

Tía Lucha whispered, "*Buenas noches, amorcitos*," then withdrew into the hall, padding back to her room in her socks.

Happy said, "Things okay?"

He smelled of tobacco and *pulque*. Godo rolled over finally, nudged himself into a sitting position, tucked a pillow into the small of his back. "Why shouldn't they be?"

Happy checked around the room, saw the duffel, glanced toward the hallway, cocking an ear for the click of Tía Lucha's door. "The thing with Puchi and Chato, that's what I meant."

Godo wondered why Efraim didn't earn mention. He was the only one worth talking about. "Went okay, I guess."

"They didn't say anything was coming up soon?"

Godo studied Happy's face. It was gaunt, eyes sinking into the skull like a bedouin's. Did the guy ever eat? "They mentioned nothing coming up no time."

"That's important. Put off anything they want you to do."

Godo recalled the tedious dry fires and other lessons out at the farmhouse, the free-form shoot-out at the barn. "Too late."

"I'm not talking target practice. I'm talking a job."

A slash of pain rifled up Godo's spine, igniting a shimmer inside his skull. He wouldn't be falling back asleep anytime soon. Damn. He wanted a beer. "You're talking to the wrong creature. I'm not in the loop there."

"Money's in the pipeline. Things are moving." Happy worried his fingers into a knot. "Pops'll be back in a week, two tops. We're good. No rush. Don't get talked into anything."

"Those two fools? Couldn't talk me into lunch."

"Keep it that way."

Incredible, Godo thought, the attitude. "And if Vasco says put me to work?"

"Put him off. Buy time." Happy reached out, took Godo's arm, a brotherly touch. "Two weeks, that's all we need."

SIXTEEN

THE CAR, A SIX-YEAR-OLD TOYOTA COROLLA, APPEARED IN THE morning, Sisco driving it, part of the arrangement with the *salvatruchos* for the trip back to the States. The money had finally come through. Roque guessed the car had been stolen up north and was making the return trip with a new VIN number and license plates, all part of Lonely's little empire. Roque could only imagine what a relief it was to unload this *cacharro* on just the right bunch of suckers. He wondered what ridiculous price they'd been milked for but that was Happy's end. He chose to believe Happy knew his business.

Tío Faustino worried over the thing throughout the day, replacing the serpentine belt, inserting new plugs, changing the oil and coolant. Test drives around San Pedro Lempa gradually increased his confidence level. Finally, late afternoon, came Roque's turn.

He slid behind the wheel and adjusted the seat, Tío sitting beside him, wiping his hands on a rag.—*She loses power a little going uphill, probably carbon in the cylinders. That's most likely causing some of the knocking too. It's not so bad with the new plugs. I haven't seen smoke, so we're not burning oil.* He tapped out a merry taradiddle on the console, then reached over to squeeze Roque's shoulder.—*Love her*, chamaco. *She's our ticket home*.

Roque got the knack of the Corolla easily, a little loose in the wheel, a leftward drift in the front end, soft brakes. They barreled down a two-lane road lined with fields of sun-browned grass and scant trees. A man in an oxcart bearing plantains passed a small abandoned house bombed with gang graffiti. A woman with a bright red water jug atop her head led her daughter by the hand, the girl staring as the car sped past, the thing no less mysterious for being familiar.

As they drove, he listened to his uncle recount what Carmela and her friends had told him the past few nights. Street vendors were being driven underground, labeled terrorists for selling pirated CDs and DVDs—Hollywood was incredibly, strangely pissed about this, forcing the government to do something—plus the growing corruption in the national police, to where the FBI admitted they could find only twenty officers worthy of trust out of two thousand they'd polygraphed. Former guerrillas, desperate for jobs, now worked security for the very same men who, twenty years ago, wanted them dead. Whole farming communities had abandoned the land because they couldn't compete with the low price of imported American corn. The spiraling cost of oil, swelling demand for meat and dairy in China and India, the use of cropland for biofuels, it was all driving up prices. Families couldn't make ends meet. The number of people starving was larger than before the war.

—*I have this terrible sense of déjà vu*, Faustino admitted.—*I'm running away to save my boy. Except this time he's saving me.*

It was after nightfall by the time they returned to the house in San Pedro Lempa. As they entered the courtyard, a figure they hadn't spotted at first rose from one of the chairs, unrecognizable in the darkness. Roque felt his heart bound into his throat but the man approached with an air of deference, clutching a small cloth bag to his chest. In an accent Roque couldn't quite place, the man said to Tío Faustino, "I believe you are Happy's father. My greetings to you." He placed a hand over his heart, bowing respectfully. "My name is Samir."

—

THEY SAT AROUND THE WOOD-PLANK TABLE BENEATH THE MANGO tree, the fragrance from Carmela's exotic flowers mixing with the scent of candle wax.

"Let me tell you something, your son was a worker, very dedicated. But also very kind, very brave." The Arab paused to take a sip of *shuco*, a hot corn sludge darkened with black-bean paste, thinned with scalding water and sweetened with raw sugar, something Carmela had worked up. "I owe him a great deal, your son. My being here tonight, not least of all."

His face—long and vaguely hourglass shaped, indented at the temples—rippled with shadow in the guttering light, his features both delicate and stern, a beak of a nose but womanly lips, sunken eyes, closely shorn hair. His age was hard to pinpoint, late thirties, early fifties, anywhere between. Given the honey color of his skin and his textbook Spanish, he might just pass for a *guanaco* at the various checkpoints, Roque thought, if he says as little as possible. His accent seemed a bit starched, vaguely Castilian. As for his English, which he preferred to use with Tío Faustino and Roque for the sake of practice, it too was oddly accented, not just with the usual clipped Arab inflections but a kind of plodding cadence, as though he'd learned the language reciting clunky poems.

"I met Happy when the country was coming apart. The imams were in bed not just with the insurgency but with organized crime. Muqtada al Sadr and his thugs took over the hospitals. If a Sunni man came in with a gunshot wound, the Jaish al Mahdi would come, accuse him of being a terrorist, take him away. His body would get found a few days later, tossed in the street or a field somewhere."

Tío Faustino hung on every word. Roque remained unconvinced. The man seemed too put together, like an actor still working into the skin of his role.

"The Shia hated the Palestinians worse than they hated the Sunnis. And I served in the war against Iran—very odd, a Palestinian in the army, but that's another story. The Persians are Shia too, so I was particularly loathsome to them. But the worst thing? What my own in-laws did to me."

Tío Faustino looked puzzled. "How—"

"Two weeks after the election, my wife's brothers came, took Fatima and our daughter away while I was at work. Admittedly, things were getting much worse. Our neighbor, he had two uncles kidnapped, a note demanding $100,000 ransom arrived. Impossible. They tried to negotiate. Next day, the two uncles show up at the morgue, drill holes everywhere. This is the Jaish al Mahdi, okay? I could tell you stories even more horrible than this, trust me."

Tío Faustino gazed into the candlelight. "War is a kind of sickness. People go mad."

"Two days later, Fatima's brothers show up while I'm away. They left a letter behind, saying they couldn't just stand by and watch their sister and niece get raped and murdered while I did nothing, as though I didn't even want to protect them. Everything I did, every dollar I earned, was for them. But none of that mattered. They took Fatima and little Shatha and their own families and fled to Syria, but they couldn't get in. They're stuck."

One of the candles burned out. Tío Faustino watched the thin curl of smoke rise. "I'm sure my son understood," he said, "how hard it was for you, your family ripped apart like that, given what he himself has been through. Being deported, I mean."

Roque wondered where Tío was going with this. It seemed a morbid kind of one-upmanship, a game of dueling miseries.

"A week later, the Jaish al Mahdi drove me out. Three of them showed up, dressed all in black, the oldest maybe twenty-one. They pounded on the door, spat at my feet when I opened it, then handed me a bullet soaked in blood, told me I had three hours to get out or die in the street. I left behind everything I owned but what I could jam into a suitcase. I began sleeping on pallets of rice at the warehouse in Abu Ghraib, until they found a bed for me in the worker compound. That was when Happy and I got to know each other. I went to work for the Salvadorans because they were the only ones left. The Spaniards, the Hondurans, the Nicaraguans, all gone. Everybody was getting out if they could. The thing was a disaster. And everybody figured the Americans bungled their way in, let them bungle their way out."

A stray dog poked its head through a hole in the hedge of *veranera* surrounding the garden, sniffing the air, eyes glimmering. Tío Faustino hissed, raised his hand in almost comic wrath. The dog shrank away. "Why didn't you try working for the Americans?"

"Of course I tried, the Americans and British both. They would have nothing to do with me. I know Israel gets blamed for everything, not wrongly in my view, but I have to believe my being Palestinian was why I was shunned. The Salvadorans, praise God, took pity on me. They were in Najaf, rebuilding the airport, the hospitals, a few small refineries. None of the roads into Najaf were safe. Muqtada al Sadr and his thugs put up their own barricades. And if they weren't shaking you down, the Badr Brigade was. I told you, your son was very brave. I grew to respect him very much. Entering the city took hours sometimes. Bribes just vanished, they did nothing, but without a bribe you sat there all night or got dragged away to a secret prison, ransomed off. Or got to star in one of those special videos, where your head disappears."

A sudden stirring in the mango tree lifted everyone's gaze. A *garrobo* scurried among the branches, scaly and brown, staring back at them with elfin dinosaur eyes.

"Not to sound morbid," Samir continued. "I just want you to understand, your son—"

A car roared up the hill, crunching to a stop in the gravel beyond the hedge. Doors opened, slammed closed. The scuffling of feet, harsh voices.

Lonely appeared, clutching Lupe by the arm with one hand, the other grabbing her hair as he dragged her forward. She bucked against his grip. Sisco lingered behind, hands buried deep in his pockets.

On impulse Roque stood up, regretting the move instantly. Who did he expect to fight, who would it save? He could feel the adrenalin crackling in his blood. Tío Faustino just sat there slack-jawed. Samir stared blankly.

Lonely shoved Lupe forward and she stumbled, trying to keep her feet. Even in the candlelight, Roque could see the fresh damage, the glistening lip, the crimped eye. He envisioned killing the two *mareros* right there, bare hands if need be, knew as well it was his powerlessness triggering the fantasy, triggering all his fantasies.

Lupe dropped uneasily to one knee, her breath ragged. Eyes blazing, Lonely stepped forward, rocking his hip as though to kick her. She recoiled from him and he laughed, then looked up and met Roque's stare.

"Like the way she looks, *jodido*? She's yours. All the way to Agua Prieta. You deliver this *pinche putilla* to a dude called El Recio. He's your man, you wanna cross over. She gets handed over to him or your uncle and Turco the motherfucker there don't make it home, get it?"

Tío Faustino rose from his chair, came around to see if Lupe needed any help. Easing the girl to her feet, he took her chin in his hand, regarded her face. She seemed responsive to the kindness. Roque thought: Hand her over, and then? Meanwhile, Samir's whole demeanor had changed. He seemed coiled, ready to lash out if need be and yet also indifferent. The look of an animal, Roque thought.

"Where are her things?" He felt the stupidity of the question instantly but couldn't help himself from clarifying: "Her clothes, I mean. Her stuff."

"Her *stuff*?" Lonely cackled like a magpie. "You wanna talk about her *stuff*?"

"You know what—"

"Pack up your own fucking *stuff* and drag your punk ass outta here, *mamón*. You gotta head for San Cristóbal. Guy you're gonna meet there, his name is Rafa. He'll be looking for your car. Pull up about half a mile shy of the border, his gas station's there, blue lantern in the window. You see the bridge up ahead, you've gone too far, turn around and go back. And try not to be too fucking obvious about it."

He took one last glance at Lupe, looking like he was gathering saliva so he could spit. Tío Faustino moved between them. Lonely grinned, turned on his heel and plodded back to the car.

Sisco lingered, hands still balled in his pockets. "You know the secret of getting past the checkpoints, right?" His eyes focused on some nebulous point outside the circle of candlelight, a grin on his lips, childish and taunting and strange. "No matter what they do, or how they ask, just keep smiling."

SEVENTEEN

THE COURTROOM DOOR WHISPERED OPEN, THUDDED CLOSED. Turning to glance over his shoulder, Lattimore spotted the strange man enter timidly under the indifferent eye of the bailiff, who sat perched on a stool at the back, thumbing through last month's *Ebony*.

The newcomer had a wonkish dishevelment, bristling salt-and-pepper hair, a close-cropped beard, gold-rimmed glasses that sat cockeyed on his face. His jacket, tie, shirt and slacks looked like they'd mugged him in the closet that morning. The man's glance met Lattimore's, followed by an unsettling smile. Lattimore turned back toward the proceedings.

"We're not asking for any more than the court provided in *U.S. v. Fort*, Your Honor." Pitcavage stood at the prosecutor's table, hands clasped behind him, a skipper on deck. His trial team, a claque of mannequins with law degrees, sat to his right. "We have no obligation to provide police reports or 302s to the defense any earlier than the Friday before testimony."

"We can't prepare an adequate defense under those restrictions, Your Honor." This came from Tony Torreta, lead defense counsel, representing Hugo "Little Brother" Rodriguez, the shot caller for the Fogtown Brujos, a Mara Salvatrucha *clica* that ran a car-theft ring and various shakedown rackets plus good old-fashioned dope in the Outer Mission and Visitacion Valley. He was on trial with two of his lieutenants for the murder of a witness in a federal racketeering trial last spring. "We get, what, two days?" Torreta continued. "Two *weekend* days at that, to track down and interview more than one hundred witnesses. In an excess of caution, or bowing to the government's paranoia, we've agreed not to share the witness names with our clients."

"An inadequate prophylactic, Your Honor. Again, *U.S. v. Fort—*"

"This sabotages a deal made only a week ago."

Feeling the pressure of the stranger's gaze boring into his neck, Lattimore decided what the hell. He rose, eased his way past two other agents in attendance and headed down the center aisle toward the courtroom door, avoiding the stranger's eye, choosing instead to cock his hand into a gun, then firing at the bailiff who glanced up from his *Ebony* just in time to die.

Lattimore waited in the corridor, figuring it would take only seconds. True enough, the door eased open, the rumpled man with the scratchy beard and off-kilter glasses materialized, breaking into an ample smile, teeth the color of butterscotch, plowing forward, hand outstretched. His footsteps echoed brightly in the empty corridor, a sound like he was tap-dancing across a shower stall.

"Jim Lattimore? My name's McIlvaine, Andy McIlvaine. I'm with the Banneret Group."

They shook hands. "Can't say I know your outfit."

"We're security specialists, out of Dallas."

Lattimore was thinking Midwest, not Texas, given the accent. And he would have guessed OGA, Other Government Agency, the new nickname for the CIA. As though changing acronyms hid anything. Maybe he was a cutout. But a security firm, what kind of cover was that?

"Might I have a moment of your time?" McIlvaine at last let go of Lattimore's hand. "It concerns your interest in a man by the name of Samir Khalid Sadiq."

Lattimore led him to the prosecution conference room. It was clubby in atmosphere and no one else was there at the moment, the day being set aside for pretrial motions and other drudgery. Lattimore gestured McIlvaine into a plump leather chair and dropped into the one opposite, saying, "Not to be rude, but could I see some form of ID?"

McIlvaine hefted his battered leather briefcase into his lap as though it contained a bowling ball, unhitched the clasps and withdrew a business card. "If you call the home office, ask for Ron Stillwagon, he was with the bureau's Houston office for quite a while. I think he might be able to fluff your comfort level."

"Give me a minute." Lattimore rose, thumbing his cell phone, but the number he entered wasn't the one on the card. He called the secretary for his unit, ran the company and its numbers past her, then the names McIlvaine and Stillwagon. "Text me back if it all checks out. Call otherwise." He flipped the phone closed, walked back to his chair and sat. "Sorry."

"Not at all. I'd do the same."

For the first time, Lattimore noticed that one of the man's ears was half an inch lower than the other. It explained the crooked glasses. He had to resist an impulse to dock his head, render the face plumb. "Mind if I ask why you're interested in Samir Khalid Sadiq?"

"We have units stationed in Iraq, doing both VIP transport and antifraud. We work closely with the bureau over there, among other agencies. One of our men in the Green Zone is an old Urgent Fury pal, the two of us were intelligence analysts with the Second Fleet, we stay in pretty regular touch. Your inquiries came to his attention and he thought, given the fact your case touches on matters relevant to my region of interest—that would be Mexico, Central America—that I might want to connect with you, see if I could be of any assistance."

Lattimore felt vaguely backdoored. The bureaucratic merry-go-round in this thing was already mind-numbing. Beyond the guys on the ground in Iraq whom this McIlvaine bird had already mentioned, there was the counterterrorism desk in Washington, the Transnational Anti-Gang Task Force in Los Angeles, and outside the bureau he'd had to involve ICE on the immigration angle—without a significant public benefit parole, Happy Orantes would get grabbed right out of Lattimore's office and deported so fast his head would spin, no matter what he had to say or who he had to offer. Then there was Homeland Security's inspector general on the corrupt border agent angle, and if they decided to pass—he was still waiting for an answer—it would be back to ICE, their office of professional responsibility. And then there was the Pentagon, the NSA, even the OGA/CIA, who'd be tracking the cousin Roque through his cell phone and informing trusted local contacts in Mexico and Central America of his whereabouts in case something went sideways. The State Department insisted on notification too, since they were permitting known criminals to enter a sovereign ally, and most likely they'd inform the MFJP, the Mexican Federal Judicial Police, the gold standard for south-of-the-border corruption, something to put off as long as possible.

He felt his cell phone vibrate in his breast pocket, pulled it out. A text: "All OK." He dropped the phone back in his pocket.

"So then, Mr. McIlvaine—"

"Andy. Please."

"What can I do for you?"

The bristly face rubbered up another butterscotch smile, further skewing his glasses. He fussed again with his briefcase clasp, rummaged about inside, finally extracting a thin sheaf of papers. With no more exertion than that, a bead of perspiration formed in the hollow of his temple, hanging there, a minor defiance of gravity. "This may still be making its way to your desk." He leaned forward, holding the documents out. "I thought I might facilitate."

Taking the papers, Lattimore noticed the cover sheet bore no agency heading or seal, just a line at the top for subject reference—in this instance, the name Samir Khalid Sadiq—then another line for the date, a third bearing a source code he couldn't decipher. He pictured the original gathering dust on somebody's desk in Baghdad. Typical, he thought, and yet the poverty of detail on the face sheet suggested clandestine channels, spooks in the ether, dead drops. OGA. How many lies would he have to sit through, he wondered, if he asked Mr. Itchy Teeter-Peepers how he got his hands on the thing?

The second page was in Arabic, the third a translation. It appeared to be a data sheet of some sort, for an employee, a contact, maybe the target of an inquiry. Lattimore's eye, trailing across the page at random, quickly settled on the word "Mukhabarat."

"You may or may not know this," McIlvaine ventured, the lone bead of sweat still hovering at eye level. "Forgive me if I'm belaboring the obvious. After the fall of Baghdad, coalition forces took control of various government ministries, including the Mukhabarat, Saddam's secret police. By the time they arrived, unfortunately, many of the files had been destroyed in the invasion's first wave of bombings. Most of the rest were boxed up by loyalists and hustled away or carted off by looters. In the weeks after Baghdad fell, some files resurfaced, many of them ransomed off to the families of men who had disappeared. Some were sold to journalists—it was practically a cottage industry. It's difficult to know the value of what remained. This, for example." He wiggled his hand at the sheaf of papers. "Your man Samir was on the payroll, that much appears certain. What does it mean? He may have been an interpreter through the foreign press office or a minder for a foreign journalist. They may have enlisted him as an informer, they kept a close eye on the Palestinians in-country. Or he could have been nothing more than a driver for one of the car companies the Mukhabarat operated." He shrugged, then crossed his legs, revealing a bright hairless shin above the bunched gray sock. "Maybe he collected payoffs. Maybe he was an assassin. Maybe this document is fake."

Lattimore had to resist an impulse to reach over and wipe the drop of sweat away, maybe straighten the man's glasses while he was at it. He handed the papers back. "You came all the way from Dallas to tell me that?"

McIlvaine's smile turned sly. "A link to the Mukhabarat is, of course, inherently significant. Top to bottom—analysts, case agents, drivers, torturers, common thugs—they were jobless after Baghdad fell. Many went to the Americans hoping for a job and got brushed off. That left the resistance, which they flocked to, angry, humiliated, out of work, but also well informed and lavishly armed since neither the Third Army nor the First Marines were assigned to guard the weapons depots."

Lattimore studied the man's eyes, which had hardened almost imperceptibly behind the old-fashioned lenses. Anyone who'd served in uniform couldn't look at that war and not turn bitter at the recklessness, the idiocy, the arrogance. But that wasn't quite relevant to the matter at hand. "The fact we can't be sure exactly who this man is as yet," he said carefully, "argues for the greater control we can exert by keeping tabs on him, which this investigation does. What would you rather have us do, let him move at will?"

Another smile from McIlvaine, less sly than indulgent. "We've learned Mr. Sadiq was sponsored by a prominent Salvadoran of Palestinian descent for his visa, not someone we know, exactly, but a friend of a friend, let's say, two or three degrees removed from people we trust. That doesn't mean he's a genius or a saint but he's on our side, as far as we can tell."

"Let me stop you for a second. Tell me again, this is all of interest to you why?"

"To be honest, I thought the more relevant issue would be its interest to you."

"My interest is obvious. Yours—"

"As I said, this is my area of expertise. I work in the private sector. When you have the fee structure we do, you'd better know your business. We can't wait to educate ourselves as circumstances dictate. We're paid to predict, not react."

"What concerns me," Lattimore said, "is why my business is your business."

"Mr. Sadiq is my business. Any potential threat in the region is. Now, may I continue?"

Lattimore felt outmaneuvered. Still, better to see where the thing was heading.

McIlvaine toggled his glasses. "Where was I? Yes, a foreign affairs officer from the embassy followed up—our embassy, down there, in Santa Elena. The sponsor said he was asked to back Samir because he'd helped the Salvadoran troops in Najaf. That's all he knew. He preferred not to say who asked him to step up for the sponsorship but claimed it was absolutely not someone who would knowingly get involved in a plot to move a terrorist across three borders into the States."

Lattimore marveled at the scant reassurance the word "knowingly" provided. Given the capacity for ignorant blundering you saw everywhere, Iraq most of all, what difference did it make what you knew or intended? Still, despite the sense of being outflanked, he took some relief from McIlvaine's news. It basically confirmed Happy's version of events.

"El Salvador," McIlvaine continued, "is relatively enlightened on immigration issues, curiously enough. During World War II, the Salvadoran embassy in Geneva issued citizenship papers to more than forty thousand Hungarian Jews. Of course, most didn't emigrate. But the citizenship documents kept them from being deported to the camps." He drummed his fingers on his briefcase. "The curse of all intelligence analysts: I'm a history buff."

"Fascinating," Lattimore said.

McIlvaine took no offense. "There's a word you use for the kind of case you're working, if I'm not mistaken, where you insert an informant into a nest of bored, restless, vaguely ill-inclined but not yet traitorous young men, with the hope that, given a little stirring of the pot, a dash of conspiratorial brio—a pledge of allegiance to al-Qaeda in a warehouse rigged for video, let's say—you can charge them all for conspiracy to commit terrorism. An acronym, am I right?"

A flume of bile lodged in Lattimore's throat. "BOG," he acknowledged.

"And that stands for . . . ?"

"Bunch of guys."

"Exactly. The full power of the American government brought to bear against . . . a bunch of guys."

"Mr. McIlvaine—"

"Boy, if that doesn't shiver Old Glory right up the flagpole, I don't know what does."

Lattimore checked his watch. He was due to meet Happy back at his office in half an hour, review his most recent tapes, which were, by and large, not just boring and repetitive but worthless. "So you didn't come all the way from Dallas just to show me an essentially meaningless one-page document."

"As I told you—"

"You came to put me in my place."

"It's no secret your bunch-of-guys cases haven't fared too well. Snitch problems."

"Snitch problems are a given."

"The Liberty City trial's a debacle. What is it now, two hung juries in a row?"

"We got verdicts across the board in Fort Dix. The Toledo case came out okay."

"Sure, with two full years of video and audio. *Two years*. Correct me if I'm wrong, but you don't have that kind of window here."

Lattimore felt himself recoil inwardly. The guy knew way too much.

"Meanwhile," McIlvaine added, "your bureau buddies went off chasing vegan bicyclists around Minneapolis trying to recruit snitches before the Republican National Convention. I'm sure that ended well. Is this the best we can do?"

Depends on who you mean by we, Lattimore supposed. "This case was vetted before I moved on it."

"It makes us look like we're making this crap up. We're not. Hezbollah has camps in the Triple Border area. They know we're watching, too, because some have fled east into the jungles of Brazil, or west into Iquique, Chile's northern desert. Hezbollah's also connected to Pablo Escobar's old cronies who now run cocaine through a paramilitary organization in Medellin called the Office of Envigado. The money gets laundered by Lebanese businessmen in Bogotá and Caracas. They have sleepers operating out of Iranian embassies all over the region. They even have websites, no joke, for their presence in several countries, including El Salvador. There's solid intelligence they're surveilling U.S. and Israeli targets throughout the subcontinent. And it's not just Hezbollah we're tracking. It's Hamas, the PLO. Given that this Samir Khalid Sadiq claims to be Palestinian, that's relevant I'd say."

"I wouldn't disagree. Look—"

"These groups are trading guns for drugs with the Mexican and Colombian cartels. The markup on cocaine alone in the Middle East is obscene. A kilo of Mexican coke costs them $6,000. You can turn it around for $100,000 in Israel, $150,000 in Saudi Arabia. Imagine what that kind of money buys. You're seeing a lot of meth over there now too, the *jihadis* use it to amp up for battle. That's serious, all of it, especially compared to *a bunch of guys*."

At last the bead of sweat slithered down from his temple into the nettles of his beard. Lattimore felt an odd relief. Still, McIlvaine made no move to wipe it away.

"We're already losing faith with American Muslims, they

think we've got spies planted in all their mosques. Imagine the intel we're losing because they no longer trust us. Another half-baked terrorism case won't help. And the more you lionize Mara Salvatrucha, the more attractive it looks to all the teenage losers needing something to buy into—"

"Mr. McIlvaine—"

"It's self-fulfilling. Make them out as the next big deal, guess what they'll become?"

Lattimore found it strange that McIlvaine would play down a threat. In his experience, the private security outfits were more than eager to turn every crackhead lowlife with access to a gun into the next Che Guevara. It was, as McIlvaine would say, their business.

"I'm not going to apologize," Lattimore said, "for going after the people we're targeting."

"Don't get me wrong. Making sure that Mr. Sadiq is who your informant claims he is? Crucial. But the idiots on this end, I mean, seriously. Linking them to terrorism?"

Lattimore took a second to check his temper. "Maybe you should've spent a little more time in court back there. I can show you some of the 302s we've got, bring you up to speed."

"Given what little I heard, I don't think the defense team would view that kindly."

"Little Brother and his rat-packers in there dragged a single mom out of her apartment on Shotwell last May, did it in front of her two little girls and just about everybody else in the neighborhood. It was a hot night, folks were out on their stoops, buying *helado* from the pushcart vendor. Kids, parents, grandparents. One of these Fogtown runts doused this young woman with lighter fluid as she begged for her life, one of the others struck a match. Take a second to imagine that, okay? The sound. The smell. Her two little girls right there. As if that wasn't bad enough, they also shot her seven times. Not out of charity. They took out her legs, so she couldn't run. They wanted her to lie there and burn, so everyone could watch. She'd identified one of Little Brother's zukes as the bagman who, every Wednesday, came into her beauty salon to collect the week's tax. We were building a case against the crew at the time. No surprise, things dried up pretty quick after that. This time we've named every third person in the neighborhood as a smokescreen, figuring they can't kill them all. I sure hope we're right. That's terrorism too."

"You don't need to phony up an Arab *jihadi* sneaking across the border to prosecute it, though, do you?"

"Whatever it takes."

"Look, street crime is destabilizing, it drives off investment, sucks up public resources, development hits a wall—granted, okay? But street crime isn't terrorism."

"To you, maybe."

"I'm not saying it isn't a problem, Lattimore. I'm arguing the problem isn't strategic." Finally, he wiped the perspiration off his cheek. "People here in the States get the vapors reading the news reports and the embassies get swamped by delegations from home wringing their hands, begging something be done. It's a waste of time. The *maras*, the *salvatruchos*, they don't own isolated tracts of land where you can build an airstrip. They don't have diplomatic immunity or connections to the military or go to the same clubs as the judges quashing warrants. The real problem is the cartels, the corruption. Real organized crime, the men with social or political connections, immune from prosecution."

"You saying Mara Salvatrucha's not connected to the cartels?"

"Right now? They're humps, mules. They provide muscle and move freight."

"And people, don't forget. They move people. Like the ones in this case, including a Palestinian we're all hoping is who we think he is."

"They couldn't move those folks without the blessing of the cartels. Running those routes on their own? Five years away at least. The cartels would skin them alive."

"Really? Five whole years. Well damn."

"I'd like—"

"They're sure as hell not five years away from running pot farmers off their land at gunpoint up in Mendocino and Humboldt counties. That's happening right now."

"I'd like to get back to talking about terrorism. Islamic terrorism."

"How come I hear Salvadorans and Hondurans tell me, when they go back to visit family, every time it's worse, the shakedowns, the muggings, the drug use, the killings."

"You're thinking like a cop."

"Whoa. Imagine that."

"Guatemala's got the best infrastructure in the region and it's a testament to one thing. Drugs. You think the World Bank put up that money? Graft is a way of life down there. Christ, it's a tradition, like cockfights and *quinceañeras*. But the *maras* don't pose anywhere near the kind of organized-crime danger they're routinely blamed for. Granted, once they're a solid cog in the trade, looking up from the ground, they're going to tell themselves they deserve better. They're going to make their move, start fighting for control and I don't mean a barrio here or there. That's when it's going to get hairy. You think Mexico's a mess? It'll look like Mother's Day in Fresno compared to what's coming."

"All the more reason to jump now."

"With a trumped-up case?"

"Mr. McIlvaine—"

"I asked you to call me Andy."

The cushion hissed as Lattimore leaned forward. "All right. Andy." A janitor poked his head in at the door, kicked the nearest wastebasket, left. "I'm not so sure we're disagreeing here. Seeing the problem from different angles, maybe. But even if I wanted to back off this case, I couldn't close it down completely. First, like I said, it's generally agreed we have better control over

Samir Sadiq's movements working this operation than we would otherwise."

"I haven't said word one about calling off that end of things."

"Second, the smugglers my CI has connections to have corrupted some border agents, we don't know who they are just yet. The inspector general over at Homeland Security—"

"Can run his own sting."

"Look—"

"You've got politicians running campaign ads where terrorists slip merrily across the Rio Grande and make a beeline for the Alamo. Is this possible? Sure. And about as likely as a meteor hitting my cat. If the chuckleheads who've bought into your snitch's scheme had one good functioning brain cell in their collective head, they'd know that. Which means a jury is less likely to see them as the menace you're making them out to be than just plain stupid."

"That doesn't mean they don't deserve what they get."

"These cases are backfiring, Lattimore. The whole counterterrorism effort looks ludicrous. If you're going to cry wolf, you better have one to show for it."

It was startling, the change in his demeanor, the hardening around the edges of the eyes, the combative snap in his posture. And with it the slovenly shabbiness dissolved. Maybe the secretary was right, the Bannaret Group was real, but Lattimore wondered if the entire encounter wasn't a charade, down to the documents the man had brought, the supposed translation. Time would tell. Maybe it was all just a way to throw him off the scent of some other problem lurking around the edges.

"The men we're investigating aren't innocents," he said. "Fools? Maybe. But they gladly jumped on board, even knowing they were involved—"

"Imagine you're a terrorist," McIlvaine said, barely able to contain himself now. "You have an engineering degree, like Mohammed Atta, and you live in Munich. Are you going to schlep to Tijuana or try to swim the Rio Grande or starve in the desert for days with a pack of *mojados* who will hand you up in a heartbeat if they get caught? No. You have a legal passport and no criminal record, you're not on any lists—that's the kind of character a real terrorist cell will send here, okay? You'll get a student visa to Canada, where you'll rent a car, drive in comfort to some spot in the 450 miles of wilderness patrolled by four Mounties and simply walk or drive across the border. It's that easy. Or maybe you'll buy a skiff with an outboard and cross a few miles above Niagara Falls, where you're as likely to get spotted as a cricket. Maybe you'll just sign up with a Bavarian travel agency for a charter flight to Vegas with a pack of blue-hairs, play the slots, cruise the buffet at the Luxor, go to a drag show, then get on a bus and vanish."

"Or bribe a border agent and cross over at Douglas, or Laredo or Calexico or—"

"In hock to a bunch of *mareros*? Too many things to go wrong. Too many idiots to pay off. It's not the style of the networks we're tracking. They're used to outsmarting Mossad. They wouldn't soil their hands with the likes of the hoons you've got your sights on here."

Maybe I'm missing something, Lattimore thought. He didn't see the bad news in all this. He didn't want to bring a real terrorist into the country, a phony one served just fine. Better, in fact. That was the point. And what the fuck was a hoon?

"Look, all you're saying, seems to me—"

"What I'm saying is that by rigging up a case where you have a bunch of losers tricked into thinking they're bringing a real terrorist into the country, you condition people to believe that this stuff is always jerry-rigged by us to make it look like we're actually doing something about terrorism when we're not. There is no threat. It's prosecution for the sake of PR, soap opera for paranoids. Five years from now, when the problem's real, who's going to believe us?"

—

AN HOUR LATER, AS LATTIMORE SAT IN A CONFERENCE ROOM REVIEWING with Happy the transcripts of his most recent tapes, he decided to pose the question that had been nagging him ever since he'd watched Andy McIlvaine disappear like a magician's assistant behind the hushed brass doors of the elevator. Nothing seemed solid now. But the phrase that haunted him most, the one that kept circling again and again through his mind, was: *You're not on any lists*. That was the man you had to worry about. Even if the Mukhabarat lead turned out to be a red herring and nothing else hinky cropped up, even if this Palestinian came up clean as a tadpole's ass, that wouldn't mean he wasn't a danger. Quite the contrary.

Tucking the last transcript back into its accordion file, he said, "This friend of yours, Mr. Sadiq. The guy whose heart you know so well. Saved your life, you say." He glanced up, a brushback stare. "I don't remember you telling me anything about him and Saddam's Gestapo. Or were you just saving that up, a little gift for later."

EIGHTEEN

A LOW-WATTAGE BULB SCREWED INTO A WALL SOCKET PROVIDED the only light in the *gasolinera*'s cramped back room, the smears left behind by greasy fingers projecting across the walls as faint blotches of shadow. A *garrobo* the size of a switchblade flicked the brown scaly quiver of its tail back and forth as it pondered how to cross the blurred lines. Remembering Sisco's parting advice on the best way to finesse the checkpoints that lay ahead—keep smiling—Roque wondered if the wag of a lizard's tail wasn't a kind of smile.

Lupe lay on the floor near the workbench, holding a slushy bag of ice to her face. For a pillow she used a plastic bag filled with underwear and a few blouses she'd bought that afternoon at a village market along the road. They'd also bought some ibuprofen and a cream with heparin; trust the local *mamacitas*, Roque thought, to know how to nurse a black eye.

A few minutes earlier, Rafa, the service-station owner, had explained that in just a short while the coyote would arrive to take Samir and Tío Faustino overland into Guatemala. Lupe, being Salvadoran, could pass through with Roque in the car using just her ID. Central Americans, he explained, can travel freely across borders from Guatemala in the north to Costa Rica in the south. She doesn't need to walk.

Samir couldn't believe that was the plan.—*Look at the girl's face! What do you think will happen at the checkpoint? They'll question her, just because they can, just to fuck with her. Then what?* He went on like that, voice rising higher with every phrase, as though pushing the words uphill. He knew his fate was tied to hers now and he hated her for it. But Rafa replied that his instructions were clear.

Ever since, the Palestinian had hammered away at Lupe.

—*Let me tell you something: They will find your family if you try to run. You want them to die? Want me to tell you how it will happen?*

—*You've made your point*, Roque said, aware he was broadcasting his attraction by taking up her defense. She just lay there, eyes closed, ignoring them both. Tío Faustino wisely had gone outside and was now stretched out beneath the Corolla's hood, working by flashlight as he tightened the belts.—*Let her rest.*

Samir, as always, ignored him.—*Whatever you've done, you must pay the price yourself.*

—*Who says she did anything?*

Samir chuckled.—*You're a child. Maybe the same age as her, but you're the child.*

—*Stop, enough, my God.* She rose up on one elbow, the bag of ice sliding off her face onto the floor with a damp thud. The battered eye remained dark with bruising, the purple skin glistening from the heparin cream. The swelling had gone down. Her lip looked normal too, except for a scab.—*Take it somewhere else, you two. I want to sleep.*

Roque studied her face as she fumbled for her ice. He hoped this was the last of Lonely's abuse, though who knew what damage a freak like that could inflict from a distance.

—*You want to sleep?* Samir couldn't help himself, couldn't hold his tongue.—*Let me tell you something. My wife's brothers tried to save her, like our young friend here dreams of saving you, but what did they accomplish? Refugee camp, it's a prison. And where can they go from there, back to Iraq? Palestinians have to register with the Ministry of the Interior every month, which is just signing up to be killed. Bodies get left out in the street, some with their faces burned away by acid, some with no hands. Just before I left, the Jaish al Mahdi stormed into this tiny radio station. All ten people who worked there, men and women both, were dragged out into the street and shot. I saw this happen with my own eyes. I watched those poor people, I knew their names, I saw them beg for their lives. So no, my wife, her brothers, they cannot return to Baghdad. And they cannot work in Syria, not legally. They've all but exhausted their savings. Fatima has to choose between medicine or food.*

He clutched his small cloth bag to his chest, rocking as he spoke.

—Know what Fatima does for money? She fasts. Yes. She has an engineering degree—think about that, an Arab woman with an engineering degree—but she fasts. She does this for rich people, men and women who can't be bothered to honor the traditions on their own. So they hire a surrogate, they hire my wife. They pay her $60 per month for a sick relative, a son who has strayed with an evil woman, a brother who has lost his business. Some just don't want to observe the Ramadan fast, so they hire Fatima to do it for them. Sometimes Shatha, my daughter, she does the fasting, because her mother is too weak. Here, I will show you a picture.

He dug into his bag, withdrew a photograph, held it out for her to take, but Lupe didn't move. Finally, to save the man embarrassment, Roque reached out for it. It was a close-up, just the two of them, mother and child, faces filling the frame, hair unveiled, raven-black and long, both of them smiling, cheek to cheek—same dimples, same eyes, same lips. He couldn't see much resemblance with the father, thought better of saying so. He tried to hand the picture back but Samir merely clutched his bag tighter.

—There is no school for Shatha. Fatima is sick from the lack of food, the lack of sleep, the despondency. But the only alternative is to become a prostitute.

—And that would kill you, wouldn't it? Lupe spoke without lifting her head, holding the ice bag in one hand, wagging a

knowing finger with the other.—*To think your dear wife's fucking other men, sucking their Arab cocks, so your daughter can eat.*

Samir shook his head with an almost boyish violence.—*She understands honor.*

—*She understands hunger.*

—*And it is the Americans, the contractors, who use the prostitutes.*

—*You use prostitutes. Admit it, Turco.*

His sunken eyes flared.—*I have never—*

—*Don't worry, your wife understands. She understands her husband is far away and men are men. She's on her own, like women everywhere.*

—*I have never used prostitutes. Never. And Fatima is not alone! All of this, this struggle to reach America, it's for her.*

—*America?* Lupe resettled her weight, nudging herself onto her back with an indulgent moan, as though self-pity was the only pleasure left.—*We're all prostitutes in America.*

—*You are wrong! You are wrong. I realize these men you fell in with, they have made you a slave. Yes, you will have to degrade yourself, sell yourself to buy your way out of their grip. You will have to endure much and suffer greatly. But you can do it. You are young. You are not the only one facing such things.*

—*Like your wife?*

—*Someday you will get to America and there things change. I'm not stupid, I know dreams are for children. Yes, there is little hope in the world. But without America, there is none. Despite everything, you will have a chance.*

At last she leaned up a little, meeting his eyes.—*What makes you think I'll live long enough to have a chance?*

—*You are too young to be so bitter.*

—*And you're too old not to realize your wife is fucking strangers to stay alive.*

—*She's not! She can't. You don't understand how it is. Her brothers would kill her.*

—She'll tell them she's out cleaning houses. Like Latinas do in the States. Like I said, in America—

Samir refused to hear more. He shot to his feet and turned away.*—I pity you. Despite all I and my family have endured, I have not despaired. I am a father, I can't give up hope. You need to do the same. Otherwise, why not just surrender to death and the devil?*

—You don't want me to die. I die, you don't make it to America. Like it or not, all the hope in the world won't save you without me.

This last bit was said to Samir's back, he'd already fled. She watched the empty doorway for a moment, then resettled herself, easing onto her side with another wincing moan, facing away from Roque.*—God, I thought he'd never leave.*

It was the first thing he could recall her saying to him, even during their recording session back in La Chacra. He could think of nothing to say in return, preferring instead to study the hollow of her back where her blouse rode up. Wiping the lather of sweat off his face, he glanced up at the clock: half past ten. Tío Faustino and Samir would head off soon. Several feet below the clock, the lizard had yet to budge.

—Stop looking at my ass.

He flinched at the sound of her voice.*—I'm not—*

The bag of ice sloshed.*—Not what?*

—I'm not playing this game. You want to think all men are alike, we're nothing but dogs—eat it, fuck it or piss on it. Be my guest. But my uncle's not like that. I'm not like that.

She huffed, glancing over her shoulder with her good eye.*—What's wrong with my ass?*

He heard an unfamiliar voice coming from outside.*—Excuse me*, he said, getting up from the floor to head out toward the sound, leaving Lupe and the lizard to themselves.

The stranger looked nothing like Roque had imagined. He wore jeans, a rugby shirt, a denim jacket way too large, plus a Dodger's cap, blue again, his only nod to MS-13. His name, Roque gathered from the conversation, was Humilde.

Samir slung his bag at his hip, the shoulder strap crossing his chest. Tío Faustino prepared to head off with nothing but the clothes on his back. He wrapped his arms around Roque in a farewell embrace. "We'll see each other tomorrow. Don't worry." Slapping Roque's back, he waited for the others to drift out of earshot before adding in a whisper: "I cannot live with my conscience, knowing what that girl in there has facing her at the end of this trip." He backed away, taking Roque's face in his hands, a shocking gesture, overly tender, except the cast of his eye was calculating, not affectionate. "We have to think of something, you and I. The problem will be El Turco."

NINETEEN

GODO WATCHED THE CLOCK, WAITING UNTIL TÍA LUCHA HAD been gone a full hour, meaning she'd be safely chained to the cash register, mid-shift, stuck till midnight, no likelihood she'd circle back home for anything. He pushed open her bedroom door, crossed to her dresser, sat on the edge of the bed. He wondered how lonely she was, not having slept with Tío Faustino for several weeks now. There was no way to know, of course. Not the kind of thing she'd discuss.

Chancing the mirror, he suffered the usual jolt, his moonscape face. Speaking of lonesome beds, he thought. Maybe, someday, I'll find myself a blind girl.

Leaning down, he tugged open the bottom dresser drawer. Tía Lucha's underwear trended toward the functional, boxy white panties, thick-foamed bras. He lifted the soft prim stacks one by one, moving them to the bedspread, then reached back in for the thing he wanted. Setting the worn manila envelope in his lap, he gingerly undid the clasp. Postcards and letters tumbled out, sent from El Salvador, people he'd never met writing about stuff he knew nothing about. It was the photos he wanted, the old ones, some brittle to the touch, some worn so smooth from handling they felt like cloth.

The ritual was always the same but no less intimate for that. He liked to begin with the oldest, one particular favorite—here it was—picturing Lucha with her little sister Graciela, his mother, in their school uniforms. They stood outside the family home, a modest cinder-block house with a clay tile roof in the village of San Pedro Nonualco. A man in a harlequin costume was holding a macaw for the girls to pet, the two sisters so unalike, Lucha with her pinched face, her sour wince, pigtails so tightly braided they looked like they hurt, Graciela with her candy-red cheeks and plummy eyes, her gap-toothed smile, her wooly black tangles.

In another picture they walked hand in hand in crisp white dresses down a meandering cobblestone street. Other girls and boys marched along with them, everyone dressed for First Communion, heading toward the colonial-era bell tower. Lucha dragged Graciela along, the older sister bulling ahead while the younger lagged behind, reaching out to touch the fierce red blossoms of a fire tree.

He moved on to the teenage years, when his mother dropped her baby fat, though not all of it, slimming down here, filling out there. Was he to feel ashamed or proud that his mother's image aroused him? Again, the contrast with her older sister practically reached out to slap you, Lucha with her twiggy shoulders and knobby wrists, the gaunt face, eyes dark and deep and sullen. But Graciela's were shiny and full and wicked. Her smile was ripe, like an orange slice. She cocked her hip just so, suggesting the hunger of a born tease. Where were they? Godo liked to imagine it the doorway to a secret lair, a place where the teenagers hid away to talk in the dark about movies, smoke, touch each other, but it was probably just the neighborhood *tienda*, selling bread and sodas and aspirin.

There was a gap then, seven years or so, no images with the savagery of the war for backdrop, nothing from the feverish trek to America. When his mother appeared again, she was holding her newborn son, Godofredo, swaddled in fleece, named for a maternal uncle. She looked weary, anemic, but strangely happy, or at least relieved. No pictures of the father.

Now came the snapshots he lived for. He was just a kid in them, a wolf-eyed scrap clinging to his mother's hand or nuzzled in her arms, their cheeks pressed close, her hair cascading down both their faces. He sometimes believed he could smell the floral tang of her shampoo, the talcum scent of her skin. Worry bags darkened both eyes, her smile wan, her skin pasty. She'd put on weight again. The lonesome grind of exile—one took comfort where one could, and in America food was easy, unlike love. Still, to Godo, she resembled perfection.

Last, the pictures of her pregnant with Roque, the killer innocent, *hijo del amor*. Again, no snaps of a dad. She offered the camera a brave smile, hand poised on the swollen belly like a last regret. I would have saved you if I could, Godo thought, and as those words lingered in his mind Happy walked in, finding him on the bed, Tía Lucha's underthings stacked beside him, a snapshot in his trembling hand.

To his credit, Happy declined to express surprise or disgust. Godo was too lost in grief to feel ashamed. They regarded each other guardedly, almost kindly.

Finally, Happy said, "I need to tell you something."

That seemed fair, Godo thought, wiping his face. One secret deserves another. He tucked the pictures back into the envelope, which he then returned to its spot at the bottom of the drawer. After carefully replacing the undergarments, he said, "Let's not talk in here," smoothing out the bedcover as he rose to leave.

Happy chose a spot at the kitchenette table, Godo plopped down on the couch. Outside, the wind chimes gonged erratically in a brisk wind.

Happy seemed tormented, running his hands through his hair. He'd let it grow back these past few weeks, to where it resembled short black fur. Godo waited him out, still in the backwash of memory, recalling the *chicas* in their starched white dresses, the *chicos* in their boxy suits, proceeding up the stone-paved street to their first holy sacrament, stepping smartly, little soldiers, all except the girl named Graciela, who got distracted, tempted by the fire tree.

He was told by one of his squaddies, who'd also been wounded and medevaced to Landstuhl after the checkpoint blast, that he'd cried out for his mother as he lay there crippled and bloody, face in shreds, Gunny Benedict vaporized. But Godo remembered none of that. All he remembered was the little bird chopper hovering overhead, rotor wash scattering dust everywhere, the door gunners aiming not just at the gathering Iraqis but the dazed, bloody marines—he remembered it, even as he feared it wasn't true.

But don't go there, he thought. Not now.

"There's something I should have told you," Happy said. "About this thing, bringing Pops back, dealing with Vasco. Somebody else is coming along too, this guy I met in Iraq. He was our terp."

Godo was having trouble understanding. Happy's eyes looked like they might melt from dread. "The guy's a *haji*?"

"He's Palestinian, lived in Baghdad. His family's in a refugee camp on the Syrian border." He reached out for the sugar bowl with both hands, as though reassured by its shape and weight. "You can't tell anyone about this."

"You sound scared."

"We're bringing an Arab across the border. What the fuck do you think that means?"

Godo blinked. An artery pulsed in his neck and he pictured it, the tall figure in woman's clothing, marching forward, so calm, a martyr . . .

"What if he's not who I think he is? What if, say for instance, he worked for the Mukhabarat? What if everything he told me's a lie, who he is, what he wants?"

Godo caught something in Happy's voice. He was holding something back. "What does he want?"

"That's the fucking point, I don't know!" Happy gripped his head again. "He saved my life. At least, that's what I thought. Maybe I got played."

Godo glanced at the clock. It was a little before nine, Tía Lucha wouldn't be home for three more hours. The trailer felt empty without her. He wondered if he should tell her that, wondered if she would want to hear such a thing from him.

"I can't figure out what you're trying to tell me, Hap. Saved your life how?"

FOR THE FIRST TIME SINCE HE'D BEEN DRIVING IN IRAQ, ALL THE TRUCKS were camouflaged.

"This is wrong, very wrong." Samir crumpled a can of Iraqi Pepsi as he followed Happy around the trailer, checking the tires and brake lines in the swirling grit. "They'll think this is a military convoy. That doubles, triples the chances of an ambush. You should say something."

"I speak up," Happy said, fingering tread to gauge its depth, "I'm fucked three times over. Lose my pay, get sacked, find myself back in El Salvador. That's not an option, I told you."

The war increasingly resembled a massive game of bait and switch. Happy had come to focus solely on not getting killed. Sure, somebody was getting fleeced and somebody else was getting rich but he just kept telling himself: It's not your problem. Besides, driving was the only relief from the boredom, which the heat made insufferable. Some of the contractors had built a driving range and a fishing pond to pass the time but those were off-limits to the Salvadorans and Filipinos who formed the truck pool. TCNs—third country nationals—were beasts of burden. Sometimes their trucks didn't even have windshields.

And yet they still dreamed of earning special status for a work visa to the U.S. It was a kind of group delusion. The company made no promises, nor did the embassy. Still, every man hoped, believing dedication and sacrifice could somehow manufacture luck.

The warehouse complex had sixty-four squat, sand-brown buildings packed inside the double-blast walls, with Alaska barriers strung with razor wire stacked along the whole perimeter for extra protection against suicide attacks and VBIEDs—car bombs. Uniformed Kurds of vague employ and armed with AK-47s glowered from their posts in the guard towers, which were mounted with belt-fed Dushka machine guns.

The drivers finished their prep, strapping down tarps on the flatbeds, tightening pineapple pins, slamming home bolts on trailer doors. They were bringing mattresses and baby incubators to the new hospital in Najaf, some desks for a rebuilt school, plus the usual drayage of rice and grain, bricks, bags of cement, drums of paint and acetone and asphalt sealant. There were sixteen guards in the convoy, four American vehicle commanders with 9mm Glocks and short-stocked Serbian Zastava M21s, the rest Colombians with Kalashnikovs. It was rumored the VCs made as much per month as a two-star general.

After final load checks against the manifest, the Kurds in the towers aimed their Dushkas and AKs into the nearby streets as the gates opened and the convoy roared out in a storm of noisy dust toward Route 10. Two security SUVs led, followed by Happy and four other trucks, another SUV, then the final five trucks and a trailing security detail. It was always the slow in-town streets that posed the greatest danger but soon they hit the highway and were sailing along, miles of shimmering asphalt, the heat a mere ninety-six ungodly degrees.

Every now and then a child ambling along the roadbed lurched off his feet and waved as the convoy rumbled past. Gestures of friendliness didn't matter; the presence of every person and vehicle got radioed up and down the convoy. Happy kept his eyes alert, checking his sectors, while Samir, noting the prevalent variety of livestock clustered along the road, talked about the proper way to butcher a goat.

They hit Baghdad at noon and rolled through the southwestern suburbs, long crowded boulevards lined with palms, the radio traffic constant up and down the line as guards and drivers called out possible threats: a *haji* with a gas can wandering into the street; a kid on a bicycle yammering into a cell phone; a clump of trash on the roadside, possible IED. One of the Colombian guards asked permission in clipped English to shoot a crane roosting in its nest atop a telephone pole. "Request denied, numbnuts," one the American VCs drawled back. Happy's throat felt like he'd swallowed pumice, stomach coiled like a fist, until they hooked up with Route 8. The road congestion cleared. He could breathe again.

The squat mud-colored houses grew shabbier and more isolated the farther south they drove. Cowbirds and vultures veered low over the canebrake rimming fetid marshes while sheep and bellowing cows scavenged through reeking landfills for food. Happy told himself he hated this place, hated its scarred blankness, its punishing dust and soul-crushing sun. At the same time, he had no difficulty imagining why it was that, centuries ago, the nomads who wandered this landscape devised a god of judgment.

The road split midway to Karbala, the convoy veered southeast onto Route 9. They crossed the Euphrates and were heading toward Karbala itself, charging through light traffic toward some nameless village, when Samir noticed the road suddenly empty. Traffic was no longer merely light, it was gone.

"Something's wrong," he said. "Up ahead, something's—"

Fifty yards ahead of the lead SUV, a dump truck roared out from behind one of the crude white houses, pulling onto the highway in a blackish cloud. It stopped, blocking the road. As the lead SUV hit its brakes, preparing to challenge the driver, the red coiling tail of an RPG slithered from a wall of canebrake thirty yards off the road. The first rocket was followed quickly by two others, the last trailing in from the opposite side of the highway. That one hit. The lead SUV exploded in a savage plume of white flame, the pressure wave from the blast rocking the windshield of Happy's rig, scattering it with gravel and shrapnel. Suddenly gunfire rained in from everywhere, not just from AKs but an RPK machine gun, the shells slamming and pinging against the trailer and cab.

"Keep going, move!" Samir crouched down in his seat, slamming one hand against the dash, the other gesturing manically for Happy to pull forward.

"There's no place to go! The road—"

"Around! Around! You can't stay here."

Happy struggled to recall his ambush training: Continue forward if possible, low gear. Use your truck to push barriers aside, aiming for a corner of any vehicle in your path. He slipped the transmission into gear, prepared to ease off the clutch, but in front of him two bloodied survivors from the first SUV, one dragging the other, struggled toward him, screaming for help, while from the second SUV the Colombians and the American VC had already taken two casualties while trying to find targets, return fire. Help them, he thought. No, continue moving forward. He froze, unable to decide.

Out of the corner of his eye, he saw a corkscrewing tail of red flame veer out of nowhere toward his tractor grill. Samir shouted, "Down!" and leaped across the seat, shielding Happy with his body as the RPG hit, rocking the entire cab off its tires, nudging it ten degrees right, shattering the windshield. Happy felt a knifing sting in both eyes, unsure what it was—tiny splinters of glass or metal or just brittle grit and dust shaken loose from the blast. Regardless, he couldn't see. The engine stalled. Then he heard the crackle of flames.

"Out! Get out!"

Samir's voice seemed swathed in cotton. Happy's eyes still felt raw, he couldn't see. He was covered in jagged shards from the splintered windshield but he grabbed at the door handle, fumbled for the lever, lifted hard, felt the door give way. Tumbling out, he plummeted ten feet to the ground, almost breaking his wrist and shoulder in the fall. Samir dropped close beside him, nearly crushing his hand, then grabbed his sleeve. "Under the trailer! Stay down."

Happy would remember the gut-coiling nausea of his terror, the stench of cordite and burning gasoline and finally blood, the continuing gunfire sending ricochets everywhere, off the asphalt, the tires, the truck's underframe. He thought: Why are they shooting at me—what have I ever done to them? We're transporting baby incubators for fuck's sake, school desks, food. Some time afterward, he would learn that the Badr Brigade and the Sadr militia, the two main Shiite paramilitary forces, were vying for control of government patronage; the attack most likely resulted from the Sadr faction hoping to undermine the Badr organization's role in funding development. But that would mean little to him later and nothing to him now.

How much time passed? Why could he still not see except through a shimmer of tears? The Colombians, Samir told him, were overwhelmed, too few gunmen, too many enemies, all invisible. Four of the other trucks, one by one, exploded in sheets of white flame, their crews dead or wounded or scattered. Then Happy smelled the trickle of diesel leaking from his fuel tank. It was a fuse. It was death waiting to happen.

He began scrambling out from under the trailer. Samir dragged him back.

"We have to get out!" Happy kicked at Samir's hands. "The gas tank!"

Tangled together, two halves of some comic beast, they scuttled into the crossfire and ran for a culvert overgrown with elephant grass running parallel to the road. What if gunmen are hiding here, Happy thought, feeling now an odd indifference to the idea of dying—at least I won't be scared. His body clawed ahead, unwilling to give up yet, prodded into the tall sharp grass by Samir. Several inches of thick brackish water, foul with excrement, sat in the bottom of the culvert, while a noxious cloud of stinging flies swarmed up from nowhere. The truck erupted then in a towering fireball, an ear-splitting blast, the shock wave knocking them onto their knees in the thick black water. Nothing cohered anymore, there were just the screams of the dying clouded by smoke, flickering silhouettes backlit by raging fire, helpless shouts of cruel insistent horror or triumph, the words in English and Spanish and, farther away, Arabic.

Samir grabbed the shoulder of Happy's filthy shirt, dragging him up onto his feet. "I see something. Come."

Happy let himself be pulled along, able to see no more than a few feet ahead, the rest of the world a riot of savage form. They ran crouching, far too long a ways it seemed, Happy with his head down, afraid to lift it for fear of one lucky shot, footfalls breaking the crusted, sunbaked sand, then the screech of rust-dry hinges, a wood gate slammed open, gravel underfoot. He smelled manure, the musk of wool, the char of a wood fire. Samir dragged him through a door, sat him down in a bed of straw. "We'll wait," he whispered, chest heaving. "Maybe somebody radioed ahead. Maybe a patrol from Karbala will come. LAVs, tanks."

Happy blinked and blinked, feeling the fine sharp dust in his eyes finally milking away. Not glass, he thought, thank God for that, but he was still unable to focus. His breath rumbled inside his chest, he coughed up dust. Then Samir grew suddenly stiff, his breath stilled. His clothing rustled, the stench of shit unfurled off his clothes as he slowly rose to his feet. Happy looked up: a reed-thin silhouette in the doorway of the barn, flowing black dishdasha, a checkered keffiyeh wrapped around his head. A Kalashnikov in his hands.

Samir spoke quietly in Arabic to the man, an old farmer perhaps. Or one of the gunmen? In the time it took to say a rushed prayer, some bargain was made, exchanged in whispers. Happy would know only that the man withdrew. Samir sat back down. "I told him we wanted nothing, we would say nothing." Happy chose to believe, sitting in silence until the churning roar of Hueys flying low echoed from the south, relief from Karbala. They left the barn behind and ran crouching back the way they'd come, through boiling smoke and the cries of the dying, waving their arms in the rotor wash and its choking storm of dust.

GODO LISTENED TO HIS COUSIN'S TALE, MARVELING AT HOW LANGUAGE told you nothing. It was the tremor in Happy's voice, the haunting emptiness in some words, the sloppy quick clutter of others, that gave him away. You can't make up that fear. And for the first time in a long while, he felt the two of them were truly kin.

"Seems to me," he said finally, "you need to know more about what went on with this farmer, this gunman, whatever he was. You could call down, have Roque hand your guy the phone, put it to him."

Happy glanced up from behind his hands. "If he lied to me back then, why not just keep lying?"

"Got a point."

"He's down there with Pops. With Roque."

Godo's eye strayed to the clock. A little past ten now, still two hours until Tía Lucha would be home. A migraine was ticking away behind his eyes. "Yeah."

"What should I do?"

Good question, Godo thought, watching as the walls inched inward a little, then inched back. He decided not to mention it to Happy. "He wants to get to the States. He's not gonna fuck up Tío Faustino or Roque, not while they're his ticket."

"What about once they're across? When he doesn't need them anymore?"

Godo kept an eye on the walls, checking for further insolence. "Seems to me you're gonna have to catch them just south of the border, right before they cross. Deal with it then."

TWENTY

ROQUE SLEPT NEAR THE DOOR, LUPE ACROSS THE ROOM, BOTH curled up on the concrete floor, nothing but newspapers and flattened cartons for comfort, the air close and hot. At some point in the interminable night, the lizard finally chose his path and vanished from the wall.

Rafa had locked them in, saying he'd be back around daybreak. They'd arouse too much suspicion, he said, trying to cross in the middle of the night. He parked the Corolla in the service bay, so no one could hot-wire it, and come morning Roque and Lupe would drive it through the checkpoint, then continue on several miles to a roadside *chalete* run by a woman named Chita. There they'd wait for Humilde to appear after a nightlong trek with Samir and Tío Faustino in tow. Simple, Roque thought, lying awake, picturing ways it could all go wrong.

He kept coming back to Tío and Lupe. Was she really the tragic cause his uncle made her out to be? All that talk about sucking Arab cock, she said it so breezily—and hadn't Lonely called her a *putilla*, a wannabe whore? She wasn't just a singer with stars in her eyes, gulled by her own ambition. She had other talents, talents Lonely got bored with, though not so bored he wasn't willing to sell them to somebody else.

Regardless, there was something broken inside her, something she'd tried to mend with fury. It made her a wild card. Maybe she'll try to run, he thought, maybe she'll want some sort of payback, a way to get even or maybe she'll just turn the rage on herself, roll into a ball, settle in for her fate. There was no way to tell.

A kind of homesickness came over him, not for Rio Mirada or Tía Lucha but Mariko, and yet the dishonesty in that seemed clear soon enough. You just want to get laid, he thought, and the feeling gave way to something else, a kind of emptiness, as though his heart had become a grave and in the grave was buried what he'd once considered love. What is it we want, he thought, that we try to find in a woman? Especially a woman who isn't fooled, who won't buy into the usual bag of tricks. Secretly we want to be seen for who we are, the rest is just show. We want love, not praise. And yet that seemed a recipe for weakness, a shortcut to failure.

And, he reminded himself, failure's not an option. Everyone is so proud of you.

He drifted off into fitful sleep and the dreams that came to him seemed slight, disjointed—except one, which echoed back to another dream, the one he'd had at Mariko's house all those weeks ago. Again there was twilight, a gun blast, the snarling dog. And yet the sense he was carrying something priceless, something he'd have to fight to keep, had changed. He saw his mother standing a little ways ahead. Her hair, usually long and densely matted in her pictures, was cut short like a nun's. She looked sickly and frail. The face, however, was unmistakable. He tried to call out but the sound caught in his throat and that was when his mother—or whoever, whatever she was—pointed to a dusty leather bag at his feet. A ridiculously large and agile tarantula pushed its way out from under the unbuckled flap, scuttering toward him.

He shot up blinking, felt the scaly presence on his neck, brushed the lizard off.

A throng of *golondrinas* chirruped in the trees outside. Not to be outdone, a rooster crowed. Roque rubbed his neck as he rose from his bed of cardboard to peer out through the sooty cobwebbed window, hoping for some trace of daylight.

RAFA APPEARED WITHIN THE HOUR AND UNLOCKED THE DOORS. THE dream had left a residue, a sense of defeat, and Roque feared what he might do if trapped inside any longer. Lupe didn't stir at first and only rose once Roque backed the Corolla out of the service bay, her hair mussed, her eyes piggish with sleep as she clutched the plastic bag of new clothes.

Rafa told them it would be best to cross the border early, before the guards working the day shift settled into their routine, but Roque got the feeling he just wanted them gone. Lupe dropped into the passenger seat, the better for appearances, he supposed, though he imagined she'd want to climb in back once the border was cleared, fall asleep again. He had a pretty good idea she'd be sleeping a lot in the coming days.

The clouds were a steely blue-gray and fat with rain, the air fresh but muggy. Twice in twenty minutes a quick thrumming shower fell, whipped by crosswinds, the downpour stopping as suddenly as it began. If that's the worst of the weather, he thought, Tío and Samir shouldn't have too bad a slog. Still, he wondered what shape and frame of mind they'd be in after trekking through pathless rough all night, rain or no rain.

The landscape was rolling windswept bluffs covered with tall brown grass, not unlike the foothills of Northern California, except there were more trees and he recognized none of them. He had no idea what bugs or other critters lurked out there, nor did he know if bandits were a problem. It was Humilde's job to steer clear of such things, for which he'd been paid through Lonely, part of Happy's end, the up-front fee. Roque had their pocket money with him, locked inside the glove box, a little less than three hundred dollars cash, enough for food and gas, they hoped.

If Tío Faustino got jacked, he'd get jacked for nothing, not that that would change the experience much.

Taking a turn too fast, Roque braked hard to miss a stalled truck sitting square in the road. The back end got away from him on the slick pavement, the car fishtailed as he overcorrected and Lupe sucked in a scared breath. Finally he got the car square, passing the breakdown, accelerating away, a knee-jerk fear of robbery. He watched as the truck grew small in his rearview. Pay attention, he told himself, heart clapping inside his chest.

A little farther on the terrain flattened out, broad fields extending for miles to either side of the highway. Scrawny cows grazed in the cane stubble amid bolts of sunlight and roaming pockets of cloud shadow. Shortly he spotted the Puente Jorge de Alvarado ahead, the bridge that spanned the Río Paz.

Trucks pulled over onto the side, engines idling, waiting for a signal to proceed across the bridge to inspection, while young women in aprons went driver to driver, selling *refrescos* and fruit juice and *pan dulce*. The atmosphere was genial. Roque's heart raced.

Once past the line of trucks and across the bridge he entered the rustic customs plaza and headed for the inbound lane marked "Tráficos Livianos," intended for cars. Lupe undid her hair, shook it out, sliding a little closer in her seat. They'd discussed none of this. She leaned over the center console, draped an arm around him and rested her head against his shoulder, the better to hide her bruises. It was all show—they were a loving pair, they'd tangled recently, he'd knocked her around, just to remind her who spoke and who listened. A man other men would understand.

The immigration agent waved the car forward. He was short, dark, muscled like a wrestler. Roque had the registration out—it was in his name, arranged by Lonely—and his passport. Lupe listlessly fished around in her pocket for her Documento Unico de Identidad, handed it to Roque, then once again buried her face sleepily into his arm.

Bowing at the window, the agent reviewed the documents cursorily, then gazed in at the couple. His eyes lingered on Lupe, a stare so intense Roque wondered if she'd stuck out her tongue. Seconds passed. Finally she glanced up, offered a drowsy smile.

Roque studied the burly agent's face. It was a knot of dark-skinned folds and creases, studded by onyx eyes, almost princely in its homeliness. He was taking too much time. I should ask if anything's wrong, Roque thought, but he couldn't get his mouth to form the words. Keep smiling, he told himself, ridiculous advice, sure to fail. Maybe he wants a bribe. No, disaster. Sit tight. It's a trick, the silence. A ruse. Wait.

Lupe squeezed his arm. "*Amorcito*," she murmured sleepily.

Still, the guard waited. Then with a brisk jolt he returned the documents, stepped back, waved the next car forward.

Roque put the car in gear and pulled away.—*Stay put for just a minute more, till he can't see us*.

Lupe said nothing, still clinging to him gently and he fought back the stir of a mindless erection. They passed the line of merchant stalls along the roadway, the vendors selling Mayan handicrafts, watermelons, lightbulbs, socks. He checked the mirror, saw the agent growing smaller, occupied now with the next car in the queue.

"Okay," he said at last.

Yawning, she lifted her head, unwrapped her arm from around his shoulder and settled back in her own seat, hands folded between her thighs, listing against the door.—*Next time*, she said, *don't just sit there like a fool. Check your hair in the mirror, jot down your mileage, pick your teeth, chew your nails—anything. He was waiting for you to say something stupid*.

—*He was looking at you, your face*.

—*Because he knew it would put you on edge. You'd get protective. You'd fuck up*.

—*Well, I didn't fuck up. Here we are. On our way*.

—*Lucky us*. She nestled tighter against her door.

He returned his focus to the road. A chain of jagged mountains loomed to the north, necklaced by immaculate clouds. A boy led a trio of coarse-haired goats along the roadbed.

He reached for the radio dial, hoping he could catch a signal. Nearly three hundred kilometers separated them from the capital but maybe there was a station to be found. He started venturing through waves of static, ghostly chords and plaintive melodies rising and fading, never quite coming whole. Finally a throaty alto came through clearly, Ana Gabriel, a mariachi tune: "Hay Unos Ojos," There Are Some Eyes. It was one of the traditional songs he'd played for his uncle and the others at Carmela's.

Lupe turned her head.—*Wait. Keep it there.*

It was a Mexican folk waltz in the *habanera* style, with Cuban and Creole touches. The lyrics were poignant if overwrought. Lupe settled back into the wedge of her seat and the door, humming softly along, closing her eyes again. When the final verse rounded to a close, she sang along softly:

Y yo les digo que mienten, mienten
Que hasta la vida daría por ti

And I tell them that they lie, they lie
That I would even give my life for you

Roque had almost forgotten how much her voice moved him, the husky sensuality, the simplicity. So suited to *ranchera*, all that betrayal and pride, love's misery, survival's regrets.

—*I'm sorry for the way I've acted these past two days.*

He felt stunned. After a moment, he managed:—*I just figured you were angry. And scared.*

She gathered up her hair in a ponytail, held it one-handed.—*Scared? Yes. But what will anger buy me?*

That didn't really seem the point, he thought. Emotions weren't currency. You couldn't trade them for better ones, no matter how badly you might want to. And who was she kidding, she'd been angry as a hornet.—*If you don't mind my asking, what made Lonely . . .* He let the question trail off gently, a prompt.

—*Fuck me up? Who says he needed a reason?*

—*I just—*

—*I got pregnant.*

Roque dodged a slung-back horse grazing in the roadside grass.—*Why beat you for that?*

—*Why do you think?*

Lonely's not the dad, he thought, he tuned her up because he was jealous. But how did they know who the father was? A girl balls more than one cat, she can point the finger where she likes, at least until the baby pops out. Then again, maybe they didn't have sex. Maybe Lonely couldn't.

—*I don't know enough about the two of you to think much of anything.*

She looked at him like he'd sprung a third eye.—*What do you mean "the two of you"? Me and Lonely. You really take me for that kind of skank?*

Roque sighed. Skank, no. But he'd always found it interesting that Tía Lucha's favorite word for being in love, *agarrado*, derived from the word for a fight, *agarrón*.—*If you're not together, I don't get it. Why slap you around if you're knocked up? What's it to him?*

She shook her head in bemused disgust.—*You really have no clue.*

—*How can I have a clue when you won't tell me anything?*

—*You have eyes in your head.*

—*Okay, fine, I'm blind. I've got bad habits too. Want to hear about them?*

—*He owns me.*

Feeling self-conscious, Roque gazed past her out the window. The terrain was more dramatic here, steep hills, jagged rock outcroppings, small misshapen trees.

—*What do you mean, he owns you?*

—*Oh for God's sake—*

—*Tell me. I mean it. I want to know.*

A cop on a motorcycle shot past them, coming over a hillcrest from the opposite direction. Off the road, a spanking-new pickup sat parked outside a windowless hovel.

—*I answered an ad for a singer, this casino in the capital? I came in, looked the place over. The lounge was packed on weekends. I thought, Wow, this could work out. I could make a name, build an audience, you know? Lonely and his* chamacos, *they worked security. I should have seen right there the thing was wrong. Nobody with real money, the kind of people who can change your life, none of them would come near a place where those fools hung out. Even the bigwigs in bed with the* maras *know better than to be seen with them. The owner of the place, he looked like he was on something, like he was sleepwalking. That should have tipped me off too.*

—*Meaning what?*

—*Meaning they'd taken the place away from him, Lonely and his crew. A protection racket, probably, taxing a piece each week, then little by little or all at once they just took over. Great places to launder money—casinos, nightclubs. I could feel something screwy but I wanted the job too bad. The owner, his name was Miguel, old man from Sonsonate, he was very sweet, very quiet. I thought he was being polite.*

Then Lonely says he likes my voice. The crowds dug me, man: Friday, Saturday night? It was a scene, I loved it. So yeah, Lonely, he wants to help my career. He'll get me a recording session, burn a CD, take it around to the radio stations. He's not always a complete shitbag, you know—he actually says this to me. I can be half nice, he says, when there's something in it for me. I fell for it. Then he told me the other half of the bargain. There's a cathouse half a block away, the customers who know about it buy chips from the casino cage then take them down, so the girls have to cash out at the casino to get paid. Harder to steal that way.

The terrain flattened out again and thirty yards beyond the next turn a sawhorse blocked the road, bearing a sign reading: PUESTO DE REGISTRO. Orange cones veered traffic to the berm, where a trio of uniformed cops waited.

The group didn't look too motivated. Two sat off in the grass, smoking, watching the clouds cross the sky, while the third, a bucktoothed *chavo* with a scraggly fade, shirttail out, waved the car on desultorily, shotgun slung from his shoulder. Dress code must be lax out here in the sticks, Roque thought as he eased past the youth and his dead eyes. If all the checkpoints are like this, he thought, we'll be home in three days. He didn't even need to smile.

He drove on a ways, checking his rearview, see if the cops changed their minds.—*So Lonely, this place, this brothel, in return for this recording gig—*

Lupe cackled.—*Recording gig. Yeah.*

There was no way to win with this girl.—*Okay, the promise of a gig, whatever. He forces you to work there. That's how he owns you.*

She turned to stare at the scraggy hills.—*Yeah. He forced me.*

Roque waited.—*What are you saying?*

—*I knew I'd screwed up by then, screwed up bad. I couldn't see a way out. Except maybe, if I got careless.*

Roque was thunderstruck.—*One of your johns?*

—*It didn't matter who. Not to me. Not then.*

—*You could've gotten AIDS.*

—*But I didn't. Lucky me.* She glanced over her shoulder, eyes like small black marbles.

—*Lonely found out.*

—*That was the first beating, the one I got right before you showed up in La Chacra. To punish me for being such a sloppy whore. He never did figure out what I was really up to. Not that it mattered. I wouldn't get an abortion—children are a gift from God, no matter how they are conceived—so he decided to make a lesson out of me.*

He wondered what the bruises were like where he couldn't see.—*You lost the baby.*

—*Who would wish a child on me where I'm going? God saw fit to show the little one some mercy. I thank Him.*

Just what the world needs, Roque thought, a devout Catholic lounge singer.—*This latest beating. What was that for?*

Lupe laughed quietly, lowering her chin.—*You really are a boy sometimes.*

—*Look*—

—*Because he can. Because he likes it. Remind me just how fucked I am.*

Up ahead, he saw the sign, hoisted over an open roadside restaurant: CHALETE DE CHITA. He pulled into the sand parking lot and turned off the ignition but didn't get out. A hint of rain still scented the wind but the clouds were high overhead, looking starchy and white, like dumplings. He wasn't sure whether to be impressed with her courage or fault her for being so stubborn. Like I'm one to judge, he thought, or she'd listen regardless.

—*Want to know what my uncle said, just as he was heading off with El Turco? He couldn't have it on his conscience, watching you get handed over to whoever these people are up in Agua Prieta. That's like him. He has the biggest heart in the world, a sad heart, a strong heart, but generous too. I know, whether or not it's your own damn fault, he will do whatever he can to help you. Now I need to ask you, are you worth it? Look me in the eye, tell me, what can you offer him back for a sacrifice like that?*

Her whole face turned to stone.—*I didn't ask for this.*

—*It's the way he is.*

—*El Turco will never*—

—*Forget El Turco.*

—*They'll find my mother, my brother.*

—*We have a few days. Call them, tell them to go, hide, stay with somebody. Ask the priest at their church, maybe. We can find some way to get them north, join you in the States.*

—With what money?

—Forget the money for now. We'll—

—Stop it! She grabbed her hair in her fists, eyes shut.*—What is wrong with you? Is your uncle as much of a child as you are?*

—Call me whatever names you like. But don't mock my uncle.

—You think it's only my family they'll go after? You think they'll leave yours alone? Not to mention you, your uncle. You think I can live with that? Assuming of course I have time to worry about such things before they kill me.

—Know why the world's so fucked up? Nobody fights back. They get used to their misery. Sometimes they fall in love with it. Some shitbird like Lonely starts fucking with them? They bargain. They deny. They cave. And it's always the assholes who get the power. The greedy, the small, the paranoid. They have the say-so. You go along or you suffer. Roque was reciting almost verbatim a rum-fueled tirade he'd received one night from Lalo, after a guitar lesson. Lalo, the great believer, the artist.*—Doesn't have to be that way. You can stand up.*

—Be my guest. But not on my account.

—You don't need to live afraid.

—What's in this for you? Okay, your uncle's got this nice-guy death wish, but what's in it for you? You want to make me a star? You think I'm gonna like you? You think I'm gonna fuck your brains out?

He took the keys out of the ignition, opened his door.*—I'm gonna get something cold to drink while we wait. You want something, let me know.*

She reached across the car, grabbed his arm.*—Stop being nice to me. Hear me? How fucking dare you.* Her grip was fierce. Tears welled in her eyes.*—Fuck you, understand? Don't be nice to me. I know what you think, how you feel, what you want. I know you better than you know yourself. Stop it.*

TWENTY-ONE

"WHERE'D THAT THING COME FROM?"

They were back at the old farmhouse, the one Efraim's people lost to the county. Manure and pond scum tanged the air, the trees thick with the twiddly chirp of sparrows, the screeching caw of blue jays. Godo was supposed to teach the crew how to clear a house today, show them how it got done in the Suck, the Green Monster, the Gun Club: the Corps. What for, exactly? Never ask a question you'd rather not know the answer to.

Vasco's crew had a history of takeovers, restaurants a favorite, the occasional home invasion. They'd put all that aside for low risk, high return: the mover scam, the mortgage hustle, the copper rip-off, none of which paid out like before, not with the economy in a ditch. Apparently they wanted to go back to what they once knew best, just kick it up a notch. Old dogs, new tricks. I'm here to train the dogs, Godo figured. Just don't let it go beyond that. Once Tío gets back, the family can wash its hands of these losers for good.

Puchi and Chato played coy the whole drive out, all glances and giggles, homely sisters with a secret. Now with the trunk popped, Godo could see what the secret was: an AK-47, a real one from the looks of it, not a semi-auto knockoff or a kit model. They were surprisingly hard to find in the States, unless you wanted to pay through the nose. Everywhere else, third world especially, they were common as kickstands.

Puchi lifted the rifle from the trunk. "Some guy, told us he worked security in Iraqistan? He sold it to us, in the parking lot at People's Fried Chicken. You know, over in Richmond, near the Empress?"

Godo felt like somebody'd plucked his spine. Worked security, he thought, contractors, and the black SUV throttled up to the checkpoint, honking its horn, Godo getting smack from the driver, giving it right back as the broad-shouldered muj in the flowing *abaya* sauntered up, Gunny Benedict stepping forward—

Shake it off, he told himself.

He refocused on the Kalashnikov, recalling the distinctive chug of the weapon, remembering too, hitting the deck, inhaling dirt as incoming rounds chewed up nearby concrete. You could always tell the ones coming straight at you by the crack.

He said, "What's the Empress?"

Puchi sighted the weapon, aiming across to the barn. "Card room, man. San Pablo Dam off-ramp, see it from the freeway. You know the one."

Guess I do, Godo thought. His memory felt like chowder sometimes.

On closer inspection he confirmed it wasn't a jigsaw model, rigged together from a parts kit like Efraim's M16s. The handguard, pistol grip, buttstock all looked authentic, even battle-scarred, virtually identical to the ones he'd seen over there. It had full auto, the true mark of illegality, with the thirty-round banana clip, a felony in California, even by mail. "You bought this in a parking lot?"

"Man, you gotta check this place out." Puchi settled the gunstock on his hip, striking a combat pose. "Like a fucking bazaar. Freaky how much hardware moves through that place."

Chato, smoke-eyed, scratched at his ear, adding, "Chicken's for the pits, though. They do something weird with it."

Godo had heard that more than a hundred thousand Kalashnikovs like this one, not to mention tens of thousand of Glocks, all intended for the Iraqi police, had vanished. Poor controls, shoddy oversight, squirrelly paper trails. Some cases, the guns found their way to the mujahideen, meaning the U.S. helped arm the insurgency, the kind of story that made you want to cry, that or kill somebody. It didn't surprise him to learn at least a few found their way back here.

"You said the guy who sold you this worked security?"

"That's what he told me, yeah."

"He say what company he was with?"

Puchi shrugged. "Didn't think to ask."

"Harmon Stern Associates, that name ever come up?"

Chato, back from his chicken reveries: "This thing good as what you carried?"

Godo sighed. The kid had a Chihuahua for a brain. "What are you talking about?"

"I hear you guys secretly wished, like, you had AKs, not M16s." Trying to sound in the know. "Don't jam so easy. Heavier round."

Godo assumed he was mimicking the guy they'd bought the gun from. "It's not as accurate," he said. "But yeah, you can rough them up, drag them through a swamp, pour sand down the barrel, even set the damn things on fire, they don't get touchy like a sixteen. Had to clean my piece at least once a day over there, twice sometimes." Back to Puchi, "How could I meet this guy, this security dude, one who sold you this thing?"

Puchi did something with his lips, a creepy pout of a grin. "We're supposed to meet him again tonight, talk about scoring more of these, depending on how we like this one."

Godo recalled Happy's warning: Don't get talked into anything. Did this qualify? He couldn't help himself, he wanted to meet this character, this fella who worked security in Iraqistan. This guy who sold banned guns out of his trunk in the parking lot of a second-rate fried-chicken house.

Goading, Chato said, "So you gonna show us how to dice the pie or what?"

"Slice," Godo corrected. He felt a migraine clawing at the backs of his eyes. "The phrase is '*slice* the pie.' "

They collected the rest of the weapons from the trunk and trooped inside the empty farmhouse. Godo took possession of the AK. Glancing around until he remembered the lay of the place, he marched them down a back hall, chose a bedroom, squared himself in front of the door.

"This spot right here? It's called the fatal funnel. Most dangerous place in the house." He snapped his fingers, rousting Chato from a daydream. "Stand clear till you have at least some idea what you're up against. Use the wall as a shield."

He demonstrated as he spoke, flattening his back against the plaster. The migraine flared white and red behind his eyes.

"First thing? Check does the door open in or out. That dictates how you sweep the room. This one opens in. Stand on the side closest to the knob—why?"

Puchi and Chato just stared, breathing through their mouths. Efraim said softly, "Fatal funnel." Godo loved the guy.

"Specially if the room's dark and the hallway's lit? Do not and I mean do *not* lean across the doorway to reach the knob. Okay. Tuck your weapon in tight against the body. Soft-check the knob." He lowered his voice to a hush. "Gentle. Don't give yourself away. If it's not locked, turn, push—don't slam it open, that'll just make it snap back."

He let the door glide back in a slow easy arc.

Chato screwed up his face. "Why not just *kick* it in? Show the motherfuckers who rules."

Godo wanted to butt-stroke him with the AK. He turned to Efraim. "You tell him why."

"Fatal funnel." It came out sounding almost philosophical.

"And if the door's not locked," Godo added, "why risk getting your ass shot?"

"Fuck you both," Chato said. "I seen it: Check out YouTube

you don't believe me. Motherfuckers are *kicking in* the fucking *doors*."

Godo decided to wrap the rest up quick: Step back from the doorway to prevent getting your weapon snatched, give yourself room to fight; shoulder your piece, crab-walk in a half circle across the fatal funnel, sweeping the room in twenty- to thirty-degree angles. "Do *not* cross your legs as you move. You trip, you're dead. Shuffle, fast—hey knucklehead, Chato, heads-up, this is slice the fucking pie—the longer you're exposed in that doorway, the more likely you end up dead. Be aggressive. You see something? Shoot. Check foreground, background, ceiling, floor—fast, fast, you linger, you're dead—then move to the next slice."

He had their full attention now. Repetition of the word "dead" tended to do that.

"Okay, you've still got the two areas at extreme angles on either side of the door, deep back near the far corners, right? Maybe nobody's there. Maybe there's one guy, you don't know which side. Maybe there's two, one on each side. You *commit*—choose one side, step into the doorway, strong-side foot forward, aim toward the space, but check back over your shoulder, *boom*, just a glance, tenth of a second tops. Be decisive, keep moving, that's your advantage. You see something, pivot, drop to a knee, fire up at the guy, chest shots, head shots. If there's two, hit the guy behind you first, then pivot back for the one in front. If you're still alive, clear the rest of the room."

He guided them through stairwells next, same fundamentals, different geometry, emphasizing decisiveness, mobility, aggression. Efraim, as always, proved the model student, careful with his footwork, mindful, precise. Next to him, even Puchi looked sorry. At times the *vato* showed real promise, the makings of a stone killer, but at some point his concentration always broke, he played down to his audience, Chato. It became just another round of what-the-fuck to them, sharp one minute, sloppy the next, no clue how easy it was to die. Christ, you didn't even need to be stupid. He'd seen it, men he knew, buddies, crashing through a doorway, responding to the shadow in the corner a snap too late. And yet only a sniveler could be so weak, he thought, as to convince himself there's a smart way to die.

TWENTY-TWO

ROQUE WATCHED THE THREE FIGURES EMERGE FROM THE SHADows of the southerly ravine. Humilde led, with Tío Faustino trudging behind with a bit of a limp. He looked thinner from a distance too, something Roque dismissed as a trick of the eye. Samir brought up the rear with an ungainly lope, clutching the soft leather bag at his hip. No *zopilotes* lazed overhead, waiting for someone to falter. A good sign, Roque supposed.

Lupe was curled up in the backseat, sleeping, pretending to sleep. He remembered what she'd said, *How dare you?* Get used too often, he supposed, kindness begins to look like nothing more than step one in getting screwed. He wanted to feel for her. He wanted to feel clean. He wasn't sure either was possible. Or wise.

He glanced back at the three men laboring up the ravine. A cooling wind caught their backs, though he suspected the day would heat up soon. By early evening they'd be in Tecún Umán, the opposite end of the country, assuming the roads were clear, no problems at the checkpoints. They were to go to the Posada Rico and ask for a man named Beto. He would take care of the border crossing into Mexico and through Chiapas.

As the three of them came within earshot, Roque considered calling out but merely waved, a gesture Tío Faustino, slogging waist-deep through swaying grass, listlessly returned, breaking into a smile. The smile of a man with a nice-guy death wish, Roque thought. Was that really such an unforgivable thing?

Humilde gestured for water as the three men staggered up and Chita, the owner of the *chalete*, plucked three bottles from a cooler and handed one to each. They drank in parched gulps, scratching at the tick bites on their legs. Tío Faustino had a particularly nasty spider bite on his ankle as well. Probing the tender flesh with his thumb, he glanced up at Roque.—*Maybe Lupe would spare some of her magic cream?*

Roque went off to ask. Rapping lightly on the glass where Lupe's head rested, he waited for her to stir, sit up, crank down the window. A funky wave of heat greeted his face.

—*My uncle was wondering if you had any of the heparin cream left.*

She mumbled something, rubbed her good eye, rummaged around in the plastic bag that held her clothes and medicine—everything she owned now. Finding the half-depleted tube, she handed it to Roque.—*What happened?*

He turned away, not answering. What do you care, he thought, biting his tongue.

Tío Faustino was holding a small jagged chunk of ice dredged from Chita's cooler against the spider bite as Roque returned. Dabbing the welt dry, he applied a smidge of cream, gingerly rubbed it in. Without glancing up, he asked,—*So how is she doing?*

Samir snorted.—*She's not your problem. Stop worrying about her.*

—*She's okay.* Roque didn't know how much he should say in front of Humilde, didn't know how much had already been said.—*She sleeps a lot.*

The coyote shook his wrist, rattling his watch around so he could check the time.—*You should get going. You'll want to reach Tecún Umán before dark. It's a bad place to get lost.*

TÍO FAUSTINO, WHO NEVER FELT MORE AT HOME THAN BEHIND THE wheel, gave in to his exhaustion and the stiff swollen ankle, telling Roque he should drive. There was a far more difficult crossing ahead that night and he wouldn't be alone in needing rest.

Lupe kept her perch in front, Samir and Tío piled in back. As the car pulled away from the *chalete* there were no farewell waves, no shouts of "*bueno suerte*." Roque wondered what had happened overnight to create such a chill, though on reflection he could understand not wanting to get too close to people you knew you'd never see again except for bad luck.

The two-lane road curved gently through rock-etched hills, small cane fields, patches of dense green forest. Roque marveled at how empty the countryside was, only the occasional *champa* of scrap and tin, so unlike El Salvador with its crowding, its overworked land, as though a switch got thrown at the border—one moment you're in India, the next you're on the moon.

In the backseat, directly behind Lupe, Tío Faustino drifted in and out of a rumbling, fidgety, leg-scratching sleep. Occasionally, giving it up, he would gaze out his window and hum softly, the inevitable "Sin Ti." From guilt, perhaps, or self-consciousness, Lupe glanced over her shoulder at him and, this was the strange part, began to hum along. Tío fought back a smile, eyes closed, humming in inadvertent harmony now, given his lamentable pitch. Finally, as though from some unspoken signal, they both began to sing, their voices barely rising above a whisper:

Sin ti
Es inútil vivir

Without you
It is useless to live

Using English, to shut Lupe out, Samir said, "Old man? You sing like a dying goat."

Tío Faustino chuckled, then winked at Lupe.—*No, my*

friend, I know what a dying goat sounds like. A whole truckload of them, actually. I'll tell you about it sometime.

The car topped a steep grade, then rushed down a blind curve into a deeply gorged valley, thick with shadow. Roque didn't spot the roadblock until too late—not soldiers, not cops. An unmarked pickup sat lengthwise in the road, right at a pinch point, the rock faces looming close to either side. There was no way to steer around. Four *pistoleros*, two in the truck bed, the other two on the ground, aimed their guns at the Corolla, bandannas masking their faces.

"Stop! Back up!" Samir pounded the seat behind Roque's head. "Now! Fast!"

Roque braked, reached for the gearshift, but then one of the *pistoleros*, aiming skyward, fired off a shot and the air in the tight ravine cracked open with the sound. Roque froze, remembering the uneasy lack of farewells or good wishes at the *chalete*. Humilde had betrayed them, set them up. No, he thought. That can't be true. Please don't let that be true.

Samir, gripping the seat back, pulled himself forward, hissing in Roque's ear: "I know you are afraid, but you have to do it. Now—reverse!"

The two masked men approached the car, twenty yards away, closing. Above them to either side, jags of weathered stone thrust upward, flecked with scrub. A black *zanate*, rousted by the gunshot from its perch on one of the overhangs, winged down and away into the swallowing darkness. Roque at last felt something turn, his hand blindly sought the gear knob, fumbled, found it—he jammed the transmission into reverse, floored the gas pedal and turned to look out through the back window as another shot rang out.

He'd gone no more than thirty yards when he realized there was a pickup behind them as well, breaking the up-road turn, barreling downhill. There were armed men standing in its truck bed too, except they had rifles, not pistols. They began firing, automatic bursts louder than the uphill pistol shots, or was that just illusion? Could terror fuck up your hearing? He felt strangely calm now, his thoughts still, his body numb, a counterweight to the visceral dread as he just kept plowing the car uphill, steering toward the inner bend of the curve, intent on dodging the downhill truck if possible, tagging it to knock the gunmen down if not. There's your plan, he told himself, feeling a kind of pride. Everyone else in the car had ducked, he heard shouting but couldn't make out words. Maybe there were none. Regardless, the only word he could fathom at that moment was "escape." It floated like a goldfish in the clear bright bowl of his mind. To live is to escape, he thought as Lupe shouted, "*¡Buzo!*" Look out.

The downhill pickup veered to miss the up-rushing car and it was only then he realized the men with the rifles had not been firing at the Corolla at all but at the *pistoleros* below. Braking, he turned to look front as the riflemen routed their adversaries, two of the masked men down on the ground, clutching wounds, the other two having fled. Roque could not see beyond the pickup blocking the road; for all he knew the two who'd run were down as well.

Down, he thought. Don't cheapen it. What you mean is dead.

The two riflemen dropped from their truck onto the asphalt, each one choosing a different wounded *pistolero*, and fired a three-shot burst point-blank. In a bizarre reversal of his previous deafness, Roque heard not only the shattering crack of the weapons but the church-bell ping of the ejected brass casings against the pavement. Then just as suddenly and perversely his hearing turned inward again, the pulse in his ears a hammering throb. He swallowed, the sound like a melon stuffed down a tube. The dying men had not begged for their lives. The killers had not waited for them to do so. Everyone understood everyone else. We're all in on the secret, Roque thought, the secret called death. The two riflemen turned uphill and began walking toward the Corolla.

"I just axed if you'd like a refill on your soda," she said.

Her voice was soft and more feminine than her size suggested. Gazing up into her face, framed by its veil, he searched for what it was that reminded him of Mobley, feeling vaguely ashamed, as though at some level his mind still believed they really did all look alike.

"Yes," Godo said, a whisper. "Please. A refill would be nice."

"It's a dollar," she said.

He dug into his pocket for the bill, thinking: ax. Who was it in the squad that used to tease Mobley about that? I axed you nicely. Don't make me ax you again.

He handed her the money and watched her bobbing hips as she ambled away. Girl can work it till you jerk it, he thought, veil or no veil. He wondered if she felt disgusted by his face.

The night Mobley died, army psyops crews roamed the city in their Humvees, cranking out the deafening sounds of men and women screaming, cats fighting, Guns N' Roses: "Welcome to the Jungle." The favorite, though, was a gut-knotting laugh, the creature from *Predator*, played with amped-up bass at a hundred decibels, echoing off the pavement and the concrete walls of the pillbox houses and apartment buildings, like the voice of some cut-rate god.

"Hey hey hey." Puchi nodded toward the parking lot, sucking loud on his straw, the dregs of his Pepsi. A gray windowless van had just pulled in. "Here comes business."

Watching as the driver got out and crossed the parking lot, Godo took notice of how underwhelming the man was. Among the contractors he'd met in Iraq, a fair number had come from special forces backgrounds; they'd kept up with the PT, rock-hard bodies, switchblade minds. Cocky, sure, but sometimes you just had to grant that. There were plenty of others, though, who'd simply grabbed the back of the gravy train and refused to let go, slack habits, washed-out eyes, the mouthy swagger of small men: users, gasbags, phonies. They didn't just lack fire dis-

TWENTY-THREE

PEOPLE'S FRIED CHICKEN WAS THE LATEST BODY SNATCHER TO inhabit the corpse of a seventies-era burger stand in an area of Richmond called the Iron Triangle, saddest neighborhood in the area's most homicidal city. The canted beams out front bristled with graffiti, a half-dozen bullet holes pocked the window glass. The parking lot's asphalt buckled so badly Godo imagined some ancient tribal curse gathering force from below, trying to break through. Where better to hawk a black market AK, he thought.

Through the smeary glass he noticed that two of the black girls working the counter wore head scarves and *abayas*: Muslims. It was a growing subculture here, a way to detox the ghetto. He felt blindsided and not a little pissed off as he grabbed the door, following the others inside, then the smell of the place hit him. What was it Chato said? *They do something weird with the chicken*. Grilled meat, lemon, tamarind paste, mint, like some of the houses he'd searched in Iraq. A jolt of terror, feeling for the trip wire, waiting for the explosion, even as he knew it wouldn't come. He checked to see no one had noticed. Wiping his palms on his shirt, he edged another step inside, let the door close behind him.

While Chato and Puchi pimp-strolled across the room to claim the corner table, Efraim went to the counter to order drinks. Godo lingered, neither here nor there, glancing up at the overhead menu and noticing the place sold only Pepsi, just like over there, Coke being linked to Zionists and the devil.

Lowering his eyes, he studied the chunky black girl in the scarf taking Efraim's order. She had Cherokee cheeks in an otherwise perfectly round face, a laugh-line squint and a blazing smile so selfless Godo could imagine joy coming to her easily. Enviable, that. Inadvertently, he searched her face for tattoos, like the Shia women wore, and shortly not just his palms but his neck and brow were cloying with sweat.

Efraim carried the drinks on a tray to the corner table and Godo followed like a pup, sat down quickly, grabbed his Pepsi. It was oversweet but the cold was what he wanted. He finished the thing in two fierce swallows.

"The fuck, homes." Puchi, chugging his ice with a straw. "Sucked that down like a junkie."

Godo wiped his lips, already craving another. Out in the parking lot, two bikers wearing Nomad patches straddled hogs, gazing down into the open trunk of a BMW owned by a catlike Asian dripping gold, hair slicked back, shades despite the darkness. The conversation was quick, close, almost intimate. Maybe thirty feet away, a trio of black hood rats—more gold, worn over a dashiki, a turtleneck, a Raiders jersey—lurked behind a Mercedes SEL, apprising another set of merchandise, staring into the open trunk, listening carefully to the owner's patter, in this case a bottle blonde in candy-red slacks and slave-maker pumps: body of a porn star, face like a dropped pie.

Fucking place is an open-air gun mart, Godo thought, wondering if any of the players out there were ATF. "How long till your guy shows up?"

Puchi leaned down to his straw like he was snorting a rail. "Ask me when he gets here."

Godo belched into his fist, looking off. The moon-faced girl was counting change into the palm of a washed-out, splay-footed woman whose body cascaded fat. Her stretch pants matched her hair curlers. Beside her, a bone-thin towheaded girl sucked on her fingers while bumping mindlessly against her mother's slab of a

thigh. It looked like some sort of gag, the two of them togeth
pecially with the moon-faced girl in the head scarf standing
beyond them, that breathtaking smile, the cash register a kin
shield, protect her from the white trash. She reminded God
someone, the counter girl, the memory just out of reach at fi
Finally, it crystallized: Mobley, Jam Slammer Mo, his squad
with the hip-hop battle anthems, Outkast's "Call the Law" t
hands-down favorite, bellowing the words into the teeth of th
shamal sandstorms from his perch at the Humvee's turret:

Just grab my gun, and let's go out
Grab my gun, and let's go out

Godo spotted the two grenades rolling toward them across the concrete floor and had time to shout out, everybody charging back at flash speed, diving for cover, but Mobley was dragging the SAW, those two-hundred-round ammo drums. The explosions tag-teamed, a sheering white one-two thunderclap followed by AK fire from somewhere near the back of the house, muzzle flashes crackling through the smoke and dust. Godo and Chavous answered with suppression fire, Gunny Benedic crawled forward toward Mobley's screams. The blast had rippe his leg in two, just above the knee, the arteries torn like threa He bled out so fast he was convulsing from shock by the tin Gunny reached him. Calling for a corpsman was pointless. Mo ley was dead before they could drag him into the courtyard, severed half leg still inside the house.

Call the law, and hold the applause

"Hey dude, she asked you a question."

It was Puchi. Godo glanced up, saw everyone grinnin kindly. At the table's edge, the moon-faced girl stood there ing.

cipline; they used their weapons like bug spray. Everything about them stank of self-delusion and the fear of weakness.

The man pulled a chair from another table and sat near Puchi, neither close enough to be part of the circle nor far enough away to seem too much a prick. He wore work boots and cargo pants, with a khaki T-shirt underneath a frayed cammie combat blouse, the name tape removed. That alone was enough to make Godo hate him. His eyes were smallish and filmy green while his skin had a raw red quality just short of a rash. He had a wisp of a mustache blurring his lip and a fistful of sag hiding his belt. His left eye drooped, suggesting some sort of nerve damage, and his left hand trembled till he jammed it in his pocket, which he did the instant he caught Godo's stare.

Puchi did introductions. The man went by Chuck. He tugged a cigarette from a pack lodged in his shirt pocket and lit up right there, using a yellow Bic. No one behind the counter so much as frowned, let alone told him to put it out; they seemed to be ignoring him, actually. Christ, Godo thought, maybe he owns the place.

"We had a chance to float the boat a little," Puchi said, slipping into some prearranged code. "I'd say everybody was happy."

"Not quite," Godo said, squaring himself in his seat. He'd been wondering how the guy got the weapons in. He'd heard tales of GIs sawing off the bottoms of oxygen tanks, slipping the AKs in, welding the bottoms back on, then loading them into shipping crates for transport back to their unit's home base, all but impossible to track to a specific soldier. Maybe Chuck here had a guy in uniform working for him, easier that way, no customs. Godo felt certain that, if he asked, he'd only get a lie for his trouble.

Improvising, just to see where it went, he said, "You get the guns in Iraq, that's one thing. If that's where you get the ammo too, there's a problem. Saddam's factories got sloppy packing cartridges, it's why they had so many misfires. So the weapons, fine.

Ammunition? Unless it's Czech or Cuban, Yugoslav, anything but Iraqi, we're not in the market."

The guy named Chuck tapped ash onto the floor. His gaze was watery and a little off-center with the sagging left eye. He turned to Puchi. "What's this guy talking about? You can buy a 7.62 round anywhere."

"Not the quantity we want," Godo said. "Not without red flags everywhere."

Chuck turned to him, squinting against his cigarette smoke. "I don't know you," he said, half matter-of-fact, half insulting.

Godo mocked up a smile. "Sure you do. All the guys at Harmon Stern knew me."

Chuck blinked, turning his cigarette in his fingers. His left hand still sat tucked away, safe in his pocket. "What's that supposed to mean?"

"You guys came through my checkpoint four times a day."

Chuck shot Puchi a glance. "What's he going on about now?"

Puchi shrugged. "He worked over there. Like you."

"So what?"

"Harmon Stern Associates." Godo rocked back in his chair a little. "Don't act like you don't know what I'm talking about."

Chuck took a short tense drag on his smoke. "I didn't work with that outfit."

No doubt the guy's lying, Godo thought. Too vague, too interior. "You sure about that?"

Chuck stood up, said to Puchi, "This is fucked up."

"Don't let him bug you, man." Puchi waved toward Godo like that might make him go away. "He came back with kind of an attitude. Not like he's the only one, am I right?"

"I'm not fucking around. I don't care where he's been. Or what happened." Chuck's eyes flicked over to Godo's face, jittered back. "He gets his shit in check or this is over."

Godo basked in the power, the situation his to dictate. What did he care if Puchi and Chato scored another AK or two? Chuck looked like he might bolt for the door, Puchi seething in silence, Efraim just sitting there, arms crossed tight. Chato, in a world of his own, fiddled with his straw, making soft trumpet sounds with his lips.

"You think I'm just messing with you?" Godo laced his fingers behind his head. "We had trouble with Harmon Stern, not just once or twice. All the time. They were like a cancer in Al Anbar when I was there. This one time in particular, they shot two unarmed *hajis* for sport, the two guys just working on their pickup along the road to Ramadi. We dealt with the blowback for days. Had a fucking riot on our hands."

"That's got nothing to do with me," Chuck said, a little stronger now.

"Convince me."

"Con*vince* you?"

"Yeah. And don't be so touchy."

Chuck dropped his butt on the floor, crushed it with his boot. "You think I'm touchy?" He leaned forward, fists on the tabletop. The inwardness had fled. "I get sick of Molly Mopes shitting on what we did. You were there? Then you know as well as I do there was damn near no way to tell a good *haji* from a muj. You could talk to a guy one day, he's friendly as a foot massage, that night you catch him carrying gasoline out to the highway to soften the asphalt, bury an IED. You want to fault somebody for shooting two guys by the side of the road? Listen up—unless you were there at that instant, unless you knew what the intel was, unless you know what those two *hajis* did, how suddenly they moved, how they acted right before the trigger got pulled, unless and until you know all that, you don't know dick. And guess what, I don't care how bad things turned after. That means nothing. Those people used any excuse they could to bitch about what we were trying to do. Ungrateful shitbags most of them. But we had a job to do and we did it. We didn't lose one package we were hired to protect. Not one. I owe nobody an apology, least of all you."

Godo waited for a second, watching as, across the room, the towheaded girl and her walrus of a mother attacked their food. "My gunny got killed because of fuckups like you."

"That's it." Chuck shoved the bad hand back in its pocket. "I don't need this." He turned toward the door and stormed out, Puchi watching his back as though waiting for that magic point when he'd stop, cool off, rethink it, come back in, if only to give Godo a ration of shit. But that didn't happen. The guy who called himself Chuck, the man Godo felt almost certain he remembered now, if not him some guy just like him, climbed into his plain gray van and peeled out so fast his rear axle leapt almost a foot off the ground when it tagged a high-crested buckle in the blacktop. The other parking-lot shoppers stopped everything, staring after the van as it fishtailed away.

Puchi turned back to Godo, eyes glazed with fury. "Vasco's gonna have your balls for that."

TWENTY-FOUR

EL CHUSQUERO, AS HIS HENCHLINGS CALLED HIM—THE COMmander—took great pride in his wooden English. "I ask only, you know, because it look so, yes? You . . ." He winked, flourishing his hand back and forth between Roque and Lupe. "And she . . ."

He had a meaty face with sleep-lidded eyes, an oft-broken nose that sloped back to a glistening forehead. His thinning black hair rustled in the downdraft from the ceiling fan. He wore a blue guayabera and khaki slacks, the crease as straight as a blade.

They were seated in his office, painted a stark white and located at the back of a traditional thick-walled house, his headquarters. The only furnishings in the room were his desk with its leather swivel chair, a huge Guatemalan flag hanging behind him on the wall and two wood chairs for Roque and Lupe.

He was the leader of the gunmen who'd come to their rescue out at the roadblock in the hills. Who he and those men were, exactly, remained somewhat foggy, though it seemed obvious by now they weren't exactly Robin Hood and his Merry Men.

The desk was arrayed with a yard-long cord of rope with two close knots in it—the better to crush the windpipe of your victim, or so the Commander had explained during their leisurely afternoon together—plus a stretch of piano wire tied to two blocks of wood, a modest if chilling collection of knives, a bayonet honed to razor sharpness, a machete similarly seasoned, a set of nunchuks, even a length of chain he called a *pirulo*. An overreliance on firearms was the mark of an amateur, he'd remarked at one point, wanting to be thought of as *muy matón*, a real killer, a point he'd driven home with an anecdote from his days with the Kaibil corps, the Guatemalan special forces. They gave each recruit a puppy at the beginning of basic training, he'd said, and that puppy was your sole responsibility until the end, when you were commanded to slit its throat. Some recruits wept, others vomited. "But I," El Chusquero intoned with exuberant pride, "I not shame me."

He'd been studying Lupe's face with unsettling fascination throughout the afternoon. Clearly he thought Roque was the culprit—and, judging from the tone of his winking insinuation, approved.

"Honestly, it wasn't me," Roque told him, trying to sound more humble than moral. He sat tuning the impossible guitar. They'd been serenading the man for hours now, ever since he'd learned they were musical.

The Commander sat back in his chair, rocking pensively, contemplating Roque's disavowal. Sunlight drilled the window ledge. The putrid, sickeningly sweet stench of *cáscaras de café*, the husks stripped away from coffee beans, thickened the stifling afternoon air, like a mix of rotting chocolate stirred with human shit.

Roque strummed the guitar to test the tuning, deciding it wouldn't get better with more fussing. Distraction had become its own kind of focus as they'd run through song after song. Luckily the Commander's tastes were unoriginal. He preferred many of the same *ranchera* ballads that Roque had played in San Pedro Lempa; what others he requested were easy enough to fake after hearing him or Lupe hum a bar or two. They tended to be about defiant pride in the face of feckless betrayal. Women came off badly in them—shrewish, cruel, duplicitous, needy—thus his fascination, Roque supposed, with Lupe's face. Meanwhile she was growing hoarse from the nonstop performance and even with the additional requests the repertoire was tediously thin. Roque had played some songs a dozen times. But there was no thought of stopping.

"This is your woman, do not tell me no." The Commander eyed Roque tauntingly. "I can see. I have eyes. More—I have ears. You play, she sings, like *lovers*." It came out with a baiting smile, an insult wrapped in a dare.

Roque was aware that, while playing, he'd thoughtlessly stolen a glance now and then at Lupe as she'd lifted her face, eyes closed, concentrating on the lyrics and her pitch. Her voice, as always, kindled something inside him and perhaps that had come out in his playing, though he'd only tried to match what he'd heard as she sang, like any good accompanist. As time had passed and the repetitions multiplied he felt he'd become increasingly attuned to the nuances of her phrasing. Now all that seemed a hopeless mistake.

Lupe broke in.—*Music is intimate by its nature*, she said. Roque had learned over the past two hours that she had an awkwardly functional if limited command of English that permitted her to pluck out certain meaningful words—like "lovers." She also had a knack for reading faces, gestures, tone of voice.—*A song can make anyone seem amorous, even two strangers, if it is done properly*.

El Chusquero squirmed. To keep from having to show Lupe any attention whatsoever and to continue hacking away at his English, he spoke to Roque: "Strangers? No. Not possible. You think I'm stupid—I no have eyes?"

For some reason, Lupe kept at it.—*I can see you too are a romantic*.

She was either daringly brilliant, Roque thought, or fiercely stupid. The Commander trained his gaze on her. The silence felt like a shroud.

—*I think you're being generous*, she continued.—*Too generous.*

Seriously. We barely know each other. She flicked her hand back and forth, herself, Roque.—*It's the songs. The songs bring the feeling out of me, out of him. Out of you.*

Rather than respond, El Chusquero turned his attention to the laptop resting on his desk among the weapons. He'd shown them a website earlier, explaining it to them, feeling it would prove instructive. He'd kept the screen averted since then but now he tapped the space bar so the screen saver melted away, revealing the background slide show, then glanced up at his two visitors with a truculent smile.

The website belonged to an incarcerated colonel named Otilio Rubén Villagrán Pozuelos, under whom the Commander said he had served in Petén during the civil war. The reasons for Colonel Villagrán's imprisonment were left vague, though it was clear the dutiful El Chusquero considered them a travesty. That didn't keep the colonel from living in relative opulence—in his earlier tutorial, the Commander had shown them pictures of his old superior's prison quarters posted on the site: a spacious and freshly painted room with a refrigerator, an entertainment center with cable TV and a stereo, a brass bed, elegantly appointed bookshelves, rugs on the floor, even a few tasteful watercolors adorning the walls. But for the lack of natural light, it almost seemed more a condo than a cell.

The slide show now in progress, however, was horrific. The pictures had been taken with cell phones during a riot inside the prison: one group of *cholos* cowing another within one of the prison sectors, wielding machetes and dart guns called *chimbas*; a prisoner trying to escape through a hole in the wall; a *cholo* grabbing the would-be escapee by the hair, raising a machete to hack at his neck. In the background, torchlight reflected the glimmer of row after row of empty mayonnaise jars, and Roque remembered Happy's letter, recalled his story of nightlong humiliation in La Esperanza, the Salvadoran prison. Roque's imaginings of that night could not come close to what

TWENTY-THREE

PEOPLE'S FRIED CHICKEN WAS THE LATEST BODY SNATCHER TO inhabit the corpse of a seventies-era burger stand in an area of Richmond called the Iron Triangle, saddest neighborhood in the area's most homicidal city. The canted beams out front bristled with graffiti, a half-dozen bullet holes pocked the window glass. The parking lot's asphalt buckled so badly Godo imagined some ancient tribal curse gathering force from below, trying to break through. Where better to hawk a black market AK, he thought.

Through the smeary glass he noticed that two of the black girls working the counter wore head scarves and *abayas*: Muslims. It was a growing subculture here, a way to detox the ghetto. He felt blindsided and not a little pissed off as he grabbed the door, following the others inside, then the smell of the place hit him. What was it Chato said? *They do something weird with the chicken*. Grilled meat, lemon, tamarind paste, mint, like some of the houses he'd searched in Iraq. A jolt of terror, feeling for the trip wire, waiting for the explosion, even as he knew it wouldn't come. He checked to see no one had noticed. Wiping his palms on his shirt, he edged another step inside, let the door close behind him.

While Chato and Puchi pimp-strolled across the room to claim the corner table, Efraim went to the counter to order drinks. Godo lingered, neither here nor there, glancing up at the overhead menu and noticing the place sold only Pepsi, just like over there, Coke being linked to Zionists and the devil.

Lowering his eyes, he studied the chunky black girl in the scarf taking Efraim's order. She had Cherokee cheeks in an otherwise perfectly round face, a laugh-line squint and a blazing smile so selfless Godo could imagine joy coming to her easily. Enviable, that. Inadvertently, he searched her face for tattoos, like the Shia women wore, and shortly not just his palms but his neck and brow were cloying with sweat.

Efraim carried the drinks on a tray to the corner table and Godo followed like a pup, sat down quickly, grabbed his Pepsi. It was oversweet but the cold was what he wanted. He finished the thing in two fierce swallows.

"The fuck, homes." Puchi, chugging his ice with a straw. "Sucked that down like a junkie."

Godo wiped his lips, already craving another. Out in the parking lot, two bikers wearing Nomad patches straddled hogs, gazing down into the open trunk of a BMW owned by a catlike Asian dripping gold, hair slicked back, shades despite the darkness. The conversation was quick, close, almost intimate. Maybe thirty feet away, a trio of black hood rats—more gold, worn over a dashiki, a turtleneck, a Raiders jersey—lurked behind a Mercedes SEL, apprising another set of merchandise, staring into the open trunk, listening carefully to the owner's patter, in this case a bottle blonde in candy-red slacks and slave-maker pumps: body of a porn star, face like a dropped pie.

Fucking place is an open-air gun mart, Godo thought, wondering if any of the players out there were ATF. "How long till your guy shows up?"

Puchi leaned down to his straw like he was snorting a rail. "Ask me when he gets here."

Godo belched into his fist, looking off. The moon-faced girl was counting change into the palm of a washed-out, splay-footed woman whose body cascaded fat. Her stretch pants matched her hair curlers. Beside her, a bone-thin towheaded girl sucked on her fingers while bumping mindlessly against her mother's slab of a thigh. It looked like some sort of gag, the two of them together, especially with the moon-faced girl in the head scarf standing just beyond them, that breathtaking smile, the cash register a kind of shield, protect her from the white trash. She reminded Godo of someone, the counter girl, the memory just out of reach at first. Finally, it crystallized: Mobley, Jam Slammer Mo, his squaddie with the hip-hop battle anthems, Outkast's "Call the Law" the hands-down favorite, bellowing the words into the teeth of the shamal sandstorms from his perch at the Humvee's turret:

Just grab my gun, and let's go out
Grab my gun, and let's go out

Godo spotted the two grenades rolling toward them across the concrete floor and had time to shout out, everybody charging back at flash speed, diving for cover, but Mobley was dragging the SAW, those two-hundred-round ammo drums. The explosions tag-teamed, a sheering white one-two thunderclap followed by AK fire from somewhere near the back of the house, muzzle flashes crackling through the smoke and dust. Godo and Chavous answered with suppression fire, Gunny Benedict crawled forward toward Mobley's screams. The blast had ripped his leg in two, just above the knee, the arteries torn like thread. He bled out so fast he was convulsing from shock by the time Gunny reached him. Calling for a corpsman was pointless. Mobley was dead before they could drag him into the courtyard, the severed half leg still inside the house.

Call the law, and hold the applause

"Hey dude, she asked you a question."

It was Puchi. Godo glanced up, saw everyone grinning, not kindly. At the table's edge, the moon-faced girl stood there waiting.

"I just axed if you'd like a refill on your soda," she said.

Her voice was soft and more feminine than her size suggested. Gazing up into her face, framed by its veil, he searched for what it was that reminded him of Mobley, feeling vaguely ashamed, as though at some level his mind still believed they really did all look alike.

"Yes," Godo said, a whisper. "Please. A refill would be nice."

"It's a dollar," she said.

He dug into his pocket for the bill, thinking: ax. Who was it in the squad that used to tease Mobley about that? I axed you nicely. Don't make me ax you again.

He handed her the money and watched her bobbing hips as she ambled away. Girl can work it till you jerk it, he thought, veil or no veil. He wondered if she felt disgusted by his face.

The night Mobley died, army psyops crews roamed the city in their Humvees, cranking out the deafening sounds of men and women screaming, cats fighting, Guns N' Roses: "Welcome to the Jungle." The favorite, though, was a gut-knotting laugh, the creature from *Predator*, played with amped-up bass at a hundred decibels, echoing off the pavement and the concrete walls of the pillbox houses and apartment buildings, like the voice of some cut-rate god.

"Hey hey hey." Puchi nodded toward the parking lot, sucking loud on his straw, the dregs of his Pepsi. A gray windowless van had just pulled in. "Here comes business."

Watching as the driver got out and crossed the parking lot, Godo took notice of how underwhelming the man was. Among the contractors he'd met in Iraq, a fair number had come from special forces backgrounds; they'd kept up with the PT, rock-hard bodies, switchblade minds. Cocky, sure, but sometimes you just had to grant that. There were plenty of others, though, who'd simply grabbed the back of the gravy train and refused to let go, slack habits, washed-out eyes, the mouthy swagger of small men: users, gasbags, phonies. They didn't just lack fire discipline; they used their weapons like bug spray. Everything about them stank of self-delusion and the fear of weakness.

The man pulled a chair from another table and sat near Puchi, neither close enough to be part of the circle nor far enough away to seem too much a prick. He wore work boots and cargo pants, with a khaki T-shirt underneath a frayed cammie combat blouse, the name tape removed. That alone was enough to make Godo hate him. His eyes were smallish and filmy green while his skin had a raw red quality just short of a rash. He had a wisp of a mustache blurring his lip and a fistful of sag hiding his belt. His left eye drooped, suggesting some sort of nerve damage, and his left hand trembled till he jammed it in his pocket, which he did the instant he caught Godo's stare.

Puchi did introductions. The man went by Chuck. He tugged a cigarette from a pack lodged in his shirt pocket and lit up right there, using a yellow Bic. No one behind the counter so much as frowned, let alone told him to put it out; they seemed to be ignoring him, actually. Christ, Godo thought, maybe he owns the place.

"We had a chance to float the boat a little," Puchi said, slipping into some prearranged code. "I'd say everybody was happy."

"Not quite," Godo said, squaring himself in his seat. He'd been wondering how the guy got the weapons in. He'd heard tales of GIs sawing off the bottoms of oxygen tanks, slipping the AKs in, welding the bottoms back on, then loading them into shipping crates for transport back to their unit's home base, all but impossible to track to a specific soldier. Maybe Chuck here had a guy in uniform working for him, easier that way, no customs. Godo felt certain that, if he asked, he'd only get a lie for his trouble.

Improvising, just to see where it went, he said, "You get the guns in Iraq, that's one thing. If that's where you get the ammo too, there's a problem. Saddam's factories got sloppy packing cartridges, it's why they had so many misfires. So the weapons, fine.

Ammunition? Unless it's Czech or Cuban, Yugoslav, anything but Iraqi, we're not in the market."

The guy named Chuck tapped ash onto the floor. His gaze was watery and a little off-center with the sagging left eye. He turned to Puchi. "What's this guy talking about? You can buy a 7.62 round anywhere."

"Not the quantity we want," Godo said. "Not without red flags everywhere."

Chuck turned to him, squinting against his cigarette smoke. "I don't know you," he said, half matter-of-fact, half insulting.

Godo mocked up a smile. "Sure you do. All the guys at Harmon Stern knew me."

Chuck blinked, turning his cigarette in his fingers. His left hand still sat tucked away, safe in his pocket. "What's that supposed to mean?"

"You guys came through my checkpoint four times a day."

Chuck shot Puchi a glance. "What's he going on about now?"

Puchi shrugged. "He worked over there. Like you."

"So what?"

"Harmon Stern Associates." Godo rocked back in his chair a little. "Don't act like you don't know what I'm talking about."

Chuck took a short tense drag on his smoke. "I didn't work with that outfit."

No doubt the guy's lying, Godo thought. Too vague, too interior. "You sure about that?"

Chuck stood up, said to Puchi, "This is fucked up."

"Don't let him bug you, man." Puchi waved toward Godo like that might make him go away. "He came back with kind of an attitude. Not like he's the only one, am I right?"

"I'm not fucking around. I don't care where he's been. Or what happened." Chuck's eyes flicked over to Godo's face, jittered back. "He gets his shit in check or this is over."

Godo basked in the power, the situation his to dictate. What did he care if Puchi and Chato scored another AK or two? Chuck looked like he might bolt for the door, Puchi seething in silence, Efraim just sitting there, arms crossed tight. Chato, in a world of his own, fiddled with his straw, making soft trumpet sounds with his lips.

"You think I'm just messing with you?" Godo laced his fingers behind his head. "We had trouble with Harmon Stern, not just once or twice. All the time. They were like a cancer in Al Anbar when I was there. This one time in particular, they shot two unarmed *hajis* for sport, the two guys just working on their pickup along the road to Ramadi. We dealt with the blowback for days. Had a fucking riot on our hands."

"That's got nothing to do with me," Chuck said, a little stronger now.

"Convince me."

"Con*vince* you?"

"Yeah. And don't be so touchy."

Chuck dropped his butt on the floor, crushed it with his boot. "You think I'm touchy?" He leaned forward, fists on the tabletop. The inwardness had fled. "I get sick of Molly Mopes shitting on what we did. You were there? Then you know as well as I do there was damn near no way to tell a good *haji* from a muj. You could talk to a guy one day, he's friendly as a foot massage, that night you catch him carrying gasoline out to the highway to soften the asphalt, bury an IED. You want to fault somebody for shooting two guys by the side of the road? Listen up—unless you were there at that instant, unless you knew what the intel was, unless you know what those two *hajis* did, how suddenly they moved, how they acted right before the trigger got pulled, unless and until you know all that, you don't know dick. And guess what, I don't care how bad things turned after. That means nothing. Those people used any excuse they could to bitch about what we were trying to do. Ungrateful shitbags most of them. But we had a job to do and we did it. We didn't lose one package we were hired to protect. Not one. I owe nobody an apology, least of all you."

Godo waited for a second, watching as, across the room, the towheaded girl and her walrus of a mother attacked their food. "My gunny got killed because of fuckups like you."

"That's it." Chuck shoved the bad hand back in its pocket. "I don't need this." He turned toward the door and stormed out, Puchi watching his back as though waiting for that magic point when he'd stop, cool off, rethink it, come back in, if only to give Godo a ration of shit. But that didn't happen. The guy who called himself Chuck, the man Godo felt almost certain he remembered now, if not him some guy just like him, climbed into his plain gray van and peeled out so fast his rear axle leapt almost a foot off the ground when it tagged a high-crested buckle in the blacktop. The other parking-lot shoppers stopped everything, staring after the van as it fishtailed away.

Puchi turned back to Godo, eyes glazed with fury. "Vasco's gonna have your balls for that."

TWENTY-FOUR

EL CHUSQUERO, AS HIS HENCHLINGS CALLED HIM—THE COMmander—took great pride in his wooden English. "I ask only, you know, because it look so, yes? You . . ." He winked, flourishing his hand back and forth between Roque and Lupe. "And she . . ."

He had a meaty face with sleep-lidded eyes, an oft-broken nose that sloped back to a glistening forehead. His thinning black hair rustled in the downdraft from the ceiling fan. He wore a blue guayabera and khaki slacks, the crease as straight as a blade.

They were seated in his office, painted a stark white and located at the back of a traditional thick-walled house, his headquarters. The only furnishings in the room were his desk with its leather swivel chair, a huge Guatemalan flag hanging behind him on the wall and two wood chairs for Roque and Lupe.

He was the leader of the gunmen who'd come to their rescue out at the roadblock in the hills. Who he and those men were, exactly, remained somewhat foggy, though it seemed obvious by now they weren't exactly Robin Hood and his Merry Men.

The desk was arrayed with a yard-long cord of rope with two close knots in it—the better to crush the windpipe of your victim, or so the Commander had explained during their leisurely afternoon together—plus a stretch of piano wire tied to two blocks of wood, a modest if chilling collection of knives, a bayonet honed to razor sharpness, a machete similarly seasoned, a set of nunchuks, even a length of chain he called a *pirulo*. An overreliance on firearms was the mark of an amateur, he'd remarked at one point, wanting to be thought of as *muy matón*, a real killer, a point he'd driven home with an anecdote from his days with the Kaibil corps, the Guatemalan special forces. They gave each recruit a puppy at the beginning of basic training, he'd said, and that puppy was your sole responsibility until the end, when you were commanded to slit its throat. Some recruits wept, others vomited. "But I," El Chusquero intoned with exuberant pride, "I not shame me."

He'd been studying Lupe's face with unsettling fascination throughout the afternoon. Clearly he thought Roque was the culprit—and, judging from the tone of his winking insinuation, approved.

"Honestly, it wasn't me," Roque told him, trying to sound more humble than moral. He sat tuning the impossible guitar. They'd been serenading the man for hours now, ever since he'd learned they were musical.

The Commander sat back in his chair, rocking pensively, contemplating Roque's disavowal. Sunlight drilled the window ledge. The putrid, sickeningly sweet stench of *cáscaras de café*, the husks stripped away from coffee beans, thickened the stifling afternoon air, like a mix of rotting chocolate stirred with human shit.

Roque strummed the guitar to test the tuning, deciding it wouldn't get better with more fussing. Distraction had become its own kind of focus as they'd run through song after song. Luckily the Commander's tastes were unoriginal. He preferred many of the same *ranchera* ballads that Roque had played in San Pedro Lempa; what others he requested were easy enough to fake after hearing him or Lupe hum a bar or two. They tended to be about defiant pride in the face of feckless betrayal. Women came off badly in them—shrewish, cruel, duplicitous, needy—thus his fascination, Roque supposed, with Lupe's face. Meanwhile she was growing hoarse from the nonstop performance and even with the additional requests the repertoire was tediously thin. Roque had played some songs a dozen times. But there was no thought of stopping.

"This is your woman, do not tell me no." The Commander eyed Roque tauntingly. "I can see. I have eyes. More—I have ears. You play, she sings, like *lovers*." It came out with a baiting smile, an insult wrapped in a dare.

Roque was aware that, while playing, he'd thoughtlessly stolen a glance now and then at Lupe as she'd lifted her face, eyes closed, concentrating on the lyrics and her pitch. Her voice, as always, kindled something inside him and perhaps that had come out in his playing, though he'd only tried to match what he'd heard as she sang, like any good accompanist. As time had passed and the repetitions multiplied he felt he'd become increasingly attuned to the nuances of her phrasing. Now all that seemed a hopeless mistake.

Lupe broke in.—*Music is intimate by its nature*, she said. Roque had learned over the past two hours that she had an awkwardly functional if limited command of English that permitted her to pluck out certain meaningful words—like "lovers." She also had a knack for reading faces, gestures, tone of voice.—*A song can make anyone seem amorous, even two strangers, if it is done properly*.

El Chusquero squirmed. To keep from having to show Lupe any attention whatsoever and to continue hacking away at his English, he spoke to Roque: "Strangers? No. Not possible. You think I'm stupid—I no have eyes?"

For some reason, Lupe kept at it.—*I can see you too are a romantic*.

She was either daringly brilliant, Roque thought, or fiercely stupid. The Commander trained his gaze on her. The silence felt like a shroud.

—*I think you're being generous*, she continued.—*Too generous.*

Seriously. We barely know each other. She flicked her hand back and forth, herself, Roque.—*It's the songs. The songs bring the feeling out of me, out of him. Out of you.*

Rather than respond, El Chusquero turned his attention to the laptop resting on his desk among the weapons. He'd shown them a website earlier, explaining it to them, feeling it would prove instructive. He'd kept the screen averted since then but now he tapped the space bar so the screen saver melted away, revealing the background slide show, then glanced up at his two visitors with a truculent smile.

The website belonged to an incarcerated colonel named Otilio Rubén Villagrán Pozuelos, under whom the Commander said he had served in Petén during the civil war. The reasons for Colonel Villagrán's imprisonment were left vague, though it was clear the dutiful El Chusquero considered them a travesty. That didn't keep the colonel from living in relative opulence—in his earlier tutorial, the Commander had shown them pictures of his old superior's prison quarters posted on the site: a spacious and freshly painted room with a refrigerator, an entertainment center with cable TV and a stereo, a brass bed, elegantly appointed bookshelves, rugs on the floor, even a few tasteful watercolors adorning the walls. But for the lack of natural light, it almost seemed more a condo than a cell.

The slide show now in progress, however, was horrific. The pictures had been taken with cell phones during a riot inside the prison: one group of *cholos* cowing another within one of the prison sectors, wielding machetes and dart guns called *chimbas*; a prisoner trying to escape through a hole in the wall; a *cholo* grabbing the would-be escapee by the hair, raising a machete to hack at his neck. In the background, torchlight reflected the glimmer of row after row of empty mayonnaise jars, and Roque remembered Happy's letter, recalled his story of nightlong humiliation in La Esperanza, the Salvadoran prison. Roque's imaginings of that night could not come close to what he was now obliged to watch. Lupe turned away; this was permitted since, after all, she was merely a woman.

El Chusquero, meaningfully turning to Spanish:—*You see the fate of our enemies.*

—*I am not your enemy,* she said.

—*You see what happens to those who mock us.*

—*I would never*—

—*Don't contradict me!*

Lupe sagely dropped her glance to the floor. A tremor fluttered along the hollow of her throat.—*I'm sorry, El Chusquero.*

Responding to an impulse from God knew where, Roque began playing softly the opening refrain of "Canción de Cuna"—Song of the Cradle—the Cuban lullaby he used to practice endlessly when he first began playing guitar. It drove Godo crazy, the constant repetition, but then gradually he always calmed down, often despite himself, succumbing to the insidious languor of the melody.

Eyes still trained on Lupe, El Chusquero reached down to a lower desk drawer and took out a small glass cage. At first Roque could not make out what lay inside, except for a quivering shudder of small black forms, two dozen or so, swarming across mounded beds of sand, in the midst of which lay a rubbery lump of hairy flesh, prey of some kind. Gradually he recognized the armored bodies, the glossy pincers, the uniquely coiled tails.

He stopped playing.

El Chusquero, employing Spanish again, so Lupe could not pretend to misunderstand:—*Let us call this the lovers' test. These, you may or may not know, are a particular kind of Guatemalan scorpion. They're not as deadly as those one encounters farther north but the sting is still quite painful, especially if there is more than one. Right now they are feeding on a tarantula we found out in the firewood. But they can always be tempted to eat whatever we give them.* He gingerly lifted the cage's glass lid.—*So here is the test: Which one of you is willing to put a hand inside? You cannot both refuse.* He stared at her bruised face.—*One must suffer so the other does not. Such is love, no?*

For some reason, Roque suddenly became acutely aware of the groaning rumble of flatbed trucks loaded high with sugarcane laboring through the village's modest *zona urbana*, that and the sulfurous smell of the *cáscaras de café*. His tongue and throat had turned stone dry. Still, after a labored swallow:—*Why are you doing this?*

Before the man could answer, Lupe jumped to her feet, approached the desk and reached out with her left hand.—*You are mistaken about us, El Chusquero. I don't know why you won't believe me. But if one of us must be the victim, let it be me. A guitarist must look after his hands, no? And we may well need to play and sing again as we make our way north, to earn a little money here and there.*

Her face was a mask of stoic indifference. Roque realized she'd understood instinctively what he hadn't, there was no way to negotiate out of this. He sat gazing at her, feeling unmanned. El Chusquero eyed her too, but with an almost merry suspicion, while the chittering mass of black bodies continued boiling over one another in their glassed-in world.

Suddenly the Commander reached out, snagged her wrist—not roughly, more like the father of a reticent bride.—*And what else, for the sake of your lover's hands, would you be willing to do for money?*

For what felt like an eternity neither of them moved, eyes locked, her breathing feathery from terror, his smile gradually draining away. Finally he tossed her hand aside and slammed the glass lid shut.—*You think I'm a sadist, a fool. That tells me who you are. What kind of woman you are. You know nothing of me, what I think, what I feel. Sit the fuck down.*

Lupe drifted back to her chair, a terrified sigh trembling up from her belly as she clasped her hands in her lap. The Commander watched, saying nothing. Finally, he turned to Roque.

—Play something, asshole. And not that weepy little number you were fucking around with before.

Roque formed his left hand around the guitar neck, searching out an intro chord, but nothing came. Every tune that entered his mind seemed charged with some secret insult. Thankfully, he was spared a decision as a knock came softly at the door. One of the henchlings peeked in, a member of the crew of riflemen from the encounter on the road, a young Mayan named Chepito.*—El Chusquero, a moment, please.* He was small and coiled tight, dressed in a bleached-out work shirt and jeans, a pistol tucked in his waistband.

The Commander took one last look at Lupe, then without comment left the room, closing the door to the hallway behind him.

Roque and Lupe turned to each other as though unsure the other was really there. Before he could say anything, she lifted a finger to her lips, darting her eyes toward the door. Always the wise one, he thought, doubly ashamed. Unable to help himself, he glanced at the scrum of small black scorpions one last time, imagining her hand in there, swarmed, stung, piped with venom. For his sake.

The Commander burst back into the room, a cell phone pressed to his ear. Gesturing curtly, he ordered Lupe and Roque out. Wasting no time, they obeyed.

They had known that while the Commander sat with them, indulging his taste for *rancheras*, his men had been busy trying to determine who the four strangers they'd saved really were. For fear of the consequences if they were discovered holding anything back, Roque had explained their arrangement—the payment to Lonely and his network of smugglers, all aligned with Mara Salvatrucha. El Chusquero had responded that the gunmen at the roadblock had been members of the *salvatruchos'* main rival, Mara Dieciocho. Someone had tipped off the *pistoleros* about the border crossing and they'd hoped to kidnap the four of them, kill them in some strikingly memorable way, post the video on the Web and discredit their enemies' operation, show that Lonely and the *salvatruchos* could protect no one, the better to move in, claim their share of the lucrative racket of moving people and product north. But none of this was entirely clear. So much of what the Commander said came larded with a caustic if dull-witted irony, as though anything he actually chose to tell you was in essence a kind of joke. And he'd said nothing about how his own men happened to come along at just the right time, nor about any *mara* affiliation of his own. Roque suspected the man had no such ties except to the incarcerated Colonel Villagrán, which brought to mind the hideous prison-riot photos. You see the fate of our enemies. But who, exactly, were those enemies? Who wasn't?

Chepito led them to a room in the basement that reeked of mildew and body odor. As though to parody the Commander's Spartan sense of decor, it was totally devoid of furniture. Tío Faustino, Samir and a third man sat cross-legged on the bare cement floor with a deck of worn playing cards, engaged in a game of canasta. The stranger was twentyish, gaunt, unshaven, his hair stiff from lack of washing and his uncut fingernails rimmed with grime. His sunken stare resembled an animal's, though from dread or hunger or just raw tedium it was hard to tell.

Lupe immediately fled to a corner, dropped to her haunches, tucked up her knees and covered her head with her arms. Samir shot her a glance of naked contempt. Tío Faustino, wiping a glaze of sweat from his face, glanced at Roque inquiringly but he responded with a shake of his head, set the guitar down with a ringing thud, then dropped to the floor himself, using the instrument for a pillow as he lay on his back, draping an arm across his eyes. He felt impossibly tired, the adrenalin jag of the past few hours draining away like a toxic dream.

Samir, using Spanish for the sake of the stranger, said to Roque:—*Guess how long our new friend here has been trapped inside this house?*

By way of introduction, the stranger interjected:—*My name is Sergio*. His voice was faint, trebly, educated.

Peeking out from under his arm, Roque saw an unwashed hand snaking through the air in his direction. Lifting himself up on an elbow, he squelched his queasiness, shook it.—*Roque*.

—*Oh I know. I've heard so much, so much about you. And Lupe*.

The girl's name arched across the room, a lobbed pitch. She did not swing.

Sergio turned back to the men.—*It's been wonderful, having someone to talk to, you have no idea. And canasta, not just solitaire. A miracle*.

He beamed like a schoolboy, clutching his fanned cards to his chest. Roque suppressed a mild case of the creeps.

—*Tell him how long you've been here*, Samir prompted.

—*Oh, yes. Yes. Nine and a half months. As of last Wednesday*.

Samir shot Roque a baleful glance, saying in English. "Let me tell you something, I'll kill somebody before I stay here nine and a half months."

—*His family can't come up with the ransom*, Tío Faustino offered.

—*It's far too much money. Far too much*. Sergio chafed a hand beneath his nose, then swept it through his hair.—*They think my family is rich. We're not. We're merchants. Appliances: stoves, refrigerators, washers, dryers. We have eight stores, in five towns, here and there across the country. But that's nothing. We own no land. We have no political connections. We do not belong to society. We work. My family has not forgotten me, don't think that. No. But the ransom is impossible. Too much, too much*.

Tío Faustino drew a card from the stock, arranged it in his hand, then placed a six of spades faceup in the discard pile. Everyone knew the stories, hostages held for seven to ten years, some killed when it became clear the family would never come up with the money, sometimes even when they did. He shuddered, thinking if mere months could reduce a man to this, what would years do? To change the subject, he leaned a little closer, lowering his voice so no one stationed at the door might overhear.—*Sergio, what is it with El Chusquero, this colonel in prison? Are these guys soldiers or gangsters?*

—*Both! Good God, both, of course. Both*. Though it wasn't yet his turn, Sergio took a second to review his hand and the melds arranged before him, tapping his cards expectantly with his filthy middle finger.—*You haven't heard of Los Zetas? Mexican commandos working for the Gulf cartel. Assassins. They were trained by Kaibil officers like El Chusquero. They're notorious.*

Roque watched Samir draw a card, puzzle over it, grimace, toss it down onto the discard pile.

Sergio was next. He drew a card, screwed up his face, played it on a meld of sevens, smiling absently at this small success.—*The military is the mafia here. The army refused American aid because it came with strings attached. Human rights conditions. They laughed at that. They got their arms from Israel, Argentina. The CIA helped of course. And unlike El Salvador, they won their war. Using butchery, indiscriminate slaughter, with spies and informants everywhere, scaring everyone into silence. Worse, complicity. That kind of power, when no one can touch you, what to do with all of that once the last shot's fired? Take over the national police, tell the Colombian and Mexican cartels you're open for business*. He laid down his discard as though applying the final touch to a painting, then folded up his hand and rapped it pensively against his chin.—*They say two-thirds of the cocaine reaching America passes through Guatemala. Maybe more.*

The door opened. Chepito appeared again, accompanied this time by another of their rescuers out on the road. The young man was armed as he had been then, a semiautomatic rifle, bearing himself with a vacant intensity. Chepito gestured for the four newcomers to follow along, nailing Sergio with a hard stare that told him to stay put. Roque dared to believe they were going to be freed, even as the price of that luck seemed clear. Sergio erupted into helpless chatter, the words tumbling out even more manically than before, almost birdlike in tenor, thanking them all for playing cards, asking that they perhaps maybe if at all possible contact his family—no one else, of course, the police, the press, nothing so bold—just his mother, his father, his sisters, let them know he was alive, inform them he was well, instruct them to do whatever they were told to do if they were contacted. He wanted to come home. He prayed every day and night to see them again.

—*Do whatever El Chusquero says*, he called out as the door clicked shut.—*Do nothing to jeopardize yourselves. Or me*.

Securing the padlock on the door, Chepito chuckled. "*Pobre hueco*." Poor faggot.

Shortly they stood assembled in the bare white room before the massive Guatemalan flag. The Commander as before sat at his desk, rocking in his chair, neither beaming nor glowering, his thumb to his mouth as he chewed the nail pensively. The array of weapons and the glass cage with its little black riot inside remained exactly where Roque had seen them last, the scorpions earning a helpless shudder from Lupe, a furtive glance from Tío Faustino, a smile of admiring revulsion from Samir. Apparently El Chusquero gave no thought to the chance someone might grab a knife or the bayonet or the nunchuks, put up a fight, make a run for the door, not with Chepito's sidekick standing behind them, his safety off.

"Well, look like is time for everyone turn over his bowl of soup," the Commander announced mystifyingly. His eyes tracked each of their faces one by one. "I admit to you that I be in touch with Señor Lonely. We talk, we understand, okay? We agree on this: You want to reach Mexico, you need my protection. This will cost five thousand dollars each person." His smile was generous. He gave the scorpion cage a meaningful pat. "I understand this is much money, but not too much, yes? Besides, in America, there is always someone with the money."

TWENTY-FIVE

THE CALL CAME IN AS HAPPY SAT AT THE WHEEL OF THE VAN, overcast afternoon, hooded dog walkers braving the wind. He was waiting for Puchi to close the deal with the latest bunch of marks, a Mexican family, hardscrabble parents with three quiet kids, thought they'd found the perfect answer in American Amigos Moving.

Increasingly, the dupes were Latinos. Less likely to make a fuss, Happy supposed, guessing at Vasco's logic. Even if they were legal, had all their documents in order, they'd be fools to risk it, take the chance that somewhere in the faceless maze of gringo justice they'd cross exactly the wrong guy, the one with an ax to grind, a sadist on a mission. Sure, maybe after a couple years and lawyer fees up the *culo* it would all end well, but you'd never get back to square one. People getting screwed, misidentified, shipped off, ignored when they tried to tell the truth, maybe just blindsided by cruel luck, their lives gutted—the number of stories had upticked crazily the past year, even on the fabled Left Coast, the People's Republic of California. Only those with nothing to lose, Happy thought, could go ahead and bitch. Better to keep your head down, move along, hide.

Case in point: the father here, a short stocky dark-skinned *obrero* from Hermosillo, gentle cat, soft-spoken, handyman by day, waiter nights and weekends. He stood there beneath the leaden sky in the tree-lined street, outside the new house, shamed before his wife and sons, counting out the extra bills into

Puchi's hand. Not even a green card can save you from this, Happy thought, and that was when the cell phone in his pants pocket began to throb.

He dug it out, checked the digital display, the number not just unfamiliar, it had one too many digits. Flipping the phone open, he pressed it to his ear, expecting some mistaken stranger or just dead air.

It was Roque. "Pablo. Hey." He sounded wrong. "We've got a situation here."

Happy spent the next two minutes trying to focus, holding back his rage and dread, as Roque set about trying to explain, as best he could, the "situation."

It seemed a gratuitous insult—the old man, kidnapped. He'd already been snatched once by the feds, wasn't that enough? Of course it meant money, quick, except there was none. He glanced in the mirror at the gentle *obrero* waiting for his furniture to appear from the back of the truck. Who was the sucker now?

He tried to take heart from Roque's voice. The more he talked, the stronger he sounded, holding it together, but how could the kid have let this thing happen? First rule of schemes, Happy thought: They fall apart. They mock you. He bit his fist to keep the nausea down, closing his eyes tight, listening until Roque had nothing to say except, "Don't call back to this number. It won't work. I'll contact you in two hours."

Disposable phone, Happy thought. It explained why he hadn't recognized the incoming number. The kidnappers, whoever they were, probably tossed Roque's cell somewhere, realizing their location could be tracked through the transmission towers. Kid didn't even need to use it, just have it on. Now that it was history, no one would know where they were, not Lattimore, not the spooks, nobody.

That too was the situation.

"And in two hours, we discuss what?"

"Getting the money together. Where to send it."

"Yeah. Look. I can see some problems there."

"Jesus." Roque's voice plummeted twenty stories. "Don't talk like that."

Suddenly Puchi and Chato were slapping their hands on the door of the truck cab, making faces. It was time to unload. On top of everything else, a faint mist had started to fall. Happy held up a finger: Gimme one minute.

"I mean, who the fuck am I supposed to hit up for twenty grand?"

There was a noise on the other end. Roque said, "Wait a minute," followed by a sound like windblown sand hitting glass, static on the line. Roque came back: "Like I said, two hours, I'll call you." The line went dead.

THE FURNITURE FELT LIKE TONNAGE AS HAPPY HELPED CARRY IT OFF the truck through the drizzle and into the small house. He ignored the shame-faced *obrero*; everybody's got problems, he told himself. Once or twice, though, as he dropped a chair into place or nudged a dresser into its spot, he caught the stare of one of the kids, a boy, the oldest, maybe twelve, thin as a birch and nothing but hate in his eyes.

As they drove back to the truck yard, the sun peeked through the gunmetal haze along the horizon. Something like a plan started taking shape in Happy's mind. The smallness of the amount, he thought, was interesting. It wasn't a real kidnap, they weren't trying to bleed the family. They must've already known we were tapped out, he thought, the fee paid to Lonely. They just want a little something to make up for their trouble. They killed a few men, from what Roque'd said, and that deserved fair compensation. The ransom was just a way to tax the *salvatruchos* without actually causing ill will. Lonely was no doubt delighted: Stick it to the *pollos*. It made it look like he'd made a deal but it cost him nothing. Every business should catch breaks like that.

He considered phoning Lattimore, hitting up the bureau for the ransom. Not like it isn't in their interest to keep this thing afloat, he thought. They had flash and drop money, twenty grand was in the realm of possibility, theoretically. Small or large, though, the amount would mean dick to Lattimore. The bureau's not a bank: Happy had actually heard him say that into the phone to some other snitch. It doesn't hand out money it doesn't expect to grab right back. You flash it for a buy, you drop it on the table during a sting, that's it. Even when a kidnapper's threatening a child, an agent's going to make the family bargain for more time, cash out a policy, work a loan on the house, whatever. The bureau always holds out, Happy'd learned, hoping you get itchy and scratch up the money on your own, helpful fuckers that they were.

Meanwhile Happy had yet to see dime one for his undercover work. The case had moved forward at a bouncing clip, while the wheels of the bureaucracy churned along at their usual speed, slow as a root canal. The money he made from Vasco barely paid expenses. Lucha was broke and he didn't want her fully in the loop regardless. She'd just fret herself into a state.

No, the only answer was Vasco, hit him up again. And he'd refuse. Too much thrown at this deal already, he'd say, with *pinche nada* to show for it. Your uncle and cousin got themselves snatched? Not my problem. Let Zipicana handle it, the cocaine kingpin with the hard-on for terror. He's the one who wants to bring the raghead across anyway, right? About time he anted up for the privilege.

And who could argue with that, Happy thought as he eased the moving van into its parking stall, secured the brake, turned off the ignition. He jumped down from the cab and went to his locker.

He left the wired flannel shirt he'd received from the bureau on its hook; he'd done no recording of Puchi and Chato in the phony mover deals for weeks. It didn't rise to the level of actual fraud, he'd been told—contractual misunderstanding, it could be said, the money at issue small-claims stuff—and thus wasn't a crime, federal or otherwise. It was getting to be an issue, the recordings. Pitcavage, the AUSA, was pushing for deeper involvement of Vasco and his crew in the terror angle: Get them to talk about helping pick out local targets, the Fed Building, Coit Tower, Golden Gate Bridge. Think of what Hollywood would want to blow up, he said, then get video of Vasco or Puchi or Chato casing out the place.

But Happy was the least chatty guy on the planet. After that initial meet with Vasco, everything felt forced. He wasn't comfortable bringing stuff up out of nowhere, it wasn't his nature. He was convinced everybody would see right through him, then what? That's why so many of his tapes were filled with brief bits of idle chat separating long, worthless silences. He never engaged and no one took the initiative to engage him. He was the world's worst rat, except he'd brought them the case of a lifetime, Mara Salvatrucha meets al-Qaeda, and he couldn't understand why they didn't seem happier with that, especially since, if Lattimore's offhand suspicions were true, if Samir wasn't really who Happy thought he was, that might very well be what they were looking at. His stomach lurched. Samir, a true *jihadi*. Christ. If that's true, he thought, I'm gonna spend the rest of my life trying to convince anybody who'll listen I was played just like everybody else. He had a pretty good idea a lot of that convincing would take place in prison.

He took his cell phone, which served as both a transmitter and a backup recorder, out of his pants pocket and placed it on the locker's upper shelf. Ironic, since he was finally about to initiate a conversation worth recording. But it just seemed best that the next few minutes not exist, not as far as the government was concerned.

Chula was coming down the stairs, dragging little Lucía behind her, as Happy made his way up. As always, the mother had a smoke lit, cigarette dangling from her lips as she stuffed a wad of bills into her purse; the child was sniffling, her eyes wet and red. Girls' night out, Happy thought, listening to the heels of Chula's pumps hammer the wood-plank steps. No words were exchanged as they passed but Chula, as always, tossed him a look of lukewarm want while Lucía, clutching her smoky stuffed bear, regarded him with the distant needy meanness he knew her for. I pity that child, he told himself, but his heart wasn't in it.

Vasco sat stewing in his usual post-Chula funk, facing the window in the lamplight, chewing a fingernail on one hand, holding a smoke in the other, white sharkskin boots propped on his desk. He'd developed a rash of some kind in the past week, a blotchy redness on his neck, and he'd scratched at it so savagely the skin was bloody and raw. A pair of Band-Aids covered the worst of it. Jiggling one foot like he needed to pee, he cocked an acid eye toward the door as he heard Happy knock, but otherwise did nothing. Happy accepted that as invitation to enter.

The coils of copper wire were gone, the mortgage flyers remained. Happy sat on the sofa and the cushion emitted a stiff vinyl sigh. "We've got kind of a situation," he began, invoking Roque's words.

To his credit, Vasco heard the story out without a single damning comment or insult. His face remained inert as once or twice he tapped his cigarette against his ashtray. When Happy was done, he said simply, "Kidnapped."

Happy nodded. "Fucked up, I know."

"And they're only asking twenty grand—total, right?"

Happy explained his understanding of things, the likelihood the money wasn't a ransom at all but a kind of secondhand fee. Vasco heard him out, then: "Doesn't matter either way. I'm not fronting any more money."

Down in the truck yard, someone dropped a tin bucket onto the concrete floor. A wail of surprise, a chuckle.

"I don't blame you," Happy said, "especially after what Godo did last night."

He was referring to the sabotage of the gun buy at People's Fried Chicken. He'd heard about it from Puchi during the shift, Chato chiming in, the usual speed-freak rag.

"Godo can kiss my ass but that's got nothing to do with this. I'm not throwing good money after bad, simple as that."

Happy folded his hands and leaned forward. The sofa cushion creaked like he'd squeezed a balloon. "I want to make good on what Godo did."

Vasco, slit-eyed, took a drag from his smoke. "What do you mean?"

"I want to make it up to you."

"Yeah? Like how?"

"Puchi told me he got the license number off the van this guy drives, the guy selling guns. I know a girl, works at the DMV, she can trace that plate to an address. Godo's been training your guys on how to use an M16, how to clear rooms, all that. Puchi and Chato can't shut up about it, they're jacked. So—what say we take this guy's house down?"

Just lay it out for the man to see, Happy told himself. Let the crime sell itself.

Vasco plucked a stray bit of tobacco off his tongue.

"Guy deals in cash," Happy prompted. "Means he'll have a wall safe. We make him hand up the combination. Probably got the guns locked away in there too or someplace else inside the house, maybe the basement, maybe the garage. Same deal. We persuade him to cooperate. What I mean is, we let Godo persuade him."

The merest smile flirted with one side of Vasco's mouth. Downstairs someone was sweeping now, Happy couldn't see who: Puchi, Chato, one of the others. The broom bristles whisked against the concrete floor. Vasco said, "What do you mean 'we'?"

"I'll be there to look after Godo, make sure he doesn't get strange, have a flashback, that sort of thing."

"You."

"Yeah."

Vasco's hand went up to scratch his neck, stopped midway. "And how does one do that exactly, keep a guy from, you know, getting strange?"

Downstairs the man with the push broom started whistling "Watermelon Man."

"I was over there too, remember. I dealt with some stuff, I told Godo all about it. He knows I understand. He'll listen to me."

Vasco stared across the room at Happy as though he was a picture not hanging quite right. "You told him all about it? How about you tell me."

Happy relayed the story of the ambush on the convoy. Vasco nodded along, then said, "Interesting. But you still want me to front you twenty grand, am I right?"

"In exchange for my old man and me shaving our points on the cocaine deal down from twenty to ten per."

Vasco cocked his head. His smile broadened a hair. "You want this bad."

It's imaginary money, Happy thought, knowing he couldn't let it sound that way. "He's my old man. Besides, I don't get him back here, there's no deal to talk about. He's the driver at the port. Without him?" He opened his hands. "That's true of you as well as me, you know."

"But you're the one with the need. You're the one begging."

"That how you want to put it?"

Vasco stubbed out his smoke, snagged his pack from the desktop, tapped out another, lit up. Nudging the cigarettes across the desk, he said, "Want one?"

TWENTY-SIX

THE FOUR OF THEM STAGGERED OUT TO THE COROLLA IN THE midmorning light, Roque dragging the guitar, Samir clutching his shoulder bag, Lupe her clothes and medicine, Tío Faustino empty-handed, all of them stiff in joint and cranky of mind from a night of miserable sleep. They'd be resuming their journey across Guatemala, trailing a pickup driven by Chepito, who would have as sidekick and secret gunman one of the other henchlings. Together, the two of them would serve as protection and emissaries of goodwill, or so said El Chusquero, who bid his guests a chirpy farewell now that the wire transfer had cleared.

"*Músico*," the Commander called out from the porch, waiting for Roque to turn. He twiddled his fingers daintily.—*Use those hands well, my brother*. He offered one last lurid smile, then disappeared inside the thick-walled house with a punctuating slap on the doorframe.

Roque tumbled into the backseat and gave shuddering thanks as the car headed off, Tío Faustino at the wheel. Guitar between his knees like a cello, he let his head fall back and closed his eyes, hoping to snatch back some of the sleep lost because of Sergio. The poor wretch had whimpered like a puppy in the dark all night, the sound inescapable in that dank airless room, keeping everyone awake. Roque loathed himself for resenting that.

He stole a heavy-lidded glance at Lupe. She too was trying to rest, curled into her corner of the backseat, legs tucked beneath her. He still marveled at her courage, knowing how perverse that would seem to a man like El Chusquero. Only a queer like Sergio, he'd say, would think of a girl as heroic. It brought to mind something Mariko had said, about a certain kind of man—often drawn to uniforms, always fond of weapons—the type of man so instinctively fearful of women he couldn't even think of intimacy without possession. The kind of man, she'd said, who wants a virgin to fuck and Mom to fight for. Roque had always assumed she was talking about her ex, the airman, Captain Detwiler. Now, however, he had a far more palpable grasp of what she'd meant. And I'm nothing like that, he realized. An orphan knows possession's a lie. The most crucial thing, by its very nature, is always missing.

Half an hour into the drive, Tío Faustino turned on the radio. As Roque drifted in and out of sleep, he caught bits and pieces of marimba workouts, old-style *cumbias*, *duranguenses*, *charangas*—even a few dolorous *rancheras*, so dear to the Commander's heart.

The next thing he knew two hours had passed and they were careening down a hillside in scattered rain into the sprawling basin that contained the capital. Despite himself, Roque felt a little awestruck. After San Salvador, he'd lowered his expectations to third-world level, but Guatemala City was a real metropolis: shimmering office towers, broad tree-lined boulevards, quaint commercial neighborhoods, choking traffic.

They stopped for lunch at a storefront cantina. Roque ordered *fortachón*, a kind of Mexican hash with pork and jalapeños, and as they sat outside beneath a green umbrella he shoveled it in heedlessly. He would have felt embarrassed if everyone else, even Lupe, weren't similarly graceless. The only interruption to the chow-down came when a man with shaggy blond hair, wearing a cockeyed ball cap and a filthy tweed jacket, tottered past them down the rain-damp sidewalk, strumming a tuneless guitar. His eyes were glassy but his smile was serene. Lupe and Tío Faustino glanced up, first at the strolling lunatic, then at Roque, and shared the day's first smile as Chepito tossed the man a quetzal.

North of the capital, the highway curved through roadcut and cane fields and rubber plantations toward the coastal lowlands. With food in everyone's bellies the mood grew less tense. Roque played along to the radio and Lupe, prodded by Tío Faustino, sang harmony to Julieta Venegas's "Canciones de Amor." When she was finished, the older man lifted his hands from the wheel to gently applaud.—*You have such a gift*, he told her, but instead of inspiring gratitude his words dropped a veil across her eyes; she turned to stare out the window and couldn't be coddled or goaded into singing again, no matter how invitingly Roque played.

The farther they drove, the greater the number of people trekking on foot along the highway. Roque wondered how far they were going—the next town, Mexico, the States. Crews of children scavenged for scraps of sugarcane that fell off trucks, shoving the reddish brown stalks into burlap bags. Breakdowns created sweltering bottlenecks. Things only worsened in the towns, where the local women stood out in the road, hawking oranges and sodas and coconuts, each with the sagging paunch of recent motherhood bulging beneath her blouse.

Only four roadblocks appeared, each manned by blue-uniformed cops who invariably waved the Corolla through with barely a glance. It was impossible to know whether this was because of El Chusquero's touted influence, communicated somehow by Chepito in the pickup just ahead, or merely the way of things. As though it matters at this point, Roque thought. Be grateful the car's moving.

They reached the border town of Tecún Umán late in the afternoon, realizing only once they were within the town proper that they had arrived on the occasion of an annual *feria*—the first Friday of Lent. The narrow streets were thronged with people drawn from all the nearby villages who came to visit the tents and arcades, haggle with the vendors, play the games. Chepito led them down a brick lane and they inched their way past merchant stalls displaying blouses, bras, shoes, toys, including eerily realistic AK-47s and Glocks made of plastic. Women working hand presses made fresh lemonade. Ears of corn boiled in deep tin pots.

Chepito found his way to a parking area, an empty lot shaded by a sprawling ceiba, where he paid an old man and his grandsons to look after the pickup and the Corolla. He then led everyone to a small posada that, from what Roque could tell, served as a way station for thieves and hookers. They gathered on the sidewalk to either side of the doorway, hulking unkempt men smoking cigarettes to the left, flirty young women in festive skirts, sipping Cokes, on the right. A few others loitered in what passed for a lobby, an open room with broad ocher walls, furnished with a card table, mismatched chairs, an electric fan.

Chepito went to the man at the card table, whispered something, waited out the reply, then collected a key, dangling it between finger and thumb as he gestured for Roque and the others to follow. The henchling, still nameless, his shirttail pulled over the pistol shoved down into his jeans, took up the rear.

The room was a closet with a cot and a bowl. The canvas of the cot bore a disturbing stain. The bowl had a used bar of soap in it. A tiny window looked out on a passageway between the posada and the next building over.

Chepito maneuvered everyone inside.—*I am going to talk with a man who works here with us. He will arrange for your crossing over to Mexico. There will be a boat, it will take you to a spot a little south of Puerto Escondido and there you'll be met and taken the rest of the way overland. I'll be back after dark. If you want something to eat or drink, there's a place in the back, out on the patio, you can get soft drinks and tortillas, maybe beer. Or they can send one of the kids out, get something from the fair. Don't go wandering around. Even with all the people out, it's still not safe, not for you.*

He met each of their glances meaningfully, then closed the door. The four of them stood there, so close each could feel the next person's breath on his or her skin. Shortly footsteps clattered on the wood stair: two sets descending, not just one. Roque felt relieved. The thought of being stuck in the cramped room, the nameless henchling standing guard, seemed too grim.

He said:—*They're arranging the crossing to Mexico? Since when?*

Tío Faustino turned to look out the small window, craning to get a glimpse of the street.—*Something cold and wet is in order, I'd say. Who will join me?*

Roque reached for the doorknob, figuring everyone was going, but Lupe plopped down on the cot, avoiding the umber stain.—*I'll stay. In case they come back.*

Not missing a beat, Samir dropped his cloth shoulder bag in the corner and settled down next to it, folding his arms, dropping his chin.—*I'll wait too. I hate crowds. If you think of it, bring me back a Pepsi.*

Lupe shot him a black glance.—*What, you're afraid I'll try to squeeze out through the window? Then what—fly away?*

—*Let me tell you something, I wouldn't put it past you.* He traced a finger across the floor, inspecting the ribbon of grime that came up.—*The window part, not the flying.*

Tío Faustino nudged Roque into the hall, smiling farewell.—*We won't be long, I promise.*

The patio area was in truth a patch of tamped-down sand with tussocks of pampas grass, shaded by a stately *conacaste*. Two giant wood spools served as tables with a scattering of plastic chairs. The bar consisted of a door spread across two sawhorses, aluminum tubs filled with ice and drinks underneath, packs of cigarettes on top: Rubio, Pasayo, Marlboro, Pall Mall. Tío Faustino bought two *tamarindos*—they came in sealed plastic bags with straws—and sat with Roque, leaning in so they could whisper, using English as an extra precaution.

"It may be a blessing in disguise, this connection with El Chusquero." A trio of shirtless boys slinked toward the table to beg. Tío Faustino shooed them off. "If we put our lot in with him from here on out, we may not have to hand the girl, Lupe, over to that sniveling little coward's connection in Agua Prieta, I can't recall the name."

"El Recio." Roque remembered it well, it meant Tough Guy. "What about Samir?"

"As long as he gets to America, he'll have no complaints."

"Are you joking? He'll have nothing but complaints. You saw him. He hates her."

"That's not—"

"He's developed this thing for her. He'll only be happy if he sees her suffer."

"Don't exaggerate. While you were upstairs serenading El Chusquero with the girl, I was down in the cellar with El Turco, okay? He's not a monster."

"You're only saying that because he saved Happy's life."

"Nonsense. He just knows, the way it stands, his fate is tied to hers."

Tío Faustino rubbed his eyes and when his hands came away Roque noticed how much older he seemed than just a few days ago. His stubble was bristly and gray, the sagging flesh beneath his eyes was the color of tea, his hands shook. Only driving seemed to soothe him and it would be days at least before he was back behind the wheel, assuming they were lucky.

"Besides," he continued, "it's not a bad idea to remember where our confidence in that pack of *salvatruchos* got us."

"Tío, who knows what El Chusquero's really up to here? He's not doing this out of kindness, it's going to cost. And Happy made it clear, there's no more money. This last payment's the end."

"Maybe we could work something out."

"No, Tío, listen to me. I know how the guy thinks. He'll

strand us in the middle of nowhere till we pay. And let me repeat: *There is no more money*."

"So you're okay then with handing that girl over to some *padrote*." Pimp.

"Good God, how can you say such a thing? I just—"

"We're not going to have a lot of choices. This one presents itself. I say we consider it. Unless you—"

Tío Faustino broke off his sentence, stiffening imperceptibly, eyes veiled. He seemed to be saying, Don't look. Shortly, however, the newcomer who'd caught his eye was grabbing a nearby chair, dragging it over to their table through the gravel. Finally, as the chair came close and the stranger plopped down, Roque glanced his direction.

TWENTY-SEVEN

HE WAS HANDSOME LIKE AN EXOTIC ANIMAL, LATE TWENTIES, *indio* features and muscular, his flat bronze face astonishingly smooth-skinned. His arms were tattooed but his hands, his face, his neck were clear. He wore a Giants cap and an immaculate T-shirt.

"Roque, Faustino—hey." Their names rolled off his tongue naturally, without affected familiarity. "I'm Beto, your *guía*. Take you from here to Agua Prieta."

Roque remembered the name, he was Lonely's man in Tecún Umán. His English was solid, the accent soft, that lilting musicality few Latinos lost.

Beto gestured to the Indian woman working refreshments for a third *tamarindo*. She dug one from her cooler, tottered over, money changed hands. It gave everyone a second to think.

Finally, Tío Faustino said, "You've lived in the States."

Beto laughed. "Yeah. Up around Salinas." He fussed with the straw for his *tamarindo*, punctured the plastic bag, took a sip. "Worked construction, I was a carpenter, till I got snagged running a stop sign. Believe that? Bad luck, man. Now I can't go back for ten years." He checked out the patio area, then a shoulder roll, a bodybuilder tic. "Getting used to it here. Life's okay. And who needs the constant paranoia, right? Crazy back there now."

Roque said, "Look, we don't know who we're supposed to be dealing with."

"Nothing's changed." Beto's eyes darted between Roque and Tío. "We're good to go."

Tío Faustino said, "How did you know where to find us?"

"This shithole?" Beto glanced up at the cracked and moldy stucco wall of the posada. A large black *pijuyo* perched on the edge of the roof. "This is my town. What goes on here's my business. Look, you guys paid for us to get you to the States. That's what I'm here to do, my leg of the trip anyway."

A group of Mayan women in traditional *traje* wandered into the courtyard from the street, clearly lost. With birdlike titters they bowed a group apology, turned around, vanished.

"This is the one day of the year you can cross over without showing documents," Beto said, explaining the crowds. "There's another fair right across the river. Mexicans come here, Guatemaltecos go there, trade goods, just for the day. Try to get farther than Tapachula, they'll nail you. But you should see the mob down along the river. Hundreds of people, these crappy little rafts, scrap wood lashed to inner tubes. It's nuts."

"It hasn't been the easiest trip for us, either." Roque ignored a warning glance from his uncle. "But you probably know that."

Beto smiled acidly, then glanced around again, making sure no one was in earshot. "Captain Quintanilla, that what you mean?"

"We never heard him called anything but El Chusquero."

Beto shook his head, whispered, "El Choo-scay-ro," like the punch line to a raunchy joke. "Toad-faced fuck. You realize that whole ambush on the road was a hoax, right? Those guys at the roadblock, they were his men, I don't care what he told you."

Roque and Tío Faustino sat there, taking that in. Finally, Tío Faustino said, "They got shot. Two of them. Straight to the head."

"No, trust me." Beto tottered his fingers, a puppeteer.

"That makes no sense," Roque said, at the same time realizing it was possible. He hadn't seen the shootings up close, everybody else ducking down inside the car, terrified. "Why go to all that trouble just to kidnap us anyway?"

"Who knows what goes through that sick fuck's head? I'm telling you it was bogus. Captain Quintanilla's way of amusing himself, jerking the chain, adding a tax for moving you through Jutiapa. He makes it look like a gang thing. Something goes wrong, one of you dies, he can walk away, hang it on us."

Tío Faustino sat back in his chair. "I can't believe this."

"Now, let me guess, I'll bet he's pushing to get you to cross over to Oaxaca with his people here. Don't do it, my friends. You'll die."

Beto struggled for a notepad stuck in his back pocket. A pencil stub was fastened to it with a rubber band. He opened it to a page where there was a crude map of the coast.

"They'll send you by boat. Pick you up around here," he pointed with the pencil, "little outside Champerico, take you to a *huequito*, a little smuggler's cove, outside Puerto Escondido. That's what they say. But how you supposed to get the rest of the way through Mexico?"

"They told us they'd take us overland," Tío Faustino said, "all the way to the States."

Beto tossed the pencil down. "Seriously? They tell you two boats, two whole boats, just vanished the last couple months? They tell you fifteen poor fucks drowned just last week? What was left of the boat washed up in pieces. Shit that floats outta Haiti's got better rep than that."

High in the *conacaste* branches, a *zanate* cawed. The *pijuyo* on the roof's edge fled. The *zanate* swooped down, took its place, a leathery curl of something, flesh maybe, in its talons.

Tío Faustino said, "How are we supposed to trust you?"

"Look, you paid, everybody got his slice, we'll get you home, okay? El Chusquero on the other hand." He sat back, crossed his arms, biceps popping. Not carpenter muscle. "Guy's a bug eater, know what I'm saying?"

Roque told himself not to fall for this but it was seductive. It didn't just sound like the truth, it was the truth, as far as he knew it. But what con wasn't salted with truth, how else would suckers buy into the bullshit? He was tired of being a sucker. "Why believe you, not these other guys? You were supposed to get us this far. Look what happened."

"Wanna go by boat? Fucking be my guest. But say they get you to Puerto Escondido—and that's a big if, okay? Like I said, you got the whole rest of Mexico to get through. They say they'll take you overland, sure, and hit you up every step of the way, one leg of the trip after the next. Pay or get left there, stranded, and hold on to your ass so it don't blow away. That what you want? You've already paid. Why pay twice, three times, four?"

"That would've been nice to hear before I had to beg twenty grand more off my cousin. So going by boat's no good. What's your plan?"

Beto opened his notebook to another page, another rough map. "Know what we call Chiapas? The Beast. More arrests there than anywhere. If it ain't the *federales*, it's the Mexican *la migra*. If it ain't them it's the paramilitaries, the vigilantes. And yeah, I'll admit it, the *maras* prey on the poor fuckers too. You pay for protection or you just fucking pay, all right? The way to get through Chiapas, honest to God, is you walk or take the bus. Both, actually." Again, using the pencil as pointer: "There are checkpoints along the way. Tapachula, Huixtla, Escuintla, Pijijiapan, Tonalá, Arriaga. You have to know where the roadblocks are or you'll still be on the bus when it gets stopped. No documents? Too bad. Get sent right back where you came from.

"Now, I'll take you overland to Arriaga. We'll get off the bus a little before the checkpoints, walk around, catch the next bus." He glanced up at Roque. "I take it you'll drive the car. Personally, I think that's a hassle. Perfectly safe on the bus, safer in my opinion, but you made your choice, Lonely got his piece of that too—I envy the cocksucker, man, the angles he plays—but fine, you got a car. You realize, they catch you moving *migrantes* in it, they can take it away? Deport you and take the car to boot, fucking American passport won't mean dick.

"Anyway, me and your uncle, the Arab and the girl, we meet up with you in Arriaga. I call my source, he tells me which routes are clear, which ones got roadblocks right now. We take the clear route, head through Oaxaca, which is the only real rough spot after Chiapas, then it's on to Mexico City where we'll take a rest. You'll need it, trust me.

"From there, things are a snap till you get to the U.S. border. Checkpoints are run by the army, you can buy your way through, fifty bucks, sixty tops, assuming they don't fall for the docs we've got for you." He sat back, closed the notebook, wrapped the rubber band around it and tucked the pencil into place. "That's something to keep in mind, okay? We got voter registration cards for you—not you," he said to Roque, "I mean the other three, you got a passport. Big mistake, phonying up a driver's license—how many Mexicans got a car? But they register to vote, get the shit knocked out of them by the local *jefe* they don't. That ID'll cure a lot of headaches, trust me. But you go ahead. You listen to what El Chusquero's man tells you. Let me know if it doesn't sound like crazy talk. It don't, you wanna do it, I wash my hands of you. But don't come back here thinking you can try us twice. This is business, not charity." He rose from his chair, puffing out his chest. "Sunset's a little before eight. I'll be back at nine. If you're here, we go. If not, good fucking luck, my friends."

TÍO FAUSTINO STOPPED ON THE NARROW STAIR AS HE AND ROQUE returned to the room. His face looked ashen. "You were very strong down there. You've changed, do you know that?"

Don't tell me, Roque thought. You're so proud. "I'm tired of being screwed with."

Tío Faustino smiled wearily. "A big part of learning you can handle yourself is knowing what it feels like to get your ass kicked."

It was too uncomfortable to fit all four of them in the room unless everybody stood, so they kept the door open and Roque sat in the hall as Tío Faustino recounted what Beto had told them. An angry fly caromed against the dingy corridor walls. The overhead light flickered. Samir unsurprisingly voted to stay with the *salvatruchos*. Lupe deferred to the group. Tío Faustino glanced over his shoulder at Roque with the same sad warmth he'd shown on the stair, at which point something crystallized.

Roque said:—*I'll agree to stay with Beto and the* salvatruchos *only if you, Samir, agree to let us work something out with El Recio in Agua Prieta. I'll buy Lupe's freedom somehow, stay behind myself, whatever it takes. But I'm not going to watch her get handed over.*

Tío ventured a quixotic smile. Samir leaned forward to say something but Lupe beat him to the opening.—*It's none of your business.*

—*I'm talking about my conscience. Whose business is it?*

—*This is unfair*, she said, *you can't—*

—*You have no idea how such things work*, Samir told Roque, *the kind of men—*

—*You're pushing your luck*, Roque said, *know that? Don't kid yourself, you could wind up stranded somewhere in the middle of Mexico, nothing but your thumb in the air and what's left of your luck in that bag of yours. Wouldn't kill you to try a little harder, be a team player.*

Samir's gaze sank into the hollows of his eyes.—*If that's how it is*, he said quietly, *but if this El Recio says no way, the girl stays behind, then what?*

—*It'll come down to money.*

—*Really? How can you be so—*

—*I'll deal with it then!* Roque's voice echoed down the bare hallway. Stupid, he thought, get it together.—*Now if we're going with Beto we need to get out of here. I don't see much to gain sticking around for Chepito if all we're going to do is say no.*

HE MADE A SHOW OF LEAVING THE OLD GUITAR IN THE LOBBY, AS though to guarantee their return, then they ambled out as a group to the fair. Crowds still swarmed the narrow streets, providing cover as the four of them drifted farther away from the posada. Tiny Mayan women marched with woven baskets atop their heads, men carried drowsy children draped across their shoulders, the rest of the throng just bobbed and swayed in the darkening twilight. Roque glanced behind every few seconds, to see who might be following, but it was impossible to tell.

They walked in aimless circles for half an hour just in case, then headed for the *feria*'s central arcade, comprised of long low tents, where concessions served food. They ordered heaping paper plates of grilled chicken, fried yucca, black beans, papaya slices for dessert, deciding to wait until nine o'clock as innocently as possible, so if Chepito happened to find them they could say convincingly they'd simply wandered out for dinner, lost track of time.

Shortly after eight, fireworks erupted over the still-crowded river, the stuttered explosions deafening. Roque took the show as cue to venture back to the posada but before he did he sat down next to Samir, who was watching a mother several tables over feed her crippled boy.

Leaning in to whisper, Roque said, "Happy told me you saved his life. He said I could rely on you. I haven't found that to be true, to be honest." Samir turned his gaze from the mother and son, his eyes hypnotic in their vacancy. "You've been a major pain in the ass as far as I'm concerned. Did Happy get it wrong?" Overhead a rocket shrieked with a quivering tail of smoke into the pitch-black sky, paused for a breath, then detonated like a thunderclap in a green-and-white starburst. The crowd gasped and cheered and sighed. Roque got up to leave. "Look after my uncle. Take care of the girl. Live up to what Happy said about you."

He worked his way back through the dwindling crowd to the posada and chose a dark spot between two vendor stalls to settle in and wait for Beto. The working girls were still gathered out front, watching the last of the fireworks. Some of the roughnecks from earlier came and went as well, refreshed with beer. A quarter before nine, Chepito and his sidekick showed up, materializing from the stragglers still wandering about. The two men vanished inside—a minute passed, then two, then five. Chepito and the other man returned to the porch, the latter carrying the cheap guitar now, holding it by the neck like a club. They questioned the hookers, one of whom pointed the way Roque and the others had taken earlier, toward the river, not the fair. Good, Roque thought, go.

A hand clamped down on his shoulder.

He shot to his feet, spun around, knocked the hand away.

"Easy, *cabrón*."

Roque's skin was slick with sweat. "I didn't know who you were."

"I get that." Beto leaned out into the street, looking each direction. "I already rounded up your uncle and the other two."

"How did you know where to find them?"

"You keep asking me that."

Roque wiped his face. "We've decided to go with you, not El Chusquero."

"Yeah. That's been explained already." Beto reached into his jeans, withdrew a box of Chiclets, shook two pieces into his palm, sharing one. "Look, I'll get your uncle and the other two across the river, we'll pick up a bus on the other side. You should go get your car before those two *huecos* looking for you figure that's where you gotta end up."

A fight broke out in the middle of the street, down the way, near the posada. The hookers started cheering, wading into the fray, bawling out the names of the adversaries: Chepe, Zumbo.

"Get to the bridge," Beto said. "Tell the border agent you're heading for Puerto Vallarta, Acapulco, someplace on the coast. Follow the highway all the way to Arriaga. Go to the railway station. There's a hotel across the street. Ask for Victor. He knows you're coming."

ROQUE GOT HIS BEARINGS AND FOUND HIS WAY BACK TO WHERE HE'D parked the Corolla. The lot was marked by Christmas lights draped between poles on either side of the entrance. Pausing in an alley across the street, he waited a moment, making sure only the old man and his grandsons were there, not Chepito, not his buddy, not someone else. He dug into his pocket, pulled out a hundred-quetzal note, then another—a little over twenty-five dollars total—checking them close in the dark to be sure of their denomination, wishing he could spare more. He'd already paid the parking fee up front when he'd arrived; this was for discretion. He crossed the street, dodging a weepy drunk, then two women dragging a handcart, and approached the grandfather who was sitting in a white plastic chair, fanning himself with his hat, his youngest grandson at his feet.

"*Hola, viejo.*" Roque folded the money into the old man's hand. "*Gracias por todo.*"

Hurrying toward the car beneath the ancient ceiba, he tried to reconnoiter the area without seeming too obvious, swatting away mosquitoes with one hand as he walked, digging out his keys with the other. He could feel the old man's eyes on his back as he opened the car door, dropped behind the wheel. The engine turned over—thank God, he thought, having feared they might have taken the distributor cap—and he put the transmission in gear, flipped on the headlights, steered his way out of the lot and into the street.

Someone started pounding on the car door with a meaty fist—Chepito's sidekick, still carrying the beat-up guitar in his other hand. He was grabbing for the handle, trying to open the door. Roque elbowed the plunger down, throwing the lock, and accelerated.

The crowds were all but gone, he could gain some actual speed, but a pair of tottering *vagabundos*, holding each other up, blocked the way twenty feet ahead. Roque blared the horn, veering to pass them on the right, hoping to squeeze between them and the sidewalk. The henchling, running alongside, cursed and kept pounding on the car window, then lifted the guitar over his head like an ax and swung it down hard, smashing it against the roof on his second try. The instrument shattered into kindling with a jangled chord, while the two drunks half lurched, half jigged out of the way, still clasping each other. Roque sped on, braking only for the corner, picking up speed again as he laid on the horn, hammering at it with his fist while he dodged the night's last revelers frozen in the tunnel of his headlights, stony Mayan faces materializing then vanishing in the corner of his eye as he prayed he didn't hit anyone, didn't harm anyone, didn't have to stop as he headed as best he could tell for the bridge into Mexico.

TWENTY-EIGHT

SHEER LUCK THE CLEANING LADY SHOWED UP TODAY, HAPPY thought, sitting in the passenger seat of the plain white van they'd borrowed from Vasco—Puchi behind the wheel, Chato in the back—the better to blend in here, parked down the block from the house.

Happy's DMV connection had come through with the plate trace: Charles T. Snell, an address in Crockett, half a mile up the hill from the sugar refinery. The house was the largest on the block but like most of the others along the street it looked a little shabby, stucco and brick with flaking trim, chimney mortar gapped in places, mismatched shingles from a roof patch. A general sense the heyday was over, an old company town gone bust.

They were there to scout the place out, reconnoiter, get some ideas about ways in, ways out. In the middle of that, the cleaning lady shows up. What else could she be but a gift?

She was Latina of course, who else cleaned houses in California anymore? He had to hope that would make the whole thing easier. They'd talk *la raza*, they'd talk *la familia*. They'd talk mutual interests, like making sure no one got hurt.

She'd been inside two hours and was finally done. Walking out to her car, an ancient Mazda, she dug her keys out of her purse, dropped them on the cracked pavement, scooped them up, opened the door. The engine turned over with a bark of smoke and the car shuddered away from the curb. Happy lifted his hand, signaling for Puchi to wait until she reached the stop sign.

"Easy," he said. "She drives like an *abuela*." A grandma.

He wished Roque would call, days since he'd heard anything. Buy a damn disposable phone, he thought, but how could he say that till the kid got one? It was like a bad joke. And Lattimore, cranking up the heat. They needed to be able to track Samir, he said, they still weren't sure his story checked out. "I tend to get tense when the radar goes blank. I'm not alone." Nobody knew where they were. The mighty eyes and ears of Uncle Sam, they'd gone blind, gone deaf. And all my wannabe superstar cousin had to do is lose his fucking cell.

They figured the cleaning lady was heading for the freeway and gave her space, then closed in once she neared the on-ramp, dropping back again once they knew her direction, trying to keep another car between them—not easy, given what a poke she was—then pulling close again as she took the El Sobrante exit. From there she drove east, weaving her way among the tightly curving streets through low hills. They lost her at one turn, caught her down the block, stopped, backed up, followed, until she parked finally outside a clapboard bungalow with a sprawling honeysuckle out front.

She got out of her car. Happy told Puchi to slow to a stop beside her.

"*Buenas, señora*," he said, an engaging smile, getting out as Chato opened the van's sliding door.

She was plain, matronly, dimpled cheeks, copper-colored ponytail. She froze in panic as Happy stepped close, grabbed her arm hard at the elbow, dragged her toward the van.

—Make a sound and I'll kill you right here.

He'd never said such a thing before. It scared him a little, hearing how like him it sounded.

Chato popped out and the two of them bundled her into the van. Happy glanced up and down the block, wondering if they'd been spotted, while Chato scrambled in behind the woman, boxing her in while he rammed the sliding door closed. Happy jumped up into the passenger seat and slammed the door shut, barking at Puchi, "Go!"

As the van sped away Happy turned around, looking the woman square in the eye, trying to muster inside him whatever it would take—menace, sympathy, a little of both—to get her to listen, get her to obey. She sat on the floor in a lump of furniture quilting, clutching her purse to her midriff, eyes like balloons. Happy reached out, took the handbag from her, needing only two gentle tugs to get her to give it up. Checking inside, he found her wallet, flipped it open, dug out her driver's license: Lourdes Trujillo, forty-one years old. He found pictures too, a pair of girls, one twelve or so, homely like her mother, the other closer to eighteen. No baby fat this one, lipstick and eyeliner, almost pretty.

"We don't want to harm you," he said, switching to English now. She'd know it, the only question was how well and the answer was important. "But we will if you don't help us. We'll hurt you, hurt your daughters. Don't make us do that."

Her eyes welled up. "I am nobody," she said, voice whispery with fear. "Help you—how? You see my car, my house. I buy food, I pay rent, there's no money left." She clenched her hands together, pointing them at Happy. "Please, whoever you are . . ."

Chato, kneeling beside her, dug into his pocket, took out a folding knife and flicked it open. Pressing the blade to her thigh, he began stroking it back and forth, teasing it closer to her crotch with each pass. "Do what he tells you, *abuela*, it'll be okay. I give you my turd of honor."

Happy, continuing his search of the purse, shoveled past her keys then stopped. The car, he thought. It would be sitting there when her daughters came home from school, their mother nowhere to be found. The girls would call the police, the cops would back-walk her day, they'd ask the contractor or his family about her, a tip-off that something was wrong.

"Go back to the house," he said.

"I'm on it." Puchi seemed to be trying to get his bearings back to the freeway.

"No. *Her* house." Happy nodded toward Lourdes. "We can't leave her car back there." He ignored Puchi's stare and took out the wad of keys—it had a plastic piglet for a bob—and tossed them into Chato's lap, thinking: Turd of honor. What the hell was *that* about? "Put the knife away, she gets you're serious. Take her car, follow us out."

Chato's eyes tightened but then Puchi hit the brakes and the van lurched to a stop. They were back at Lourdes's house.

"Go on," Happy said, gentler now.

Chato sulked his way out of the van, Lourdes staring at his back as the door slid shut, then Happy snapped his fingers to get her attention. "I apologize," he said. "I mean it, we don't want to harm you. We need you. I'll explain as we drive."

GODO AND EFRAIM SPENT THE MORNING ALONE INSIDE THE ABANDONED farmhouse, breaking down the weapons, cleaning them, loading the magazines, every moment or so blowing into their hands for warmth. There was no electricity, no heat. Even the septic was fucked up, so they went out behind the barn to piss and, once apiece, take a windy dump. Now Efraim was gone, off to grab lunch for the crew—Happy and Puchi and Chato were due soon—while Godo stayed behind to wrap up.

There was a time when the slow taking apart and piecing back together, the wiping and swabbing and brushing, the nutty smell of the oil, would have soothed him. All that crap about don't get talked into anything, he thought. Now Happy says it has to get done, not just done, done like tomorrow.

He knew about the ransom, knew Vasco stepped up to pay it and that gave him rights, the sly fuck. But he also felt guilty, wondering what might have been if he'd been the one down there, not Roque. Maybe he'd have gotten them out of whatever spot they'd blundered into. But that was fantasy. You're damaged, he told himself. The damaged get left behind.

He supposed he should count himself lucky he was able to chip in at all. He was the weapon wizard, the gun guru, maybe he should take pride in that. For a while there he'd felt reasonably in control, a lid on the monster, even the nightmares settled down some. Then came the run-in with Chuck. That's when the hinges started working loose again.

Strange, him being the target of this thing. Godo found some poetry in that. Serves him right, let him suffer, suffer for all the grief his kind caused, all the mayhem, all the blood. Suffer for Gunny Benedict. Because as the Chevy Blazer with the tinted windows bulled ahead of the rattletrap Cressida with its single headlight and the *haji* family huddled inside, Godo stepping forward, blocking the Blazer's path, demanding docs, needing to check them against the names on his BOLO list, he'd spotted in the back, passenger side, one of the armed men, a face increasingly whole in his memory—this guy, this contractor, this Chuck—just as the searing white flash switched off the world and the explosion ripped it to shreds.

So much for poetry, he thought, rising to his feet, the scent of the gun oil in his nostrils and the slickness on his hands. Looking out the window, he watched a sudden burst of wind thrash the walnut trees and for a second heard the chugging rotors of the little bird chopper hovering over the blast site amid the screams of the wounded, his included, felt in his mouth the grating dust from the rotor wash. Wiping his numb fingers with a rag, he thought: I can't function like this, I'll fuck this thing up and that's not an option. Using his sleeve he mopped the sweat off his face—check it out, he thought, I'm sweating and it's maybe fifty degrees, tops—then he bent down to the final M16, pushed the takedown pins into position, refitted the handguards into place, slammed home the magazine.

The three sixteens would go to Puchi, Efraim and Happy;

Godo would use the Kalashnikov. Chato would get the Mossberg.

As he was bagging the brushes and rags and barrel rods he heard not Efraim's pickup but another vehicle he didn't recognize thunder up the drive, churning gravel. He edged toward the front window, peeking out at the white van pulling to a stop. Puchi sat behind the wheel, Happy beside him. As he stood there looking out, a flaring ghost of white light rippled across the backs of his eyes; his mouth went dry and he felt certain he wasn't just imagining it, the taste of dust.

Funny, he thought, how you hear people say: My body has a mind of its own. What am I supposed to do, he wondered, when it's my mind that has a mind of its own?

He wasn't prepared for the woman. Happy dragged her forward from the van, not roughly but not kindly, either.

"This is Lourdes," he said once they were all inside. "She's decided to help us out."

HAPPY PLOPPED DOWN WITH HER ON THE FLOOR IN ONE OF THE smaller rooms. He'd explained to her during the drive why she was so important, speaking to her in English, making her use it with him, practicing their back and forth, figuring if they reverted to Spanish during the robbery the family would suspect she was involved all along. "There's no stopping what's going to happen, Lourdes, one way or another, we're going to do what we need to do. But you can change *how* it happens. Without you, people get hurt." It had taken awhile, convincing her there was no escape, but the drive was long and he'd ultimately worn her down. There would be no way to beg or wish or talk her way out of it, except to tell him what he wanted.

Strange, he thought, how things were lining up. There was reason to breathe easy. Sure, the thing was crazy but you heard stories all the time, snitches working both sides. And the government always looked the other way. They were greedy, like everybody else. They wanted what they wanted, wanted it big, wanted it yesterday.

When it came time to take the stand, he'd tell the jury: I had to do it, they gave me no choice. It was all Vasco's idea. Ladies and gentlemen, the only way to get my father back to the States was to go along with the plan, this stupid home invasion. My father was kidnapped, we needed the ransom, the government wouldn't front the money. What was I supposed to do? But I was afraid that, if I told Mr. Lattimore what I was doing, the government would pull the plug, my father and cousin would get stranded. My father, he's not a young man, he could die down there just waiting, while I'm scrambling around trying to scratch up the money all legit. It was a lot of money, more than my family could put together. And this was the only way to keep the case on track. We don't bring my father and Samir to the States, the thing falls apart. I was doing the prosecution a favor.

I did it for my family. I did it for the government. I did it for this country I love so much.

Remember, he thought, you won't be the one on trial. It will all work out, so long as nobody gets hurt.

Efraim returned with *tortas* for lunch and Happy sent him right back out for paper and pens. They shared a sandwich and a soda, he and Lourdes, while the others ate in another room. The intimacy was intentional on his part and apparently welcome on hers, she seemed to hearten a little. Her nibbles turned to bites, she settled into her body.

He asked about her life and in a voice that gradually lost some of its fearful whisper she explained she was from Santa Clara del Cobre in Michoacán, a village known for its copper artisans. Many in her family were in the trade but she had no such skill and so, when she was twenty-one, she traveled north to work. She'd been in California twenty years, wanted to improve her English but could never get to adult school regularly. Both her daughters were born here, their father left five years ago for another woman. He sent money sometimes. "He a weak man, not a bad man," she said. "Señor Snell—he is weak *and* bad."

Happy sensed it, the turn. Don't overplay it, he thought. "How you mean?"

She corkscrewed her hips, trying to get comfortable. "This family I work for them three years now maybe. But him I talk no more five, six times, okay? He away at work when I there. But each time him, me talk, he treat me like I am stupid. Treat his wife, Veronica, like that too. Yell at her like she is a child. To myself, I think, how lucky for her if he die in Iraq. But he come back. And he is worse. Veronica, she cry sometimes, talk to me, tell me his business. I not supposed to see them, the guns—they all in the basement, I don't go there—but she show me. She is very strange, Veronica, very lonely. She drink." She picked at a bit of lettuce caught in her teeth. "She crazy a little too, I think."

Happy stopped chewing. "Crazy dangerous?"

"No." Her copper-colored ponytail wagged back and forth. "Crazy scared."

He took a sip of soda, passed the bottle to her. The house felt as cold as a cave. "You understand, Lourdes, those guns, the ones in the basement, it's all against the law."

She nodded timidly, took a sip, handed the bottle back.

"He won't complain to the police. He knows he'll have to lie about what we came for, about what we take. He won't risk that. Better to lose the money, the guns, than risk that. They find out what he does, who he sells to, the taxes he doesn't pay? He goes to prison."

Her eyes drilled his face. "He not need the police, a man like that. He come for me, my daughters. He come alone."

"When we tie up the family, Lourdes, we'll tie you up too, make it look—"

"He have this hate, this thing inside him—"

"You'll have to tell him you don't know nothing. You'll have to convince him." A conspiratorial wink. "Don't tell me you haven't lied before."

"He will come, hurt me. Hurt my girls."

"You're going to have to be an actress, Lourdes." He felt a surge of impatience, fueled by guilt, pitying her, resenting her for it. "There's no other way, I'm sorry."

Out in the front room, a sudden spate of goofy laughter: Puchi, Chato. Not Godo.

"Why you do this?" Her hand drifted across the space to touch his hand. Her fingers were ice-cold. "You are different, not like them, out there, those *pellejos*, those *chusmas*." Lowlifes. "I can tell you have family, you love somebody, somebody love you—"

One of those *chusmas* is my cousin, he thought of telling her, though he imagined Godo's face had made an impression that wouldn't get undone with words. Then the front door opened and closed—Efraim, back from the store. Happy pulled his hand from under hers. "You're right, I have family. You wonder why I'm doing this? For them."

Efraim appeared in the doorway but Happy realized something else needed saying. He asked for just another moment. Efraim, clutching the bag with Happy's paper and pens inside, glanced curiously at the woman as though trying to determine if she was still their prisoner or something else now, then set the bag on the floor and shuffled down the hall, joining the others just as another spurt of idiot laughter erupted.

Happy turned back to Lourdes. "Once this is done, Snell won't harm you or your daughters. You have my word."

OVER THE NEXT TWO HOURS HE HAD HER DRAW OUT THE FLOOR PLAN for the house, upstairs, ground floor, basement. During the day, Snell worked as a claims adjuster out in the east county, an hour's drive away most days, given traffic. Lourdes had only seen him at the house once since he'd come back from Iraq. She didn't know what time he got home in the evening, didn't know where any guns might be other than that one locked room in the cellar. She'd never come across any in the closets, under the bed; there were no display cases upstairs. Snell had a safe down in the basement as well but Veronica, the one time she'd shown the place to Lourdes, had admitted she didn't know the combination.

The couple had two children, but they'd be at school till four or so—a boy of thirteen named Samuel, a girl of nine named Samantha.

"Two Sams." It was Godo. They were all in the room together now, watching her chart out the house. "Weird."

"It is a strange family," Lourdes replied.

TWENTY-NINE

HAPPY TOLD LOURDES TO CALL HER DAUGHTERS AND SAY THAT one of her housecleaning clients had been in a bad wreck. The woman was in the hospital, she'd be there overnight; the husband was away, couldn't get a flight back till tomorrow. The family needed Lourdes to stay with thc kids. "They pay me," Lourdes assured her oldest, whose name was Carla, "a lot." Then the younger daughter, Angelica, got on the phone and Happy thought it would never end, back and forth: a kitten, the dentist, homework, a boy named Terrell. Finally he made a cutting gesture to his throat and Lourdes told her daughter she had to go.

"Your daughter's needy," Happy said as she flipped closed her cell.

Lourdes sank into herself. "She's at that age."

It was decided she'd stay at the farmhouse, with Happy and Efraim trading shifts watching her. Efraim went off to fetch blankets and a kerosene lamp and one more meal. They'd do the takeover tomorrow, show up in the van, wearing coveralls from Vasco's moving operation, get inside the house in the morning, tie up the wife and Lourdes, raid the secret room, then wait for first the kids to come home, then Snell, force him to open the safe. If they were patient, they'd be fine. Once Efraim was back, they ran through everybody's role, rehearsing as best they could as it grew dark and even colder in the empty farmhouse: Chato watching the front door; Puchi clearing the ground-floor rooms then guarding the back; Godo and Efraim upstairs to clear the bedrooms; Happy in the living room with Lourdes, a pistol to her head.

As they practiced their run-throughs, Godo seemed distracted, one minute almost incandescent in his focus, the next wrapped inside himself so tight he looked like he might lock up in a kind of trance. The problem wasn't physical—the infection in his leg had settled down, he moved okay, looked strong. Happy drew him aside as he was doing a final weapon check, gestured toward the door. "Outside for a minute?"

The night was damp, a rustling roar from the walnut trees whipping around in the wind. The clouds were plump in the moonless sky. Chafing their arms against the cold, they tested their way along the gravel to where the van and pickup were parked, out of earshot from the house.

Happy lit up a smoke, needing two matches in the wind. He took one long drag, then said, "What's wrong?"

Godo was still rubbing his arms. "Who says anything's wrong?"

"Don't fuck with me, not now. This is too important."

"I know how important it is."

"Then tell me the truth. What's eating you?"

Godo's breathing became slightly labored, then he coughed. "Hard to talk about."

"That's why it's important to talk about it."

"Who are you now—Dr. Happy?"

"This about Iraq?"

"What isn't? Fuck you, by the way."

"Tell me about it."

"I don't—"

"I told you my story. You think I was proud? I felt like a total chickenshit. But something's got you by the nuts, it's got some power over you. Tell me about it. It'll lose some of that power, I promise."

A smile crept across Godo's pitted face. "Where'd you learn that—Oprah?"

"Listen to me. You're the one I gotta lean on, Godo. You're the one who gets it. I can't have you going in and out. Every second, you gotta be there."

"I know what I gotta do."

"It ain't a question of what you know. It's a question of what's gonna get in the way at exactly the wrong time if you don't wrestle it to the fucking ground. Now talk to me about it."

HIS UNIT WAS NEARING THE END OF THEIR SHIFT ON FALLUJAH'S WESTern outskirts, a flash checkpoint, no concertina wire, no sandbags, no glow sticks, just the Humvee with the engine running for the sake of the headlights, the diesel fumes increasingly noxious as the hours passed. Dawn smeared a thickening mustard haze across the east while overhead the night sky softened from black to a gritty shade of brown. The sand beneath their feet crunched with every step.

The usual shabby low-slung houses bordered the road, while beyond them, emerging in murky silhouette, were palm and eucalyptus trees, elephant grass, a distant camel, a water buffalo. Soon the day's first prayers would blast by loudspeaker, courtesy of the local muezzin, from the nearest minaret, same thing all across the city, mosques that during the battle served as secret armories, pillboxes, sniper hides.

It was always a toss-up, which would start first, the morning prayers or the daybreak dog barking. Everybody'd come to hate the dogs, but shooting them for sport was a no go—the locals saw it as cruelty, not pest control—so Godo held his fire as he caught sight of a slinking form maybe twenty yards behind the Hummer, sniffing its way forward, a skeleton with a tail and a nose. The wind was brisk, the dust thick, the cold piercing; all this time in-country, he still hadn't adjusted to the sixty-degree temperature swings on any given day.

Among themselves, the marines sometimes joked that they'd made Fallujah the safest city in Iraq—by reducing it to a pile of rocks. On the plus side, there were fewer bats. As for the ruin, it wasn't like they'd had much choice, given the way the mujahideen had prepped the battle space, the way they'd chosen to fight. Now, with the elections over, the new year in full swing, civilians were testing their way back into the city to sort through the wreckage and recover what remained of their lives.

Military-age males—MAMs, they got called, another joke—were fingerprinted, given retina scans, issued special ID cards they had to display whenever confronted. Few vehicles were allowed inside the city limits and the ones that were got tossed inside out, nothing left to chance. It was drudgery, it was tense, it was the fucking pits. It was the shores of goddamn Tripoli.

The problem was Ramadi. Thirty miles west, it hadn't suffered the holocaust. A loose-knit bloc of insurgent gangs ruled the souk, the mosques, the winding alleyways where things got bartered for a favor down the line or sold outright for cash. Route 10, the open road between the cities, was the biggest but by no means only ratline connecting the two locales. Every way in and out of the city had to be tamped down tight.

Meanwhile, the gradual influx of redevelopment money had brought a certain breed of carpetbagger to Al Anbar, negotiating deals on landfills and power plants and water-treatment facilities, few of which seemed to be getting built. The men with the bags of money and the big ideas had to get around, though, and they did, with their well-paid condottieri, dressed in cargo pants and flak jackets and Oakley shades, armed to the tits and charging around the country in their SUVs at ninety miles an hour, slowing for no one, running down dogs and sheep, old men and kids. Accidental deaths alone had caused untold grief for the marines. Intelligence dried up, resistance to the simplest request became routine, defying orders became a badge of honor, especially for MAMs.

Then a team of contractors with an outfit named Harmon Stern Associates gunned down two Sunni men repairing their pickup on the road between Ramadi and Fallujah. Iraqis near the scene said the two men shot down did nothing. Tribal leaders and imams pressed for a face-to-face with the colonel, they wanted justice. They were assured the men responsible would be apprehended but promised nothing more. A BOLO—be on the lookout—went out with the names of the contractors. Every unit throwing down a checkpoint knew what to do if the men showed up on their watch.

Chavous manned the up gun on the Hummer. Godo and Benedict and Pimentel and the new guy, Bobby Salgado—Mobley's replacement, a transfer from the Three Five—did the hassle work on the ground.

Salgado hadn't been welcomed much, not like it was anyone's fault. The loss of Mobley still pissed everybody off but it wasn't just that. You knew the next guy could get lit the same way, so why bond? The buddy-up camaraderie of the invasion and the first flush of battle got countermanded by death. Goodbye only got harder if you bothered too much over hello, so everybody just gave a nod, figured the new guy knew his job. If not, he'd get told.

Turned out Salgado—a true *vato loco*, Sycamore Street Midnighter from Huntington Beach—had some piss up his spine. He hadn't enjoyed the color-blind unit cohesion Godo had so far. His previous platoon had included two die-hard haters and that's all they needed, the one to back the other up when launching off on some phobic jag of anti-Latino bullshit. They were just as outrageous to the blacks but that wasn't Salgado's problem. He was still hot over the constant niggling wetback pepper-belly nacho-nigger bullshit. He told Godo not to be stupid.

"These cats ain't your friends," he said one night over a cold MRE. "Don't get your *cholo* ass in a bind and forget that."

Godo pretended to give that deep thought. He wasn't sure what to make of Salgado. Kind of guy, he thought, who might pitch himself off a roof, convinced all he wanted was a better view. "Mobley fought his black ass off for me, I watched him die. Chavous is a fucking redneck but he never failed me once. Ditto Pimentel, who's crazy but that comes in handy sometimes. And I'd lay down my life for Gunny Benedict."

Salgado bit open a gravy packet. "You're a fool you think it's gonna stay that way."

"Maybe you should wait, give this team its due."

Salgado licked a smear of brown gunk off his finger. "Say you're right, *cabrón*. Don't change the fact they be looking to deport your whole fucking family before you get home."

"Too late." Godo chuckled acidly. "They already snatched my cousin." It's the reason I'm here, he thought, but why share that?

Salgado fired up that crazed stare he was known for, like his focus was the only thing keeping the world from coming unglued. "Then you know. You fucking know. What you do over here don't translate to shit. For real, man, ain't no fucking brown heroes. You go home in a box they'll kick the damn thing over into Mexico for burial."

"I'm not Mexican."

"You know what I'm saying."

It was the two of them manning the forward positions that morning at the checkpoint, Gunny Benedict staggered behind. Pimentel had their six. They stopped every vehicle and demanded access cards and weapon permits, especially the bongo trucks—cutaway VW vans, a favorite of the so-called desert foxes, generally friendly paramilitaries who wore chocolate chip cammies, flak vests, balaclavas. The unit's BOLO list included not just the names of the Harmon Stern contractors but several dozen suspected insurgents, any of whom, if encountered at the checkpoint, were to get gagged and bagged and delivered to RCT-1 HQ.

The night had been relatively quiet, though, only a couple cases of misunderstanding, taken care of when Godo or Salgado, having their shout-and-show ignored, moved to shoot: a warning round at the deck each time, one follow-up bullet to the grill of a Mercedes sedan that refused to slow down. The driver was an old man, confused—he jabbered and wept when they dragged him out of the car, threw him down in the dust for a search. The rest of the night they threw back Rip Its and tamped foot to foot, slapping their arms and bodies trying to stay warm, chipping away at the silence between them with practice of the little Arabic they knew: *O-guf! Tera armeek* for "Stop! Or I'll shoot"; *Interesiada* for "Get out of the car"; *Urfai edik* for "Put your hands up"; *Inshallah* for "Allah be willing"; and their personal nonoperational favorites: *kus* ("pussy"), *zip* ("penis"), *theiz* ("ass").

Traffic started picking up about 0500 and got increasingly jammed as dawn leached across the sky. The family in the Cressida with the one working headlight reached the head of the line and Salgado stepped forward, asking the driver for documents. Godo eyed the rest of the queue, five vehicles deep, his weapon in condition one: a chambered round, bolt forward, ejection-port cover closed, safety on. He was ready to thumb down the safety at the merest hint of trouble and was in a bad mood regardless, the days on end without washing during the siege having created a case of cancer-level crotch rot, lingering for weeks now. He'd scratched himself bloody in his sleep, only making things worse, so now he was obsessively rousting himself awake at night, lurching up in his bedroll if he was lucky enough to drift off at all. He hadn't slept more than twenty minutes at a stretch since he couldn't remember when and in the semi-hallucinatory edginess that had come to characterize his state of mind, he often found himself revisiting Mobley's death, the house they turned to smoke and ruin afterward. It wasn't the fiery itch from his balls to his ass crack or the war in general or the idiot command or the ungrateful locals or even the pitiless creeps they called the enemy that kept Godo so pissed off lately. It wasn't even the nagging dead or the skeletal dogs they seemed to inhabit. It was the fact that, after weeks of shabby sleep, he couldn't feel the center of himself anymore. He had this daydream in which he was a kite that someone had let go of, God maybe, this little jet of bright paper and balsa wood bucking around in a cold wind, just a matter of time before it came crashing down.

Back in the here and now, though, there was nothing especially screwy to get worked up about. The slender Iraqi in the coin-gray suit behind the wheel of the Cressida was merely slow, not suspicious, fumbling for his documents with his wife beside him, two kids in the back.

It was that lack of zip, though, that upset the Chevy Blazer right behind. The driver started hammering his horn, five blasts, ten—it only upset the slowpoke father more, his wife in her *hijāb* headscarf craning around to squint into the headlight glare. Then the Blazer surged up and out, jockeying forward to squeeze past the Cressida, nudging the bumper and flattening Salgado against the driver-side door.

Godo charged into the SUV's path and shouldered his sixteen. Chavous fired off an air burst from the Humvee's .50cal, tracers flaring into the ash-brown sky in a hypnotic arc, landing somewhere near the camel. Godo called out, "Whoa the fuck, asshole," and the Blazer finally lurched to a stop, kicking up a shower of pebbled dust. Turning his face away, he saw the same emaciated dog, closer now, trembling beside the Hummer's rear wheel. He resisted an impulse to reach down to his crotch and dig at his itch, at the same time feeling something unclick along his spine, a shimmer of pent-up rage shooting through him and he had to check the safety on his weapon, fearing he might fire out of pure gall. He hacked up an egg-size clot of crusty air, spat, checked again to be sure Chavous had him covered, then eased toward the Blazer's driver-side door, shouting, "The fuck you thinking, shit dick?"

The driver cranked down his window: older cat, maybe fifty, wire-gray hair, probably police back home, maybe a vet, eyes a bloodshot brown, mustache and sideburns straight out of *Death Wish*. "Got a convoy out at Akashat, they're a squad short. Thing's gotta move in an hour. Let us through."

"Akashat? You're heading the wrong way."

"We got another man to pick up. Come on. Serious. We got exactly no time to waste."

Oh boo the fuck hoo, Godo thought, fighting a sudden twitch in his eye. Somewhere in the distance a chopper rotored over the city, invisible in the swirling dust and russet sky. Behind him the dog made a thin mewling sound. "Back the fuck up to where you were or you'll spend the whole damn day here."

Salgado, jacked up from almost getting run over, blistered the Cressida's driver with obscenities, like it was all his fault.

The Blazer's wheelman said to Godo, "Look—"

"You jumped the goddamn line."

"You hear me? There's a convoy, ready to move—"

"Access cards and permits." Godo shot out his hand, glancing past the driver at the others. The guy in the passenger seat looked half in the bag, sunglasses staring straight ahead, weapon clenched between his knees. Behind him sat the rest of the team, three men abreast in the backseat, equally hungover from the general slump and cast of their eyes, every one of them dressed in the same contractor drag, like there was a store out there somewhere in the desert where they all got outfitted.

Gunny Benedict duck-walked forward to calm Salgado down and provide a forward presence. A gust of keening wind sugared everything in grit.

"Listen." The Blazer driver leaned forward, like it was the distance between them causing the trouble. "Time window's closing here."

In a moment of insomniac, rage-laced weirdness, Godo pictured the man growing a snout. "You with Harmon Stern?"

The driver's jaw tightened. The bloodshot eyes turned hard. "What's your problem?"

Good as a yes, Godo thought. "Access cards and permits."

"Look. You know who we are."

"Fuck I do. Access—"

"We're on the same side, damn it."

Godo glanced away, like the guy wasn't worth eye contact, spotting that same dog edging ever closer, nosing the ground for garbage, then he coughed up another wad of dust-choked phlegm. For a second he thought he saw a flurry of black-winged bats veering in crazy arcs in the dawn-lit east. He blinked—nothing there. The dog, though, was real, he felt pretty sure of that. "Cards and weapon permits, every man in the vehicle. Now."

"You're being an asshole."

Godo couldn't help himself, he laughed. "Coming from you?"

Salgado had the Cressida driver out of the car now, opening his trunk. Gunny Benedict spotted a pedestrian trekking forward from the hazy darkness, past the other vehicles in the queue, a strangely tall and awkward woman in a black *abaya*, her head and face wrapped in a white *niqaab*, only her eyes uncovered.

The Blazer driver, trying to regroup, ventured a buddy-up smile. "Okay, you win. But there's no need for this hassle, okay?" He nodded toward the front bumper. "How about you write down the plate number, we'll be outta your hair."

It was galling, the crap they thought you'd swallow. "How about you shit backwards on this attitude you got and do like I told you." The aggression was camouflage, he was trembling from adrenalin. Above and beyond the contractor's bullshit there was something about the walk-up bothering him, putting him on edge—plus the wastrel dog. For just a second he caught

Gunny Benedict's dusty blue eyes as he glanced over his shoulder, first at Salgado, then Godo, checking his men, taking care.

Do your job, Godo thought, another over-the-shoulder glance at Chavous then turning back to the Blazer. "My man there on the .50cal? He'll send a few live ones through your windshield you try to move, so you're going no place till you comply—we clear? Now cards and permits, I'm not asking again."

The driver cocked his head around, tracking Gunny Benedict advancing toward the odd-looking woman, ordering her to stop. Godo felt it stronger now, still not knowing why. His whole body felt like an antenna for the willies. He thought of shouting something but didn't want to come off half-cocked. Gunny knew his business.

The driver said, "That your team leader there?"

Godo snapped back. "You don't get to choose who you deal with, asshole."

The guy laughed, slapped the arm of the hunched man beside him. Back to Godo: "Touch a nerve there, did I, Poncho? Your sergeant know what a wound-up little girl you are?"

"What my sergeant knows, Elmer, is I need to see your fucking access cards and—" In the corner of his eye, Godo saw the gawky woman slip past Benedict, reaching inside the black *abaya* one-handed. The slinking dog began to bark.

"Know what?" The driver jammed the Blazer in gear. "I'm calling your bluff, hotshot."

At the sound of the engaged transmission Godo snapped. "That's it, faggot. Out of the fucking vehicle." He pulled open the Blazer's door with the dog's barking growing louder, fiercer, just as a man's pitched cry broke from behind the woman's veil: "*Inshallah!*"

Two weeks later, the doctors in Landstuhl would tell him that simple thing—yanking back the door—probably saved his life. They'd also tell him that Gunnery Sergeant Raymond Benedict, among several others, marines and civilians both, didn't make it. It was up to Godo to imagine the details. And he'd been doing that, while pretty much trying not to, ever since.

GODO COULDN'T SAY IT WAS RELIEF HE FELT, OR IF IT WAS, RELIEF AT what exactly. Exorcising the demon, maybe, whatever the hell that meant. Relief he'd gotten through the story without sniveling like a bitch. He'd never said any of that out loud before, not that he could remember and he doubted he'd forget such a thing. Maybe in the ward at Landstuhl, when the morphine made him daffy. In the cold moonlight Happy's face looked a little less grimly calculating, a little more accepting. Godo tried to tell himself that wasn't pity. He wouldn't take pity, not from Happy, not from anybody.

"You blame yourself."

Godo shivered. "Minute I felt something wrong, you know? I shoulda lit that fucker up."

"You do that over there? Wax women?"

"He wasn't no woman, Hap, that's the—"

"You didn't know that, is my point."

"No. No. Some level, I knew. It was *wrong*, you know?"

"You guessed, Godo. You suspected. And you take out a woman on a bad guess, think of the shit you'da been in."

Godo shook his head helplessly, miserably. "You're not getting it."

"You're letting hindsight fuck with you. Time don't work like that."

"Wow. That's deep."

"Go ahead and mock, asshole. I'm trying to help you."

"I got locked in, you know? The crap between me and that damn driver." Godo looked up into the night sky, the fat clouds, the spray of stars. "So fucking like me."

"No, what's like you? Letting it eat at you like this. There's nothing you coulda done. I know you wish there was but . . ." Happy let his voice trail off suggestively, the silence into which all wishes vanish. "Sure as shit no way you can change it now."

"Stop fucking telling me that."

"I'll stop when you look me in the eye, convince me you've got this shit squared away. I told you, I'm gonna need you tomorrow. You're the one I gotta rely on. Tell me I can do that."

Godo felt chilled to the bone. "There's something else," he murmured.

"Like what?"

"I'm not saying I can explain it, but more and more I picture this guy, this Snell, I see his face in that Blazer—backseat, passenger side. I swear to God it was him."

Happy didn't say anything at first, just pulled his cigarettes from his back pocket, tapped one out, crouched over to light up, then glanced toward the house. The kerosene lantern Efraim had brought back flickered in the living room where everyone was gathered, its waxy light shuddering along the bare walls. "Don't take this wrong, okay? But you been through what you been through, your mind is gonna fuck you up. It's gonna want to explain what can't get explained. Try to make sense of the crazy bullshit. All right? But it ain't the guy. You're making it up."

"You can't know that."

"I know this, okay? You go in there tomorrow thinking what we gotta get done has anything to do with what happened back there—I'm sorry man, I get it, this sergeant who bit it, he meant something to you, it's totally fucked what happened—but you go in there with this on your mind, we're all screwed. You can't make it right. You sure as hell ain't gonna make it right you walk in there tomorrow looking for payback. It's a job. We gotta keep it clean. Somebody gets hurt, the whole thing spins outta control and we're seriously fucked that happens. Keep it simple. We're jacking an asshole, period. He's smart, he hands everything up, everybody lives for another day, right? He's stupid, we improvise. I'm betting he's smart. And I'm betting he's not your guy. Even if he was, he wasn't the one driving, right, the prick who got in your face?"

Godo was gnawing on his lip. "Maybe he was one of the guys on our BOLO list."

"So what if he was? Besides, that was true, you'd remember the name."

"Maybe, maybe not." Godo winced, feeling lost. "I dunno . . ."

Happy sucked on his cigarette, face turning red in the ash glow. "Sure you do. You're just blocking it out because you want to get even."

"Listen, there were rumors of counterfeit access cards being used by some of the contractors, access levels jacked up to G-15, gave them the right to enter weapon storage. They'd get their hands on Russian and Iranian stuff, MAG-58s and AKMs, some German MP5s, sell it on the black market there. I wonder if this guy didn't figure a way to get stuff like that shipped over. You hear what I'm saying?"

"Godo—"

"It makes sense. Admit it, it's possible."

"Fuck, anything is possible. Look, put it to rest, man. It's over, you've talked it out. It don't have the power over you no more. It can't. Am I right?"

Godo knew what answer Happy was after, felt less sure he could give it to him. But he nodded assent, wanting not to talk about it anymore. Another rush of wind rocked the branches of the walnut trees, a chorus of whispers. Glancing toward the house, he thought he saw, beyond the rubbery lantern glow through the picture window, a small tumbling shadow flutter up and away from under the eaves. An exorcised demon, maybe. He couldn't shake the feeling it was the wrong demon.

THIRTY

THE NOONDAY SUN HAMMERED SHADOWS TO THE GROUND LIKE sheets of tin, while inside the musty room a slow trail of furry brown ants caravanned along the wall. Roque sat hunched at the window, squinting into the light, chin resting on his crossed arms, waiting for the Chamula woman to come along, the one who came down from her *paraje* in the hills every day to sell firewood or chickens or her specialty: popcorn. *Las palomitas*, she called it. Little doves.

She was one of three distractions he'd found for himself in as many days, holed up in Arriaga at this so-called hotel. In truth, the place was a *picadero*, a cross between a flophouse and a shooting gallery, where his contact, a nod named Victor, hung out with his fellow *salvatruchos* and spike-jockeys all day.

It was a testament to the fear the *mareros* instilled in the locals, despite the druggy excesses, that Roque could park the Corolla on the street with no fear of its being messed with. Even the cops and vigilantes, not to mention the dozens of strangers straggling through town, knew enough to give it a wide berth. Still, he kept the distributor cap locked up in the trunk and watched the car whenever he could, fearing that the one time he let his guard down would be exactly when something happened.

The second distraction he'd afforded himself since arriving came courtesy of a dog-eared Peterson Field Guide, left behind in Julio's *taberna* down the street by a birder trekking through the area. Roque paged through the color plates with bored devotion, mesmerized by the otherworldly names: loons, honeycreepers, limpkins and coots, jacanas and nightjars—also known as goatsuckers—bushtits and trogons and black chachalacas.

The mystery of the thing was this: The birds seemed to exist nowhere but inside the book. The only winged creatures he'd seen in town were vultures and blackbirds: grackles and cowbirds, if he'd identified them correctly, the latter being a brood parasite, explaining why it had driven off virtually every other species, pushing them up into the mountains.

Kill the young, he thought. The key to success.

He missed the guitar, its stubborn tuning, its thin sound. He remembered the clanging racket it made when Chepito's sidekick smashed it against the roof, the Corolla barreling down the crowded street, horn blasting, scattering the fairgoers. It taught him something, that escape. The importance of idiot will. Refusing to give in. He felt a little larger in spirit now, a little bolder, a little more *buxo*, as Tía Lucha would put it—quick on his feet.

There was nothing quick here, just tedium. He'd asked Victor if he could buy a disposable cell phone somewhere to check in with Happy, maybe even talk with Tía Lucha, but the idea got nixed.—*No such thing as wiretaps or warrants here*, Victor had said, *cops just listen in whenever they fucking feel like it. Forget a cell until you're north of Oaxaca*. Roque had wanted to respond: Right, and you guys communicate how? But it seemed best not to push it, the same way asking too many questions felt not just stupid but dangerous. Still, he missed everybody. It would be ten o'clock there, two hours behind. Tía would be at work. God only knew where Happy or Godo might be.

Again he glanced up and down the street, hoping to spot the Chamula woman. The first time he'd seen her, she'd been wearing a black-and-white poncho, typical of the women from San Juan Chamula, so he'd been told, and she'd carried a few chickens by their feet, a bundle of firewood on her back, an infant strapped to her chest with two more clinging to her skirt. The next time, yesterday, she'd been dressed in traditional Mayan *traje*, a boldly colored *china poblana* skirt, a lavishly embroidered overblouse called a *huipil*. That was when he'd seen her selling her little doves. He couldn't say for sure why that had moved him so deeply but he'd gone down, bought several greasy bags of cold rubbery popcorn off her. It wasn't peanut butter but it would do.

In the easterly distance a virginal sky topped the alpine highlands and cliff-scarred plateaus. Corn and sorghum fields checkered the lowlands all the way to the marigold fields nearer town. The yellow of their blossoms, he'd learned, was considered the shade of death. It looked so welcoming here. The flower fields yielded to the garbage dump on the town's edge, which in turn gave way to the sprawling rail yard with its tumbledown station across the street, its adobe walls slathered with graffiti.

Glancing one last time up and down the empty sun-blasted street, Roque finally decided it was time to check in with Victor.

He was holding court in the spacious room on the ground floor that the *picadero*'s denizens grandly called the ballroom. The windows were covered with ragged sheets of tacked-up plastic, creating a stuffy gloom. The spikes were all male, half a dozen or so in all, varying in age from around twelve—kill the young, Roque reminded himself—to mid-thirties, sprawled on soiled mattresses or just bedsheets scattered across the floor, the *muchachos* bleary from smack or just there to watch TV, an old Sony with a built-in DVD player perched on cinder blocks in the corner. A few *salvatruchos* were hanging out as well, shirtless, their torsos black and red with tattoos, contenting themselves with beer or *chicha*, a fiery corn liquor sold everywhere.

Victor, tragically handsome, sculpted bone and nappy hair, sprawled sideways in the room's only armchair, black-soled feet dangling over the arm and bobbing lazily as he dug beneath his nails with a hairpin. His eyelids hung at half-mast, jaw slack, a white plastic rosary draped around his neck. A pirated DVD of

Mel Gibson's *Apocalypto* was playing on the TV, and as far as Roque could tell, the *picadero* gang watched little else, mesmerized by all that color-saturated sadism, the cool tattoos and wicked costumes, the spooky nihilism and debauched scarification and ooga-booga religiosity, as though it weren't box-office bullshit but a kind of Mayan home movie.

Meanwhile, two *salvatruchos* near the doorway where Roque stood were going back and forth with the latest horror stories.

—Yesterday these five pollos *got shaken down in broad daylight by some local cops, right? Out front of the church. Then guess what—those cops got jacked by state cops not five minutes later.*

—Cops are fucking thieves.

—Shit, man, I'm a thief. But I am what I am, I don't pretend to be nothing else.

—Listen to this. Two nights ago, we were running the tops of the boxcars heading up from Tapachula, okay? Came across this pack of hicks from, I dunno, Nicaragua I think. Funny fucking accent, everything like twee twee twee. Anyway, we tell them, you ride the train, you pay the freight. They said they had no money. So we beat them stupid, stripped the fuckers naked. They had their money in their shorts, like we wouldn't find it there. Then because they lied we tossed them off. So long, suckers.

—You hear about that guy who slipped trying to pull himself up into a boxcar out here the other night?

—Guy who fell under the wheel?

—Cut him in two. He's lying there, watching the rest of the train roll over him, screaming. Fucker finally bled to death, but man . . .

—You saw it?

—I was chasing the cocksucker.

—No fucking way.

—What's more important, your money or your life?

—People, man. So fucking stupid.

—Reminds me. That Honduran girl?

—The one got raped?

—*The one got gangbanged while they shot her boyfriend right in front of her.*

—*I heard that was cops.*

—*It was the fucking vigilantes, man.*

—*No, I heard cops.*

Roque listened to this last bit and tried not to think of Lupe. She and the others had been due in town yesterday, no word from Beto or anyone else about the delay. He knew how many stops the group would have to make: Get off the bus, trek around a checkpoint, maybe miles of detour. It was anybody's guess how long they might have to wait, hiding in the fields, waiting until the time was right, dodging God only knew how many patrols, legal and illegal—local police, state police, private security thugs, vigilantes, *federales*, Grupo Beta, the army, the Mexican *migra*; the anti-immigrant backlash here made the Minute Man reaction along the California-Texas corridor look like Welcome Wagon—then heading back to the road, flagging down the next bus whenever it happened by.

Catching Victor's gaze, he gestured that he was heading out. Victor responded with a swacked grin and a fiddly wave.

ROQUE CHECKED TO BE SURE THERE WERE NO COPS OR OTHER ARMED men around, then headed up the block. A group of urchins materialized, begging. He'd learned the trick to saying no: nothing out loud, just a slow wagging of the finger back and forth, mysteriously effective. The kids made faces but retreated, scattering a handful of chickens pecking the dust.

He felt light-headed from sleeplessness. The *picadero* with its unholy stench, its meandering ant trails, its festering mattresses, it was the perfect spot for insomnia. In the long hours awake at night he'd found himself beset with increasingly shameless fantasies of Lupe, in which their lovemaking became tormented, ravenous, desperate. At times it had been difficult to know what exactly he was picturing, sex or a smackdown. What was it about this place, he thought, that caused such tormented obsessions?

He headed toward Julio's *taberna*, walking distance—more to the point, in visual range of the car. Julio's was the third and last of Roque's distractions.

After the blinding sunlight, the dimness felt welcome. Two field workers from one of the nearby plantations nursed beers at the end of the bar, their sweat-stained straw hats tipped back on their heads. A ceiling fan stirred the air around, unable to dispel the odors of leaky refrigeration and piss. What sunlight filtered in through the quarreled amber windows dissolved in the shadowy interior, surrendering its heat, a mystery Roque accepted gratefully.

Seeing him enter, Julio broke off feeding his parrot and dug out a can of 7UP from his ice chest, setting it atop the bar for Roque.

Julio cracked a smile.—*Still can't find your way out of town?*

—*I'm waiting for the bushtits and trogons to show up*. He popped open the icy wet can.—*How are things?*

Julio shrugged.—*Why complain, the worst is yet to come*. Returning to his stool, he swept away the bits of seed husks littering the bar beneath the parrot perch.

Roque chugged back a mouthful of 7UP, ambling to the small corner stage where a guitar and a vihuela rested against the wall. He earned his drinks and a lunch of red beans and rice by playing for several hours each afternoon, sometimes teaming up with Julio for a duet, the barkeep on the vihuela, a smaller guitar used for mariachi ensembles, tuned high like a ukulele.

Julio, an able if not quite inspired musician himself, at one point had offered to give Roque the guitar as a gift.—*When you become famous, you can tell people about this place, how I saw your stardom ahead of you. And the only thing between you and fame, my young friend, is bad luck and the devil.*

Julio was bearish with a soup-catcher mustache and a wild

mop of curls. Mestizo by heritage—half-caste, Spanish speaking—he was courteous but wary, that instinctive *mejicano* reserve, at least until dusk stole the bite from the day's heat, at which point he indulged in a few jolts of mescal chased with beer.

The night before, regaling his new talented friend from *Gringolandia* with the crazy *mixto* accent, he'd intoned:—*We* mejicanos *take great pride in losing. We don't just have a capacity for suffering—everyone does—we enjoy it, like the Russians*. Then he'd broken into song, a ballad by the legendary mariachi Juan Gabriel, sung in a beery tenor.—*I just forgot again that you never loved me*.

Roque had to admit he felt tempted to take the man up on his offer, make off with the guitar, but it struck him as unseemly. Julio was lonely, bored, stuck here in Chiapas with nothing but daydreams and his parrot and a nightly drunk to amuse himself. And that would not change. Time was stuck. To that extent, Julio, like some creature from myth, seemed eternal, which meant it would be unwise to take a gift from him unless the consequences were clear up front.

Roque grabbed a chair and set the guitar in his lap, figuring he'd change things around a little today, rock out, jam on some Santana or Maná, maybe a little Aerosmith or even Steve Earle, whose tunes he'd learned from the edgier folkies at open mikes. Lalo had always told him, listen to everything, dismiss nothing; the key to creativity lies in two simple words: *Steal wisely*.

He got no further than tuning, though, before he sensed a sudden tension in the room. Glancing up, he saw Julio reaching beneath the bar for his *bastón*, a kind of billy club. Thinking that some immigrants were at the door, hoping for a handout, he glanced that direction, only to see the Chamula woman waiting there, one of her daughters by her side, the child a miniature of her mother, down to the *china poblana* skirt, the beautifully embroidered *huipil*. They both held woven baskets filled with bags of popcorn.

The mother called out: "*Las palomitas, señor*," her Spanish brittle, heavily accented.

—*I told you*, Julio bellowed, slamming his hand on the bar, scaring the bird.—*Not in here. Out!*

—*It's okay*, Roque said, returning the guitar to its spot along the wall.—*I want to buy a couple bags off her*.

As though to prompt him, the woman said again, "*Las palomitas*," her voice a kind of singsong, feigning innocence.

Julio, incredulous:—*Don't encourage these people*. He reached up to stroke the parrot, soothe it.—*She's probably drunk on pox*. He pronounced it "posh"—the local home brew.

—*I'll take care of it*, Roque said. He gestured for the woman to back away from the door, he'd meet her in the street.

To his back, Julio said:—*If she steals from you, don't cry to me*. The two field workers chimed in with a wheezy little spate of laughter.

From snatches of conversation he'd overheard at the *picadero* and the bar the past three days, Roque had gathered that the Chamulas were the largest, poorest, most hostile of the Tzotzil tribes in the area. He'd learned too that the name Tzotzil meant "people of the bat"; in their folklore there were ancient stories of black winged creatures who escaped from the mountain caves at night, kidnapping women, eating children, but the old folks said those creatures didn't exist anymore. The last were seen forty years ago. This was all a grand joke to Julio and his pals. They considered the Indians layabouts, thieves, drunks, which seemed only too predictable, since they themselves were mixed blood.

As Roque reached into his pocket the woman's eyes never left him, nor did her daughter's. He could only guess at their respective ages; they seemed not so much mother and child as two reflections of the same idea. He pulled what coins he had and a few wrinkled pesos from his pocket, bought three bags of popcorn from the woman, who clearly wished he'd buy more. That was when the idea came to him.

"*Venga conmigo*," he said—Come with me—pronouncing the words slowly, in case her comprehension of Spanish was as rough as her pronunciation.

He led her and her daughter inside the *picadero*, making a funny face so they wouldn't be frightened. They entered the ballroom with *Apocalypto* at its midpoint, the parade of the bound slaves into the limestone city with its clouds of white dust, the bloodthirsty crowd in primitive exotica, the cynical priest in his towering headdress prancing atop the sacrificial ziggurat. Roque clapped his hands loud, shouting, "*Oye, cholos*." Hey, guys.

Heads turned, Victor's among them. People of the bat, Roque thought. He presented the tiny Chamula woman and her daughter.

—What's a movie without popcorn?

He snatched bags from the woven baskets the woman and her daughter carried and tossed them around the room, gesturing with his finger and thumb that payment was due. As he waited for the money to materialize he suppressed an impulse to add: You clowns want to commune with your Mayan roots? Here she is.

THIRTY-ONE

LOURDES LOCKED HER CAR, TRUDGED UP THE STEEP DRIVE TO THE front door, put her finger to the bell. She glanced once Happy's direction, despite his having told her not to, not under any circumstances, but why get angry? He knew how scared she was.

They'd bonded, he and Lourdes, talking on and off throughout the night. She'd said he reminded her of a friend of her brother's she'd known back in Santa Clara del Cobre, a young man who'd gone off to El Norte a short time before she had. She hadn't seen him since but that was the way it was, you grow up with someone, learn to know them, perhaps come to love them, then they leave to make a better life but for you it's a kind of death, because so often, almost always, they never come back. Happy had let her go on like that for hours, playing the sympathetic heavy, letting her wear herself out with talk, then watching her sleep balled up like a cat until it was Efraim's turn to keep an eye on her.

A misty winter dampness filmed the ground, the asphalt, the parked cars. His bones felt like tin from the chill. Strange, he thought, how screwed up his inner barometer had become, all that time in Iraq. Maybe he'd head somewhere good and hot when all this was over.

The front door to the contractor's house opened, Lourdes said something quick to whoever was there, then vanished inside. Happy racked the Glock's slide to chamber a round, alerting the others sitting in back to get ready, grab the duffels with the guns.

Stuffing the pistol under his belt, he zipped closed his coveralls and glanced at the cell phone on the seat beside him, waiting for it to trill.

"I NO KNOW WHAT I DO WITH IT, VERONICA. MY WATCH, I MEAN. I SO sorry, I feel stupid, I no want bother you."

Lourdes stood there in the entry, same clothes as yesterday, unwashed hair. I'm a disaster, she thought, remembering the phrase from a movie she'd stayed up to watch a few nights back, the girls in bed so she couldn't ask them what it meant. She glanced up to check how her script, such as she'd managed it, was playing, at the same time noticing the odd burned smell in the air. "I think I must leave it behind yesterday, when I come and clean. Maybe I look around, I no take time, I promise . . ."

The smell was smoke. Veronica said, "We had a teeny little accident at the stove this morning." She was girlishly small and achingly thin, sunken eyes, an insomniac pallor, her head a frizzy eruption of sage-colored hair. The ghost of an angry girl, Lourdes thought, that is what she looks like, what she always looks like. "Samantha has some awful sort of flu, she can't keep anything down. I was trying to scramble her some eggs."

Lourdes detected a second smell, the familiar whiff of alcohol, Veronica's breath, at the same time thinking: The girl is here, I need to tell them. She pointed toward the kitchen. "You need me help you clean?"

Veronica ignored the question, plucking idly at her frayed hair. She tried to chuckle but her voice caught. The self-pity in her eyes splintered. "Charlie's going to kill me . . ."

What was she talking about? "Veronica—"

"Christ, he blames me for everything. What am I supposed to do? *It was an accident*. Okay? If you had any idea what a misery this is, how hard—"

"Veronica, I'm not understand—"

"And for what?" She waved listlessly then laughed so bitterly Lourdes shrank from the sound. "Go on, look around. I haven't seen your stupid watch but maybe it's here somewhere."

Veronica turned toward the kitchen, staggering with her first step, recovering with the next. Then Lourdes's cell phone rang. Waiting until Veronica was out of earshot, she flipped it open.

—What's taking so long?

—The girl is here, not just the mother.

In the kitchen, Veronica kicked something metal—a pan, from the sound—across the linoleum floor.

—Where are they in the house?

—The girl is in her room, I think. I have not seen her yet. Veronica is in the kitchen.

—Find out where the girl is.

—The girl, she is sick.

—I understand that, but . . . What the hell . . . ?

His voice rose sharply then fell away and she heard squealing tires—a car banged into the driveway, chattering brakes, a door slamming. Swallowing the knot in her throat, she drifted toward the picture window, peered past the curtains and saw the husband charging through the drizzle up the walk, hair and necktie flailing in the wind, his face flushed with rage.

Charlie's going to kill me . . .

Into the phone, she said:*—You see him, he is—*

—Stick to your story. I'll call you back.

The front door slammed open, the husband burst in, breathing through his mouth from the rushed climb up the drive, hair shaggy and damp, skin florid. Spotting Lourdes, he pulled up short. She still held her phone.

"What are you doing here?"

For the merest instant she considered confessing everything, the five *vatos* outside waiting to rob him, ready to kill him. But she could not trust him to understand. And her girls, what would happen?

"I think," she announced, "I leave my watch here yesterday. I come back, look for it."

He'd already abandoned his question, neck craning toward the stairs, the hallway. Veronica drifted out of the kitchen.

He said, "What the hell have you done?"

"I want you to listen," she began.

"Sam said you damn near set the house on fire."

"That's a lie. I was trying to cook—"

"She told you she was *sick*, she puked up half of last week, she didn't *want*—"

"I just thought—"

"She said you were drunk."

The mask dissolved. She turned away. "I'm not listening to—"

The husband lurched forward, grabbed her arm. "Don't you turn your back on me."

Lourdes, suddenly light-headed, reached out for the nearest chair at the same moment her phone rang again—only then did she realize it was still in her hand—the sound startling her so badly she nearly dropped it.

—What's happening?

—They're having a fight.

—Can you open the door?

—I don't . . . I . . .

—Nothing's changed. Do as I told you. Just the way we discussed. It's going to be okay. I won't let anything happen to you. I promise.

The phone went dead. In a daze she backed toward the door. She swallowed another clot of air then called out, or thought she called out, that she would come back some other time to look for her watch.

HAPPY FLIPPED HIS CELL PHONE CLOSED AND TURNED TO THE OTHERS. "*Vamos, bravos*."

He considered calling it off, but till when—tomorrow? Next

week? Lourdes couldn't handle it, they couldn't handle her, she'd bolt, she'd crumble, she'd beg them nonstop, crazy, infuriating: Let me go . . . And her girls, they'd call the law, all that.

He met the others on the street. "Change in plans. This guy Chuck, he's in the house, so is one of the kids. The girl. We gotta take them down all at once, not one at a time. It's gonna be okay. Look, everybody but Godo, you go to the same positions we practiced. Efraim, you got the upstairs bedrooms, you take the girl, make sure she don't call 911. Godo, you look for this Chuck guy, you handle him, right?" His words met stares, each one with its own distinctive fear or surprise or numb resolve. "Okay then. Be smart, stay sharp."

As they reached the porch they pulled down their balaclavas, dragged the weapons out of the duffel bags, slammed the magazines home, flipped off the safeties. Happy gave the ready signal just as Lourdes opened the door and backed out, saying, "I call before I come back . . ."

FOR THE PAST HOUR, CROUCHED IN THE BACK OF THE TRUCK, GODO HAD tried to convince himself there was a right way to do this thing, reminding himself this wasn't Joe Citizen they were taking down but filth, one of *them,* the arrogant sloppy goat fuckers who, almost singlehandedly, botched the war. Happy wanted no one dead. Fine, the way it ought to be. Don't just avenge Gunny Benedict, make him proud—assert control, overwhelming force, stay alert, maintain discipline. He could trust Efraim, he wanted to trust Puchi, Chato was wack. Shoot him if need be, he told himself. Better him than the wife or the girl.

As the front door swung open, he rushed in at the lead, using the AK to track the space left to right, ground floor to the stair, feeling the eerie déjà vu he'd expected but luckily not haunted by it, the ghosts present but silent—Gunny Benedict, Salgado, Mobley, the Iraqi family in the Cressida—as though he were split in two, the old Godo, the guy standing here. Then he spotted him, the contractor, Chuck, frozen in place, halfway up the stairs, gripping his wife's dress with one hand, the other clenched into a fist. He stood there fright-eyed, hunched over the woman, then survival kicked in, he dropped her like a bag of sand and charged up the stairs but Godo was already closing, adrenalin purging all weakness from his bum leg as he moved to contact, taking the steps two at a time, forging past the wife who covered her head and rolled out of his way to keep from being trampled.

The contractor reached the first doorway, the master bedroom, before Godo gun-butted him from behind, knocked him to his knees. He heard Efraim in the hall behind him, running to the other bedrooms to secure them, take care of the girl, while downstairs Happy hooked his arm around Lourdes's throat, shouting, "Stay calm! Nobody gets hurt, you do as you're told."

Chuck the contractor scrambled to his knees, wobbly but clawing at his pant cuff. Godo moved in, planting his foot down hard on the man's calf, feeling the ankle rig beneath his boot. "Leave it!" He prodded with the tip of the AK's barrel, a poke in the small of the other man's back, then reached down, felt for the holster, unhitched the strap, pulled the chrome-plated .25 free and shoved it into the pocket of his coveralls.

"Take us down to the safe, open it up."

Chuck tried to drag his leg out from under Godo's weight. "What are you talking about? There is no safe."

Godo studied his face. It was him, he thought, the guy in the back, passenger side, the Blazer at the checkpoint. Him or someone just like him. Applying a little more pressure on the leg, he said, "Don't be stupid."

The man's eyes narrowed. "I know who you are."

Godo's mouth went dry. Knows me how, People's Fried Chicken or the checkpoint? Maybe it was the weapon, the AK, he'd sold it to Puchi after all. Lifting his boot, "Get up."

"Or what, you're going to kill me? Then what, genius?"

Godo made an instant read and figured two things: One, threatening the wife would go nowhere, the guy was thumping her when they busted in, he could care less. Christ, might even be grateful. Two, that left the girl or Thumper here himself and he wasn't gonna be impressed with mere displays, it was gonna take pain, which meant a change in the ROE. Nobody Gets Hurt had to downgrade to Nobody Gets Hurt Too Bad.

He took out the .25 and fired into the man's calf. The burned tang of cordite, a strangled scream, floret of blood on the trouser leg.

Godo shouted down to Happy, "It's okay. It's me." Then, turning back, a soft voice: "Infield hit, Chuckles. Man on base."

Face white with pain, that sour breath, the guy hissed, "You're dead, I fucking swear."

Godo fired a second round, the right bicep this time. Another gargled scream. More blood, not too much. "Sacrifice bunt, perfect execution, third-base line. Runner on first advances. We have a man in scoring position." His face beneath the balaclava itched, damp with sweat. Somebody on the stair struggled with the wife, the screech of duct tape. "The safe downstairs, shit dick, or the girl's next."

"I told you—"

Greedy selfish motherfucker, Godo thought. "Bring me the girl!"

"You punk fuck."

"The girl! Now!"

Godo felt good, in the hunt, balls in a swing, spine like a sparkler. It was Fourth of July. Proof through the night. He was alive. Then he remembered: He knows me. Which tracks back to Puchi, to Cható, to Vasco. *Estamos chingados*. We're fucked.

Efraim dragged the girl into the doorway, flannel PJs, blue socks, her hands bound behind her back with the thick silver tape, another strip spooled around her head, pinning her hair against her head, gagging her. It made her eyes pop. She was waifish like the mother and crying.

Godo grabbed her arm, jerked her close, staring down at her father. "Daddy wants you to know, whatever's down there in that safe of his? It's, like, way more important than you."

Chuck tried to wet his lips, tongue clicking. "Sammi?"

"You, he don't give a shit about. He's handed you up to me." Godo pushed her down so she couldn't avoid her old man's blood, then thumbed back the hammer on the .25. "Man on second, Pops, nobody out. Fly ball, deep center, throw to the plate." He pressed the barrel to the sobbing girl's head. "You make the call."

EFRAIM REMAINED UPSTAIRS WITH THE WOMEN, LOURDES AND THE wife, with Chato on the back door, Puchi the front. Couldn't leave Chato alone with two bound and gagged women, no matter how homely they were, not without a tacit green light to use his dick for a DNA dispenser. Happy and Godo dragged Chuck downstairs, a couple makeshift bandages for his wounds, and they brought the daughter with them, eyes puffy and red, face slick with tears and gouts of snot.

The cellar room conjured bunker, not sanctuary, low-end paneling with a fake pine veneer, an oval braided rug, an office-salvage desk. Nice array of guns, though, the ones racked on the walls all legal, shotguns mostly, a civilian-issue AR-15, a Korean War vintage M1, a Winchester .30–30 deer rifle with a 3–9 scope. The pistols were displayed in a locked glass case.

Wishing he could draw Happy aside, Godo wanted to tell him that Thumper here, Mr. Chuckles, he may have recognized his voice. The original plan had called for Happy to talk, maybe Efraim, no one else, precisely because the guy could make everybody else. That's what happens, Godo thought, when things get rocked on the fly. The endgame blurs, you miss the most goddamn obvious things. Then again there was the weapon, he may have figured it out from that alone, though one AK looked pretty much like the next. He's not going to the law, he reminded himself. Too much to lose, too much he'd have to lie about. Which meant if this thing went south, it wouldn't be later, it wouldn't be cops, it would be right here, in this room.

He didn't see a safe. The paneling had no obvious defects to suggest a false wall, the gun cabinet hid nothing. That left the rug. With Happy training the Glock on the girl, Chuck slumped in the desk chair looking on, Godo shouldered the desk aside, lifted the rug, found the cutout square in the concrete, a notch for a hand grip, the wavy outline of the newer cement like a water stain. Figuring the thing was booby-trapped, he dragged Chuckles from his swivel chair, dropped him near the hidey-hole and cocked the .25.

"Open the safe but don't reach inside. You do, I blow the back of your head open. And my buddy here does your girl."

His right arm weakened, the bandage seeping blood, Chuck struggled with his left to lift the heavy concrete panel—one try, two, barely budging it upward. Godo leaned down, flipped the back of Chuck's ear with the pistol's snub barrel, then pressed it to the hollow at the back of his skull. "You're not fooling anybody."

The man went back to his task, redoubled his effort or pretended to, hefting the concrete slab out of its form-fit hole, pushing it aside with a wincing grunt. The safe lay below, bearing a nameplate: Churchill. It had taken some real work, Godo thought, cutting through the old floor, digging a hole deep enough, planting the safe, squaring it plumb in the hole, reworking the cement. He wondered if Chuck had done it all himself. He seemed the type, industrious, thorough, paranoid.

"Open it up now."

Reaching down, Chuck leaned to the side a little for the sake of the light, making sure he could see the numbers on the dial as he worked the tumblers, clumsy again, left-handed. His daughter, in Happy's grip, shuddered and blinked, watching closely like everyone else. Three alternating spins, a pull of the lever, he drew back the door. Figuring there was a gun inside for just this sort of situation, Godo pressed the .25 to the man's head. "Back on out, sit down."

The man crabbed his way to the swivel chair and dropped into it, his breathing shallow and rough, the bloodstains on his sleeve and pant leg larger now. Godo gestured for Happy to bring the daughter over, sit her on her father's lap, and as she got dragged from one spot to the other he noticed, for the first time, the Rorschach of dampness in the crotch of her pajamas. He felt a sudden meek sympathy. He remembered blowing ballast his first time in combat, Al Gharraf, his MOPP suit drenched with piss. Some guys in his unit crapped themselves. The indignities of war. Of warriors.

He lifted the barrel of the .25 until it was level with the bridge of the contractor's nose. "You got that safe rigged—there a trip wire, a flash-bang, anything else in that hole—you better tell me now."

Dry-mouthed still, Chuck worked his tongue around, trying to talk. His girl sat perched on his knee, gazing at the floor. Ashamed. Don't be, Godo wanted to tell her. He traded glances with Happy, stepping back and letting the .25 drop as his cousin lifted the Glock in its place, pressed it to the contractor's head and spoke for the first time Godo could remember since the start of the robbery.

"Anything goes off," he said, "you die. And I promise, the girl gets it too, the wife, cleaning lady, everybody. You got one way out. Take it."

The girl started crying again, breathy tears, eyes shut tight, like she was trying to catch herself, hold back. Godo flashed on a house raid in Fallujah, the unit acting on a tip about a weapons cache, finding only a Shia woman with facial tattoos, a line of big colored dots along her chin and eyebrows, standing in the kitchen with her simpleton daughter who wore a shabby white linen dress and bit her arm to stifle her sobs, trying to be brave as the marines tore her home apart. Something about this girl here, Sammi her dad called her, she was the portal. Then became now, the claustrophobic shadows and the adrenalin fever and the smell of lentils and goat fat and mint, all of it, flooding his senses. Don't do this, he thought, trying to shake it off, but it was already too late. The misgiving and dread lingered. They belonged.

"There's a sensor," Chuck said finally. The anger remained but it swam around in his eyes untethered. "Sets off a frag grenade inside the hole. Hit the switch just inside and on the top, push it back. That clears it."

Godo studied him a second, looking for deceit, then lifted the Kalashnikov's strap from around his neck, set the rifle on the floor, went to the hole, knelt down, peered inside. "I don't see a switch."

"It's tucked inside the door. On top like I said. Have to feel for it."

Godo checked that Happy had his gun up, hammer back. Godo reached down, put his hand inside the safe, curled his hand up and around, felt for the toggle. Just as a sixth sense told him no, back out, the flash went off, blinding him. The explosion came next, that fraction of a second that saved him, otherwise the hand would be no hand. Still, he felt the scorching wave rip through the glove and his skin caught fire or seemed to, the strange gum-stretch of time with its impersonal calm even as he knew he was yowling with pain, the gravity of shock and a muddy ring in his head, the after-blast, through which he could hear a fleshy drumming tock, the rotors of the little bird chopper overhead and he braced for the storm of dust, until he understood the sound was just blood, pulsing in his ears. He feared he might weep. He could make out scuffling, the Glock's fierce crack, once, twice, and he snapped back through the funnel of time to now, then glass shattering, the gun cabinet, the barklike grunts of hand-to-hand, Happy and Chuck going at it, the thud of flesh against something hard, the side of a skull maybe, a throaty cry of pain and then the Glock again, three times now.

It got quiet.

The hand, his right, felt like he'd boiled it, fingers clenched so tight, a claw. His ears kept humming, a keening pitch, punctuated by the strangled howls of the girl, almost inhuman now, muffled by the tape gag she'd half worked loose just by screaming.

He blinked, tried to see but there was just a wincing blur, things shifting, outlines stripped apart and bleeding color. He waved his hand through the vaporous muck. In time he could make out Happy, upright, mostly so, leaning against the cabinet with its sawtooth glass, all broken, the girl in her pajamas huddled nearby. Happy's sleeve was dark and that meant blood. His chest bellowed in and out as he tried to draw breath through the balaclava's soggy black wool.

No sign of the contractor. Had he run?

He felt it first, the foot. He nudged it trying to stand, gathered his balance, saw the man finally, sprawled on the floor facedown, one side of his face a bloody knit of ripped flesh and jagged bone. Close-quarter impact from the Glock, Godo could put that together at least. One of the shotguns lay just beyond the dead man's hand and Godo figured he'd pushed the girl up from his lap for distraction, shoved her into Happy, reached for the rack, pulled the weapon down.

Godo heard himself say, "You all right?"

Happy looked at his sleeve as though discovering for the first time he had an arm. "Cut it on the glass." He pressed his hand to the bloody cloth. "You?"

PERCHED IN THE VAN'S PASSENGER SEAT, CHATO COULDN'T HELP HIMself, lifting his hand to slap high fives, grinning like the luckiest guy alive. Puchi, behind the wheel, obliged him distractedly, offering him a raised palm. Godo and Happy, the wounded, sat in back with Efraim, who rummaged through the duffel bags filled with weapons they'd taken off the walls of the cellar room. They'd left the safe alone—why risk a second blast?—even passed on the desk and the display cabinet, anything with a door, not worth it, scrambling to grab what was there in plain view. But that was a haul. They'd come for weapons and needed something to show for their trouble. They'd left the girl and the two women tied hand and foot, made sure their gags were tight, gathered up all the cell phones and cut the cord on every landline they found.

Happy, squeezing the cut on his arm, trying to stanch the blood, thought of Lourdes. Asking her to bear up with just a robbery in the picture was one thing, especially given who the target was, but they'd left a body behind and it wasn't just Happy the law would come after. The whole crew was looking at felony homicide. That'd wipe the smile off Chato's face, once he got his head around what it meant. And sure, Crockett was small-time, locals hadn't seen this big a thing in who knew how long, but that just meant they'd call in the wise men. Word would reach Lattimore faster than rats up a rope. And they'd grind poor Lourdes down, no way she'd hold out. And that meant no immunity, no citizenship, no nothing. He'd gambled, a long shot, no point crying. But it meant going on the run. That's how quick, he thought, the future dies. Not that he didn't know that already.

He glanced toward Godo. The burned hand was sickly red in places, charred in others, blisters bubbling up. He sat there flexing it, open, closed, wincing from the pain but not stopping, staring at the thing like he could heal it with his mind alone. That was Godo. Pity the ugly fucker, the guy was nothing if not stubborn. God knows he could take punishment and he had the instincts of a puma—who else could have stuck his arm in that hole and not lost the whole damn thing? Too bad it wouldn't count for more.

At the farmhouse they split up. Chato and Puchi kept the van, taking the weapons to Vasco with a report on why there wasn't more. Efraim drove off in his own car. Godo and Happy lingered in the rusted Ford pickup with the Arizona plates.

Neither spoke for what felt like an eternity, Happy sitting with his keys in his lap, Godo still working his hand like a prosthetic he couldn't quite get the hang of. The sky remained leaden and the wind blew from the north but the rain had stopped. Blue jays cawed in the walnut trees. A splintering shaft of sunlight broke through a coral-hued, *cuquita*-shaped gash in the cloud cover, like something off a pornographic prayer card.

"The guy back there," Happy said finally, "the guy I killed—was that really the cat you thought he was? You know the one I mean. At the checkpoint."

Godo stopped messing with his hand for a moment, staring out the windshield. A blue jay buzzed something zigzagging through the tall grass, a ground squirrel probably, maybe a vole. He shrugged. "Won't bring Gunny Benedict back if it was."

"That wasn't really why I asked."

"The man deserved what he got. If that's any comfort. And if not, it should be."

Happy watched a second jay join the first, dive-bombing their invisible prey. "I can't stick around here," he said.

With his good hand Godo reached into the pocket of his coveralls, took out a bandanna, and wiped away some fluid leeching out of his blisters. "Take me with you."

"You need that hand looked after."

"The hand's a fucking giveaway. Once the cops talk to the girl they'll check every ER in the state, then move on to every state nearby."

"There's clinics that'll keep it quiet."

"Not once this thing hits the news."

Happy felt the usual boil of nausea churning in his gut. "I'm heading to Mexico."

"I can handle that." Godo wrapped the bandanna around his charred and blistered hand, fashioned a knot using his good hand and his teeth. "We'll get my guns and meds at the trailer."

"Your hand like that? What good are your guns?"

"The hand'll heal. Till then, you can shoot." He smiled, remembering. "I couldn't see much of what happened, but I saw the result. Brought the fucking heat, *primo*."

Happy shook his head. "I can't go back to the trailer. Don't wanna risk running into Tía Lucha. Don't want to explain, don't want any naggy fucking bullshit, I just—"

With his good hand, Godo reached across the space between them, touched Happy's wounded arm. The sleeve was crusty with dried blood. "She's at work."

"I can't look after you."

"I don't expect you to."

Happy felt like he was swirling down a drain. "You can't leave a note for Tía, neither. You leave a note, she'll just go off, you know how she does. Better she doesn't know."

Godo turned away, looking out at the barn pocked with bullet holes, the grassy hills beyond, the lurid downshaft of light. He began to whistle a gentle tune and after a second Happy recognized it, "Canción de Cuna," a lullaby Roque had practiced damn near to death when he was first learning guitar. It used to drive Godo batshit. Funny, him thinking of it now.

Godo said, "They tell you in basic that, first time you're in combat, you're gonna experience this thing called battle distortion. Time comes to a stop. Or you see things so clear it's like they're magnified or some shit. Maybe all of a sudden your memory goes blank. Some guys hallucinate, I fucking kid you not. Nothing like a squaddie with a SAW tearing up shit that isn't there. But I had none of that. I had this weird disconnect between sight and sound, I could see okay but my hearing cut out, not entirely, but like I'd plugged up my ears real bad somehow. And in that, like, silence I heard the tune I was just whistling, the one Roque used to play. And you know what? It calmed me down. I told myself I wasn't gonna die, I couldn't die, I had to come home, tell Roque what'd happened. I had to come home for Tía and your dad. I didn't feel so scared then."

Happy remembered the ambush on his convoy, the numbness he didn't recognize as blind terror till after. He hadn't thought of the family at all. That only came later, death and its lessons, wanting to make things up to the old man, wanting to do good by him, show him he understood now, the sacrifice, the love. "Why tell me this?"

Godo turned, eyes like stones in the hamburger face. "I know you don't want me along, Pablo. But you can't leave me behind. Not with this." He presented the wrapped hand. "And no way I'm doing time, not on Vasco's ticket. Bad enough these scars, the fucking leg. But I was the one who got you sent away the first time. I can't face your old man again, tell him one more time, Hey Tío, your son's fucked, guess who's to blame." He reached out again for his cousin's arm, laid his hand gently near the wound. "We'll meet up with your dad and Roque in some cantina before they cross the border, one last boys' night out, all of us together. We'll figure out if this *haji* friend of yours is for real. Right?"

He withdrew the hand and slapped the old Ford's dash, lifting a whisper of dust.

"Come on, *cabrón*. Drive."

THIRTY-TWO

THE FOUR OF THEM ARRIVED ON THE BUS A LITTLE AFTER SUNdown, caked with road grime, wobbly from hunger and thirst but with fewer bug bites than the last crossing. They took turns in a bathroom upstairs, splashing water around, faces, torsos, armpits, while Beto made it clear they were stopping only momentarily. They needed to make Juchitán as soon as possible; from there he'd know which route they would take north through Oaxaca and beyond.

Given Tío Faustino's exhaustion, Roque again assumed driving duties, Beto taking the seat beside him, the other three in back. He suffered a vague wish to say goodbye to Julio but he realized the sudden vanishings of strangers from Arriaga would be nothing new.

Checking his rearview, he saw the three of them—Samir, Lupe, Tío Faustino—in uneasy slumber, Lupe leaning against Tío Faustino's shoulder, her head sliding vaguely toward his chest, while his uncle protectively circled an arm around her shoulder. Roque felt grateful the two of them had grown closer, at the same time secretly wishing it were him back there.

They reached Juchitán a little before midnight and Roque was surprised by its sprawl. Beto gave him directions away from the old center of the city to a more industrial district near the bay, but before they veered too far afield of the nightlife they passed several bars where astonishingly large women, dressed elegantly in traditional *traje*, sat in chatty clusters at outside tables, fanning themselves in the lamplight. Taking stock of one particularly hefty *mamacita* wearing a ballooning green pleated skirt, a white *huipil*, even a mantilla, Beto chuckled. "You don't know about this, I'll bet. This town is famous for its homos. There's like three thousand *muxes*—that's the Zapotec word—who live here. It's a matriarchal society, queer sons are considered good luck, as long as you only have one. Mothers like them because they don't marry and go away. They're usually good earners too. And because virgin girls are still prized down here as brides, a lot of guys pop their cherries on *muxes*."

He directed Roque into a nest of warehouses near the water and finally down a dark *callejón* to a nameless bar. Opening the passenger-side door, he said to keep the motor running, he wouldn't be long. Roque switched off the headlights, threw the transmission into park and slid down in his seat, watching as Beto pulled back the bar's narrow tin door and vanished inside.

A weather-worn poster for Zayda Peña, a singer, was tacked up to the bar's outside wall. Roque recognized the name from news reports. She was one of a dozen or so musicians on the *grupero* scene, Mexico's version of country-western, who'd been murdered the past few years. Some of those killed had recorded *narcocorridos*, ballads touting the escapades of drug lords, a surefire way to piss off rivals. None of the murders had been solved. As though to drive that point home, somebody'd shredded the poster with the tip of a knife to where it looked as though a giant cat had come along to sharpen its claws on Zayda's face.

Glancing over his shoulder, he caught Lupe disentangling herself from Tío Faustino's arm, stretching, yawning, finger-combing her hair. You're such a sap, he thought, mesmerized. At the same time he realized he could be looking at the next Zayda Peña. You pay for the company you keep. And yet when somebody walks up, says he loves your act, tells you he wants to bankroll you, turn your dream into your future, knowing as you do how hard you've worked, how few musicians catch a break, how many give it up or lose their way, is it really such a sin to say yes? Is it really a sign of virtue to shrink away, turn down what, for all you know, is the last real chance you'll get?

The door to the bar opened again but it wasn't Beto who emerged. A wiry man with a burdened slouch and artfully slicked-back hair stepped out into the street and rummaged a cigarette pack from his hip pocket. As his match flared, Roque got a glimpse of his features: less Mayan, more mestizo, with strangely bulging eyes like the clown Chimbombín.

But that wasn't the troubling part. This wasn't California. The guy didn't need to step outside to grab a smoke.

Roque eased his hand toward the gearshift, ready to slam it into drive, leave Beto behind if need be, waiting for the bug-eyed stranger to make a sudden move.

Beto strode out of the bar and past the other man without a glance. The passenger door opened, the overhead light flared on, the door slammed shut. He just sat there in the dashboard glow for a moment, his exotically handsome face a mask.

Finally: "They've got checkpoints all over the inland roads. Strange. Usually they focus on one, the others are clear, switch it around every few days. We have to keep on the coastal route all the way through Oaxaca, past Puerto Escondido."

It took a second for the name to register. Roque said, "That's where the boats run by El Chusquero—"

"Tell me something I don't know." Beto leaned over, checked the gas gauge, then glanced up and finally noticed the bug-eyed man with the greaser hair. "What's this turd want?"

Finishing his cigarette, the stranger tossed down his butt, crushed it with his boot and shuffled back inside the bar.

Tío Faustino edged forward. "You think that gangster—Captain Quintanilla, El Chusquero, whatever he's calling himself today—you think he has something to do with closing down the inland roads? Maybe he's paid somebody off. Maybe he has connections inside the military here, or the police. There could be somebody waiting for us up ahead."

Beto stared at the bar's tin door. "No. Fucking coincidence, that's all. Bad luck." Reaching his arm out the window, he slapped the side of the door hard three times. "Come on. Let's move it."

A FEW MILES OUTSIDE OF TOWN THEY ENCOUNTERED THE INFAMOUS wind, notorious for jackknifing trucks. The barrancas below were a graveyard, Beto said, not just the semis but the cars they dragged with them over the cliffs. Tío Faustino took the wheel. Despite a hairy sideways jolt now and then, he kept the Corolla on course, whistling under his breath to soothe his nerves, then asking Lupe to keep him awake with a song or two. Stirring herself from her inwardness, she resorted to the usual repertoire, "Es Demasiado Tarde," It's Too Late, coming first, sung sotto voce, almost a whisper, then "El Camino," The Road:

De lejos vengo yo a verte
a conseguir lo que quiero
Aunque la vida me cueste.

I've come from far away to see you
to get what I long for
Even if it costs me my life

They passed through Salina Cruz hours before dawn but the city was already stirring, the refineries bristling with light, bakery trucks roaming the streets. The road out of town followed the coastal hills for miles, the winds again rocking the car back and forth as Roque huddled against the door, trying to grab some sleep.

As they passed a dirt lane a pair of headlights flashed on, then a pickup eased out onto the road behind them, followed by a second pickup trailing the first.

Beto turned around in his seat, looking back through the rear window. "If you can pick up speed," he told Tío Faustino, "it might be a good idea."

Samir wiped at his nose with the back of his hand, a fear reflex. Lupe glanced over her shoulder, her face both brightened and shadowed by the oncoming headlights. Following her eyes, Roque could make out the silhouettes of men standing in the first pickup's truck bed, clutching the railing along the sides with one hand, weapons in the other.

Tío Faustino accelerated, taking the switchbacks fast and tight, hoping to lose the pickups that way—they'd have to slow down at each sharp turn or risk losing the men holding on in back. But even with his best efforts, come every straightaway the two small trucks made up lost ground, though the second seemed to lag seriously behind the first. Finally the crack of gunfire, bullets whistling past.

"You gotta outrun them to the next roadblock," Beto told Tío Faustino.

"How do I do that? How far—"

"I don't fucking know"—Beto pounding on the dash—"just go."

The highway dropped toward the beach and they passed into a sudden mass of fog. Tío Faustino braked, cranked down his window, leaned out to see the course of the pavement, guiding himself that way as he tried to maintain some speed. The road rose again suddenly, curving inland, the fog thinned and he hit the gas, hoping this was his chance finally to gain some real advantage. Then the road hairpinned back toward shore, he touched the brake as he entered the turn then accelerated, hugging the curve, only to see through the mist, once the road straightened, the outline of a something massive in the middle of the road. He got out the words "*pinche putos*" before everyone slammed forward from the impact and the cow barreled over the hood, shattering the windshield with the sound of an exploding bomb, continuing over the roof. The car fishtailed, careening off the road in a spin and nearly tumbling over as the wheels dropped into a rock-strewn culvert just beyond the asphalt, slamming hard to a stop. Every head snapped in recoil. Tío Faustino's face came away from the steering wheel bloody.

Beto brushed off shards of glass with one hand while the other slammed the door, "Go! Go! Go!" But Tío sat there dazed, blood streaming from his nose, a deep gash along his cheek.

Gathering his wits, Roque said, "I'll drive," but he barely had his car door open before the first pickup cleared the bend. The cow's carcass remained twisted across the road, the driver turned sharp to avoid it, almost tipped over, then overcorrected and this time sent the small truck tumbling, the men in back still aboard as the thing went over, crushed before they could jump free. The pickup rolled over and over, ending with its wheels in the air. An eerie stillness followed, just hissing steam, the wind rushing through the hillside grass, the surf below.

Jumping from the Corolla's backseat, Samir called out, "Their guns."

Beto and Roque followed, edging toward the truck, checking to see if anyone still alive might shoot. Only two of the men seemed conscious, they both moaned horribly. The other three, two in the cab, one on the road, were badly bloodied and still. There were two rifles scattered across the road, Samir picked up one, Beto the other, while Roque checked inside the cabin to see if either of the two trapped men were alive. Neither had worn a seat belt and they both lay tangled between the dash and their seats, bloody and dazed and frosted with shards of broken glass. Roque checked for weapons, saw none, then from behind Samir edged him aside. Lifting the rifle to his shoulder, the Iraqi fired two rounds point-blank into each man's skull.

Seeing the look on Roque's face, he said, "Better them than you," then headed for one of the two men sprawled out on the asphalt. "Or am I wrong?" There was an almost feral indifference in his eyes. "There's another rifle around here somewhere. Find it before the second truck shows up."

Near the Corolla, Lupe was tending to Tío Faustino, still dazed, head lolling on his shoulder, and she dabbed at his facial wounds with the corner of her shirt while Samir, with Beto looking on passively, assured himself the remaining three men from the truck were dead, an insurance round to each skull. Roque felt like he might get sick, then caught the shrill grind of the second pickup downshifting into the bend. He scoured the ground, looking for the rifle Samir was sure lay somewhere nearby, while the Arab took up position in the middle of the road, shouldering his weapon.

The second pickup rounded the curve and Samir opened fire, at the same time circling quickly toward his right, the truck's left, leaving the cone of the headlights and making himself a moving target while aiming at the driver, head shots with his first two rounds, then taking on the men in back who'd begun to return fire. Roque, on his hands and knees, continued his frantic search of the ground until Lupe screamed, the sound torquing his head her direction. She stood there against the Corolla, trying to hold Tío Faustino up as he slid down the fender to the ground, shuddering visibly as he clutched at the blood streaming from his throat. Please no, Roque thought, while Beto—standing in the road between Roque and the car, firing away—had his head jerked back suddenly like he'd been head-butted, then he dropped hard to his knees, eyes glazed, brow furrowed as though he were contemplating some impossible thought, a portion of his skull drilled open just above the eye.

Roque knelt there paralyzed until Samir shouted, "Help me, grab a gun, shoot, shoot, fucking hell . . ." The Arab continued moving through the darkness in the same wide circle, muzzle flash like a flaming spark in the night. He'd picked off two of the gunmen in the truck bed, the third clung to the railing with one hand, the other clutching his shoulder. The man still alive inside the cab was shooting wildly out his window on the passenger side as the pickup drifted on, its driver dead. Roque lunged toward Beto's body—it lay in a strange lump, folded forward, as though he'd fallen asleep in the middle of a prayer—and pried the rifle from his hands.

He'd never held a gun before, never aimed one, never fired one. How hard can it be, he thought, raising it to his shoulder, aiming vaguely toward the pickup's windshield, pulling the trigger. The noise was ear-splitting, the butt plate bit into his shoulder and ricocheted hard against his jaw even as the weapon almost jumped out of his hands. He nearly tumbled flat but collected his legs as the brass shell casing pinged against the blacktop. Jerking the weapon back to his shoulder, he re-aimed, forcing himself to ignore the bullets whistling past, willing himself not to look at his uncle or Lupe, not now, not yet. Following Samir's example he began circling to his right, crouching as he pulled the trigger, once, twice, again, aiming toward the pickup cabin, not seeing faces, just shapes, firing over and over with no idea if he was hitting anything and then the rifle clicked helplessly. He was standing to the side of the pickup, dazed, his entire body cold with sweat. Only then did he notice the quiet: no gunfire. Just Lupe's muffled sobs, the moans from one or two of the gunmen and once again the ocean wind, the swaying hillside grass, the surf below.

He threw down the rifle and ran to his uncle while the two-tap reports of Samir's coups de grace punctuated the stillness.

Holding his uncle's head in her lap, Lupe pressed hard against the wound, blood seeping up between her fingers as she murmured frantically, "*No, no, no . . .*" A tourniquet was out of the question, no way to tightly bandage the wound and stay the bleeding without cutting off his air. His eyes rolled back behind fluttering eyelids, a mindless twitch in his hands.

—*Here, let me*, Roque said, nudging Lupe's hand aside, seeing the wound for the first time, lit by the glow from the pickup's headlights, an inch-long rip in the flesh of the throat, black and wet, the bullet having sliced an artery, the blood a throbbing stream. Only then did he see how soaked through Lupe's jeans were. He reached around the back of his uncle's neck, felt for the exit wound, fingered a tear in the skin twice the size of the one in front, the blood pouring out. He tried to press against both wounds at once but his uncle's eyes glistened whitely, his breathing was shallow, his skin waxy and cool. Lupe wept faintly, her face smeared with blood where she'd wiped away tears. She began whispering, "*Lo siento*," I'm sorry, over and over and Roque whispered that it wasn't her fault but she merely shook her head, closed her eyes and pounded her head with her fists.

Samir approached from behind, dragging the butt of his rifle against the pitted asphalt. Roque looked up over his shoulder into the Arab's face.

"We need to get him to a hospital."

"There isn't time." Samir's voice was soft and sad and strangely peaceful. "Pray for him. That is what he needs from you now."

Roque felt it then, the slackening of his uncle's musculature, the stillness in his chest. Lupe's whimpering grew louder, her eyes pressed shut and she pounded at her head even harder until Roque reached up, took her wrist.—*Don't*.

—*He was so kind to me*.

—*He wouldn't want it*.

He felt Samir's hand in his armpit, snagging a fistful of cloth, pulling him to his feet. He had to fight off an impulse to swing around, leading with his elbow, catch the Arab square in the face. What would that atone? Their eyes met. Samir said, "I need you to help me."

"You're quite the killer."

"I told you, I was in the army. Now—"

"My brother says the Iraqis were piss-poor shots. You were like—"

"Your brother doesn't know everything. Now come, I need your help."

Roque wiped his bloody hands on his pants and followed Samir toward the second pickup, still relatively intact. He smelled the lingering stench of cordite, the salt off the ocean.

Samir shuddered from exhaustion. "We'll load the bodies into the Corolla."

"Why?"

"Set fire to the car, let them think it's us."

Roque turned toward a sudden rustling sound. Beyond the headlights' glow, he caught the vague outline of a *zopilote* rucking its wings as it planted itself on the edge of the kill zone.

Turning back to Samir: "They'll figure it out sooner or later, the other truck—"

"It will buy us time. We're going to need it."

They set to work, dragging bodies from the truck, shoving them into the car, tossing in Beto too, a filthy business all around, the blood, the piss, the gore, the shit—men don't die in real life like they do in the movies, Roque thought. Twice, he needed to stop, walk to the edge of the road, hurl. Then they heard the distant grinding of gears, the whine of an engine downshifting into the approaching turn. A truck was coming. Samir took one of the rifles, waved Roque and Lupe out of sight, then knelt by the back of the second pickup, waited for the headlights to appear. He fired twice into the air. The truck lurched to a stop, the hissing shriek of brakes, the clatter of gears—the driver backed up, his rig vanishing back beyond the turn.

"Hurry," Samir said. "He may have a shortwave, a cell phone."

They finished packing the car with the dead, stopping at five, then collected their own few belongings from the trunk. Samir found a jerry can of gas behind the rollover pickup's passenger seat and he doused the Corolla while Roque and Lupe dragged Tío Faustino's body to the intact pickup and laid him out in the truck bed, covering him with a tarp they found bundled up there. Using matches he scoured from Beto's pocket, Samir set the Corolla ablaze, then collected all the weapons lying on the ground, tossed them in the back of the pickup under the tarp with Tío Faustino's body, jumped in at the passenger-side door and said, "Drive! Now!"

They were beyond the first bend when the Corolla's gas tank blew, the roar deafening and the plume of flame reaching high into the predawn darkness, rendering in harsh silhouette the intervening hills with their shaggy crown of windblown grass. The buzzard rose into the sky, fleeing the fireball, visible only briefly at the edges of the rippling light. Roque pushed the truck as fast as he could, peering past the two holes in the windshield, a spiderweb pattern surrounding each one, reaching over when he could to console Lupe, telling her again it was not her fault, there was nothing she could do, until finally she fell still and sat there, staring out through the same shattered windshield.

PART III

THIRTY-THREE

IT WAS LUPE'S IDEA TO STOP AT THE CHURCH.

They'd driven for an hour, daybreak brightening a cloud-jumbled sky, but once they passed the village of Barra de la Cruz they knew trusting their luck any longer was foolhardy. The Bahías de Huatulco lay ahead with their tony resorts; sooner or later they'd reach a checkpoint and it wouldn't much matter who manned it, the police or the army, vigilantes or paramilitaries, not with the ambushers' weapons and Tío Faustino's body in the truck bed.

The sign for the church pointed up a steep and rutted dirt lane shaded by majestic ceibas with their hand-shaped leaf clusters, the peaks of the Sierra Madre del Sur in the distance. There was a notice posted beneath the sign, a declaration from the local archbishop, warning of a con man working the area, impersonating a priest and performing sacred functions—confessions, deathbed absolutions, baptisms, even weddings—for a fee. Atop the hill, the church sat in a clearing surrounded by cornfields—a short steeple lacking a cross, walls the yellow of egg yolks, wood shutters painted an electric blue. Shaped differently, Roque thought, it might have passed for an Easter egg.

Lupe gestured to Samir to let her out.—*Let me talk to the priest.*

Samir didn't move.—*What will you tell him?*

Her face was weary with grief.—*I'll say we got attacked by bandits along the road. We have someone we need to bury. He was a good man* . . . She trembled, choking something back.—*He deserves to buried by the church, he deserves to be blessed and prayed for.*

—*Look at you.* Samir eyed her blouse, her jeans, caked with dried blood.—*He'll think you're crazy. Worse, he'll think*—

With the fury of a child, she began slapping at his head, his chest, his shoulder.—*Let me out, asshole. Now. Out of my way* . . .

Samir obliged, if only to escape the indignity. She slid across the seat into the gathering sunlight and stormed off, even her ponytail clotted with blood. Samir slid his hand around his face, chafing the stubble, eyeing her as she climbed the wood-plank steps to the church's front doors. They were locked. She rattled them hard, testing to be sure, then ventured around back, to an add-on section that looked as though it might be the rectory. A modest cemetery lay beyond.

As she vanished around the corner, the Arab leaned his weight against the pickup's open door, as though only that were keeping him upright.

"We can't drive this truck much farther." Roque checked the gas gauge, an eighth of a tank remaining, but that wasn't what he was getting at. "We get to a roadblock, it won't just be the bullet holes we have to answer for. Even if we bury my uncle's body here, ditch the guns—"

"You seriously want to continue without weapons?"

"The worst is behind us."

"Says who?"

"The truck's registered in somebody else's name. That alone, boom, we're done. And for all we know those men we killed were police, military, someone else we'll have to answer for."

Samir squinted against the dusty wind. "All this I already know."

"Fine." Roque opened his door, dragged himself out from behind the wheel and stretched his legs. His clothing, too, was crusted with dried blood. Turning to the truck bed, he checked the tarp covering the weapons and Tío Faustino's body, tugging at the corners. He lacked the nerve to peek underneath. "Since you already know everything, solve the problem."

"We'll catch a bus at the nearest town up the road, head for Mexico City. We'll catch another bus there for Agua Prieta."

"We're sitting ducks on the bus. If those really were cops back there, soldiers, paramilitaries, whatever, word will spread. They'll be looking for us everywhere. On a bus we have nowhere to run."

"You asked my solution, I gave it to you. You don't like it . . ." He shrugged.

"We can call Victor, back in Arriaga, he might—"

"Who does he know we do not know ourselves? I bet he was bought off. They probably want his skin because we are not already dead."

"You think he betrayed his own, betrayed Beto."

"Let me tell you something, this kind of animal we're dealing with? We paid all that money for nothing. When the gangsters take charge, everything turns to chaos. Trust me, I have seen it with my own eyes. We would be fools to stay with them."

Despite his fury, Roque felt encouraged by this turn. If Samir was giving up on the *salvatruchos* down here, maybe he'd given up on making the connection with El Recio in Agua Prieta as well. That meant Lupe was free. After all, they were dead. Their bodies were back there on the road, burned to cinders in the Corolla. "You saying we're on our own?"

"I am saying we need to be careful. We need—" He winced, something in his eye. He rubbed at it, face naked with fatigue. "Honestly? I have no clue what we need."

Lupe reappeared, trailed by a man in street clothes, not a cassock. He looked younger than Roque expected, more trim and fit too, though he wore perhaps the world's nerdiest pair of glasses. He headed straight for the truck bed and glanced down at the wind-rucked tarp. No one said anything. Up close, the man's face told a more complex story. He had wary eyes and a sensual mouth but a strong jaw, a fighter's misshapen nose. His thinning brown hair curled around his ears and he had an educated air, though with a worker's ropy musculature and rough hands. Finally, he looked up and met Roque's eyes.—*He was your uncle?*

Roque glanced toward Lupe, but she looked away rather than meet his gaze. Turning back to the man, he nodded.

—*We can bury him here if you like. Preparing him for transport elsewhere, to be buried in the United States, let's say, will take time. And the involvement of the authorities.*

He paused there, everyone conceding what he declined to add.

—*I'm Father Ruano, by the way. Or Father Luis. Whichever you prefer.*

—*I think it's fine, we bury him here.* Roque's voice was so hushed he had to repeat himself.—*I'll let my aunt know where she can visit the grave. We can visit it together . . .* His voice trailed away, as though heading off to find some truth in what he'd just said.

—*All right, then.* The priest backed away from the truck, pointing vaguely toward the cemetery.—*If you carry him behind the church, I will get the shovels. We will have to dig ourselves. That's not a problem, I assume.*

BY MIDMORNING THEY'D FINISHED THE GRAVE, WORKING IN CONCERT, even the priest pitching in. Though baked hard from the tropical sun, the ground was sandy with little rock or clay to break through. They covered their noses and mouths with bandannas against the fine coarse dust, while Lupe murmured the rosary over and over, the monotony of the prayers only intensifying the monotony of the work. Not that anyone complained. It seemed fitting that things should go slow and hard. It rendered the effort devotional. And it distracted them from the *zopilotes* riding the thermals overhead.

The vultures weren't the only visitors from the sky. Swarms of monarch butterflies, migrants themselves, descended from the foothills in the southerly downdrafts. Some of the birds Roque had seen in the plates of his Peterson Field Guide made appearances here; he spotted petrels, frigate birds.

He grew numb as his shovel bit into the dirt, wondering if the pain that gnawed at his arms and the small of his back, the blisters breaking open on his palms, weren't all conspiring to fashion a wall between what he needed to do and what he hoped to feel. In time, though, memories rose up to deliver a little shock of feeling, one recollection in particular standing out, the afternoon of his twelfth birthday.

Until then he'd been practicing guitar on loaners from friends. Then Lalo went to the trouble of stopping by the house to meet Tía Lucha, touting her nephew's talent. "He's a natural, *señora*, an intelligent ear, excellent dexterity, he learns quickly and, at least when it comes to music"—and here he shot Roque a reproving glance—"exhibits considerable discipline." His problems at school were roundly known, though he was an avid reader—science fiction, crime stories, comics, even some precocious porn. Tía Lucha feared that deeper involvement in music would only mean more skipped classes, more trouble. Tío Faustino, though, did not hesitate. He went to the store with Lalo, asked which guitar he would recommend. Lalo would later confide to Roque that his uncle was almost obsequiously polite, as workers from his part of the world so often are with the educated, and perhaps out of pride made no mention of cost. The courtship between Faustino and Lucha was still fresh at that point and Roque had no doubt the gift was intended as much to impress his aunt as him. No one had ever spent so much money on his behalf, certainly not for a gift. Tía Lucha looked on with a miserly expression as Roque opened the hard-shell case, lifted the nylon-string guitar from its red plush bed, played a bit of "Canción de Cuna," just enough to piss off Godo. "Learn another fucking tune," he moaned and Tía Lucha threatened a backhand for his cursing. Tío Faustino merely sat there with a hopeful smile, black grime beneath his fingernails from replacing the rings on his truck, his curly hair mussed, waiting for Roque to thank him.

A woodworker from a nearby village delivered a pine coffin on a mule-drawn cart and they lifted the body into it, hammered the lid shut, then lowered it into the grave using ropes. It all went too quickly for Roque to make much of his last glance at his uncle's body. Father Luis retrieved his stole and missal from the rectory and said a few prayers that consoled no one. Lupe wept softly, hand clasped across her mouth. Roque, feeling gutted, just stared into the grave, vaguely reassured by Lupe's emotion, tapping into it secondhand. I will miss you, he nearly said aloud, but caught himself, for he felt the sorrow welling up and knew, once he gave in, there would be no end to it. Then the priest concluded his prayers, the men grabbed their tools again and began to toss back the dirt they'd just dug, the thud of each shovelful atop the coffin like a footfall on some invisible stair.

When they were finished, Father Luis said quietly:—*I'm sure we all could use something to eat*. He led them into the rectory's dining room—a crucifix and the Virgin of Guadalupe on the rough plaster wall, a modest cedar table with a white linen cloth. His tiny Mixtec housekeeper set out bowls of corn porridge called *atole*, tortillas with bean paste and *mole*, limes and salt, plus sliced fruit and a basket of *chapulines*, spicy fried grasshoppers. The woman's name was Dolor and she reminded Roque of the Chamula woman selling popcorn in Arriaga. Samir wolfed down his food, Lupe fussed with hers mindlessly, Roque felt more possessed by his thirst than his appetite. No one but the priest bothered with the grasshoppers.

Once the housekeeper collected the plates and fled to the kitchen, Father Luis looked around the table, registering each face as he enjoyed his dessert, dipping a hunk of soft white bread in a cup of Oaxacan hot chocolate.—*You are not the first migrants who have landed on our doorstep in serious trouble. Perhaps I'm mistaken, but I can't help imagining you have a special problem.* He lifted one of his hands; unlike Roque, he'd suffered no blisters. —*I do not need to know what it is. I would, however, like to know if I'm vaguely correct.*

The weapons had raised an eyebrow or two during the day, as had Samir's accent. Roque had an accent too, of course, but his was easily explained.

—*The only thing special about our problem*, Roque said, *is that the people we paid to get us to the States have been unable to protect us. Their competitors, their enemies, whoever it was out there on the road last night, they've been after us almost from the start. And yet, from what I know about how things are down here, there's nothing really special about that at all.*

The priest dipped another morsel of bread in his chocolate. —*The government is secretly in league with the Americans. It uses the federal police and the military to push back against the waves of people surging up from the south, who are doing nothing more than voting with their feet. And if the gangs rob the migrants or murder them? If the vigilantes or the paramilitaries torture them, then turn them over to the authorities? Nothing happens. It's become a criminal system, there is no other word for it. Everyone is dirty.*

He brushed a trail of crumbs from the tablecloth into his palm, scowling as he dusted them into his empty coffee cup.

—*I believe I may know someone who can help you. He's an American who lives up the way, a bit of a character, very storied life, if I'm to accept as true all he's told me, which is probably foolish. My point is, I think he could find some way to be of assistance.* He smiled abstractly, peering over the thick black ledge of his glasses.—*If, however, I have read the situation incorrectly and you simply want to continue north on your own, you are of course free to do so. But I must warn you, the guns are a mistake. They will not protect you. One way or another, they will betray you.*

THIRTY-FOUR

THEY HID THE PICKUP IN THE RECTORY GARAGE AFTER FATHER Luis drove off. Come nightfall they'd drive it back down the coastal road a ways and push it over the first convenient cliff.

The issue of the guns was seemingly resolved when Samir claimed only a pistol and one of the Kalashnikovs.—*You have not had to survive what we have*, he'd told Father Luis.—*I mean no disrespect but prayers would not have saved us. And I am a man who prays*. The priest had countered that if they were caught with weapons at a checkpoint they wouldn't be sent back to where they'd started, they'd be packed off to jail—and a Mexican jail was nowhere a foreigner wanted to be. Nor could it be known he had guns at the church. Ever since the teachers strike two years back, there were paramilitaries roaming the countryside looking for subversives. Goons and off-duty police murdered at will: organizers, activists, journalists, including an American. The governor boasted an army of thugs and everywhere he went violence broke out, invariably blamed on his opponents. Priests were always suspect, especially those who, like him, served the *pinches nacos*—the fucking Indians.

—*If someone finds weapons here, they will burn this church to the ground. Too bad for whoever happens to be inside at the time*.

And so it was decided another grave needed digging, a shallow one, into which not most but all the guns disappeared.

Once the work was done, Dolor showed them to a washroom with a large tin tub, a cake of lye soap and a bucket of well water, asking for their clothes; she would dissolve the blood with hydrogen peroxide, then wash everything and hang it out in the sun. Lupe had only blouses and underwear to change into and so hid herself away in a spare room after washing the blood from her hair, sponging the rest of her body clean, handing up her filthy clothes. The old woman hefted the tub out into the yard and dumped the dirty water, then refreshened the bucket from the well and gestured for Samir. He was even worse off, only the clothes on his back, rank from weeks of relentless wear; once he had a chance to scrub the grime off his body, he modestly handed everything he'd been wearing through a gap in the washroom door. Roque went last; he stripped, passed his clothes to the housekeeper, then went to the tin washtub and began to lather his hands with the knife-cut square of grainy soap.

From his spot on the floor where he sat naked, arms folded across his knees, Samir said, "I have been thinking about what we discussed before, what to do from here, who to trust. Even if the priest links us up with this American he knows, we still have to get across the border. Without money, that's impossible, unless we stay with our original plan. That fee is already paid. And no offense, I understand you are grieving, but there is one less among us now. They can hardly complain. Perhaps they won't even make us hand up the girl. It's possible, you know."

Roque glanced over his shoulder as he lathered his hands. The Arab was chewing on his thumb, worrying it like a bone. "You'd do that?"

"Let me tell you something, I have never wanted harm for that girl. Never. I just accepted things as they were. I understood I had little control of my fate. The same is true for her, so which of us is free to weep?"

Like that's the issue, Roque thought. "You said you'd lost confidence in the *salvatruchos*."

"They can't be expected to foresee everything or protect us from every evil. Who knows who those men on the road were?"

He inspected the reddened horn of his thumb. "Maybe they were El Chusquero's, maybe they were Mara Dieciocho, maybe they were police or soldiers or just common thieves."

Roque gripped the edge of the washtub, looking down into the water murky with soap scum. "I won't agree to handing Lupe over. I was against it before but now, no, it's impossible. Not with my uncle . . . It's bad enough I failed him, I can't fail her too. His ghost will haunt me the rest of my life."

Samir chuckled. "So you're one who believes in ghosts now."

"You know what I mean."

"You think I don't understand how you feel? Let me tell you something, I too suffer the loss of your uncle. He was a very kind, very hopeful, very brave man. I see his son in him, him in his son. I know, I know, they are very different too but I see the similarities. I will miss him—yes, as little as I knew him, I will miss him. And I think I know enough about him to guess that he would also not want to know that by refusing to honor our promise, we have condemned my wife and my little girl, Shatha, to the misery of their life in Al Tanf. They will die there. It is only a question of when."

We all have to die someplace, Roque thought. "I'm sure he would've felt for your wife and child. But he expressed to me a particular concern for Lupe."

"That is the choice, yes? Lupe or my family. Obviously, my choice is clear. And not because I am heartless. Should you become a husband, a father, you will feel what I feel."

"You know," Roque said, turning around so his nakedness faced the Arab's, "when I was waiting in Arriaga, I heard that it's not just evangelicals making inroads down here but Muslims as well. Not so much here in Oaxaca but farther south, Chiapas, in the mountains. Mosques have been cropping up more and more the past few years, that was the gossip anyway, teaching Arabic to Chamula kids who don't even know Spanish yet. Maybe you could come back here with your family, settle in the hills, teach. Life could be worse."

Using his shoe, Samir crushed a furry red spider crawling toward him on the cement floor. "That is always easy for the other man to say."

"It's better your family stay in that camp?"

"Given everything that's happened, you honestly believe I would want my family here? Would you bring yours?" He scraped the spider's remains off his shoe. "Sure, why not? You'd be closer to your uncle's grave."

"Don't mock."

"Don't make such ridiculous suggestions."

Roque turned back to the tub, glancing down into the scummy water again, his reflection a misshapen blur. Finishing up his wash, he soon heard the soft wheeze of the Arab's breath whistling through his teeth. Glancing over his shoulder, he saw Samir still sitting there, legs tucked up, arms locked around his knees but his head had dropped. He'd fallen fast asleep.

ROQUE PULLED JEANS AND UNDERSHORTS AND A T-SHIRT FROM HIS knapsack, dressing like a backdoor man slipping out before daylight, Samir dozing away. The clothes weren't clean but they'd serve until Dolor was done with the wash. Standing for a moment in the doorway, he watched across the parched hardpan of the churchyard as the tiny Mixtec woman pinned up the damp wrinkled clothes, shirt sleeves and pant legs bucking in the wind.

He idled through the rectory with its concrete floors, coarse plaster walls, bare plank ceilings. It was the stillness, though, that struck him. Lifting his head he silently prayed not to God or any of the saints or angels but to his uncle and his mother. His prayer was brief: Help me. He felt weak and lost and, in that moment, a little dishonest but there was no harm in trying, he supposed.

Then he caught the muffled keen of Lupe's sobs beyond a thick wood door.

A smallness inside him wondered what she had to cry about. What secrets had she and Tío shared during their trek from Tecún Umán to Arriaga? He wondered if they'd talked about him. What a needy little shit you are, he thought. Was that your uncle's job, be your pimp?

He eased toward the door, pressed his ear to the wood. Knocking quietly, "Lupe?"

No answer, just snuffling. The door clicked open. Through the gap he spotted a narrow bed of wood planks, a thin straw tick for a mattress. He didn't see Lupe till he edged his way in, easing back the door. She closed it quickly behind him, standing there naked.

Her damp hair hung tangled across her shoulders, down her chest and back, her breasts peeking through the uncombed strands. Her face was streaked with old tears, fresh ones welled in her eyes. She stepped into his arms, laying her head upon his chest, hands listless at her sides. He held her, pressed his cheek to her drying hair, thick with the fatty smell of the soap. They stood like that until she laced her fingers in his, guided him to the bed, attended to his zipper, pulled off his T-shirt. Neither of them spoke. This isn't love, he told himself, this is grief, her eyes told him that. And yet touch had never felt so familiar, so necessary. She made room for him and they lay side by side, straw rustling inside the tick as they settled in. Bits of straw poked through the burlap like a hundred pinpricks but when he reached out her skin was smooth and warm and met his sore hand, raw with blisters, with a welcoming tremble. All those times he'd fantasized about sharing her bed, catching her off guard with his know-how, the deft little tricks Mariko had taught him, that all felt obscene now. Open the fuck up, he told himself. No more moody loner, no more hotshot with the sad guitar. Let her in.

She kissed clumsily and the thrill of that startled him. He

could taste on her breath a hint of the lemon slices Dolor had stirred into the pitcher during their afternoon meal, along with the vague tin taste of the pitcher itself. He could smell, beneath the mask of soap, a lingering tang of sweat and her growing wetness. She slid beneath him, lifted her legs and wrapped them around his hips, guided him in. No foreplay, no romance, this wasn't about that. He opened her slowly, shallow at first, deepening his movements bit by bit, rocking his hips gently until the two of them felt locked together. A sense of having found something, not blindly, foretold. He let the sadness come in waves and he rode them toward her, one by one, and she wept out loud as she came, pulling him tight, locking her legs around him, pushing her body hard against his, a dozen rough little jolts or more, jabbing in time with her sobs, then finally she dropped back on the burlap tick, covered her face with her hands. He wanted to tell her no, please, let me see your face, but before he could, she whispered:—*I promise I will keep this baby. If God wills it should grow inside me and live, I will keep it and name it Faustino. Or Faustina. I will remember. I will always remember. I am not a bad person. I am stupid and vain and weak but I am not evil. I'm so sorry. I'm sorry, I'm sorry . . .*

THIRTY-FIVE

A DOZEN SQUAD CARS JAMMED THE STREET ON THE HILL ABOVE the sugar refinery, strobes flashing blue and red in the afternoon fog, plus another half-dozen unmarked sedans, a canine van, the coroner's wagon. The TV crews were being held back for now but they'd get cut loose soon enough. All we're missing, Lattimore thought, is the caterer.

He was standing on the porch with the detective from Crockett, one of just two on the local force; they rotated in and out of patrol on a quarterly schedule. This guy's name was Dunn—chunky, a workhorse, black loafers, blue suit. They were waiting as a uniform marched up the drive, carrying the pictures requested from Rio Mirada PD.

Lattimore took the manila envelope from the officer and unwound the thread, opened it, shaking out the contents, frontal and profile in-custody shots of Pablo "Happy" Orantes and Godofredo Montalvo, taken from their arrest on pot charges two years back. He felt a curious mix of dread and mystification at the sight of Happy's face, a vaguely guilty sadness at Godo's. He remembered the young man well, not just from his name cropping up in the undercover tapes but from that day at the trailer park, when he stood there with his pitted face and a Remington pump-loader, holding off two gung-ho morons from ICE. A miracle all three of them hadn't died right there. Two marines from his own battalion had taken a similar turn after Desert Storm—a standoff with guns, one with a hostage—and they'd seen far less to justify it, though how did one measure such things?

Dunn waved toward the photos like a lazy magician. "Anything you can tell me?"

They were debriefing the surviving victims here at the scene because they only had two interview rooms at the station. The pictures were for six-packs they were showing to the cleaning lady, who had broken down the instant she was alone in a room with a cop, begging him and everyone else to understand, she'd been forced into the scheme, they'd threatened her girls. For now everyone, Lattimore included, was willing to accept that. She was cooperating, hoping to forestall deportation. They'd tell her the bad news on that front once they were done with her.

Lattimore puffed his cheeks. "They're cousins, more or less. Not the easiest family to unravel." He pronounced Godo's full name, tried to explain the connection, him and Happy.

Dunn regarded him stonily. "Let's stick with 'cousins,' shall we?"

"This one, Montalvo, he doesn't look like this now. Came back from Iraq looking like a woodpecker mistook him for a stump, shrapnel wounds all over his face."

"But this Orantes mutt, the ringleader, he was your boy?"

Lattimore glanced up. The man was thickly jowled, his stubble and brush cut the same dull gray. His eyes lay burrowed in creased flesh. "My CI."

"Right," Dunn said. "No offense meant."

Lattimore had already endured his first quick interview with OPR; they were trawling through the case files now, seeing what laws or guidelines had gotten short shrift in his handling of things. He felt confident he'd survive the scrutiny—Pete Orpilla, his supe, had his back and for now things felt tense but not hysterical. This mess had come out of the blue, no hint that Happy had been side-balling him but that didn't mean somebody wouldn't want his head. All it would take is one call, a congressman, a mayor, somebody with juice paying back a favor. In the time it took to pick up a phone, his career could be history. Maybe that was just. It was possible, without even knowing it, he'd lost interest in the thing, gotten sloppy. Maybe he was just too old—at forty-four, an eye-opener.

Dunn gargled a knot of phlegm loose from his sinuses and spat. "Like I said, anything you could tell me?"

Lattimore shrugged. "Hard to know what to say. Happy was inward, suspicious, a plodder, not a showboat. He was in this for his family, that's what he said anyway. Wanted everybody back together, home safe for good." How could I, he thought, misread that so badly? "Never asked for much, listened when you told him things, followed orders."

Dunn, glancing over his shoulder at the house, "Until today, I expect."

"Exactly."

"Maybe he was saving all his chits up for this."

Lattimore shivered the pictures back inside the envelope. "That's crossed my mind."

The cleaning lady had already identified Ramon "Puchi" Parada and Manuel "Chato" López in photo six-packs, no such luck with Vasco Ramírez. So far it looked like he'd kept his hands clean of the actual rough stuff, not that it had kept him from fleeing. They'd found his car abandoned at the Greyhound lot in Rio Mirada, about two hundred yards from the garbage bin where he'd dumped his cell phone. God only knew where he was headed, San Diego most likely, after that a brisk walk across the border.

Earlier that afternoon, Lattimore had come down hard on both the truck yard and Vasco's home, only to find the icy wife, who'd already lawyered up, and the strange and sickly daughter. The wife had screamed obscenities at any agent who so much as cracked a door. "Where's your fucking warrant?"—over and over, top of her lungs, like somebody'd pulled a string, and Lattimore must have told her fifty times they had a warrant, an arrest warrant for her husband, in response to which he got called every variety of fucker and faggot in the Latin bitch lexicon: *puto*, *pendejo*, *chingado*, *jodido*, *culero*, *maricón*, *mariquita*, *mariposón*, with *hijueputa* and *hijo de la verga* and *hijo de la chingada* thrown in just for the sake of thoroughness. Through all of that the little girl sat stock-still on the couch, clutching a stuffed bear reeking of cigarettes, eyes as mournful as a basset hound's. Compared to that, he supposed, you could nominate Lourdes the cleaning lady for mother of the year. Too bad that didn't decide who got sent packing.

Using the envelope, he gestured to the door. "Shall we?"

The techs had already scraped and sampled everything they wanted, there was no need to put on the booties. Lourdes was sitting in the kitchen, a chunky woman cop standing guard. Dunn collected the sergeant who'd done the original photo displays and Lattimore gave him the pictures of Happy and Godo, told him to work them into six-packs for a follow-up.

They ambled into the kitchen and pulled up chairs across from Lourdes. Having cried herself out, her eyes were raw; her face, though, was a closed door. She sat there, hands clasped, waiting for the next bad thing to happen. Dunn smiled and did his magic-hand thing again as the sergeant arrived and placed the six-packs on the table.

He said, "We'd like you to go through some more pictures, Lourdes," pronouncing it *Lurdz*. "We're not saying the men you haven't been able to identify yet are in here or not. We'd just like you to look them through—no pressure, no problem one way or the other, we appreciate all you've done so far—look them through and see if any of the faces ring a bell, okay?"

She swept an invisible strand of hair off her face. "My daughters—"

"We've sent someone from CPS to watch over your daughters. They're fine."

"I would like to talk to them."

Dunn's smile slid a little downhill. "Let's go through the pictures first, Lourdes. These men are at large. You want us to catch them, right?"

She turned her attention to her task. On the third set she stopped, looked, blinked. "This one." She pointed, bottom center. Happy. "He the one who talk to me. The leader, I think. We talk a lot. All night."

Dunn took a pen from his inside pocket, thumbed the plunger. "Take a good look, Lourdes. No rush. Be certain."

She shook her head. "It is him. I know. His eyes. The chin." She docked her head a little. "Hair, yes, this is different. And he look older now, more thin . . ."

That's it, Lattimore thought, let her talk herself out of her own ID. "Lourdes—"

She waved her hands, fending off doubt. "It is him. I sure."

Dunn pulled that set aside, jotted down the group and position numbers. She went on, picking through the photo sets. Reaching the one with Godo, she looked it over, paused, looked it over again, then moved on. So much for that theory, Lattimore thought. She was already scouring the next group when her face bunched up, she went back, looked at the last set again.

"Him," she said, pointing out Godo. "I not recognize him first time. He different now." She circled her hand about her own face. "*Picoteado*. I see him out there, the farmhouse, with the others. He was the big one I tell you about. Quiet. He was quiet."

From behind, a uniform cleared his throat. "Agent Lattimore?" A finger drumbeat on the doorframe. "AUSA Pitcavage just signed in at the barricade. Said you should meet him outside?"

LATTIMORE WAITED ON THE PORCH, WATCHING PITCAVAGE ADVANCE through the swirls of blue-and-red light. He had another attorney in tow, a corn-silk blonde in a smart gray suit, no overcoat, bucking the wind with a power stride, holding her hair out of her face with one hand, the other clutching her briefcase. Pitcavage came empty-handed, like a pasha. They climbed the driveway, the woman impressively sure-footed in her pumps. She had a Midwestern prettiness, everything in its place, dull as a prairie. Nice pair though, Lattimore thought, something even the suit couldn't hide.

Pitcavage gestured him off the porch for a private conclave, shooting the blonde a knowing glance that told her to stay put. Like a collie, she obeyed. Ambling toward the garage, hands in his pockets, he waited for Lattimore. Overhead, a turkey vulture sailed toward the strait.

Pitcavage crossed his arms and made sure none of the local cops was within earshot. "Anything new on where Mr. Orantes might be?"

Lattimore shook his head and tried to straighten up, assume full height, if only to reassert that crucial inch over the lawyer. "You mean from what I've found out here?"

"I mean from what you've found out, period."

"His cell phone tracks to somewhere out in the wetlands, little north of here."

Pitcavage cocked an eyebrow. "We couldn't be so lucky he's lying right there beside it, could we." It wasn't a question.

"I suppose we could get the locals to dredge around, look for a weighted body." He found himself ambivalent on the merits of finding Happy dead.

"Ask," Pitcavage said, pulling a stick of gum from his pocket, peeling away the foil.

"Sure."

"If he's alive—and halfway smart—he's in Mexico already, maybe El Salvador." He balled up the foil wrapper, dropped it discreetly, chewing noisily. "He's got connections down there, or am I wrong?"

"Of a sort, yeah."

"You see him running somewhere else?"

"No. El Salvador, because it's familiar. Mexico, because it's Mexico."

"He gets caught, tries to use his CI status to buy his way out? The lid comes off this thing and there won't be any putting it back on." Pitcavage crossed his arms, the unhappy prince. "We become the idiots who green-lighted a comical case with a bent snitch. That's something I can live without. Which reminds me: You've shut the thing down. Or Orpilla has?"

"Of course."

"But you've still got two of the relatives, the CI's father, his cousin or something, wandering around Central America somewhere."

"Along with the interpreter, the Iraqi, Palestinian, whatever. Samir Khalid Sadiq."

Pitcavage winced. "Fuck me."

"They were in Guatemala last time we knew for certain. The cell phone we had a bead on went dead about a week ago."

"A *week*?"

"Jon—"

"And your CI had what to say about that?"

"Said his cousin turned the phone off, save the battery. It's not like they're staying in Sheratons down there, 220 wall sockets everywhere they stop."

"And you believed him?"

Lattimore felt a sagging weight, pulling him down, losing the crucial inch. "At that point, I had no reason not to."

"A week. Jesus."

"Not a whole week. Four days. Maybe five."

Pitcavage pinched the bridge of his nose. Posturing. "Give me your sense of the locals."

Toeing a clump of dead grass rooted in a crack in the driveway, Lattimore said, "I haven't caught wind of any axes to grind, if that's what you mean."

"They're not going to ass-fuck us in the press?"

There's a picture, Lattimore thought. "Not yet."

"Until they can't close the thing. Then they'll start pointing fingers, say one of the two still at large was a federal informant. Oh how lovely that will be."

"Like I said, I'm not sensing any agendas."

"Make sure it stays that way. Let them know, as far as cooperation's concerned, anything and everything's on the table. It's not going to be the usual one-way street. They want you to sharpen pencils, you do it. They want you to blow every drunk in the holding tank—"

Another picture. "There any chance we can get a wiretap on the aunt's phone? She may be the only point of contact between our CI and the three guys heading north for the border. That's likely our best bet for getting a bead on everybody."

"Under Title III? Not a chance." Pitcavage went to spit out his gum, caught himself; it was a crime scene, after all. He glanced down at the foil wrapper but didn't pick it up. "Prove to me her phone's being used to advance criminal activity, show me there's no other way to advance the investigation, maybe. But not if we're fishing. Locals might have better luck under state law, which returns us to the subject of making nice. Keep them happy. For your own sake if no one else's."

He clapped Lattimore on the back with staged camaraderie, then turned and strode back toward the street, signaling the ample blonde in the prim gray suit to come along. Lattimore wondered how long they'd been lovers.

He went back in, saw Dunn wrapping up with Lourdes, gestured him into the living room. He worked up a good-buddy smile. "I know somebody you're going to want to talk to."

TWO NIGHTS NOW, GODO STILL HADN'T COME HOME, NO CALL, NO MESsage on the machine. Lucha decided to remake his bed as though that might conjure him back. The sheet felt papery crisp beneath her hands as she spread it flat, tucked it tight, that bracing smell. For a moment at least she felt something like hope, even happiness, opening a window to let in some air. What a stench that boy could have, so much worse since he came back from the war. Not just the wounds. He didn't take care of himself. She grabbed the trash basket and went around the room, collecting balled-up tissues, shredded bits of newspaper—he did this as he watched TV, like a hamster lining its cage—candy wrappers, beer cans. Next she gathered his dirty clothes into a pile, shrinking from the smell. Finding one particularly rank tennis shoe, she hunted for its mate, got down on her knees, checked beneath the bed. The shotgun and pistol were gone. She checked the nightstand, rifling open the drawer. That gun wasn't there, either, nor the pills.

Don't get worked up over nothing, she told herself, sitting on the bed. He'd talked the past few weeks about going out with a group of friends, target practice, the shooting range, showing them a proper respect for their weapons. He said it helped him get over his nerves, so noises didn't make him jump quite so much. And he had, she thought, seemed more relaxed, more focused, stronger. Then, like that—poof, gone, no word. It was like him in some sense, so thoughtless, so unpredictable. And yet she couldn't shake a bad feeling. Her dreams had been strange and violent but that had been true since they'd sent Faustino away and it had only grown worse after Roque went down to bring him back. She spent all day trying not to think of what might happen to them, only to have it float up without warning in her sleep.

Then there was Happy. He came and went, sometimes the crack of dawn, sometimes the dead of night, careful to the point of paranoia. Still, his visits were a comfort. He'd changed, grown more respectful. More like his father. He too had vanished, not a glimpse of him for days.

Her loneliness seemed heavier, harder to bear. She felt afraid.

A moment later—was it longer?—the phone rang and she tripped over her own feet, banging into the doorway, running to answer it. Gripping the receiver with both hands, she shouted into the mouthpiece, "*Sí. ¿Aló?*"

"Tía Lucha?"

It was Roque. He sounded odd. Different.

—Where are you?

—Tía . . .

—Tell me—where are you?

—Somewhere in Mexico. Tía—

—Are you all right?

—Is Happy there?

Why would he want to speak to Pablito?*—I haven't seen him for days. The same for your brother. Roque—*

—Godo's not there?

—No one is here. I am here. What's wrong? Talk to me. For the sake of God and his angels, she thought, get a grip on yourself. The line went still for a moment, just the hiss of static.*—Roque?*

—Tío Faustino . . .

His voice trailed away. Lucha felt her stomach turn to stone. The taste of copper rose from her throat, her ulcer. As though she were suddenly standing somewhere else in the room, she heard herself say:*—No.*

—Tío Faustino is dead, Tía. I'm sorry.

She braced herself against the table. *No . . .*

—There were bandits on the road, hired killers, somebody. I don't know who it was. I don't know why they attacked us. We buried Tío in a cemetery here, behind a church, the priest has been very kind. I'm so sorry, Tía. I wanted to bring him home for you. I wanted . . .

The hand holding the receiver drifted downward as Lucha stared at the Día de los Muertos figurines on her display shelf, the skeletal mariachis, the unicyclist, the doctor and nurse with their patient in his bed. The truck driver. The bride and groom. Come

November, she would have to choose which grave to decorate for the holiday, her sister's close to home here or Faustino's far away in Mexico.

Setting the phone down gently, she glided back to her room, unaware of her own footfalls, and pulled open the closet doors. Faustino's clothes hung there tidily, waiting for his return. One shirt in particular caught her eye, her favorite. It was long-sleeved and white with pearl buttons, gold piping across the shoulders and at the cuffs, a cowboy shirt, but the collar had a subtle touch of embroidery along the edge, very delicate and yet manly. Faustino, with all his simplicity, his rustic manners, his ample belly, had always looked so elegant in it, so handsome. He wore it sometimes when they went out to dinner and the waitresses always smiled at him. And I would get jealous, she reminded herself, and then we would argue. She lifted the sleeve to her cheek, closed her eyes, waited. What kind of monster are you, she thought, unable to muster a single tear for your *marido*?

A knock came hard at the trailer door and it felt like a hand plunging into her chest. The shirtsleeve dropped, she was stumbling toward the sound, saw the phone hanging by its cord where she'd dropped it. A voice called out, "Police! Open up!"

THIRTY-SIX

"NO OFFENSE, MIND YOU, BUT I CAN'T BELIEVE YOU HONESTLY thought you could pay some clown at one end of the pipeline and think he'd get you all the way home. Those days are over, folks. Have been for a while."

His name was Rick Bergen, the resourceful American eccentric the priest had collected. Floating somewhere in his middle years, he was suntanned, well fed but not pudgy with a full head of ash-blond hair. Laugh lines creased his eyes, a handclap of a smile.

They were gathered around the dining-room table, Bergen and Lupe and Roque and Samir. Father Luis had gone off to bless a local fisherman's *lancha*; Dolor was mending altar linens in the sacristy. The basket of *chapulines* sat at the center of the table, back for an encore. Everyone but Bergen ignored them, though his enthusiasm was almost infectious.

"I relied on my cousin to arrange that side of things," Roque managed to say. He still felt only half there, the other half still on the phone, waiting for Tía Lucha to come back on the line.

"Your cousin misunderstood the playing field," Bergen said.

The man dressed, Roque thought, as though hoping to be invisible: simple sport shirt, tan linen slacks, no jewelry beyond a weatherproof watch. He could have vanished in any crowd of expats. When asked what it was he did, he'd replied simply that he "tried to help out here and there." At one point he let slip that he was a pilot, or had been.

Roque stared at the tiny basket of fried grasshoppers as though the things might come alive. "My cousin paid the same people to come across just a few months ago." He heard his voice as though he were sitting in a different room. "It worked out okay then."

Bergen snagged a fistful of *chapulines* from the basket, tumbled them like dice in his palm, popped a few in his mouth. "Your cousin got lucky."

Across the table, Lupe had drifted off into her own world, unable to follow the English. When she glanced up, Roque ventured an absent smile. Pregnant, he thought as she timidly smiled back. I won't punk out like my old man, end up nothing but a question.

Samir slouched in his seat, one arm hooked across his chair back, eyeing Bergen like he was poisonous. "Okay. We are unlucky. Are you here to help or call us names?"

Bergen chafed his hands to rid them of lingering bits of insect. "I'd say that depends. I need to know a little more about who I'm dealing with. You in particular." His eyes shuttered with vaguely hostile mirth. "And don't lie to me. I've spent some time in your part of the world, not just this one. I don't fool easy."

Samir, thin-skinned as always, rose to the bait. "Let me tell you something, I have not lied to you. What have I had time to lie about? You have been blah-blah-de-blah ever since you walked in the door."

That seemed only to amuse Bergen further. "From what I hear, you proved yourself better than average with a weapon out there the other night. You held off an ambush almost single-handed."

"Not true." Samir nodded toward Roque. "I had help."

Bergen's smile lamped down a notch. "You've got a military background. You're an Iraqi Arab. You told that much to Father Luis. You either come clean with me or you can find your own fucking way to America."

Even Lupe, lost behind the language barrier, detected the change in temperature. She glanced back and forth between the two men, who were locking eyes, then turned to Roque for reassurance. He offered a shrug, still feeling strangely disembodied, as though floating over the table, watching himself.

"I was in the war with Persia," Samir said finally with a flutter of his hand, as though nothing could be more matter-of-fact.

"Excuse me but I find that puzzling," Bergen said. "Palestinians normally didn't serve in the Iraqi military, even in the war with Iran."

"How do you know these things?"

"Like I said, I'm no stranger to that part of the world. Besides which, I'm a pilot. You spend a lot of time hanging around airfields, waiting for people and things—or money—to show up. Plenty of time to catch up on your reading."

Samir leaned in toward the table. "A pilot for who—the airlines? The CIA? The cartels?"

Bergen chortled, it was all grand fun. "We'll talk about me when the time comes. How did you wind up in the army?"

"When will come the time to talk about you? Why not now?"

"I'm not the one looking for a favor."

Outside, Father Luis's ancient Volkswagen puttered up the gravel drive from the coastal road. Somewhere, a dog started barking.

"So that's how it is," Samir said. "We're in need, at your mercy. You know all the promises we have had. And what we paid to get them. Until you show me you have something real to offer, not just more promises, I have nothing to say."

A faint scent of gasoline wafted in through the open window as the door to Father Luis's Volkswagen slammed shut and his footsteps crunched the gravel. Nodding that direction, Bergen said, "The padre vouches for me. Who vouches for you?"

"And what do I know of this priest?"

As though on cue, Father Luis appeared in the doorway, nodding toward his company, oblivious to what they were saying. Dusting off his glasses with a handkerchief, he looked in need of a nap and a shave. Roque wondered if Samir might not be on to something: What did they know of this man? Returning his glasses to his face, the priest blinked and smiled, then shuffled off to join Dolor in the sacristy.

"Oh what the hell, let's move the ball down the field." Bergen made one last attack on the basket of *chapulines*, tipping it toward him, looking for the last few tidbits. "No, I did not fly for the airlines. I was trained in the air force, served my first tour at Ramstein which, as you may or may not know, has airlift and supply responsibilities for the Middle East. I got transferred to Davis-Monthan in Tucson just in time for the invasion of Panama, Operation Just Cause—or as we called it, Operation Just Because. I bagged out of the service after my second tour and found work in Phoenix, flying businessmen around, them and whoever they wanted to impress or bribe or screw. Flew all over the Southwest, plus Cancún, Belize, Baja, down here. You meet a lot of colorful people in the air, especially in a Gulfstream. I met a few who had some seriously out-of-the-way projects, so far out in the middle of bumfuck nowhere the roads were a rumor. I got work hauling in gasoline, food, clothes—and no, I didn't fly back with a hold full of dope. Never. It was a pretty decent living for a while, until the men I transacted with left for a meeting one afternoon in Colima and never came back. That happens down here, as I'm sure you can guess. I didn't care much for the men who took their place. Since then, I've been improvising."

A boy attending a small herd of goats along a path through the cornfield started tooting a recorder. Beyond him, the sky seemed triumphantly blue, streaked with bright cloud.

Samir said, "Why settle here?"

"I'd been to the area off and on, carting clients down here to the beaches or up to Oaxaca de Juárez for the art. I bought myself some property through a *presta nombre*, a name lender. Foreigners can't own property within fifty clicks of the coast and I didn't want to go through a *fideicomiso*, a bank trust. Had plans to build myself the beach house of my dreams. It's a charming place. People think goats are the devil, black dogs are good luck, mescal cures diarrhea and skunk meat clears up acne.

"Anyhoo, prices started going through the roof the past few years and greed never sleeps. My *presta nombre* got himself in serious need of a kidney that never materialized—don't think I didn't try to find him one—and under Mexican law his heirs inherit the property, not me. His widow and kids knew a bargain when it fell out of the sky. But I like it here, didn't feel like letting them run me off. They want to cheat me, they can look me in the eye. Not that that's a problem, mind you. The Mexican conscience knows how to adapt. Thousands of years of getting screwed will do that."

Outside, the boy with the recorder had mercifully wandered out of earshot with his goats, which may or may not have been devils.

"Now that's my story, or the part that's relevant. Let's get back to how you wound up in the Iraqi military."

Samir made a token snort of protest, fluttered his hands. Then he settled deeper into his chair. "I didn't want to, believe me. Saddam was just throwing bodies at the front, same as the Persians."

"All wars are lousy," Bergen offered, "but that one—"

"It was butchery. Obscene. But I came to realize there was no choice, it was enlist or else. I was studying English and Spanish at university, was beginning some classes in Portuguese, Italian. I wanted to work in radio, maybe TV. But the Mukhabarat, they had other ideas. They came to where I was living—my first apartment, overlooking the Tigris, I had just turned twenty—and they drove me to their ministry near the Al-Wasati hospital.

I was put in an interview room on the top floor, at the end of a long hallway of cells, and they made me wait for hours, the door locked.

"Finally a captain came in and sat down. A guard stood behind him at the door. The captain had a folder and he very politely apologized for any inconvenience. He was plump and bald and wore reading glasses and I thought to myself how much he looked like one of my professors. And just as I was thinking this he asked how I enjoyed my classes, like he could read my mind. I told him I liked them very much, I hoped to perhaps work for the foreign ministry. You know, make it look like we were on the same team.

"He asked if any foreigners had approached me, any reason at all. I said no, none. He seemed disappointed. I was afraid he didn't believe me. Then he asked that I contact him should I receive any job or research offers by noncitizens, even visiting professors. Even Arabs. I of course agreed, even though I knew what this meant. If I didn't report some contact, I would be the one under suspicion. But there was no one to report. I'd have to hand up someone innocent."

Lupe yawned—so much talk, none she could understand—then formed a cradle with her arms and laid down her head.

"I went home, tried to think of what to do. You have to understand what it was like, living under Saddam. Once you were a target there was no place to hide. At some point it came to me: Why not join the army? The war had been dragging on for eight years, Iraq fighting for a stalemate, the Persians fighting to win. Without the Americans we would have been done for. But the Kurds were mounting skirmishes in the north, the Shia in the south—this, I realized, was why the Mukhabarat had come for me. They were becoming suspicious of all outsiders in the country. If I enlisted, it's not like they'd turn me away. They were executing ordinary Iraqis who refused to serve, then making the families pay for the bullet. I realized my friend the captain might think I only joined to be a spy but I could not afford to do nothing. I had to prove my loyalty. This was the only way I could see to do that without harming someone else."

"Except in battle," Bergen noted.

"The Persians are dogs. I was at the front, I saw with my own eyes what they did. Don't lecture me."

Bergen's smile froze. "So you enlisted—"

"I was put into the infantry just before the offensive in Shalamcheh. I was lucky, my sergeant was a good soldier. The irony? He had been a cop in America. I'm serious. Dearborn, Michigan. He knew how to shoot, something none of the other recruits ever learned. It was criminal how badly trained the army was. Lucky for us, the Iranians were no better. We fought them hand to hand, sometimes just hacking and beating each other with our weapons because we'd run out of ammunition. There is no word in any language for what that is like. I became an animal, the men around me became animals.

"The offensive was our first victory in years. Then the Iranians struck back with incredible ferocity, we lost tens of thousands of men. I was fortunate, my position was not gassed. But I knew men who were. The Iranians of course said we were the ones who used gas—and who knows, maybe they were right. I would not put it past Saddam to gas his own troops. But we managed to hold out, regroup, and within the week we went on the attack again, recaptured the Majnoon oil fields, then Halabja. Soon the war was over, Iran agreed to peace. I came home a hero. People were so proud we'd actually, at long last, pushed back, regained some of the country's pride."

"But that didn't satisfy the Mukhabarat," Bergen guessed.

"I was back in school maybe two months when they came around again. There were incredible purges going on in the country, people disappearing right and left, not just Shia and Kurds. I was taken to the ministry again, a different room, this one on the second floor, but the same captain came in, sat down.

My file was much larger at this point. They must have been watching me in the army. Just like before, he asked me how my classes were going. Honey would have melted on his tongue. I was more scared in that room than I had been at the front.

"Finally I asked, 'What do I have to do to convince you I am no enemy of the regime?' He seemed offended but that lasted only an instant. He said I had to know someone in the Palestinian community who had spoken out against the war, against Saddam. And there it was. My way out. All I had to do was give them a name. I had joined the army for nothing. They wanted to terrorize the whole Palestinian community, remind us that our safety under Saddam was a gift, not a right.

"So I went home, thought about who I would betray. Given what I saw in the war, I was no longer quite so squeamish about doing what I had to do to survive—do you understand? There was a man named Salah Hassan, he had a little business repairing radios and televisions and vacuum sweepers. I knew, when the war was going badly, he had demanded that some of his customers pay him in Saudi riyals—better yet, pounds or dollars if they had them. This was considered a crime in Saddam's Iraq, a kind of money laundering. Worse, subversion. So I told my friend the captain about it. A few nights later, while I lay awake in my bed, I heard the cars pull up outside the repairman's house, I heard them pound on his door. I heard him speak very respectfully, very cordially to the men who took him away. And after that night, my problems with the Mukhabarat ended."

Lupe, head still lolling on her arms, uttered a drowsy, uncomprehending sigh. Samir fussed absently with his hands. Bergen said, "I don't mean to be contrary, but from what I know of intelligence agencies, they don't tend to let go. They keep coming back—"

"You misunderstand." Samir seemed strangely uncoiled, even relaxed. "The Palestinian community in Baghdad had caused no problems during the war. The Mukhabarat just wanted to make a point. We were not beyond their reach."

"You'd told them you had ambitions to work in the foreign ministry."

"I can only assume the captain saw through that. Regardless, I wanted nothing to do with working for the regime. I got my degree and found work with *Al-Zawra*, the country's main newspaper, translating wire-service pieces for publication."

"*Al-Zawra* was owned by Uday, Saddam's son."

"Yes, but I had nothing to do with any of that. Let me tell you something, in Iraq you could not work for the media in any form and not have contact with someone who knew someone—you understand? But I was a very small fish. I kept to myself, bothering no one. And no one bothered me. That is the truth. Choose to believe it or not. But if you are worried I am some kind of *jihadi*, let me tell you something. I worked for the coalition as an interpreter, it's how I got to know this one's cousin." A bob of his chin toward Roque. "I did what I could to help America. All I want is to get across the border, make my case for asylum and try as best I can to rebuild my life and help my family. If you do not want to help me, I will find some other way. But I will not be denied. On my honor as a husband and father, I will see this through."

Bergen sat there a moment then pushed up from the table. "Excuse me a sec." He collected the empty *chapulín* basket and ambled off toward the kitchen. Samir dug the heels of his hands into his eye sockets and rubbed. Lupe stirred and stretched, rising from her nap.

Roque said:—*You okay?*

She tucked a strand of hair behind her ear and smiled. —*What's everybody been blabbering about?*

—*True confessions*. He shrugged apologetically for Samir's sake.—*I'll tell you later*.

—*Okay*. The smile lingered.

Samir looked back and forth between them.—*What's this?*

—*What business is it of yours?* She nailed him with a stare.

—*You know what business of mine it is.*

—*He's lost his uncle. Have some pity.*

—*I'm neither blind nor stupid. Pity?*

—*Listen, I'll do what I please, feel what I please. What are you going to do—kill me?*

Bergen returned, bearing Dolor's tin pitcher and four glasses. "Figured all this time, flapping our jaws, somebody might be thirsty." He filled each of the four glasses with water and passed them around. "Don't worry," he added. "It's bottled."

Resuming his seat, he regarded Lupe now.—*What's this about our Arab friend here killing you?* His Spanish was clumsily accented, the same Rocky Mountain twang as his English.

Roque explained the situation to him, the expected connection with El Recio in Agua Prieta, Samir's crossing in exchange for Lupe. Bergen's gaze traveled the table.

—*And that's acceptable to all concerned?*

—*Acceptable?* Roque acted insulted.—*My uncle hated the idea. I'll do anything to see it doesn't happen.*

Samir drained his glass. "You should hear yourself. Fine. I'm tired of arguing with you. If you think you know some way back home with no money, no connections, just that noble heart of yours, be my guest. Leave me here. I'll fend for myself. But I wonder what it will be like for you, when you come face-to-face with your cousin Happy again and he learns not only that his father is dead but that you froze like a little boy when it came time to defend him. You needed me to snap you out of it, get you to act like a man, but by then it was too late. And then you left me behind. Will you be noble enough to tell him the truth?"

He reached out for the pitcher, poured himself more water. Lupe turned to Roque.—*What is happening?*

Before Roque could answer, Bergen stepped in.—*Seems to me you folks have a thing or two to work out. There's no way I'm taking you anywhere with this going on. I don't need the hassle. You find common cause or I leave now and that's that. And Father Luis can't put you up forever. People are going to come looking for you. Then what?*

Samir, finally surrendering, switched to Spanish, letting Lupe in.—*I said it before, all we have from you so far is promises, same as we've had from every thief and deadbeat along the way. Why should we trust you? What's the special trick you know that will make our problems vanish?*

Bergen considered the question, taking a leisurely sip of water, then lowered his glass and offered that jolting smile.—*You're right, I know a trick. Pretty simple trick, actually. When I drive up to a checkpoint, I flash this happy white face. I show them my Utah license, the Beehive State. Plain old vanilla, that's me. Maybe this trip I'm a teacher on sabbatical indulging my wanderlust. Maybe I'm a Mormon, hoping to save your souls. Regardless, far more likely as not—I know this from long experience, my friend—they're going to wave me right on through.*

THIRTY-SEVEN

RIDING ALONE IN THE BACKSEAT, LUCHA HAD TO FIGHT BACK the nausea bubbling up in her stomach, fearing she might get sick. She told herself to breathe but the car had a sour smell, like food that had spoiled.

They'd ransacked the trailer, telling her nothing, just handing her a piece of paper that made no sense. She knew not to stand in their way. Armed men, you object, you suffer. Then these two stepped forward through the bedlam, told her they wanted her to come with them.

She knew the handsome one from that day *la migra* raided the trailer park. He was the one who calmed everyone down, talked sense into Godo. Lattimore, his name was. The other one, the driver—Dunn, his card read—was unfamiliar. He was homely and yet full of himself, the kind of man Graciela used to mock with . . . what was the phrase? *Sapo guapo*. Handsome toad. Every few minutes he hawked up mucus, cranked down his window, spat onto the road. *Qué grencho*. What a hick.

Lattimore talked into his cell, confirmed something, slapped the small black phone shut. He turned in his seat to face her, wearing a thoughtful smile that his eyes betrayed.

"Sorry for that interruption. Your nephew, Godo, and your son-in-law, Pablo—"

"He is not my son-in-law."

"All right. Excuse me. Pablo, let's just call him that. The last time you saw him was?"

She looked out the window. They'd crossed the bridge spanning the Carquinez Strait and were veering down the first off-ramp, the one for Crockett. It was almost dark now, the bridge's new span lit up like a monument and shrouded with wind-driven mist, the distant house lights glowing against the fog-bound hill. Directly below the bridge, the sugar refinery's massive neon sign anchored the small downtown with its abandoned railhead and lonely dock and ghostly warehouses. "I told you. I am afraid. I have temporary protected status and my green-card application is pending but nothing is certain these days. I do not want to do anything to harm my chances. I wish to have a lawyer with me when I talk to you."

She kept to herself the fact that her heart was breaking.

"You're not a suspect, Lucha."

"Lucha is what my family calls me. My name is Élida."

The man's smile weakened. His eyes remained unchanged. "You're not a suspect, Élida."

Dunn cranked down his window again, a burst of cold air, smelling of brackish water and eucalyptus, a hint of the oil refinery over the hill in Rodeo. "You're not a citizen, either." A punctuating spit. The window shuddered back up. "Your right to a lawyer's not absolute."

"I wish," she repeated, "to have a lawyer when I talk to you."

"I understand," Lattimore said, stepping back in. "But this isn't El Salvador, especially the El Salvador you left behind. I mean, sure, we're cops, not dancers. But we're not here to hurt you. We just want the truth."

He thinks I'm stupid, Lucha thought. Like all he has to do is keep chattering away and I will forget about a lawyer. Will they ever stop insulting us?

"The warrant's a little sketchy on what this is all about, so let me explain a few things. Witnesses place Pablo Orantes and your nephew Godo at the scene of a home invasion this morning. The thing went pretty badly off the rails. The homeowner's dead. His nine-year-old daughter's in pretty bad shape too, not physically, but her dad was gunned down right in front of her. We're still putting things together but it seems pretty clear that Pablo was the ringleader. Godo wasn't just along for the ride, though. He was in deep, especially on the violence end."

She felt like she'd misunderstood. He couldn't have said what she just heard. "Excuse me, I do not—"

"We need to find both these young men. I could lie to you, try to trick you, say we just want to talk to them. But I don't want to do that. They're in very serious trouble. That trouble won't go away. They need to come in, give themselves up, tell us what happened. It could get a great deal worse for both of them if they don't do the right thing now. I can understand how frightened they might be. I would be, in their shoes. I can imagine why they did it, hoping to score enough money to get Pablo's father back from El Salvador. Or maybe somebody else put them up to it, Vasco Ramírez, let's say." He paused, as though to see how she reacted to the name. It meant nothing to her, she just sat there. "They're going to be caught, Élida. They won't walk away free. They need to talk to me or Detective Dunn here, tell us everything. I promise, they'll be treated fairly."

She could no longer look at his face. Such a cruel and devious thing to do, take advantage of her grief, play on her conscience, so soon after hearing that Faustino was dead—did they know that? Were they piling one misery on top of the other, just to get her to say something, get her to tell them where Godo was, where Pablito was? As if she knew. As if, supposing everything he'd just said had actually taken place, those two would tell her anything about it.

By the time she realized what was happening she couldn't stop it, the vomit churned up into her throat and out of her mouth, sour and hot, showering across the seat and onto the floor mats. Her skin was flushed, she felt repulsive, childish, naked.

"Don't worry, ma'am." It was Dunn, his voice surprisingly

gentle. "You're probably the third person this month who's lost his lunch back there. But I bet you figured that out already."

THEY HELPED HER WALK FROM THE CAR, ONE ON EACH ARM, LEADING her up the steep driveway and into the house. Everyone stared as she came through the door; their gazes weren't kind. There were strange markings everywhere, circles drawn on the floor and walls, smudges of soot-like powder. Police officers milled about as though they had nowhere else to go. She wavered, feeling sick again but there was nothing left to bring up. Lattimore, sensing her unsteadiness, tightened his hold on her arm. A midair feeling, about to fall—from where?

Lattimore addressed one of the uniformed officers. "The girl still here?"

The officer glanced offhandedly at Lucha, then shook his head. "She was acting a little loose on deck. Mom pitched a fit, be glad you weren't here. Meds all around, that's what they wanted. Sergeant said screw it, take her to Kaiser in Martinez, patrol car drove them over about an hour ago. Son went with them. He came home from school while you were gone."

Lattimore frowned like he was adding up a sum. "Housekeeper's still here, right?"

"Lourdes? For now. DHS called, they put dibs on her."

Lucha felt Lattimore's grip slacken. "DHS? Christ, what the . . . They're going to deport her. Best wit we've got, only one—" He cut himself short, glancing to Lucha and Dunn then back at the officer, looking sheepish, tense. "Never mind. Not your problem."

"She's still in there," he pointed, "you want to talk to her."

"Yeah. Good. Thanks."

Lattimore guided Lucha into a spacious, dimly lit kitchen. A greasy black stain coated the wall above the stove, the lingering smell of a grease fire. A *mejicana* sat napping at the table. Lucha felt a shudder of contempt. The woman was short like a stump, flabby arms, pudgy hands, dyed hair. She looks like one of those troll dolls, Lucha thought, even as she recognized the scorn for what it was. Fear. What has this *puta cochina* said, what does she know?

The woman lifted her head, rubbing her eyes, blinking, then staring at Lucha with the same instant distrust. They were opposites, they were mirrors.

Lattimore said, "Élida, this is Lourdes. She was kidnapped yesterday morning by Pablo Orantes and two other young men, Puchi Parada and Chato López, shortly after she finished cleaning this house. They threatened to kill her daughters if she didn't help them rob the family who lives here. She was here when the robbery took place, when Mr. Snell, the owner, was murdered. As if all that wasn't bad enough, she's now in trouble with immigration. She's not lucky like you, temporary protected status, green card in the pipeline. She may get sent away with no chance of ever coming back. I'll do what I can but I don't have much pull. What will happen to her daughters is anybody's guess. In any event, I thought you might like to meet her, or she might like to meet you, seeing as your nephew and stepson—"

"I told you—"

"—were the leaders in the robbery. She picked out—"

"My *marido* is dead." The words escaped before she even had the thought formed. Everyone stared. "Faustino. He was murdered by bandits in Mexico. Yesterday. We were together six years." She looked at Lourdes with an indifference that felt limitless. "I have nothing to say to this woman."

ON THE DRIVE BACK TO THE TRAILER, LATTIMORE TOLD HER THAT HE knew about Roque, how he had been driving north through Mexico with Faustino, intending to bring him back home. He did not say how he'd learned this and she felt too numb to ask, staring out the car window, seeing nothing but blurred lights and hulking shapes. He told her he was sorry about Faustino's death—whatever his sources, she thought, the *chivatos* had not filled him in on that—but Roque's involvement made him an accomplice in a conspiracy. She needed to consider that carefully. Everyone would suffer if she did not step forward, tell the truth.

"I will get in touch with a lawyer tomorrow," she murmured. "I will see what advice he has to give. He or I will contact you." Or not, she thought.

After they dropped her off at the trailer, she stood for a moment listening to her wind chimes, enjoying them, resenting them. How many little treasures, she wondered, how many fleeting joys slip past as we fail to pay attention?

Inside the trailer, she couldn't get her bearings. She moved from spot to spot as though looking for something but had no idea what it was. The next thing she knew she was standing in the doorway to his bedroom, looking at the freshly made bed, thinking: My lonely funny Godo, always the wily one, the character, the demon. Do you remember, *m'ijo*, that time you got so angry when your mother did herself up like a tart and went out, another night at the bar, leaving us alone together like always? How quiet you became, so intense, but I didn't see that for what it was. Then, behind my back, you found the scissors. By the time I realized you were up to something you'd torn her pillow to shreds, stabbing at it, ripping it, like some crazed little fiend. I grabbed the scissors away and slapped you so hard. You did not cry, though. You bit your lip, daring me to hit you again. I shouted, What do you think you're doing? But you said nothing, glaring at me. I slapped you once more, harder still. Tears ran down your face but you refused to wipe them away. I dragged you to the couch, told you to sit. If you move, I said, I will beat you like a mule. Later, when your mother stumbled in with the man she dragged home that night, I was lying in bed and I heard the door to my room open, felt you slip into the bed behind me in the dark. For once, I did not shoo you back to your room. I felt guilty and, yes, alone. We lay there, me on my side, my back to you, you on the edge of the bed, so still, and we listened as your mother and her man went at it. Do you remember what I told you? Your mother is going to get pregnant, I said. You are going to have a little brother, maybe a little sister—how are you going to handle that, *m'ijo*? Only then did you cry. And I did not turn over to comfort you. I let you cry yourself to sleep, thinking: Now, my little monster, now you will learn what it really means to want what is impossible.

The loneliness became unbearable. Shrugging back into the coat she'd just removed, she went out to the car, drove over to Food 4 Less.

A sense of nakedness swept through her as she marched in, everyone glancing up. Did they know what had happened? How? Maybe they were just surprised, it was her day off after all. Only then did it occur to her that she hadn't put on her makeup. She'd worn her normal face, her dark *indígena* face. She was the only woman she knew who went to such trouble anymore but only a fool trusts the open-mindedness of strangers. After a moment of stunned silence, Regina the checker broke into an uneasy smile. Alion the bag boy raised a power fist. The others quickly turned back to what they were doing.

The manager's office lay back off the storage room. She climbed the three wood steps to the door and knocked. A muffled voice called from within, "It's open."

The manager on duty was named Rafael, a muscular Tongan with a high tight fade, a meticulously groomed Fu Manchu. His necktie was loose at his unbuttoned collar, one of his shirttails had worked itself free. A half-eaten *lumpia* laced with brown Chinese mustard and the discarded banana leaf from a *patupat*, both courtesy of the Filipino bakery next door, sat in a Styrofoam container on his desk. "Lucha, hey—whazzup?" He too stared for a moment at her face, then gestured her into a chair.

Lucha hugged her purse to her belly, taking a second to compose herself. A fly careened about the remains of Rafael's dinner. "I am going to need extra shifts," she said, "if you can." It seemed wise to stop there. No need to explain what the money was for—mention a lawyer, there would be no end to the rumors.

"Shouldn't be a problem." Rafael wiped his lips with a napkin. "Let's take a looky-look at the schedule." He plucked a clipboard from the top of the file cabinet behind him, pushed back the top page. "Gina's been screaming for time off, her kid's got some kinda skin problem. You want her Wednesday ten to six, Friday noon to close?"

Lucha realized at that moment that in just a short while she would be returning to the empty trailer, spending the night there, nothing and no one to distract her from what she was feeling. And what would happen when these people found out what Godo and Happy had done—would she still have a job?

"Lucha?"

She snapped to. "I'm sorry. Could you say that again?"

"You okay?"

"Yes. Yes. Tired, maybe."

He repeated the shifts he had to offer. She said, "Starting when?"

"Day after tomorrow. That soon enough?"

"That would be fine." She considered asking for an advance on her paycheck but felt she stood a better chance by asking Monroe, the day-shift manager. He liked her—she reminded him of a babysitter he'd had growing up in Chula Vista, he said—and the extra shifts would serve as a kind of collateral.

"Hey, almost forgot." Rafael picked up his pad of message slips, ripped one free, tossed it across his desk. It fluttered to the floor, he said, "Sorry," and Lucha said, "It's all right," and they both bent to pick it up. Lucha got there first. It contained one word, "Pablo," and a phone number. Rafael said, "That came in through the message center maybe, I dunno, two o'clock?"

She stared at the handwriting as though it came from another world. Leaving his office, she walked though the store waving a curt goodbye to everyone, whether they looked up or not, then went outside to the pay phone in front of the store, opened her pocketbook, took out her change purse and inserted three quarters into the slot. A disposable phone, she thought, that was his style. He picked up on the second ring.

—You lied to me, you son of a bitch. You told me Godo wasn't involved in anything and that was a goddamn lie. You got him into this and now he can't get out and shut up! Shut up and listen to me! They took me to the house in Crockett, told me about the robbery, the man you killed. I had to face the woman you kidnapped you selfish little shit, she may never see her daughters again. And now let me guess, you need my help. Well let me tell you *something—your father is dead too, how's that? Roque called me today, he told me, your father is dead, killed by bandits. Bandits like you. Look what you've done. This whole thing was your idea. You always thought you were smart. You've never been smart. You've always been the stupid one. The worthless one. Don't come back, understand? If I so much as see you I will call the police, if I don't kill you myself.*

She slammed the phone so hard against its chrome-plated stirrup it banged out of her hand. She fumbled for it, got it under control, redoubled her grip, then slammed it home again, over and over, harder, faster, time and time again until the plastic earpiece shattered, exposing the copper coils and tin diaphragm beneath. She threw it down, staring in disgust.

From behind Alion the bag boy said, "Fuck, Lucha. Be trippin'."

She pivoted toward the parking lot, finger-raking her hair to hide her face, chin down, sucking in jolts of air as she stormed to her car.

THIRTY-EIGHT

A SINGLE BARE BULB SCREWED INTO A WALL SOCKET LIT THE bathroom mirror. El Recio, naked except for tattered slippers and a silvery brown boa constrictor coiled around his shoulders, leaned over the basin, brushing his teeth. Happy stood in the doorway, waiting. A small desert gecko hid in the corner, outside the snake's reach, lurking behind a coffee can stuffed with foul tissues, the toilet barely usable because of the trickling water pressure.

Beyond the bracing whiff of shit, the house smelled of fresh cement, rotten fruit rinds and raw sewage from outside. They were in one of the new developments, if that was the word, on the outskirts of Agua Prieta. Happy had driven two straight days to get here, checking into a transient hotel downtown with Godo, then discreetly asking around, finding his way to El Recio. He was light-headed from lack of food, his body humming with adrenalin and foul with sweat.

El Recio drooled a thin white spume into the sink. "Don't know what you're talking about, *güey*. Ain't heard nothing from nobody down south about moving your people across." He'd spent most of his life banging around Tucson, his accent flat and hard. "You say you paid them? News to me. I ain't seen nothing. Ain't heard nothing." He affected a shrug, not wanting to disturb the snake. "Way it is."

Happy only half heard, Tía Lucha's voice still echoing inside his brain: The stupid one. The worthless one. Let the scrawny bitch talk, he thought, she's not your mother. Your mother was a hero, she died on Guazapa volcano.

El Recio rinsed, spat, then stuck the toothbrush behind his ear. He had a manly, misshapen, bone-smooth head and stood tall for a *mejicano*, over six feet, but so skinny his veins popped. He gave the snake an attentive, leisurely stroke. "You want to get somebody over the wall, you know the freight. Fifteen hundred a head."

"I already paid," Happy heard himself say. "Twelve large per."

"Not me you didn't."

"It's a lot of money. It was supposed to get them all the way."

"Look, you got a beef with Lonely, go down and talk to him about it." He gestured for Happy to make way, he and the snake were coming out.

"You know I can't do that."

"Call, then." He edged past and shuffled bow-legged toward the front room, the tattoos down his back blending with the boa's mottled scales.

Happy, following: "Every number I got, plug's been pulled. Best I get is a ring nobody answers. If you got a number—"

"Last time I say this, right? *Ain't* my fucking *problem*." Entering the front room, he regaled the rest of the company with a hearty scratch of his balls. Over his shoulder: "You paid twelve thousand per head—for real? Man, those faggots musta seen you comin'."

Them or you, Happy thought. He couldn't figure out who exactly was screwing him. The fact Lonely couldn't be reached smacked of rip-off and yet maybe there'd been a raid down there, everybody popped or driven underground, something El Recio, sly motherfucker, would no doubt recognize as the genius of luck. He could say anything, demand whatever, who'd contradict him—how could he not know how much got paid and why? Either way, Happy thought, I'm stuck. And the kicker? My old man's dead. All that money and trouble to keep him safe. A restless sorrow fluttered inside his chest. He saw the wisdom of keeping that to himself. It would only make him look weak.

The front room was bare except for a large-screen TV, a leather sofa, an armchair that didn't match. El Recio's two underlings had commandeered the couch, nursing beers and watching some rerun of *The Shield*, Spanish subtitles. One was named Kiki, freckled and wiry, his long black hair knotted in a bun atop his head like a samurai. The other, Osvaldo, was thirtyish, dumpy suit, roach-killer boots, one of those close-cropped beards so trendy a few years back. A girl sat by herself in the armchair, throwing back Jägerbombers—Ripple with a shot of Jägermeister over ice. She had thin Asian eyes carved into a stony Latina face and wore a party dress, no shoes. It wasn't clear who she belonged to.

Happy said quietly, "Look, about the fifteen hundred." He was thinking of Samir. Roque could cross on his own with his passport. "No way I can get my hands—"

El Recio, back still turned, cut him off. "You can work, right?"

Happy'd told him about the home invasion. In the half-assed logic of machismo, it was less important the thing went bad than he and Godo walked out alive. It created expectations. He still suffered flashbacks—the contractor lying on his side, face ripped open, the girl screaming through the duct tape—and yet he could barely recall a single moment of the drive south. "Yeah. I can work."

"Good." El Recio gestured to the girl. She obliged with a huffing frown, hoisted her glass, uncrossed her legs and wrestled herself onto her feet, taking no notice of his nakedness. The chair clear, he uncoiled the boa from his shoulders, gentled it down into the deserted warm spot, then continued with Happy. " 'Cuz I think I got something maybe could suit you."

Happy's cell phone rang. In unison, the two on the couch

glanced up, the stubbled one growling, "*Afuera, pendejo*." Take it outside, asshole. Heading for the door, Happy checked the incoming-call display. Tía Lucha was the only person he'd contacted so far on this phone, but this wasn't a callback. He didn't know who it was.

Letting his eyes adjust to the darkness, he stepped first across the open ditch ripe with filth that ran downhill to the sewer linkage, then past the concrete *pila* topped with potable water, filmed with mosquito larvae. Across the muddy roadbed, unfinished houses loomed in shadow, wands of rebar fingering skyward in the moonlight. Down the road, a few lived-in houses sported satellite dishes, courtesy of El Recio, so his own wouldn't tip off the police.

He flipped the phone open, put it to his ear, waited.

"Happy—that you?" It was Roque.

A nervous rage crackled up Happy's spine. "Tell me what happened."

"Happy—"

"You know what I mean."

Roque stammered out an explanation—a cow in the road, two trucks of gunmen, it all sounding too fucked up to disbelieve. "Tío got hurt in the accident, he was dazed, it made him an easy target. We all would've died if not for Samir. He was like a killing machine."

Wait, Happy thought, that can't be right. He recalled the ambush on the road to Karbala, when Samir saved his life. The Arab never grabbed a gun, not off the wounded, not off the dead, he never even tried. He ran and hid, then talked his way out. He lied to me, Happy thought. He's lied to me all along and so has Lonely and every other glad-handing cocksucker who said he was doing me a favor. There are no favors.

Roque broke back in: "Tía Lucha said Godo's with you."

"Not this minute." He glanced around, looking to see if anyone was listening in. The night was disconcertingly quiet. Come daylight, the neighborhood would burst with the hiss and rumble of propane wagons and water trucks, the shriek of postman whistles, the jingle of bells on the *helado* wagons, the hawker calls from men and women selling newspapers, corncobs, goat-cheek tacos, broiled tripe. "But yeah, Godo's here."

"Where's here?"

"Agua Prieta."

"What are you doing—"

"We're waiting for you." Across the way, a crow perched atop one of the exposed rods of rebar fluttered its long black wings in the moonlight. "Listen, no more calls to Tía Lucha, understand? The phone might be bugged. Things've taken an odd turn the past couple days. I'll explain when I see you."

WHEN HE RETURNED TO THE HOTEL HE FOUND GODO SITTING CROSS-legged on the floor of their tiny room, facing a girl maybe six or seven years old. She was wrapping his hand in fresh gauze with only a candle to see by.

Godo glanced up at the doorway. "Hey, *primo*." Nodding to the girl, "This is Paca."

The child spun her head around, pigtails flying. She was rail thin with an incongruously round face, like a human lollipop, except she had fever-dream eyes. Her smile was short a tooth.

Happy nodded hello. Then, to Godo, "She got a mother?"

"You mean around?" Godo took the end of the gauze from the girl, tucked it in, finishing the wrap. "Mom's out working." He glanced up meaningfully. There were only a few things a woman could do in this town for quick money. "They're making their fourth go at the border."

Happy sat down on his cot, gnawed by weariness but too wired to sleep. Four tries, he thought, Christ.

"Last three times, funny enough, they've walked right into the arms of *la migra*. Their *guía* says it's just bad luck. Fucker.

They're decoys, he's running a load of dope some other route once he's got the border boys chasing his *pollos* around."

"Stuff happens." Happy lay flat. In the candlelight the ceiling looked like a rippling pond.

Godo placed his bandaged hand atop the girl's head and scrubbed affectionately. She pointed toward the cot, beaming. "Hap pee?"

"Yes. Happy." Godo smiled proudly. "I've been teaching her some English."

"Slaphappy," the girl chirped.

"Hey! *Recuerdas*. Good."

"Naphappy! Craphappy!" She bounced with delight, accenting the second syllable, not the first, thinking in Spanish.

Happy lifted himself onto one elbow. "Those aren't words."

"They oughta be. You've never been naphappy?"

"Laphappy! Sappycrap!"

"Can I talk to you alone?"

Godo broke the news to Paca. Like a little soldier, no pout, no pretending she hadn't heard, she jumped to her feet, brushed off her skirt and padded out, shooting back an over-the-shoulder smile with its little notch of blackness—her happygap, Happy thought.

"Get the door, okay?"

Godo rose, did as asked, then sat on the opposite cot. "What's up?"

"El Recio says he never got paid. I've gotta scratch up another fifteen hundred to get Samir across."

Godo looked puzzled. "You sound like you resent it."

"The money? Fuck yeah. This shit never ends."

"Not the money. Samir. You sound like you loathe the fucker. Change your mind about getting him across?"

It's that obvious, Happy thought. Not good. "Roque got in touch, by the way."

Godo made an odd sound, grunt and snort and chuckle all rolled into one. "How goes the golden child?"

"He told me what happened. With Pops. It doesn't sound like it was his fault."

"Since when are you so forgiving?"

Happy let that go. "The way he described it, I don't see it going down much different if it was you or me who'd been there. You, maybe."

"Stop beating yourself up. Like I made some big difference back at Fucked Chuck's house." He rested his bandaged hand on his thigh, palm up, staring into it. "Unlucky Chuck."

"What is it with you and this rhyming shit?"

"I'm bored stupid here. Thought I was gonna die from fucking tedium before Paca showed up."

There are worse ways to go, Happy thought. "Well, knock it off. We got stuff to discuss." He told him about El Recio's offer, the job he'd proposed. "He wanted to know if you were interested. I told him your hand was still messed up."

Godo's pocked face looked like a mask in the candlelight. "My hand's fine."

"Wrapped up like that?"

"I can carry my weight."

"I wanted you kept out of it."

Godo chewed on that for a bit. "You ashamed of me?"

"I'm trying to be thoughtful, *pendejo*. Everything you been through?"

"You my mother now?"

Drop it, Happy told himself. "That's not my point." He glanced up at the watery shadows again, feeling as though, if he stared long enough, they might speak. "You still get nightmares?"

Godo reached beneath his cot. "You know I do. And not just at night." He checked the duffel holding his guns. "Thing back in Crockett eating you?"

Happy wanted to close his eyes but felt afraid. He could hear the dying man's blood, smell the girl's screams. "Stuff just comes out of nowhere."

Godo settled back on his own cot, lacing his fingers beneath his head. "Sorry to tell you this, *cabrón*, but that's gonna be part of the mental furniture from now on." He nudged off his shoes. "Welcome to the house."

THIRTY-NINE

THEY HIT THEIR FIRST CHECKPOINT WITHIN HALF AN HOUR OF setting out, between Puente Copalita and the turnoff to the beaches at Huatulco. Contrary to Bergen's prediction, he wasn't waved breezily through. He was directed to the berm. He was told to have everyone step out of the van.

Roque was struck by how young the soldiers looked; even the lieutenant interrogating Bergen appeared to be no older than twenty. He reminded himself of Sisco's advice regarding moments like this—keep smiling—as he watched a German shepherd sniff the undercarriage of the Eurovan, straining his leash. Meanwhile, maybe twenty feet away, a group of especially entrepreneurial local women dressed in festive *pozahuancos* were selling fruit, snakes, even an iguana on a rope, in the event the detainees might want to take the opportunity for some impulse shopping. One woman waved frantically at a cluster of bees swarming her bucket of sweet *panochas*. It was midmorning, still reasonably mild with the breeze off the ocean, but Roque couldn't help himself, he was sweating like a thief.

The pimpled soldier who took his passport flipped to the border stamps.—*You've come up from El Salvador, through Guatemala*.

His voice was reedy with forced authority. Roque acknowledged the observation while the soldier checked his face and arms for tattoos, told him to open his shirt so he could inspect his torso as well. Roque obliged: clean. The young soldier, expressionless, handed back his passport, then moved on to Samir.

Thanks to Beto's *compas* in Tecún Umán, both the Arab and Lupe had voter registration cards from Veracruz, mocked up with the obligatory lousy picture, one of the few ways the *salvatruchos* had actually come through. Bergen, fearing their accents might nevertheless give away the charade, had enlisted the company of a frog-faced local named Pingo who, as far as Roque could tell, was on board chiefly to blow smoke.

—*We're headed for Nogales, get work permits from the union, you know?* He almost crackled as he talked, mesmerist eye contact, homely smile.—*Gonna pick cantaloupes in Yuma. Used to be you had to go through recruiters, couple hundred a permit, goddamn shakedown. With the union, the growers pay. For real. Least that's how it's supposed to work. Not like the recruiters gonna cave without a fight. Fucking gangsters. Couple union dudes been shot, I heard.*

The pimply soldier paid Pingo little mind, choosing instead to glance back and forth—Samir's face, his ID picture, looking for something, lingering, then all of a sudden handing the voter reg card back. Moving on to Lupe he repeated the process, mimicking his own actions so unimaginatively Roque caught on finally it was all just mindless rote. The guy barely glanced at Pingo's ID. Roque felt his shoulders unbind.

Then the lieutenant told Bergen to open the back of the van.

The whole reason the American was traveling north was to deliver a vanload of art to a dealer he knew in California. That was his story, anyway.

—*You know how it is, Captain*, he told the lieutenant, *ever since the troublemakers caused all the problems here in Oaxaca, the tourist trade has dried up. No one comes to the galleries anymore. You have some of the most talented artists in the region on the verge of going broke*. He removed a cardboard tube from the back, popped open one end, shook out the canvas that was rolled up inside.—*Here, let me show you something*.

The lieutenant nosed around the boxes of tin ornaments, copal wood carvings, hand-painted masks and figurines, ceramic bowls and pitchers, then called for the dog handler to bring the shepherd around. The animal hiked his forepaws onto the bumper, probed the nearest boxes with his snout.

Bergen, undeterred, unrolled the painting.—*Look at that. The colors remind me of Chagall. But the artist is from here, just over the mountain in Zimatlán. Now here's a question for you, Captain: How much do you think this painting is worth?* He paused, as though to give the lieutenant time to think, playing the thing out, milking it.—*Up north, it will fetch five thousand dollars. Five thousand. Imagine what that means to this artist and his family.*

Roque had to grant the man his bullshit. What he was leaving unsaid was that the artists whose work he was carrying north had exclusive contracts with fiercely competitive local galleries. You could get blacklisted if any of the curators figured out they were getting backdoored. But nothing was moving here and the artists had mouths to feed, supplies to buy. So on the sly Bergen had offered to broker their work to a gallery in Santa Monica, for which he was getting three times the normal commission—calculated on the 500 percent markup on the other end—but what could they do? A smaller slice of something still beat a bigger slice of nothing.

The point, though, was Bergen had an angle. God only knew what else he was up to, Roque thought, half expecting the German shepherd to alert on the boxes piled in back—there'd be pot or scag or crank in there, courtesy of Bergen's old paymasters, maybe Pingo the joker.

The dog dropped down onto the pavement. No alert. The lieutenant curtly gestured the American and his curious pack of fellow travelers back onto the road, then marched toward the next waiting vehicle, his retinue of baby-faced soldiers traipsing along behind.

Bergen rolled up his painting and suggested with a glance that everyone climb back into the Eurovan with as much oomph as they could muster. As they pulled onto the highway, he studied his rearview mirror and said, "My guess is that's the worst we'll have to handle."

"That's not what you said before." Sitting in back on the passenger side, Roque leaned out his window, tenting his shirt to dry his skin. "You said they'd just wave us through."

"I made no promises."

"Yeah. I can see why."

To the west, immaculate beaches melted away into emerald green water frothed with surf. Pelicans strafed the waves for food. The southern end of the Sierra Madres dropped into the sea. Roque wished he could enjoy it all but he could only think of who wasn't there to enjoy it with him. He'd abandoned his uncle to a lonely grave, far from everyone he loved. It brought to mind his strained conversation with Happy. So much anger, so little grief, but that was hardly surprising. Things have taken an odd turn, he'd said, there might be a bug on Tía Lucha's phone. What had they gone and done, why head for Agua Prieta? And whose side would they take when it came time to talk El Recio into letting Lupe go?

THE VAN CAME UP BEHIND A SIXTEEN-WHEELER WITH ENGLISH GRAFFITI spray-painted across the back of its trailer:

Tourists:
Oaxaca is Temporarily Closed.
It will Reopen as Soon as There is Justice.

"That reminds me," Bergen said. "I did a little nosing around about what happened to you folks on the highway the other night. Appears you were mistaken for somebody else. The governor here is facing something that, in its own modest way, feels like full-fledged rebellion. He sure sees it that way, and he's not been shy responding, which is why tourism's in the toilet.

"Word apparently reached him or someone in his camp that members of the EZLN—the Zapatistas, the guerrillas from the next state down, Chiapas—were coming to powwow with the local opposition on tactics. There were rumors of a new general strike. The powers that be decided to nip that little fucker in the bud and they had their men waiting out there on the road."

Roque glanced toward Lupe, who was staring out at the hypnotic surf. "Why chase us? What made us so suspicious?"

"It's my understanding," Bergen said, "that the folks who could answer your question best are unavailable." A turn toward the sun sent a shock of white glare across the windshield. Bergen flipped down his visor. "I can tell you this much, if those phony IDs you guys picked up from your *salvatrucho* pals were from Chiapas instead of Veracruz? We'd still be back there at that checkpoint, most likely facedown on the pavement."

Roque caught a whiff of himself, realizing only then just how scared he'd been. "How come we didn't hear any of this from you before?"

Bergen glanced over his shoulder, his customary smile at half-mast. "You aren't seriously complaining, are you?"

Roque blanched. "No. I'm not."

"Good." Bergen slowed for a *tope* and a pack of women swarmed the windows on each side, holding up bags of oranges, cold drinks, miscellaneous *chácharas*. The windows filled with eager hands, the voices almost accusing in their urgency.

Once the van picked up speed again, Bergen said, "I'll tell you a story. About the way things are here. I have this friend, delightful lady, used to run a restaurant in Oaxaca de Juárez. Best pork with *mancha manteles mole* you'll ever know. One morning she was walking to her bank to make the daily deposit when the Policía Federal Preventiva rolled in. This was November 2006, during the teachers' strike. The PFP came to teach the teachers a lesson. Batons, rubber bullets, tear gas, the whole trick bag. Alix, my friend, she tried to help somebody who'd been tear-gassed, dabbing their eyes with a hankie dipped in Coca-Cola. Trust me, it works. Anyway, she got snatched up by the PFP along with everybody else, dragged to a van, thrown inside with ten other women. One cop said they were going to get taken out in a helicopter and dropped into the ocean. That's not an idle threat down here. It's not folklore, either. It gets done. Good news is, it didn't get done that day.

"Cops took them to the women's prison in Miahuatlán, not that things were swell there, either. Alix got questioned, to use the usual euphemism, and the man in charge used a blanket when he kicked her so he wouldn't leave marks. She was charged with assaulting police, sedition, destruction of public property. Mind you, I'm talking a nice middle-aged lady here, maybe weighs 110 after a heavy breakfast, who was trying to help somebody who was hurt. She closed up her restaurant after that. No more pork with *mancha manteles mole*. Haven't heard from her in over a year."

The driver of the truck just ahead signaled that Bergen could pass. He downshifted, wound the Eurovan out in third gear, then ventured his move into the oncoming lane.

"What I'm saying is, that's the state of things you folks walked into. Just so you know."

Thanks for the tip, Roque thought, sinking in his seat. It was like they were trapped in some hellish video game where the longer they played the more their enemies multiplied.

They hit two more checkpoints in short order, one just before Puerto Angel, the second at the lighthouse turnoff right before Puerto Escondido. Bergen's magic seemed to be taking hold, they got waved through each time. After that their biggest problems were road washouts and wandering livestock until they passed Pinotepa Nacional—another checkpoint, but though they got stopped the soldier simply reached in, opened the glove box, checked inside for a pistol or drugs, then directed the van into the slow-moving queue for a giant X-ray machine, its white crane-like boom arching over the road.

By midafternoon they reached Acapulco—or Narcopulco as it often got called these days, Bergen said. The cartels were jockeying for control of the port, with the predictable rise in body count, at least until the army got sent in. Things were returning to normal, more or less, or the illusion of normal. The southern end of town looked shopworn and sad, the northern more stylish and new. Pingo, from his perch up front, pointed to the top of one particularly stunning cliff with shameless reverence.—*Check it out, that's Sly Stallone's house*.

Come twilight they pulled into a modest roadside hotel half a mile beyond a pig-filled swamp just outside Zihuatenejo—only a dozen or so rooms, high walls isolating each of the entrances, an armed guard stationed in the parking lot, another at the office door. Bergen explained it was a *casa de citas*; patrons paid by the hour, not the night, a favorite spot for a poke with the mistress. "I know the folks who run this place," he said, killing the ignition, lodging the emergency brake. Beyond the hotel, the hillside rose with lush thickets of nameless greenery, crowned with mango and thorn trees. Across the highway, fishing boats thronged a network of docks. "It's clean, it's discreet, the van will be safe. And I'm guessing, given prior experience, you're not all that eager to travel the roads at night. Me, neither."

FORTY

EL RECIO PUT HAPPY ON THE FRONT DOOR, KIKI WITH HIS TOP-knot watched the back. Osvaldo with his dumpy suit and roach killers joined El Recio and another man, Hilario, in the kitchen where they got to play butcher.

How had he put it: I think I got something maybe could suit you.

Happy couldn't tell if this was their standard MO or whether they'd taken inspiration from what he'd described of the Crockett takeover. Maybe they wanted to see how he'd react. Using duct tape, they'd tied and gagged the cop and his wife and their son to chairs. The boy was seven maybe, blue fleece pajamas, matching blue socks. The pajamas had little bucking broncos on them. The parents were naked.

El Recio made the parents watch as Hilario did the boy, using wire cutters and grain alcohol and a box of wood matches. Happy leaned against the wall, back turned to what was happening, but he could hear, he could smell. His memory emptied its sewer, he was back inside that claustrophobic room with Snell and his daughter and he would have sold his soul to get away except how do you outrun what's inside you? Keep your eyes on the street, he told himself, focus on what's out there, even if it's nothing. Especially if it's nothing.

He threw back another slug of *tejuino* to buck up his nerve. It scalded his mouth and throat and simmered in his gut. El Recio said the Indians fermented it by putting a ball of human shit inside a cheesecloth and burying it in the corn mash, letting it molder. He clutched the bottle, fearing he might vomit. Worse, faint. What would happen, he wondered, if I went in there, tried to stop it? Nothing. Everybody would just get to watch me die too.

The cop was bent, just not bent enough apparently. He'd talked to somebody, a shipment got stopped—of what? Migrants? Drugs? Guns? Happy wasn't told, the wisdom of murder. He knew only this: Muffled screams howled into thick swaths of tape—the boy, his mother, his stupid on-the-take-but-suddenly-honest cop father—the rocking of wood chairs against the floor as the parents struggled to free themselves, the acrid smell of burned flesh and scorched fleece and smoke, but Happy was there and not there, unable to get the girl out of his head, like she was living under his skin, struggling to get out, her eyes so huge when he shot her old man, then kicking herself into the corner, trying to get away—from him, from her dying old man, from *it*.

In the kitchen, El Recio sang in a clownish baritone:

> *Hoy es mi día*
> *Voy a alegrar toda el alma mía*

There were no questions to ask, nothing to learn. This was a message. The killing would go slowly, over hours, then the rumor mill would kick in and every other cop in Sonora would learn that the boy died first, died horribly and slowly in unthinkable pain, followed hours later by his mother, most likely driven crazy by then, and only several hours after that, at the cusp of dawn, by the father, the man whose chickenshit conscience could be blamed for it all. After that, who with a badge wouldn't take the money?

There was a lull in the kitchen. Happy dared a glance over his shoulder. Hilario was wiping his hands with a towel, Osvaldo lit up a smoke. El Recio stepped into the doorway, looking skeletal without the snake.

He approached slowly, almost wearily and Happy wondered what depths got tapped in the torturing of a child, then recoiled at his own phony righteousness. A birdlike hand reached out, resting on Happy's shoulder.

"Didn't have time to tell you," El Recio said. "Finally got word about Lonely. Now, what I heard, it's like secondhand, thirdhand, some don't even make sense, all right? But word I got is damn near his whole clique went down." His lips were drawn. A vein the size of a night crawler throbbed on the side of his shaved skull. "Cops sent the riot squad in, storm-trooper shit, snipers and dogs and choppers overhead, shut the whole barrio down, went door to door like it's fucking Baghdad. You know how those assholes love a show. Lonely and ten other dudes, slammed with gang beefs and that's like no bail, no luck, no hope, know what I'm saying?"

Happy had expected this explanation. It was most likely true and thus the perfect lie. The weightless hand lifted off Happy's shoulder, vanished into a pocket, reappeared with an asthma inhaler. Two quick pumps: bob of the Adam's apple, hiss of albuterol. He didn't seem particularly short of breath. Maybe he just liked the taste.

"And here's the shit, *güey*. Way I hear it, this Guatemalan *comandante* your cousin got tangled up with, this clown named El Chusquero?"

"I know who you mean." Happy worried his hands around the *tejuino* bottle, the rough glass reassuringly solid. "We had to wire down money to pay him off."

"Yeah, well, he's the one who made the call. Maybe it's bullshit, you know how some of these idiots think, but this is what I'm hearing, all right? Supposedly this El Chusquero cocksucker got fucked out of some deal by your cousin, they was supposed to take some boat up the Mexican coast or some shit—"

"I heard about this, look—"

"Just listen, all right? Your cousin and uncle, they skipped out, last minute, and this El Chusquero asshole said: Okay motherfuckers, try this. He picked up the phone, tapped some old pals in uniform down in El Salvador, called in a favor, whatever. And the hammer came down."

Another thumb-punch on the inhaler, eyelids fluttering, a clenching swallow of mist.

"So, like, even if you did have some deal with Lonely, it's useless now. I swear to God, I never heard word one, never saw a fucking dime, and now I'm not gonna, no matter what. Sorry, just the way it is."

He slipped the inhaler back into his pant pocket, rubbed at his eye. From the kitchen, ragged sobs.

"*Chécalo*, there's guys who seriously want to fuck your cousin up, given all the shit that came down back in San Salvador."

"Look, Roque's not perfect, I get that." Happy again had to bite back mention of his father's death. "But way I hear it, Roque turned down this El Chusquero to honor the deal with Lonely. So why's he in the shit for that?"

"Law of unintended consequences, just the way it is. Besides which, there's some girl supposedly in the picture too. I never heard about this till yesterday, some chick Lonely sent up to gain a little juice with Don Pato."

"I don't know who that is."

"You don't need to know. I need to know. Right? Just like I need to know who ropes the *pollos*, who rounds up the *guías*, who watches over the safe houses and makes the bribes and launders the money. I need to know all that because they rely on me. They rely on me to enforce the motherfucking law, right? You need to know one thing—what I tell you."

"Look, I'm sorry. I didn't mean—"

"I'm just making a point, okay? Don Pato knows about this girl coming up with your cousin. He knows what's supposed to happen. I don't make it happen, I look weak. I can't afford that. I look weak, next day I'm dead."

Happy realized finally what El Recio was saying. "I don't know why Roque would have a problem handing this girl over." Thinking: Now who sounds weak?

"Things happen, you know? I hear she's like crack for the eyes, *güey*, and she's got a voice. You know how all the big shots down here wanna be sung about. You're nothing unless there's a *corrido* on the radio pimping you up. There's talk this *pichona* and your cousin, like, connected or some such shit."

"You want me to talk to Roque, explain what the deal is?"

"When the time comes. Maybe, yeah. Meanwhile I got some bad news on another front."

Osvaldo appeared in the kitchen doorway, a disheveled silhouette, and made a chittering sound with his tongue and teeth. El Recio, without turning, gestured for patience. "*Momentito, cabrón*." Reaching again into a pocket, this time he withdrew not the inhaler but a small plastic bag of salted plums called *saladitos*. They smelled like something plucked from the inside of a pig and brined in lye. He lifted one to his mouth, tilted the bag toward Happy, shrugged when the offer was declined, then continued. "This Arab dude you wanted to bring across. There's a problem. An American showed up last week, frumpy motherfucker, kinda fat with crooked glasses, lugging this big old briefcase with him, he met up with Don Pato over dinner at El Gallo. Again, okay, I don't know everything, but the fat guy was, like, way interested in this friend of yours and some kinda deal got made. Just so you know, the Americans are pissing blood over the way things are down here. Too many bodies, too much news about it, and the news is, like, freaky. They're willing to go with a winner, even tip their hand, pick a favorite, if it means things calm down. None of this is official, it's all secret-handshake spook shit, but whoever the winner turns out to be—and this guy was here to say they'd be happy with Don Pato—he's gotta understand, we can't be moving ragheads across the border. Them, we turn over to this frumpy fat motherfucker and his people. Hear what I'm saying?"

He saved my life, Happy thought, wondering if he should believe that anymore. "What happens to him after you turn him over?"

"Not your problem, *güey*." The skeletal hand returned to Happy's shoulder, a lingering squeeze. Deep in their sockets, El Recio's red-veined eyes warmed. "You stepped up tonight. I wanted to see you carry your weight. You done good. You're part of the picture now, right?" He licked bits of *saladito* off his teeth. "You got no place to go to up north, there's serious heat on you there. And there's people down south now want your fucking head, or your cousin's head. Yours'll do in a pinch, hear what I'm saying? Best idea you got, stay here with me. Don Pato, the others I mentioned, they're serious cats—run the whole goddamn show, this stretch of the border. Anything moves across, it's got their brand on it, otherwise you die. I do what's necessary, they watch my back. Same thing with you and me. Be cool, stand up, don't give me nothing to worry about, I'll look the fuck after you. I'll get your cousin across. The rest can't be helped."

From the kitchen doorway, Osvaldo made his tetchy little sound again. The mother was mewling hysterically behind her gag. Hilario backhanded her but she wouldn't settle down.

"Back to business," El Recio said, stuffing the bag of *saladitos* back in his pocket. "We'll talk more over breakfast."

THOUGH THE WATER WAS TEPID THE SHOWERS FELT LIKE LUXURY—first Lupe, then Roque, finally Samir, each of them scrubbing off the grit and stickiness and toweling dry in the small spare room, nothing but a twin bed for furniture. What else was needed, given its usual hourly occupants? Bergen took a room for himself, Pingo would sleep in the van. The tally of money owed was inching upward—three hundred dollars per person for the ride, which Bergen said would barely cover gas, even at Pemex prices, then the room, food. They'd already pooled their money and handed over what they'd had, the rest being due on credit, for which Roque gave his address, the names of both Tía Lucha and Lalo as guarantors of his debt. Bergen had never promised charity but it all added up so fast. Still, Roque supposed, better that than paying out to some *salvatrucho* or *pandillero* who'd just keep the shakedown going forever back home. He got it now, it wasn't just that nothing was free. The moment you agreed to pay, you opened the door to hell. Bergen was simply a friendlier breed of devil.

Lupe joined him outside and they sat together beneath a roadside mango tree, gazing through the darkness and the day's last traffic at the fishing fleet moored to its lantern-lit docks. The breeze carried the scents of sea salt and beach rot and the echoes of beery laughter.

—*We should have gone for a swim before the shower*, he said.

Using both hands, Lupe spread her damp hair to let the wind help dry it, lifting her face toward the starlight. The bruising from Lonely's beating had all but healed.—*It's stupid to swim at night. You can't get your bearings.*

—*There's plenty of light from the bar, the docks.*

—*The waves can be dangerous*. Her voice was adamant, almost shrill.—*I heard of a woman whose neck was broken just a few months ago and she was a very strong swimmer. The undertow kills several people every year.*

For a second, he felt ridiculous. Then he figured it out.—*You don't know how to swim.*

She shrugged, shook her hair.—*Let me guess. You want to teach me.*

—*I wasn't trying to insult you.*

—*I'm sorry. It's just . . .* She glanced up into the dark tree.—

We both know what's coming. I'm tired of thinking about it. Get me a mango, would you?

Climbing up a ways to one of the middling branches—the lower ones were picked clean—he tugged a plump mango from its rubbery stem and tossed it to her, then scrambled back down. Using her nails, she peeled away the skin so they could trade bites. Soon their faces were tacky with juice and pulp.

Between swallows, he said:—*I'm going to need another shower.*

She slipped her sticky hand in his, their fingers interlocking. He tilted his head to venture a kiss, only to see Samir approaching, chafing his burred black hair with a towel.

—*I am sorry to interrupt*, he announced, sounding more flustered than contrite.—*I have been thinking today, very much, very long, about our situation. I have thought of what Fatima would want of me. I have prayed. And I am here to tell you I am ashamed of how I have behaved. Yes, I need very much to reach America—not for my sake. My family's. But I have been thoughtless, even cruel, in how I have spoken. It needn't be so. I had a chance earlier to talk with Pingo. He knows a man at the border, his uncle, he lives in a town called Naco, who could help us get across. There would be no need to deal with this El Recio character in Agua Prieta. For all they know we burned up in the car, right? Who can say differently, how soon? Months it will take, longer most likely, for them to determine for certain who it was in that car. Again, yes, there is the issue of money and Happy has told you there is none, fine, but things change. You, Roque, can pass over as you please, perhaps you could head home, ask among friends or family. I could wait with Lupe in Naco*. He stood with his shoulders folded forward, as though preparing to bow. His deep-set eyes lacked their usual indignation.—*I am agreeable, is what I am saying. I no longer want us to fight among ourselves. It is wrong.*

No more was said about it. But later, when the three of them settled in for the night inside the tiny stifling room, Samir took the floor in a sign of goodwill. Roque and Lupe negotiated the narrow bed, spooning though fully clothed, his stomach pressed into the hollow of her back as she pillowed her head on his arm. In time their breathing synchronized, drowsiness settled in. Samir fell asleep first, though, snoring with a chesty rasp. Perhaps we don't know what's coming after all, Roque thought, and shortly Lupe took his hand, nudged it inside her jeans, pressing it against the downy warm curls, holding it there in a gesture of possession, him of her, her of him.

FROM HIS TABLE NEAR THE BACK, LATTIMORE SPOTTED HIM IN THE doorway, the distinctively scruffy beard and hair, the rumpled suit, the cockeyed glasses, the clownishly fat and battered briefcase—McIlvaine, the security man from Dallas, what was his company's name—Bayonet? The man made eye contact, offering his tea-colored smile, then began picking his way through the tables and Lattimore felt his stomach plunge with an almost punitive sense of dread. His sandwich turned into a soggy wad of nausea in his hands. Banneret, he thought, that was it.

"Jim!" McIlvaine thrust out his hand. "Mind if I sit?"

Lattimore nodded to the open chair, setting his oozy sandwich down and reaching for a napkin. "Let me admire your investigative skills—you found me how?"

"Inspired guesswork." McIlvaine reached across to a nearby table where a menu sat unused and plucked it for his own use. "The receptionist said you were out, the hour suggested lunch, I decided to wander around the area, take my chances." He pushed up his glasses, reading a nearby chalkboard listing specials.

"That's all you wanted, company for lunch?"

"No need to sound so put-upon. I'm not expecting a fanfare but I do have news I think you'll find useful, if you haven't already received it."

Lattimore, resisting a smile, took a sip of his lukewarm coffee. Since the screwup with Happy the information chain had gone into lockdown. The case was infamous, no one wanted his name near it. Memos and e-mails gathered dust somewhere out in the bureaucratic nowhere. Not one single agent outside the country would return his calls. "I'm all ears," he said.

Folding his hands across his midriff, McIlvaine settled into his chair. "I heard the news, the bad business on your end. Quite a cock-up, as our British friends would say."

"Yes." Lattimore tasted the grit of his coffee dregs. "British friends, one can't have too many of those."

"Oddly enough, you're near half right." The waitress bustled past and he caught her eye, tipping his menu back and forth as a signal. "Turns out my friend in the Green Zone knew a Brit journalist doing a story on the Al Tanf refugee camp. He got in touch, I scratched out a list of questions, ones I thought you'd want answered given our previous discussion. Well, unhappily but not too surprisingly, he came up empty. There is no record of a woman named Fatima Sadiq in the Al Tanf refugee camp, nor any woman named Fatima with a daughter named Shatha, or more generally a woman married to an interpreter working for the coalition, the Salvadorans in Najaf specifically. Nothing, nada. Sorry. Now who knows how doggedly this Brit asked his questions—it wasn't really his focus, after all, just one of those quid pro quos one accepts in a war zone."

The waitress materialized. McIlvaine ordered a grilled liverwurst and Swiss on corn rye with pepperoncini and onions, mustard not mayo, coleslaw side, iced tea with extra lemon, then handed her the menu and watched her flee.

Lattimore, prompting, "Andy?"

"Where was I . . ." He adjusted his glasses, glanced at his watch. "Ah yes. Perhaps your Samir's Fatima, if she exists, has moved to another camp, Trebil for instance. Maybe she's gone back to Baghdad, meaning she could be God only knows where.

These are not people who trust the government or the press, the Palestinians, I mean. They feel very much hunted and betrayed. But there's something else too. Something rather curious."

A busboy delivered a dewy tumbler of iced tea and a saucer of lemon slices. McIlvaine fussed the straw from its wrapper. The busboy, a Latino, vaguely reminded Lattimore of Happy's cousin Roque and he suffered a sudden flash of misgiving, wondering where the kid might be.

"My friend spoke to a contact he's developed, a man once very well appointed within the Mukhabarat. Obviously, this is very sensitive. I can't tell you any more than that about the man."

Like I could burn him from here, Lattimore thought.

"But he remembered a Palestinian named Salah Hassan from the al-Baladiyat neighborhood. The man was arrested for trafficking in foreign currencies sometime after the end of the Iran-Iraq War." He began squeezing lemon into his tea, one wedge, two. "Curiously enough, this Salah Hassan had a wife named Fatima and a daughter named Shatha. And after her husband's imprisonment—they cut off his hand, like they do with thieves, then stuck him in a prison somewhere to be forgotten—the woman, this Fatima, she not surprisingly fell on very hard times. There are brothels in Baghdad, obviously, though they're known to favor green lights, not red. Apparently this Fatima had a small but very devout clientele. But once Saddam's regime fell and the Mahdi militias began their persecution of the Palestinians, which became quite indiscriminate after the bombing of the Al-Askari mosque in Samarra, she grabbed her daughter and fled the area and no one is willing to admit they know where she ran off to. Assuming anyone knows. Maybe one of those devoted patrons stepped up, whisked her off to his tent in Araby."

The waitress returned to the table, this time with McIlvaine's sandwich and coleslaw. Setting it down, she turned her attention to the remains of Lattimore's lunch and cocked an eyebrow. He leaned back so she could clear. Earlier, he'd considered flirting—

innocently, of course, unless she responded—but McIlvaine was like a sexual black hole. Once she was gone: "This source of your friend's, any chance he got a look at the document you showed me, the one linking Samir to the Mukhabarat?"

McIlvaine stuffed a paper napkin into his collar, gripped half his sandwich in both hands and leaned forward over his plate. "It's a contact sheet, that's all. At some point he was brought in for an interview. That's all you can infer from it reliably. Whether there were others—contacts I mean, interviews—it's impossible to tell. Sorry, nothing else on that end to report."

Lattimore smiled absently, wondering how long courtesy would demand he sit there watching the other man eat. Hearing the unmistakable popping growl of a Harley 110 V-Twin outside, then the distinctive *potato potato potato* of its idle as it backed to the curb, he felt an immediate pang of longing—the empty road, freedom. It occurred to him that Samir might have been one of this Fatima's devoted johns, one whose ardor went haywire, to the point he married her in his mind, plotted to get her and her daughter out of Iraq forever. He was clawing his way to America, trying to find her the future she deserved, one for which she would be slavishly grateful, if he could ever find out where she was. Weirder things had happened, he supposed, especially when pussy was involved.

"By the way," McIlvaine said, speaking through a mouthful of liverwurst, "any idea where our would-be terrorist might be at the moment?"

FORTY-ONE

THEY ROSE EARLY AND DROVE THROUGH MILE AFTER DEEP-GREEN mile of banana, papaya and mango groves on their way north from Lázaro Cárdenas with its massive industrial port.

"They used to call this stretch of road Bandido Alley," Bergen said at one point. "The whole state of Michoacán was pretty much a playground for the Valencia cartel. Then the army came in, put up roadblocks, cracked down on drug labs, burned pot fields. Drove the trouble off the coast and into the hills, at least until after dark. No guarantee it won't come back, of course, but for now I think we're safe."

The checkpoints grew fewer in number over time and the Eurovan invariably got waved through. As the sunlight hit its noonday pitch the terrain grew dramatic, the road winding steeply along mountainsides that dropped off into crashing waves. When the road leveled out again the vine-covered hills to the east were wreathed in filmy cloud, the palm-rimmed beaches to the west almost monotonous in their perfection, untouched by tourism or development. On some the surf was wild and unwelcoming, on others it dissolved in a rumbling hiss onto vacant sand. Roque began to understand the stubborn pride of Mexicans, as well as their despair.

They stopped for gas in a beachfront hamlet, buying it from a bowlegged woman smoking a pipe who siphoned it from a drum. A little farther on they lunched on fresh ceviche at a seafood bar and stocked up on water for the afternoon heat.

The hours grew hallucinatory, dissolving into sweaty sunlit dreams of roadside shrines, wild hillsides, makeshift cornfields, thatched *enramadas* and *palapas*, interspersed with signs marking iguana crossings, armadillo crossings, warnings against hunting raccoons.

Once, they found themselves bestilled inside a pastel cloud of butterflies.

When they struggled through Manzanillo with its cruise-ship crowds, Bergen told the story of a woman known as Mountain Girl, one of Kesey's Merry Pranksters, who gave birth to her daughter Sunshine in the decrepit local hospital, only to flee her room one night when beach crabs, crazed by the full moon, stormed the newborn's bed.

Colima dissolved into Jalisco, the villages thinned out and the Costa Alegre began, with its sculpted mansions on the cliffs and scowling guards at the gates: crisp uniforms, wraparound shades, machine guns. "Nice place to visit," Bergen cracked, "if you're Mick Jagger."

As the sun dropped into the ocean beyond the Bahía de Banderas, Puerto Vallarta came and went in a blur of colonial-era cobblestone streets, roadside market stalls, the rebuilt promenade. "Just a little ways more," Bergen said, to explain why he wasn't stopping. "I know I've warned off driving at night but we're so damn close. Keep your fingers crossed."

They took the main highway toward Tepic, then cut off toward the coast, the road a rustic two-lane obstacle course of cavernous potholes, fearless chickens, slinking dogs. Here and there between nameless hamlets a bar appeared, nothing but a box of concrete trimmed with Christmas lights and barbed wire, a jukebox throbbing inside—*cumbia*, *chuntaro*, *grupero*—while outside jubilant drunks wandered the roadbed or stone-eyed men stood with arms crossed, watching the strange van rumble past.

The isolated stretches grew longer, the darkness so thick it felt like their headlights were boring a tunnel and they were barreling through it, jostled by the bad road, swarmed with dust.

It was in one of those mid-hamlet stretches of pitch-black night that the headlights appeared behind them. They seemed to float independently, buoyed by the darkness like fireflies, then the engines could be heard and Roque realized they were motorcycles. Shortly everyone turned around to look.

"They're getting closer," Roque said.

"I'm aware of that," Bergen replied.

Soon the pack was right behind, eight of them riding two abreast, the riders' silhouettes in the dust clouds, muscular arms slung from ape hangers, wind-raked hair. Samir stared at them, face skeletal in the joggling light. "And you said leave the weapons behind."

Bergen dodged a rat-size tarantula scuttling across the road. "You think we'd even have gotten this far, past all those checkpoints, if there'd been a gun in this van?"

"What good will it have done," Samir said, voice rising, "to get this far only to end here?"

"Relax, ace. We haven't reached the end. Far from it."

The motorcycles made no move to pass but seemed content to herd the van along from behind. Soon the salty tang of the surf broke through the smells of gasoline and dust. Just off the road, at the end of a rutted lane lined with sprawling jacarandas and guava trees, another bunkerlike building sat, barred windows glowing with caramel-colored light. Another two dozen motorcycles sat outside, a ragtag collection of café racers, dirt bikes, crotch rockets, choppers, rice burners, trikes. When Bergen hit his signal and braked for the turn, Samir leaned forward and hissed, "What in the name of God are you doing?"

Bergen downshifted and the van lurched, slowing. "Stopping for the night," he said. "Unless you have somewhere else in mind."

He pulled into a sandy spot beneath a sagging palm and killed the motor. The riders backed their bikes into the line outside the clubhouse, the revving engines a thunder roll in the settling dust. Some of the other members filled the lamp-lit doorway, tossing beers to the new arrivals. Beyond them, a fire roared in a barbecue pit.

Samir hand-mopped sweat from his stubbled face. "You know these people?"

Bergen opened the door and the overhead light flickered on, fixing the Arab's expression. "I think that would be a reasonable inference." His voice was free of mockery. "You know, a little gratitude wouldn't kill you."

As everyone else extricated themselves from the van, Bergen opened the back and withdrew one of the cardboard tubes with a rolled-up painting inside, then thumped it against his leg as he strolled toward the clubhouse entrance, the others straggling behind. The surf tumbled onto the shore beyond the tree line, breaking on the beach in surges of foam, the sharp scent of brine mingling with that of wood smoke and roasting fish.

A scrum of bikers waited outside the glowing frame of the doorway. Bergen held the cardboard tube aloft and called out to the nearest one, a princely muscular *vato* with swept-back hair and a soul patch furring his lower lip.—*I have a little art for you, Chelo. A masterpiece.*

BERGEN SAT DOWN AT ONE OF THE LONG HAND-CARVED TABLES AND several bikers joined him, including the one named Chelo, the leader. Roque and Lupe and Pingo and Samir, all but ignored, stood there idly until one of the bikers flashed a dentally challenged smile and gestured them grandly to an empty table. As Bergen unrolled his painting Roque took a second to get his bearings—an old Wurlitzer jukebox, two pool tables, a few bumper pinball machines. The bar looked like it had been salvaged from elsewhere and a banner hanging behind it read:

Los Mocosos Locos—San Blas, Nayarit

The bikers themselves were refreshingly stereotypical—shaved heads on some, tangled manes for the rest, a spattering of Fu Manchus, two or three chest-length beards, bandannas, harness boots, black leather chaps and vests with the club's colors emblazoned across the back: a whorl-eyed skull over crossed six-shooters. It was like walking into a remake of *Angels Unchained*, except the skin shaded darker, the swagger wasn't half as pompous and everybody spoke Spanish. Still, Bergen looked like a golf coach in their midst, with Roque and the rest his scraggly fourfold shadow.

As Bergen unrolled the painting—it was the same one he'd shown at the roadblocks, the one he compared to Chagall—Chelo reached into the pocket of his leather vest and withdrew a jeweler's loupe and a razor blade. Bergen and one of the other bikers held the painting flat; Chelo set the loupe down onto the canvas and lowered his eye to the lens. Roque, sensing what he was about to watch but unable to believe it, traded a brief stunned glance first with Lupe then Samir—only Pingo seemed unbothered—then turned back in time to see Chelo, calm as a surgeon, razor a perfectly straight section from the canvas inch by inch. When the narrow strip was clear he handed it to one of the others, who coiled it around his neck like a chain of raffle tickets, then Chelo bent over the painting again, adjusted his loupe, found the next invisible demarcation and repeated the process, painstakingly trimming another strip from the canvas, the same width as the last.

Bergen glanced up once, winked at Roque, then returned his focus to his slowly vanishing masterpiece. One of the women, almost busting out of her leathers, came by with a bucket of iced beers and settled it onto the table for Roque and the others, while another brought a plate of mango slices, with roasted shrimp and mahimahi and *pargo*, marinated in lemon and chilies. The four of them dug in shamelessly, wolfing their food down with their hands, intermittently turning back to watch as bit by bit the painting vanished, carved into long shreds, each of which then got piecemealed further into squares the size of postage stamps. Fucking hell, Roque thought, backhanding the slop from his chin, we've been bluffing through checkpoints for two whole days with a couple hundred hits of blotter acid.

No money exchanged hands, Roque noticed, this was a long-standing deal, credit not an issue. A bit of a character, Father Luis had called Bergen, with a very storied life. That and then some, Roque thought. And what of the priest himself? Maybe he was the impersonator warned about on the poster at the entrance to his own damn church. If so, Roque thought, my uncle lies in his cemetery, consecrated by a phony sacrament. Bringing the point home was the current procession of Los Mocosos Locos idling in, approaching their leader and collecting a hit of acid into their cupped palms, swallowing it down like a communion wafer, then heading back outside for the fire pit.

Bergen ambled over to the table where Roque and the others sat, working on their third plate of roasted fish and shrimp.

—*Looks tasty*. He plucked a fatty charred hunk of *pargo* from the plate, chewed with gusto.—*Everybody happy?*

No one said anything. If they weren't stunned from what they'd just observed they were tipsy from the beer, sated from the food.

Turning to Samir, Bergen lowered his voice. "You can thank me anytime."

Samir looked incensed. "You used us."

"That a joke? I'm doing you a favor."

"We were a distraction. A decoy."

Pingo, sensing the change in drift despite the use of English, excused himself, grabbing an extra beer from the ice bucket and steering a path outside. Bergen's smile withered. "Listen, you ungrateful prick. Think of where you'd be right now without my help. If not dead, damn close. You might also consider that, should any of these good people get the idea you've got a problem with what you just watched—they get the vaguest notion you're the talkative sort, as in better off facedown in a ditch somewhere—they won't ask my permission. Now cheer the fuck up." He slapped Samir's shoulder like a sales manager coaxing the new guy onto the floor. "You've just been fed and you've got a place to sleep tonight. Because of me. Put it in perspective, Samir." He pronounced it *smear*. "Or I'll tell these nice folks you've got something you'd like to say."

He reached for the bucket, collected the final beer, then turned to Roque and Lupe.—*You two aren't above singing for your supper, I hope.*

THE GUITAR WAS BEHIND THE BAR, A GUILD DREADNOUGHT WITH fairly new strings. As Roque tuned and played a few test chords he smiled at the crisp sweet highs, the rich booming lows, a beautiful ax, Bluegrass Jubilee. He joined Lupe out among the others who circled the fire. The acid was starting to hit, a number of the bikers were staring into the flames as though seeing within them their own spirit faces; some picked through the charred crackling skin of the fish they'd just eaten, as though it held some mystic portent; others just sat and smiled, hugging their knees, heads eased back. The rest milled about, beers in hand, bestowing warm *abrazos* to every brother they met.

For the sake of visibility and projection above the crackling fire, they fashioned a mini-stage from four wood chairs, then hoisted Lupe onto it, perched like a surfer on an unsteady wave. Roque sat in a fifth chair to her side. He strummed the opening chords of "Sabor a Mí," suggesting they open with that. Lupe nodded her assent and, as the introduction gently concluded, lifted her chin, closed her eyes and began the first verse.

It took a bar or two for her voice to find its center and the lyrics at first seemed lost in the roar of the fire and the distant surf. As the chorus came around, though, she had the crowd with her, a few even daring to sing along:

No pretendo ser tu dueño
No soy nada, yo no tengo vanidad

I don't pretend to be your master
I am nothing, I have no vanity

Their voices spurred her on. The next verse bloomed with even deeper feeling and as she came back around to the chorus the others chimed in more devoutly, their gravelly voices harmonizing in tone if not pitch. As the song concluded, the klatch of tripping bikers erupted into whistling applause. A few wiped away tears.

Lupe leaned down toward Roque, gathering her hair away from her face. " 'Sin Ti'," she whispered.

He felt stunned.—*Are you sure?*

She didn't answer. Instead she stood up straight again on the rickety platform of chairs and called out:—*On our way north, we lost someone. His name was Faustino. He was the uncle of Roque here. He was very kind to me. He believed in me. I would like to sing this next song in his memory. It meant a lot to him, because he too lost someone, lost her long ago.*

She signaled to Roque that she was ready. He played the introductory chords, a lump in his throat—how is she going to sing, he wondered—but as her cue came around she closed her eyes, balled her hands into fists and lifted her face toward the night:

Sin ti
No podré vivir jamás

Without you
I will never be able to live

He had heard her sing often over the past few weeks, under so many different circumstances. He had not yet heard her sing like this. You're going to break these crusty bastards' hearts, he thought, if not mine. Had he not loved her already, he would have been helpless then. Again the bikers sang along on the chorus, their voices a growling background hum. They understood. They knew loss, they knew remembrance, even tripping their brains out, and this time, as Roque ended with a strumming flourish and Lupe wiped her face, their applause was a benediction.

That night the two of them slept in a corner of the clubhouse, tucked inside a single musty sleeping bag, pressed together, legs entwined. The others lay nearby, so there would be no lovemaking, but she lay her head upon his heart and he stroked her smoke-scented hair until sleep claimed first her, then him. Outside, the fire raged all night, bikers milling in and out, seeking beer or food, their voices subdued in a nameless reverence. Once, when Roque eased awake, startled by some sound, he noticed through fluttering eyelids that Samir was sitting against the wall, clutching his knees, staring at the two of them snuggled together, his face veiled with shadow.

FORTY-TWO

TWO DAYS AFTER THEY DID THE COP AND HIS FAMILY THE BOA got sick. The thing wasn't eating. El Recio implored it, cooed to it, tried all its favorite snacks—live fetal rats, baby mice, bunnies—let it coil up in its favorite chair, stroked its mottled scales. He said they felt cold. How else the fuck they gonna feel, Happy thought, it's a goddamn snake. But he knew what was happening, suspected even El Recio knew. God doesn't take it out on you when you sin, that wasn't how it worked. He's not content with an uneasy conscience, he wants to push you into the flames, strip you of everything but the desire to die, watch you beg. And so he takes it out not on you but on those you love—wasn't that what you'd done to him?

El Recio threw on a shirt, said they were going out. He wanted to buy a heat lamp.

"You'll burn him up," Happy said. "Why not just put him in the oven?"

El Recio froze. "What'd you just say?"

Happy caught the hinge in El Recio's voice. The eyes, though, were far worse.

"I said you might burn him up."

"Her."

Get me out of this, Happy thought. "Her. Sorry. You might burn—"

"You said stick her in the oven."

"I didn't mean it like that. I was trying—"

"You want to eat La Princesa?"

"No. No. Look, I just came by to talk about those houses—"

"Want to eat my baby?"

On and on it went, Happy constantly trying to get back to what he came to say—an offer he wanted to make, a favor if looked at right—but the skinny *calvo* just turned everything into drama. Finally, like a hotheaded *madrecita*, he shoved Happy down the hallway, out the door, tears in his eyes, screaming not to come back until he could show some human feeling.

Happy stood there in the mud-washed street, staring across the ripening sewer trench as the door slammed shut, the noise scattering the crows that'd perched in a paloverde tree in the empty lot next door. Cupping his hands, he shouted, "*Lo siento*." I'm sorry.

Through the door, El Recio bellowed back: "*Me vale madre*." I don't give a damn.

On their way back from the job the other night, El Recio had told Osvaldo to stop the car as they passed a cluster of empty houses halfway between Cananea and Agua Prieta. Ghostly in the moonlight, they were part of a project that was only half finished, like so much of Mexico, at least the parts Happy had seen. El Recio said he and a partner were going in on three of the properties and he was worried about thieves, vandals.

Happy and Godo had gotten the sense they were drawing too much attention at the hotel, sooner or later someone could come around, find out about the weapons and God only knew where that would end. So Happy had figured they'd go down, squat in one of El Recio's houses, ward off anybody who came around to rip out the copper or the woodwork or the rebar or anything else they could turn around for cash. He didn't exactly say no, Happy told himself. If worse comes to worst, I'll buy him a new fucking snake.

He wandered about the fringes of Agua Prieta, bought some *tamalitos* at a vendor truck and headed back to the hotel. The girl, Paca, was there again, another round of English. From the sound of things, the lesson plan was a little more basic today: roof and window, shirt versus blouse, fork knife spoon. Apparently the mother had come by yesterday, thanking Godo, helping rewrap the gauze on his hand. He seemed more relaxed. Maybe he'd gotten laid.

As Godo fingered open the tinfoil wrap of his *tamalitos*, Happy's cell began to trill. Their eyes met, Happy dug the phone from his pocket. Again, an unknown exchange. If anyone was using this to track where I am, he figured, they'd have found me by now. He flipped the phone open, put his ear to the welcoming hiss.

"Happy? It's me."

Happy mouthed Roque's name, letting Godo know who it was. "Where are you?"

"The bus station in Guaymas."

Southern Sonora, Happy thought, though over on the Sea of Cortez. "Not so far."

"No. We'll be there soon. Look, Hap—"

"Samir there?" He thought of what El Recio had said, about the Americans, the deal they'd struck with Don Pato. How to explain that, after the man had come so close.

"Yeah. He's good. Pain in the ass sometimes but good. Look, there's something—"

"And let's not forget the girl—Lupe, am I right?"

The hiss surged, thrumming like a hive. "I was about to tell you about that."

"Kinda late in the game, wouldn't you say?" Happy felt a curious absence of anger. Still, the point needed to be made.

Roque said, "How did you hear about her?"

"That's not an answer."

"It's not like you and I had a chance to talk much the past week."

"That's not an answer, neither."

"Tío and I were trying to figure something out. A way to help her. It's complicated."

"I know."

"What do you know?"

"Who she belongs to. They're waiting for her."

Another silence, longer this time. "Yeah, well, that's what I wanted to talk to you about."

"It's not negotiable."

"With who—them or you?"

Happy felt his chest clench, like someone had tightened a screw. "I don't deserve that."

"I'm sorry. It's just, if you knew what we'd been through—"

"I could say the same. So could Godo."

A door slammed down the hall, then footsteps. Two men tramped toward the stair, one a murmur, the other a braying laugh. Their shadows flickered in the crack beneath the door.

"What do want from me, Hap? I didn't tell you about Lupe because I wasn't sure what to say. I am now. This guy we met in Oaxaca, he has an uncle who's a cop in Naco. He can help us get across, no El Recio."

Happy went cold—a cop? "You don't know," he said, wrestling the memory back into its hole, "what you're playing at."

"As far as anybody knows, we all died in the ambush with Tío. Five bodies burned up inside our car, no way they've ID'd who's who yet. You can say you got a call from Tía Lucha, she heard from Oaxaca about the car. Understand? We're dead. There's no one to hand over."

The tightening in his chest loosened a little, making him feel light-headed. The thing could work, he thought. It was lunacy, it was tempting the devil. But . . .

"Samir there? Something I'd like to talk to him about."

"Can it wait? The bus is leaving and I need to know where we can meet up with you."

He glanced over at Godo, fingers smeared with cheese and grease from the *tamalito*. The ugly one, he thought, the broken one. And I'm the stupid, worthless one.

Then there was Roque. The magical one.

"There's a place south of town," he said. "I'll give you directions."

ROQUE HUNG UP THE PHONE, OPENED THE FOLDING GLASS DOOR TO THE phone booth and followed Lupe and Samir to the bus. Bergen had dropped them at the station, handed them some cash for tickets plus a little extra for food. Pingo had gone with him—all that talk of hooking up with the union in Nogales for a work permit, utter bullshit—but he'd given them his uncle's name and contact information in Naco.—*He's solid*, he'd said, *he's tough. He won't screw you*.

Samir glanced over his shoulder as they passed through waves of diesel exhaust from the idling buses.—*What did he say?* The Arab had reverted to pest since they'd left San Blas, his impatience a kind of itch that everybody was obliged to scratch.

—*He's looking forward to seeing you again*.

—*No problems?*

After all they'd endured, it seemed the most ludicrous question imaginable.

The bus was a throbbing tube of road-worn chrome, twenty years old at least, but luxurious compared to the chicken buses they'd seen farther south. Roque and Lupe climbed on board and sat near the front, plopping down side by side in vinyl seats patched with tape, clasping hands, hers cool inside his, trading the occasional smile. Samir sat alone behind them, so restless Roque felt like reaching around and smacking him one. Not that he wasn't anxious himself. The driver sprawled in his seat, reading a wrestling magazine as he waited for stragglers, the time of departure apparently far more fluid than they'd feared. All that rush, he thought, now we sit, knowing it wasn't the delay bothering him. Something he'd heard in Happy's voice—or rather, something he hadn't heard—it unnerved him. The words over the phone had seemed adrift, beyond weary, no feeling, no heart. Everyone's been through a lot, he reminded himself, Happy's comeback, feeling a twinge of shame. He'd expected to get dumped on, cursed, called a weakling and a failure for letting Tío die, then felt vaguely undone when it didn't happen. Come on, he thought, resisting an urge to bark at the driver, let's go, feeling the nearness of home as an urgency, at the same time knowing he was simply afraid.

FORTY-THREE

EVEN THE BUS DRIVER SEEMED CONFUSED, NOTHING BUT A CLUSter of half-finished houses, the middle of nowhere. Twilight only enhanced the desolation. Spidery ocotillos and crook-armed saguaros manned the surrounding plain, at the edge of which dust devils swirled in the cool winds funneling down from the mountains. Overhead, a lone hawk caught an updraft and soared in its flux, a small black afterthought in a blackening sky.

The driver rechecked his odometer, confirmed they'd traveled the distance from Cananea that Roque had mentioned, then opened the door, wishing them luck as they gathered their things and shuttled out onto the roadbed. None of the other passengers looked at them. To make eye contact was, ironically, to become visible, and everyone bore a secret, even the children. Their bodies were freight, their lives for sale. The bus pulled away in a plume of black exhaust, its headlights plowing the dusk, and Roque couldn't help but wonder if they'd been tricked.

Shortly, he realized they weren't alone. On the stoop outside one of the unfinished houses a scrawny *huelepega* with matted black hair stuffed his face inside a brown paper bag, sucking up the glue fumes inside. A pack of dogs sulked nearby, trembling, sniffing the air. Then came a pistol shot—the dogs scattered, the gluehead crushed his bag to his chest, jerked to his feet and shambled off into the scrub.

Where in God's name is he running, Roque thought, wondering if they should follow.

The gunman revealed himself, easing around the corner of one of the nearer houses. Pistol at his side, he approached with trancelike slowness, offering no greeting.

Samir put his hand to his heart. "It has been so long, my friend. My God, you terrified us."

Happy stopped short, no reply, only a drifting smile, cut loose from the eyes. Turning toward Roque, he said simply, "Hey," his voice raspy and soft.

Roque said, "You okay?"

"The girl," Happy said. "She speak English?"

"Not much." Roque reached for her hand. "Not well."

Happy looked at their clasped hands, then her face, regarding her as though she were a problem he couldn't hope to solve. "Remind me, her name?"

A sudden wind kicked up whips of dust. Everyone shielded their eyes.

"Lupe," Roque said.

Realizing they were talking about her, she offered a shy smile. Happy turned away, gesturing with the pistol for everyone to follow as he led them back to the last house, the only one with a roof as far as Roque could tell. Inside, the walls were bare—no cabinets, no trim, no fixtures—the floors naked sheets of plywood that gave a little underfoot, a spooky sensation in the gathering dark. Cinder blocks sat propped on end like stools, nails lay scattered here and there amid trails of sawdust and cigarette butts and empty pint bottles. Even with the openings where windows should have been letting in air from outside, the room stank like an ashtray.

"How you like the place?" Happy glanced around like he was thinking of buying. "You wouldn't believe what they want for it."

Roque wondered where Godo was, the thought of seeing him again cropping up in his mind like a stone in his shoe these past few days. Missing him, wanting no part of him. First their mother, then Tío, who to blame? Who else?

Happy went on, "Came here to watch the place for the guy who owns it. Can't figure out if we were too early or too late."

Roque heard it. We. "So Godo's here somewhere."

From behind, a thundering: "Call the law!" He filled the doorway, shouldering a duffel. A ragged slide down his arm to the floor—whatever was inside clattered dully. Noticing the look on everyone's face, he grinned. "Hold the applause."

Roque felt a sudden coil of inner heat, so much held in check over the last few weeks, all of it now boiling up. "You sorry motherfucker!"

"Stop sniveling." Godo spread his arms. "Time for *abrazos*."

Roque didn't move. He couldn't. "Stop fucking around." His glance darted toward Lupe, who seemed baffled. Me too, he wanted to tell her.

Godo approached. "Who says I'm fucking around?"

"You're being a dick."

"Because I want a hug from my *hermanito*?"

Before Roque could answer Godo swallowed him up in his arms, a warm musty funk rising from his body as he rocked a little back and forth. In a whisper, so no one else could hear: "I know you're fucked up about losing Tío. Don't carry it with you. Let that shit go."

For a moment, Roque couldn't believe what he'd heard. Who was this person, what had he done with Godo? He swallowed a surge of weepiness and managed to say, "I'm sorry."

"I know." Godo pressed his head against Roque's. "Whole lotta sorry to go around. Not just you. It was all of us. We all lost Tío. Don't carry that alone." He gave two fierce slaps to Roque's back and let him go. Loudly, for the others: "There. That so fucking unbearable?"

Dazedly, Roque embraced Happy as well, for the sake of symmetry if nothing else. Introductions went around. Samir, as always impatient, asked if they were crossing that night.

"I need to talk to you about something," Happy said. The way it came out, everyone sank. "The people we arranged things through to begin with—I know, we don't owe them nothing at this point but hear me out—they know something about you. An American showed up, talked to the *patrón* who runs things along this stretch of the border. You're supposed to get handed over to him, this American. He represents some company out of Dallas."

Samir's deep-set eyes drew back even further. He clutched his bag. "No."

"There's all variety of shit going on here behind the scenes, Samir, I can't control none of that. But Godo and me, we can't go home no more. You don't go with these people, this honcho from Dallas, we're up for grabs."

Samir looked like a touch might knock him down. "I saved your life."

Happy looked away. "I've been wanting to ask you about that, actually."

"Ask me—"

"Roque tells me you're damn handy with a gun. Funny how I never saw that side of you. Not even when we were in the middle of a firefight."

"You don't understand."

"I figured you'd say that."

Lupe, sensing a wrong turn somewhere, looked to Roque for reassurance but he had none to give. Godo blocked the door.

"This American, this man from Dallas." Samir pointed, as though the city were only a short walk away. "He is CIA. You give me to him"—a finger snap—"I disappear."

"I don't know that."

"They will hood me, torture me. I'll end up in some secret prison. Worse, get handed over to someone else, the Egyptians, the Thais. Let them do the dirty work."

"Why would they do that?"

"Because they *can*."

Happy reached into his back pocket, withdrew a mangled pack of Marlboros, shook one free, lipped it. "Maybe all they want to do is talk." The cigarette bobbing. "That be so terrible?"

"And tell them what?"

"Whatever." Using a Zippo, Happy lit up, shrugged. "Everything."

"And if I have nothing to tell them, nothing they want to hear, what do you think happens? Think they believe me?"

"Could be they want you to infiltrate a mosque, maybe a sleeper cell, maybe just a bunch of deadbeats hanging around some café, talking tough about jihad. You want asylum? Looks like you'll have to earn it."

Samir turned one way, another, looking for a way out. "You don't understand."

Happy exhaled a long plume of smoke. "You keep saying that."

A nervous laugh, disbelief. "What else can I say?"

"No one understands. Not as far as you're concerned."

"Why are you angry with me?"

"I'm not—"

"What have I done? Why betray me like this?"

Happy took another long drag. "Who are you, really? Let's start there."

Again, the hand across the heart. "I have never once lied—"

"I have no idea who you are."

Roque glanced toward the door, wondering what if anything Godo felt about all this, but except for a vague impatience there was nothing in his expression to read. Sure the Arab was a pain in the ass but this was over the top. "Happy, what are you getting at?"

"Butt out, Roque."

"No. You don't tell me that, not after everything—"

"This don't concern—"

"This isn't *necessary*, okay? I told you, this guy in Naco—"

"For fuck's sake, you stupid? He's a cop! I don't care whose uncle he is. You gotta trust me on this, you go to this guy to get you across, you'll never be heard from again. Okay? Especially with our friend here in tow." He gestured toward Samir, then Lupe. "Same with her."

"Happy—"

"The *patrón* wants a songbird, Roque. They all do down here. One of the perks of being *el mero mero*. He'll make her a star. Life could be fucking worse."

"Now you're the one who sounds stupid."

"Not like they're gonna pimp her out, okay? Everybody's being so fucking dramatic."

Again, Lupe looked to Roque for some reassurance. There was none to find. She turned to Happy, incensed, scared.—*Tell me what is happening. Not him. Me.*

Before Happy could answer, a caravan of four SUVs turned off the road into the development, headlights raking the forward houses as the engines throttled down for the switch from pavement to gravel.

Roque turned back to Happy, took a step toward him. "What have you done?"

Happy didn't move. A twinge of his eye, a blink. "I have no clue who that is."

Samir lunged toward one of the windows, hiking his leg over the sill, ducking down. He was halfway out when Godo sailed across the room, caught him, grabbing him by the shirttail first, then a crippling punch to the small of the back, like some instinct from the war had taken hold. Lupe, seeing the door unguarded, bolted, she was gone before Roque could stop her. He grabbed his knapsack, followed, glancing back from the doorway as Godo headlocked Samir, twisting him to the floor. Happy just stood there, tip of his cigarette a curl of ash as he stared in the general direction of the oncoming vehicles, looking as though to move would be an admission of something he still felt a need to keep private.

THE DARKNESS ACROSS THE DESERT FLOOR FELT IMPENETRABLE, WORSE than inside the house, but once his eyes adjusted Roque caught Lupe's silhouette vanishing past a snarl of cacti. He hurried after her just as the SUVs braked and men poured out. Over his shoulder, he recognized the *huelepega* from earlier, passing through the headlight glare, looking not quite so feeble now. They'd known, he thought. They had a lookout.

He caught up with Lupe, snagged her arm. She fought back, throwing an elbow, a wild kick.—*Let go!*

—*Quiet! Get down.*

He dragged her behind a thicket of underbrush circling the base of a massive saguaro, its barbed arms snaking up and out in all directions. They both panted from exertion, trying to stifle the sound. The dogs from earlier had reappeared around the house and now skittered away as perhaps a dozen men surrounded it, all of them armed. Headlights lit up the house from two sides. From somewhere in the foothills a coyote howled, then one of the men called out, addressing Happy by his given name.

—*PABLO, STOP BEING SUCH A HOPELESS ASSHOLE. COME ON OUT.*

Happy, recognizing the voice, figured the Spanish was a play to the others, the men setting up the kill zone. Doesn't matter what I say or don't say, he thought, it's all an act. This is what I get for mocking a snake.

Godo gestured everyone down, out of the light streaming in through the windows, then belly-crawled to his duffel, shook it open and began pulling out the weapons, the shotgun, the Kalashnikov, the pistols. He flexed his gauze-wrapped hand, then slammed a magazine into the AK, the others already loaded. To Happy, he said, "I'm assuming you know who's out there."

A burst of machine-gun fire ripped along the outer walls of the house, a few rounds pitching in through the window, tearing pieces of cinder block away like shrapnel and leaving clouds of chalky dust behind.

Happy said, "The ones I told you about."

—Come on, Pablo. What, you think I wouldn't figure this shit out, all that crap about wanting to do me a favor? You got the Arab and the girl in there. I understand, I do. Nothing terrible is going to happen to them. Nothing terrible will happen to you. Play it smart.

"Where's Roque?" Godo asked.

"The girl ran out. He went after her."

"They think she's in here." Using his teeth, Godo began tearing the gauze away from his hand, peeling it off in shreds. Shortly, he broke into a smile. "They got away, her and Roque."

The lucky one, Happy thought. The magical one.

"I won't go with those men," Samir said. He lay across the room, staring at the glassless, light-filled window. "A man cannot choose when he will die, only how."

Godo flexed his naked hand, still black and red from its burns. "That's deep." He wiped a smear of ointment onto his pant leg. "Kinda premature, though."

"Don't hand me over to them. Kill me. Say it was self-defense."

"They're going to kill us," Happy said, talking to neither of them in particular. "He thinks I went behind his back. That can't be forgiven. There's nothing to say. I can't make it right, not with them. And I've seen how they kill people."

Godo picked up the shotgun, chuckling miserably as he racked a load of nine-shot into the chamber. "*Vamos rumbo a la chingada*." We're on our way to join the fucked. He turned to Samir and hefted the Kalashnikov. "I hear you know how to use one of these."

The Arab began to crawl across the room, inching on hands

and knees, butt high, head low, made it halfway across when another spray of machine-gun fire, this one longer, rocked the small house. He dove down, covering his head as bullets rang against the tin roof and tore away more of the wall. Once the firing stopped he scurried the rest of the way, joining Godo near the door as the dust swirled and drifted overhead.

—I'm not fucking around no more, Pablo. Hands on your head, you and everybody else, one by one through the door, or we gonna smoke you out.

"That sounds like an MP5." Godo edged closer toward the door, hoping for a peek. "They'll have trouble with muzzle lift. Bitchin' little gun, though."

"They're off-duty cops, soldiers," Happy said. "Maybe even special forces."

"The Bean Berets," Godo said.

Samir cradled the AK-47 with a kind of weary admiration. "I wish I had a bayonet."

Godo chuckled again, a little less miserably. "Good attitude."

"Give me the Glock," Happy said. "It's the one I know best."

Godo slid the pistol across the plywood floor. "Don't plug yourself in the leg."

Happy leaned forward for it, dropped the magazine, made sure it was fully loaded, then slammed it home again. The chamber already held a round. Don't plug yourself, he thought, Glock leg, they called it, the safety in the trigger, so touchy even cops shot themselves.

Godo slid the Smith and Wesson .357 after, nodding for Happy to take it, then stuck the Beretta 9mm into his own waistband. Searching the duffel for an extra mag for the AK, he found it, banged it against the floor, then tossed it to Samir. "You'll have more firepower than the two of us combined. Otherwise I'd offer you a pistol too."

"It's okay," Samir said, jamming the magazine into his trousers at the small of his back. "Pistols are for officers."

Godo smiled. "You left-handed or right?"

Samir lifted his right hand, jiggled it.

"Okay, I'll go first. I'll circle left, draw fire. You circle right, aim for the muzzle flashes. Happy? From the sound of things, I'd guess the guy who's talking out there, El Recio, he's almost a straight shot from the door, maybe twenty yards. You focus on him. Take him out, maybe the others will call it a day. If all goes well, we'll meet back at the pickup."

"Godo—"

"There is no plan B."

A canister tumbled in through the door, spinning once or twice as it spit a billowing plume of blue smoke. Godo rose into a crouch, bounced twice. "Everybody good?" He lifted the shotgun to his shoulder. "Honor, gentlemen. Think like a killer. Act like you're already dead."

HE WAS HIT TWICE BEFORE HE WAS THROUGH THE DOOR BUT HE'D expected that. You measure a warrior by the damage he inflicts, yes, but also by what he withstands. Gunny Benedict taught him that, just as he taught him that pain is illusion, it's only there to fool you, hold you back. One round caught him in the ribs, the other the thigh. Adrenalin kept him upright, moving to contact. He spotted for muzzle flash, fired, pumped, fired, trying to stay out of the headlights' center but always moving, arcing left. He saw a man spin down, another cover his face and drop his weapon, silhouettes cowering by their SUVs. The battle distortion he'd known before returned, the disconnect between sight and sound, feeling like a promise, harkening back to Al Gharraf, Diwaniyah, Fallujah, and in the sudden stillness he heard the plucking of guitar strings, "Canción de Cuna," Roque's Cuban lullaby. It gave him heart, even as machine-gun fire raked his knees and he twisted down into powdery dirt and razor-sharp rocks, struggled to rise, caught another round in the neck and one more in his skull. Blinding, the last. He rolled onto his side, racked, fired, racked again, aiming into the silence until there were no more rounds in the magazine and he dragged the Beretta from his waistband, tried again to sight a target, taking fire like a pincushion and unable to feel the trigger against his finger or the hand at the end of his arm, unable to hold up his head while his throat filled with blood and the headlight glow swelled like an incoming wave. Once the wave crested he saw it, suspecting it had been there all along, suspended in the young girl's hand. The bright red blossom of the fire tree.

SAMIR DOVE OUT THE DOORWAY FIRING ON FULL AUTO, THE HEAVY AK rounds splintering glass, carving up metal. Targeting on muzzle flash in the drifting smoke, he spotted one gunman, fired, took him down, sighted on another, fired, resisting the upward pull of the barrel. Another kill. He caught them by surprise, all eyes focused on Godo. We'll meet back at the pickup, he thought, daring to picture the off-campus cottage, brickwork and vines, the woman kneeling in her garden, the girl practicing clarinet inside, the library shelves lined with *Don Quixote*, *Ulysses*, *Life on the Mississippi*, *Yo el Supremo*, then a spray of bullets, like a sudden cloud of wasps, encircling, tightening, closing. He felt the slash of pain across his back even as he fired and took down one more gunman but the weakness came right after, legs jibbing, no strength. He fought to right himself and just that pause left him open. Another blistering stripe, this one up his chest and into his face, he spun backward. What he feared became what he knew—Fatima, Shatha, forgive me my lies, my weakness, my failure—even as he drew himself up, hefted the rifle above his head like an ax and charged the faceless invader before him.

Inshallah . . .

—

HAPPY GAGGED AS THE BLUE SMOKE THICKENED, REMINDING HIMSELF that all he'd wanted was to be a better son. Rising to his feet, he firmed his grip on the Glock in his right hand, then with his left drew the Smithy from under his belt. He felt a sudden terror that no one would remember him—mother, father, both dead—he would not be missed by any living thing. Roque, maybe. Run, he thought, run fucker, you and your woman, make it across and remember me.

He dove out the door and headed as best he could tell straight for El Recio, guessing the spot where his voice had come from. Sure enough, there he stood, taking cover behind the door of one of the SUVs, watching Godo convulsing on the ground. Samir was off to the right somewhere. Was Osvaldo there? Kiki? Hilario? Were there ghosts to account for? Happy charged, firing two-handed, making half the distance before the gaunt bald asthmatic even knew he was there. I've never loved anything, he realized, as much as this fuckface loves his damn snake. The rest of the distance collapsed and he was pounding with the pistol butts, bashing the face, erasing that smile, crushing the throat, fighting off the hands of the other men trying to drag him off and remembering the song the bastard had sung that night, in the cop's kitchen, as they forced the parents to watch their little boy get burned alive:

Hoy es mi día
Voy a alegrar toda el alma mía

Today is my day
I'm going to fill my soul with joy

FORTY-FOUR

THEY FLAGGED DOWN A BUS ABOUT A MILE NORTH OF THE HOUSE. Lupe, sensing the opportunity in the gunfight, had slipped off during the worst of it, when Godo went down. Roque didn't follow, not then, he couldn't. Instead, jumping up idiotically, he'd called out or screamed, made some sort of sound, no memory now exactly of what; his throat still felt scorched. He might as well have stayed quiet for all the good it had done; no one heard him over the gunfire. At some point he turned, scrambled after Lupe, remembering none of that, either. But on the bus his memory revived, seeking its vengeance. Images clapped and hammered inside his brain, flashes of the bloodshed, his brother, his cousin, the maddening Arab, then wave after wave of shame and guilt, panic attacks, stabbing blame: You ran. You survived.

They stepped off the bus at the turnoff to Naco, then thumbed a ride from a fat-bellied trucker in a Stetson who turned out to be an *evangélico*, witnessing them gustily during the drive then dropping them off at his storefront church. They stayed long enough to justify a fistful of cookies chased with scalding coffee, then muddled their way to the bus terminal, knowing they'd find phones there. Reading the number off the torn corner of a paper bag, Roque dialed Pingo's uncle, the cop from Naco.

His name was Melchior. At the invocation of his nephew's name he agreed to meet at a taqueria near a small park three blocks from the port of entry but he couldn't get free until late the next day.—*I'm sorry*, he said, *I have work, my family. But tomorrow, yes, we'll get together*.

The storefront church had closed up by the time they returned so they found a place to hide for the night in the alley around back, Lupe's head in Roque's lap. Neither slept.

Come dawn they bought coffee and *pan dulce* at a nearby *panadería* and breakfasted standing beneath the awning of a pawnshop catering to those needing cash to cross over. The store didn't open until eight but already people were coming up alone or in groups, peering in through the ironwork.

Once the church opened its doors they sat near the back in folding chairs, suffering the heated exhortations of the preacher from his lectern or indulging the quieter testimonials of the churchwomen, offering sweets, bestowing unsolicited advice, reading at length out loud from their Bibles. Finally, come four o'clock, they made their way to the taqueria and waited.

He showed up with a gun on his hip and a badge on his belt, no uniform. Driving a rust-tagged Cutlass twenty years old, he took them east out of town toward the Mule Mountains, the peaks stitching north across the border, then pulled off the highway onto a rough dirt lane that trailed away among jagged rocks crowned with creosote bushes and paloverde, parking on a bluff in the middle of nowhere.

He glanced left and right, ahead and behind.—*I don't know what Pingo promised. But everything has changed up here. You don't have coyotes working the border solo like before, they're either dead or they've signed on as* guías *with the cartels, who use the gangs as enforcers. A man I know, a cop like me, he and his family were tortured and killed the other night—what he did or didn't do exactly I don't know, but everyone in the corridor heard the news. There was a boy, seven years old, the stories of what they did to him . . . I have a family. I will not let that happen to them*.

—*I'd never ask such a thing*, Roque said. He glanced sidelong at Lupe sitting alone in the backseat. He doubted he had ever felt so tired.

—Life means nothing to these fucks. If you're lucky you just get used as decoys. The others, they take your money, make you a promise, then disappear, or take you into the desert and leave you there. Even the decent ones shake you down for more once they get you across.

—But isn't there some way, without dealing with this El Recio, that we could make the crossing?

—I know this El Recio—know of him, I should say. If you owe him? Pay.

—We did pay. Now he's claiming we didn't. He won't let Lupe cross regardless.

Melchior shook his head.*—I don't envy you. But I don't know how to help you, either.*

—What if we cross somewhere else? Farther west. Nogales. Maybe California.

—It's harder there than here. And ask yourself, can you outrun word from El Recio's spies if you get spotted? If there's a price on your head, you can bet there are people looking for you. Bus drivers, street vendors, cabbies, bartenders, you don't know who's taking the money, playing along. More than you can imagine, believe me.

With her chin, Lupe gestured to the mountains straight ahead.*—There has to be a way across through there.*

—Sure, there's a way. And you can take your chances. But once you reach the border they have hidden infrared cameras, thermal sensors that pick up your body heat, seismic sensors that hear your footsteps. They've got border guards with night-vision goggles stationed every half mile in places, not to mention the fucking fence. At the end of this road right here, about a mile or so up the canyon, there's a pass that runs along the western slope of those hills, straight ahead, not too steep, not too difficult, but cold as fuck at night and that's when you have to cross. That's also when the snakes come out, rattlers and

sidewinders, the tarantulas, the scorpions. The pass disappears into those trees, then winds down on the far side beyond the border. The fence doesn't reach that far up the mountain, that's how you get through. But remember, most people who cross reach a designated snatch spot, get scooped up and taken to a safe house. You don't have somebody waiting. You'll be stranded over there with miles and miles to walk and the border patrol will be onto you before you even get to a major road—if you're lucky. If you're not lucky, you walk until you die. Your only chance is to reach someone's house, break in and hide, maybe steal a car, head for Tucson or Phoenix. Or you can try to find a church, beg for someone's help. But your chances are slim. The gringos *have lost all pity. Ask for so much as a drink of water they'll turn you in. Or shoot you.*

Lupe leaned forward in the backseat, gripped Melchior's shoulder.—*It can't be as impossible as you say. Thousands get across every year, every month.*

—*Because the cartels have millions for bribes, they corrupt the border guards. Those guards leak word about when and where a spot will be clear. Yes, thousands get across. But thousands get caught, too. The cartels determine who gets lucky, who gets screwed. And the screwed will be back, paying over and over.*

Lupe moved her hand from Melchior's shoulder to Roque's. —*Come on. We'll walk. He says there's a pass at the end of this road. It's still light enough, we can find it. What good will sitting here do us? The longer we—*

Glancing up into the rearview mirror, she saw Melchior's eyes flare with dread. Spinning around, she saw the headlights in the twilight, the churning plume of dust.

Melchior turned to Roque and raised his hands.—*Take my gun, hold it on me.* When Roque just sat there baffled, Melchior shouted:—*Take my fucking gun and hold it on me!*

Roque did as he was told, glancing through the rear window at the approaching vehicle—a black Chevy Suburban with tinted glass, lurching as it hit the rocks and ditches along the unpaved road. Melchior reached around behind him, opened his door, stepped out of the car with his hands held high so everyone in the approaching Suburban could see.—*There is a flashlight in the glove compartment. You'll need it—but be careful not to use it too much, they'll spot you from twenty miles away coming down the mountain. Now get behind the wheel, drive like hell to the end of this road, then run for the trees up the hill.* He stumbled backward in the dusty gravel.—*If you ever see Pingo again? Tell him to forget my name.*

The crack of a pistol shot, then the bullet whistling overhead: Melchior dove for the ground, Roque lurched across the center console, got behind the wheel, turned the ignition, lodged the gearshift into drive and shoved the gas pedal to the floor just as a second shot pierced the back window. Lupe screamed. Roque ventured a quick over-the-shoulder glance and spotted blood as the car fishtailed up the soft rutted road.

—*Are you all right?* He palmed the wheel, righting the car.

She didn't answer, crouched down on the seat. The back window was webbed with fissures spiraling out from the bullet hole. The Cutlass lurched into a rut, dug out again, chewing up rocks, veiled in clouds of dust as it continued up the impossible road. Roque glanced back again, saw her right hand grabbing her left shoulder, threads of blood between her fingers.—*It's all right*, she hissed.—*Hurry, go!*

He considered some sort of evasive back and forth but, given the ruinous condition of the road, the vagueness of the path, he feared he might just as easily wander into a bullet's path as out of one. Speed, he thought, get away from them, create distance so you have time to run.

He gunned the engine, steering around the worst craters and biggest rocks but otherwise barreling straight ahead, checking his mirror from time to time, trying to see if, through the shifting clouds of dust, he was managing any real separation. The sound of more gunshots but only one bullet landed, hitting the trunk with a pinging *thoont*. He soared over a sudden crest, a brief gut-fluttering weightlessness, then the chassis crashed down again, first the rear, then the front, tires biting into the rocky sand as he regained control, accelerated out of another fishtail and charged forward.

In the backseat Lupe was breathing fast and shallow but made no other sound, lying flat to keep from getting shot twice. Roque thought of his uncle, wondered what advice he'd give, thought about Godo too, Happy and Samir, vowing to himself he wouldn't punk out now, wouldn't shame them, then saw ahead the pine and oak trees marking the first ascent of the foothills. A low outcropping of marbled rock loomed a mere hundred yards ahead, he reached for the glove compartment, slapped it open, rummaged around for the flashlight, all the while gripping the wheel with his left hand, steering straight ahead at full speed. Over his shoulder, he shouted at Lupe: "*¡Listo!*"

As he approached the road's end he fishtailed the car around so that it faced the way they'd just come. He shouted for Lupe to get out, waited for her to shove open the rear door and flee the car, then got out himself, found a rock the size of a melon, lodged it onto the gas pedal, threw the gearshift into drive. Following Lupe, he scrambled up the rocks toward the tree line. The Cutlass lumbered off, picking up speed as it lurched downhill, forcing the approaching Blazer to stop, turn, dodge the huge bouncing downhill missile until it slammed into a sprawling jut of scrub-nested saguaros with a dusty clanking thud.

Lupe faltered as Roque came up behind and he caught her sleeve, dragged her upright as still another shot rang out, the bullet whistling past them into the trees—a snapped branch, a shower of dry pine needles. He pulled her roughly after him, the rocks beneath their feet razor-edged in places, in others soft and flinty, powdered with dust, littered with pellet-shaped acorns. As they reached the edge of the forest he caught the welcoming tang of resin.

Below, the Blazer careened to a lurching stop, followed by three more gunshots, strangely wild, then a sudden silent impulse told him: Stop! He drew up in his tracks, used his body as a shield to keep Lupe behind him, just as he felt the rippling concussion of air, like an invisible current pulsing in front of him. The bullet missed by inches.

A clipped throaty voice called out:—*Roque Montalvo! We've got your cousin.*

He hurried beneath the tree canopy and pushed Lupe behind him before turning back, thinking: Spanish, clever, work on both our consciences, play one against the other. A tall spidery man with a shaved head leaned against the SUV, clutching his midsection, his movements stitched with pain. A smaller man dressed in black with long flowing hair climbed out from behind the wheel, flourishing a pistol. A third man in a suit and cowboy boots dragged from the backseat a fourth and final man, this one with his hands tied behind his back: Happy. He staggered blindly, weak from a beating, his shirt dark with blood. The man in the suit pressed a pistol to his head and drove him to his knees, the spindly bald one calling out:—*Come back down, you and the girl. Otherwise . . .*

Roque still held Melchior's pistol. From this distance, though, he doubted he'd hit anyone, no matter how carefully he aimed. He might be able to slow them down if they chose to climb up after them but that was the best he could hope for. The air felt cool in the tree shade. Another hour or so, the sun would set.

Happy threw back his head, a soulless voice, "Fuck them, *chamaco*. Run!"

Using his pistol, the one in the suit cracked down hard, the back of the skull. Happy crumpled, toppling onto his side in the dust.

—*Is this what you want?* The tall one bent over, coughed, waved a limp hand toward Happy.—*Come on. Think. You won't make it, you know that, right? I know just where that trail comes out.*

All I gotta do, make one call, they'll be there on the other side, waiting. Stop dicking around, give your cousin a chance here.

From behind, Lupe, her voice tight with pain:—*I can't ask you to do this.*

He could smell the stale coppery odor on her breath.—*Then don't ask.*

She tried to brush past.—*I owe it to his father.*

Roque stopped her with his arm, holding her back—he could feel her draining strength.—*They're going to kill you, if you're lucky. Kill us all. Who's that repay?*

Her eyes met his and yet he couldn't feel himself within their gaze.—*I've brought nothing but sorrow to your family.*

—*What's happened, we brought on ourselves. Happy knows that better than anybody.*

—*It's asking too much.*

—*You're not asking anything. Now trust me.*

He braced himself against one of the trees, lifted Melchior's gun and steadied it, closing one eye, squinting to aim with the other. For the merest instant he revisited the day that Tío Faustino moved in, bringing his fourteen-year-old son along with him. He wasn't known as Happy yet, that would come later, but even then he was cool and watchful and defiantly sullen. Godo hated him at first glance but that was Godo. Roque wondered if he'd bother to laugh if somebody told a joke. Tía Lucha made *pozole* for dinner, a hominy stew with chunks of pork, and no one spoke during the meal, spoons traveling from bowl to mouth uninterrupted except for Tío Faustino's increasingly hopeless stabs at chat. At one point, Roque's eyes rose from the table and he caught the taciturn newcomer, the boy named Pablo, staring. The eyes were black and deep and hard. Roque couldn't help himself, maybe it was fear, maybe it was daring, maybe the simple human need to connect, but he smiled. And for a fleeting second he saw a softening in that unavailing gaze, the slightest lifting of the mask.

If I can just hit one of them, he thought, Happy will know I didn't simply abandon him. The one in the suit presented the best target. If he missed, he might hit Happy, but he doubted whatever agony he caused would add much to what was sure to follow. He drew a bead, fixing the middle of the man's chest in the V-shaped notch of the sight. He took in a breath, held it, pulling gently, slowly, three times in succession. As always, he was amazed at how loud it was. Even more astonishing, the one in the suit flinched and staggered and clutched at his neck, tripping over his own feet and toppling clumsily to the rocky ground as though suddenly butted by an invisible goat. The other two scattered, searching for cover.

I won't stay and pretend I can do better than that, he thought. I won't stick around and watch as they kill him. He turned toward Lupe. She was clutching her shoulder and the bloodstain on her shirt had grown beyond the spread of her hand. If we can get halfway by nightfall, he thought, we might have a chance. He no longer bothered with hope. Everything now reduced to will and luck. He took her free hand, pulled her behind him as he resumed their climb through the trees.—*My cousin understands.*

FORTY-FIVE

THE CHOPPER SET DOWN A HUNDRED YARDS FROM THE CIRCUS OF strobe lights swirling across the desert plain, the law-enforcement vehicles encircling a small enclave of unfinished houses, the capital of nowhere. Lattimore and the others aboard crouched and ran through the rotor wash and churning dust toward the nearest of the houses while the Mexican PC-6 that had escorted them since crossing the border tailed away, puttering off in a northerly loop.

It was just past sunset, not quite dark, the western sky a crimson fantasy of low swirled cloud getting swallowed up by night. He'd flown from San Francisco on a moment's notice aboard an agency Gulfstream, a rare extravagance, arriving in Tucson a mere hour ago, met at the airstrip by an FBI liaison named Potter who'd steered him immediately to the helipad. They were joined there by a crew of ICE agents, like Lattimore wearing raid jackets with their agency affiliation emblazoned across the back, plus a few brush-cut military sorts Lattimore learned were DIA, two tight-lipped civilians who were clearly spooks, bringing Andy McIlvaine to mind—he'd dropped off the planet since their impromptu lunch—all of them sent here to lend some form of credibility to what he could only assume would be a dog and pony show of inimitable Mexican overkill.

They were met by a uniformed police officer who snapped to with a crisp salute, then led them through the idling crowds of chattering cops to the one roofed house in the tiny development, inside which a battery of tungsten lights transformed the shoddy interior into a brilliant if sordid photo shoot. Near the far wall, the bullet-riddled body of an Arabic-looking male lay sprawled in conspicuously little blood amid the scattered cinder blocks, the sawdust, the litter of nails. Beside him, in even worse shape if such a thing was possible, lay Happy Orantes's cousin, the ex-marine with the torn-up face, Godo. The whisking hum and whirr of cameras battled with the rumble of generators and a wafting stentorian narrative provided by a *jefe de grupo* of the MFJP, the federal judicial police. The *jefe*, bedecked in stiffly creased khakis, hands clasped in the small of his back, appeared to be in control of the proceedings.

With the arrival of the Americans he took a break from his interview and swept forward, hand extended, face crafted into a catlike smile. The cameras followed him as though drawn by gravity. His name tape read "Orozco."

"Welcome, gentlemen." His English was soft, Southwestern. "I was just telling the members of the press about our operation, our good fortune in discovering a suspected terrorist before he was able to cross into your country."

Lattimore only half listened to the rest—the anonymous tip that led them to this house, the fierce standoff and eventual commando assault, the regrettable but unavoidable death of the terrorist and a gang member who'd fought to protect him. Out of some nagging perversity he wanted to point out how obvious it was the bodies had been dragged in from somewhere else but doubted anyone would care much. The skin of the story would never get peeled back, no one wanted to see what festered underneath. It was one of those tales, the kind all sorts of people want too much to hear—why bother much over details? And though Lattimore finally had in his possession the paperwork from the Baghdad office that could lay waste to the vast edifice of bullshit the *jefe* was erecting, he lacked authority to share. The bureau wanted no part of making its efforts in this farce a matter of public record. Let the Mexicans claim victory. Let them raise the specter of terrorists at our door, without us or them having to prove much. The feigned threat served the purpose of truth—or what the geniuses in D.C. wanted known as truth. Besides, Lattimore knew he'd bargained on much the same indifference to what was real, what was pumped-up nonsense. There were no innocents in the room.

Regardless, it would matter only to him that a woman named Fatima Hassan with a teenage daughter named Shatha, both using forged papers and assumed names, had finally been located and interviewed at the refugee camp at Al Tanf. The pseudonyms accounted for the delay in proper identification. Fatima confirmed she was the widow of Salah Hassan, who had disappeared in the custody of the Mukhabarat when her daughter was a child. Her husband was charged with money laundering and never emerged from prison. She further confirmed, after evidence was provided, that she worked at a Baghdad brothel after her husband's arrest, did so for some years, and that her forged identity papers had been provided by the criminal syndicate that ran the brothel and provided protection for her and the other women working there.

Asked if she knew of a Samir Khalid Sadiq, she conceded that she did; like her, he was part of the Palestinian community in Iraq. Pressed on the matter, she admitted as well that he had been a client, a particularly loyal one—obsessive, perhaps, was a better word, but his generosity not just to her but to her daughter had convinced her to look past his infatuation. She said she knew he had been a soldier during the war with Iran, was fluent in both English and Spanish, and worked for a local TV station translating news wire items or so he had always told her. After the U.S. invasion, he made a promise to help her emigrate to America. With the war's dislocations, however, she lost touch with him.

When asked if she was aware that this same Samir Khalid

Sadiq had been the informant who had identified her husband to the Mukhabarat, she fell silent for several minutes. When she finally spoke, she said simply, "I forgave him long ago, just as he forgave me." She declined to say more.

"We have reliable information," Orozco announced, turning toward the cameras with that same feline smile, "that the Arab was in contact with local *pandilleros*." Gang members. "This was how he expected to get across, with their assistance. And as I have said, one of them died here with him. We are following up on this and hope to have more arrests in due time."

A predictable move, Lattimore thought, keep the thing open-ended, so you could draw it out until memories faded, the next god-awful whatever stole the headlines. If necessary, nail a few tattooed bozos, drag them past the cameras and call it a day.

He wondered what had become of Happy, what had become of his cousin, wondered if he would ever know or if, in the final analysis, it mattered. He turned away from Orozco and the wall of lights, murmured a path through the other Americans and headed for the door, hoping the oppressive closeness of the scene wouldn't follow him outside as he tried to think of how he might get Godo's body shipped back to his aunt.

COME NIGHTFALL THEY WERE STILL CLIMBING. LUPE'S BREATHING HAD become more labored, her skin felt cool to the touch. Even with his arm around her she stumbled and staggered and nearly fell when the path veered sharply or a tree root rose up through the dusty bed of bullet-shaped acorns and dry pine needles. He tried not to use the flashlight too often. Once, though, as they'd come upon what he'd thought was a dung pile, a sudden stab of light had caused the thing to stir, then slither off—a sidewinder, coiled to strike. He'd once heard that a pregnant woman causes snakes to sleep as you pass and he wondered if he should take this as a sign. Another time, hearing the low snarling growl of a mountain lion, he'd fired the pistol into the tree canopy, scattering birds and scaring the animal off into the underbrush.

They couldn't stay lucky all night, he thought, nor risk so much noise. His skin tingled with imagined bugs, against which he just kept walking, arm locked tight around Lupe's waist, their hips pressed flush, moving along the narrow twisting hillside trail like a single clumsy four-legged beast. Every ten steps or so, he switched on the flashlight, got his bearings along the path, turned it off.

The path had led them across one rise after the other, sometimes a leisurely upward grade, other times as steep as a ladder, descending only briefly before resuming uphill, to the point he would have given anything to feel the ground dropping off into a reliable, continuous downgrade. His leg muscles burned, the small of his back was a tight ball of pain. He could only imagine what misery Lupe was enduring in silence.

They'd brought no water. They'd had no time, they hadn't known Melchior would drive them out to the foothills and leave them to run or die. Roque wondered if the man was still alive, if his act, the feigned robbery, had fooled the others. He had no such doubts about Happy. He'd heard the gunshots as he and Lupe climbed beneath the tree canopy deeper into the hills. There's no one left but me and Tía Lucha, he thought. Me and Tía and now this one, Lupe.

They came to another rock face, rising like a wall from the truncated path. Flipping on the flashlight briefly, he saw exposed roots and small rock ledges that might provide a fingerhold here, a foothold there. He would have to feel for them in the dark. The bluff extended indefinitely in each direction, there would be no getting around it that he could see. It rose only twenty feet or so, hardly an impossible climb.

Switching off the light he turned to Lupe.—*What do you think?*

His eyes readjusted to the dark as he waited for her reply. He could just make out the lines of her face. Though quick, her breath had settled into a rhythm and her left arm hung limp, the shoulder of her shirt crusted with blood.—*I can try*. She licked her parched lips.

—*You can hold on to my belt, watch where I put my hands and feet.*

She flexed her left hand, testing its strength, wincing.—*Let's hurry.*

On again briefly with the flashlight—he mapped out his strategy in his mind's eye—then off. He reached for the highest root he could without jumping, dug into a crevice in the rock with his toe, waited for Lupe to grab his belt, then hoisted himself up. Catching his balance, he felt for the next exposed root, got his hand around it, found a second foothold and pulled himself up again, this time feeling Lupe's weight until she scrambled for her own hold below him.

—*You're okay?*

—*I'm fine, yes.* The words a hiss of air against her teeth. —*Quick. Please.*

He patted and pulled his way upward, until finally his hand reached the top of the bluff. He searched the ledge blindly, hoping for another root to grab hold of, only to encounter a scaly scuttling thing. Before he could pull back his hand the poisonous sting flared down into his arm like a streak of molten wire. He shouted in pain then said, "*¡Bajo! ¡Bajo!*"

They tumbled to the bottom, her first, him on top, tangling up as they tried to scramble to their feet. His hand burned, he shook it as he reached for the flashlight, flipped it on. The wounds were small but deep, two of them, vaguely parallel. A spider not a scorpion, he thought, probably a tarantula. It would be painful, not dangerous but he couldn't imagine trying the climb again—he doubted his grip would hold, especially with Lupe's added weight, and for all he knew there was a nest of them up there, not just one.

—*Let's wait here a moment while I think things through*. He cradled his bad hand, chewing his lip.—*Maybe there's another way*. But he knew there wasn't. They could try their luck, slash through the trees, see if somehow, somewhere, they stumbled upon another path down the mountainside. But if such a path existed why would this one be here—who forged dead ends up the sides of mountains?

He tried the flashlight again, looked left, looked right, saw only the dense forest and the mountain wall, the twenty-foot bluff that might as well be a mile high. His hand felt afire, his whole arm had turned weak but the pain was only half of it. He remembered his Day of the Dead benedictions with Tía Lucha, her steadfast conviction that her sister, his mother, lay just beyond a veil of incomprehension—someday they would all gather together again, laugh, sing, weep. When young, he had believed, not so much now. But maybe that wasn't the point. Could there possibly be anything waiting beyond death that would be so much worse than this?

He heard a rustling off to his left. Another mountain lion, he thought, or the same one, it had been tracking them all along. That's how it will happen, he thought, a predator smelling the blood. He moved the flashlight to his left hand, his good hand, then drawing Melchior's pistol from his belt with his swollen aching right. He didn't know how many bullets were left.

To hell with being seen, he thought, turning the flashlight on and pointing it at the noise, discovering not a mountain lion but a small raccoonlike face protruding from the broad-leafed greenery—immense and probing eyes, a whitish snout, a long curling tail like a monkey's. A coatimundi. He'd never seen one except on nature shows. They stared at each other for a moment, long enough for Roque to believe he heard someone say the single word: Here.

To Lupe:—*Did you just say something?*

She stirred from a daze.—*No*.

The animal withdrew into the underbrush and Roque puzzled at that, wondering why he'd not seen a way to escape in that direction before. Here, he thought, remembering the voice, unable to place it, following its direction, breaking through the scrub and pointing the beam of the flashlight down into a deep and narrow ravine, terraced with rock, dotted with scrub and spindly trees, opening at the bottom into a densely overgrown blackness.

Only then did he remember the dreams, especially the second, that night at Rafa's service station before they crossed from El Salvador into Guatemala—the image of his sickly mother beckoning him forward, the tarantula.

—*We're going this way*. He gestured with the flashlight for Lupe to follow. They would scoot down the rock ledge into the crevasse, come out somewhere lower on the mountainside, take their chances that way, forge a path of their own through the forest if need be.

—*I'll go first*. He got down on his haunches, tucked the pistol away, clutched the flashlight. The drop was long and steep and he could almost feel himself tumbling head over foot but he kept his weight back, plummeting like a sled. He crashed into tree roots and nettled plants, sharp outcroppings of rock, finally hitting bottom with a crunching thud.

He bounced up, fearing he might be bitten by something unseen, then pointed the flashlight up the cluttered rock face. The beam caught her peering fearfully over the ledge.

—*It's all right*, he called upward.—*Follow the light down*.

It took her a moment to get into position and when she rocketed down it seemed for a moment she too might begin to tumble head over heels but she stiffened into a blade, continuing down. At the bottom he broke her fall and the two of them hurtled recklessly into nearby scrub. Dazed, they untangled themselves, rose to their feet, swaying.

Roque pointed the flashlight toward the mouth of the ravine.—*This way*.

There was no path to follow, no way to tell the right direction, an excellent plan for getting lost, but he focused on one tree and then the one behind it, fashioning as straight a line as he could, taking heart from the downward slope of his footfalls and figuring once they were off the mountain he'd get his bearings. Maybe they'd still be in Mexico when that happened, if so they'd somehow turn themselves north and go. It was the best plan he had now. An idle touch of Lupe's shoulder revealed the wound was seeping again. Her breath came in coughing gasps more often, her steps fell heavy, she tripped and staggered to keep up, sometimes gripping his belt.

Time dissolved. The minutes dragged like hours and the hours collapsed into minutes. He heard only the rush of blood in his ears and the crunching monotony of his footsteps, hers behind him, the chafing rustle of her breath in her throat, interrupted now and again by the yipping barks of unseen coyotes. He couldn't pinpoint when it happened, but the oaks and pines gave way to mesquite and paloverde and tormented Joshua trees, the earth turned a coppery red in the flashlight beam, thickets of spindly ocotillos and tall agave spears rose up from the desert floor. For the first time in hours he realized how cold it was, his shivering a kind of irritated happiness, forcing him awake.

In the distance he saw a pinpoint of light—maybe from a house, maybe a church. It remained unchanging and he set his course by it, keeping it always in sight, increasing his pace.

They came to a barbed-wire fence—the border?—struggled through it, shirts snagging, and ten steps beyond she finally collapsed, falling first to her knees then her side. She winced from pain and curled up, teeth clenched, rocking, trying to will herself into numbness he thought as he stood over her, grabbing at her wrist, her arm, telling her to get up, please, try. He barely recognized his own voice. To the east, dawn smeared a cold white line along the hillcrests. A raven soared overhead, black against blue, tilting wing to wing in the tumbling wind. In the distance, a lone mule grazed in the scrub.

—You have to get up. We're almost there.

She said nothing, struggling to find some purchase, gathering strength, pulling herself to her knees. Hooking her good arm around his shoulder, he hoisted her the rest of the way up but her eyes rolled back, her knees buckled. He nearly fell, dragged to the ground after her, but he redoubled his hold and pulled her upward, leaning her body against his.*—Let's sing*, he said, *something we both know. The way you sang for the bikers, you were so beautiful, so brave. You're my hero, know that? You're so much stronger than me. Come on. We'll sing.*

In a tuneless whisper he flailed at the melody—"Sin Ti," what else?—butchering the lyrics. By the time he realized a dog was barking he'd been registering the sound in the back of his mind for a minute or longer—like the wind, the cold, and yet a haunting reminder too of his dreams—twilight, the stickiness of blood, the barren plain. Something precious he'd have to fight to keep. He redoubled his focus on the old sad song, on her dragging steps, her sliding weight. He could see it now in the dawn light, a sprawling ranch-style house. The dog was lurching at the end of a chain, frothing as it barked. He opened his shirt in order to get to the gun. The one last thing in his dream not yet revealed: a gun blast. But he didn't want to shoot the dog, wanted no harm to anyone or anything now. He wanted only to stop, rest, have someone look at Lupe's shoulder, clean and dress the wound. And after? That was impossible to picture.

"*¡Alto! Tengo una escopeta. Esta es propiedad privada.*"

Roque glanced up. For the first time he saw the tall lean silhouette marching forward. A man. His voice had mileage on it but his Spanish was wooden and nasal. He held a weapon—*una escopeta*. A shotgun. No, Roque thought, please, trying with all his might to pick up his pace. If the man can just see us up close he'll understand.

"I said stop! *Alto*, damn it. Won't say it again. Next thing I do is shoot."

Roque remembered the first time he saw her, sitting in the corner of Lonely's makeshift recording studio, her face bruised, her eyes fierce and untrusting. He remembered hearing her voice that day, the throaty heartbreak in it, the way it awakened something tragic and gentle and wise inside him. We've come too far, he thought. Not even God is that cruel.

The tall rangy man with the shotgun charged forward. He shouldered the weapon.

Summoning the words from a place inside him, a place he couldn't be sure existed even a few hours ago, Roque called out: "Don't shoot! Help us . . . please . . . I'm an American . . ."

He felt the full force of her weight against him as she lost consciousness. He buckled sideways with her fall, then the shotgun blast.

PART IV

BUNKERED IN HIS KITCHEN, STARING OUT THE SMALL CURTAINED window above the sink, the rancher watched the two figures milling about the drag line just beyond his property. One of the two was suited up in Border Patrol tan, the other wore a blue raid jacket over street clothes, the back emblazoned with large white letters he couldn't read from this distance. An SUV with that distinctive rack of lights on top stood off by the side.

They were inspecting the ground, looking for tracks. The skills of the local cutters were legend, the number of ants on a candy wrapper like a clock, telling how long since the litterbug blundered through. So the stories went, anyway. The rancher had no reason to doubt them. He dragged a calloused palm across his stubble. The tracks would lead straight this direction, blood trails too, the questions would start. Questions he wanted no part of.

He turned from the window, wondering at the things that trip you up, unraveling the promise of life right before your eyes, testing you. Audrey, he thought, there had always been Audrey or it felt like always and all he'd ever wanted was to make sure she was safe. You can't make another person happy, that's their affair to manage, but with luck, yes, their safety you might manage. But, God bless her, she had been happy. He felt humbled by that.

He wasn't one to put stock in fairness but there was a point beyond which the unfairness seemed nothing short of vicious.

He tried a mental tally, good versus bad, a lifetime's worth, but the exercise felt pointless—how does one weigh the good against death? As for testing his mettle, his spine, his spirit, it was years since any of that mattered. I'm an old man, he thought. He would have been grateful—insane, down-on-his-knees grateful—for yeah, sure, just a touch of dumb luck.

Following the murmur of voices down the hall, he stopped in the door to the guest room. The girl lay on the bed, fluttering in and out of bad sleep. Audrey sat beside her, holding her hand, talking to Doc Emerick. The boy sat in the corner, his right hand bandaged, looking at the girl like every breath was a signal. An empty jar of peanut butter sat between his feet, a spoon inside; he'd plowed through the stuff like a swarm of termites through damp pine.

The rancher had fired his first round into the air, to let them know he was serious, but the girl had already gone down. The boy dropped to his knees, first to see to the girl, then to plead at the top of his lungs for their lives. His English lacked accent, though he was clearly Hispanic. Audrey, hearing the boy, said, "Good God, Lyndell, help them."

"Get back inside, damn it. He's armed."

"Tell him to toss the gun off someplace."

He eased forward, shotgun trained on the boy. "Toss off that gun," mimicking her words, too scared to think up another way to say it.

The boy looked down at his midriff like he was angry the thing was there, then plucked the gun from under his belt and heaved it into the scrub. "She's been shot," he said, his voice hoarse and dry, a bobcat hiss. "Her shoulder."

He helped the boy bring her inside, figuring they'd call the Border Patrol and have them handle it, but Audrey would have none of that. She sensed something between the two of them—she was uncanny that way, more so since the sickness—and she refused to let him call the law before she had some idea if she was right. But they couldn't wait caring for the girl, so she'd called Doc Emerick and he'd come straightaway, thinking the emergency had to do with her, Audrey, not some stranger. He'd even brought the morphine drip he'd promised, the final morbid tool, thinking that was the reason for her call.

She'd pulled him aside when he first saw the girl. "I know what you're gonna say, John Emerick. I know you've got obligations under the law. But there are other laws. You've known me over thirty years. Don't make me die with this girl on my conscience. I can handle the cancer, I can handle the chemo and the endless string of bad news, handle all of it. I can't handle turning that girl back to whatever it was that drove her so hard, so far."

And so the doctor sutured the girl's wound, shot her full of antibiotics, hydrated her with fluids. While he did, the boy murmured the tale of all he and the girl had been through. And if Lyndell hadn't spent his life married to a woman like Audrey he might've said: Well, that's unfortunate and all but too bad, sorry, law's the law, straighten it out where you came from. Except the boy came from here and the girl's going back was a death sentence. He could no more load that onto Audrey's conscience than the doc could.

Audrey glanced up at him from her chair, still gripping the girl's hand. "Lyndell, this young man is gonna call his aunt. She lives up near Frisco and she's gonna come down in her car. Too risky, them taking the bus. And I doubt this girl could make that kind of trip anyhow. Show Roque, that's his name, show him where he can use the phone, would you?"

The boy glanced up with foxlike eyes. Lyndell nodded for him to get up and come along. He figured the phone in the kitchen would do. He led the boy back, pointed to the wall mount.

The boy said, "I want to make this up to you." Lyndell raised his hand, trying to cut the boy off, but, "We wouldn't have made it this far if people we met along the way hadn't been kind here and there. None more so than you."

Lyndell made a show of clearing his throat, thinking the boy had the presence of somebody twice his age. "Sounds of it, you met plenty of unkind too."

The boy seemed to drift away for a second. "Just more reason to be grateful. I want you to know, I don't take this for granted. I'll find some way to repay you."

Flustered, Lyndell went to the sink for a glass of water he lacked any thirst for. Looking out across the scrub, he saw the two men out by the Border Patrol SUV, Rooster barking at them, chain rattling as he darted back and forth. The two men were pointing along a line that led straight to the back porch. Lyndell felt his pulse jump. "You might want to hurry up with that call," he said.

LATTIMORE LISTENED TO THE SIGNCUTTER, WHOSE NAME WAS IRETON, extol his expertise. "We've seen this thing we call foamers? Guys tie squares of foam to their feet, thinking it won't leave tracks. Idiots—you have weight, you'll leave an imprint, and if it's not windblown or caved in, it's recent. Like these. Even in the desert, there's moisture, that's what holds the form. No sign of tracks crossing them, a centipede, a snake. That means they're recent. This set—I'd say it's a girl, or a woman, given the size of the shoe—the drag in the left foot and the heavy implant of the right, all that tells me she's hurt. And the steps so close together, the bigger one's holding up the hurt one. They've kicked up rocks, you can see where they used to be, the sand's paler. Sun bakes the hardpan so it's almost like a varnish."

He pointed along the drag, the track of brushed desert sand the Border Patrol created exactly for this purpose, to see where walkers had crossed, leaving their distinctive trails. These two—

and only two, he thought, one a girl, not knowing what to make of that yet—they hadn't bothered with a brushout, dragging a tree branch behind to wipe out their tracks. Like Ireton said, at least one of them, the girl, was barely standing. Even a city boy like Lattimore could see that.

"You say you got a tip about these two?"

"Indeed." Ireton flipped another stone over, checked the coloration of the earth beneath. "A call, plus they set off some sensors nearer the foothills. Wasn't the spot we were expecting, given the tip, which just goes to show you."

Lattimore waited for more, a little tutorial on the unreliability of informants. It didn't come. "The call, who was it from?"

Ireton looked up from the ground, a trained eye, trained on Lattimore. "Somebody on the other side. No name. Probably some *pandillero*, felt like he was screwed out of his money."

Lattimore pointed along the tortured line the tracks formed, aiming toward the lone house half a mile off. There were traces of blood along the way. "So I guess we ask the folks up there if anybody stumbled through."

Ireton shook his head. "You can bet they stopped. Like I said, the one that's hurt, she's hurt bad. If they made it all the way to the house, good for them. Any farther? I'd be amazed."

Lattimore nodded obligingly but the charade was wearing thin. Anonymous call my ass, he thought, rising from his crouch, dusting off his hands. "Let's go pay a visit," he said.

THE DOCTOR WASN'T GONE TEN MINUTES BEFORE THE TWO LAWMEN showed up on the front step. Lyndell closed the door to the guest room and told them all to stay quiet, he'd deal with this.

The one in city clothes was taller and older than the one in uniform. They both had that sad sort of gotcha in their eyes, like they were so damn sorry they had to ruin things.

"Mr. Desmond? I'm Donny Ireton with the Douglas Station,

Border Patrol? This here's Special Agent Jim Lattimore, FBI. We're tracking a couple walkers, came over the mountains last night. One of them looks like she was pretty badly hurt. Think it's a she, given the tracks, maybe a boy. They lead right up to your house here. I was wondering, anybody stop here this morning, asking for water or medicine or . . ."

The question hovered between them for a moment, like a dare.

"Only one here who needs medicine," he said, "would be my wife. She's got the cancer. Takes chemo twice a week, through this port they sewed into her shoulder? Not like it's done any good. Just makes her sicker, you ask me. Hell of a thing."

The two lawmen made a feeble show of sympathy. Ireton again: "You didn't see anybody?"

"I'm kinda busy with other things."

The city one, FBI agent, Lattimore, was studying Lyndell's face.

"Things ain't been easy here in a while," he added, telling himself inwardly: Shut up. Surest sign of a liar, he talks too much.

Ireton said, "I gotta tell you, Mr. Desmond, it looks like they headed straight for your door. And weren't in good enough shape to get much farther."

"Like I said, I been preoccupied."

Ireton tried to steal a glance inside the house. "Would you mind if I spoke to your wife?"

Lyndell rose up full height—the years hadn't worn him down, not like some men his age. "What part of cancer did you not understand, young man?"

"Mr. Desmond?" It was Lattimore. "I can imagine what it must be like, having two strangers show up at your door at the crack of dawn, one hurt, both of them with God only knows what kind of story as to how they wound up here. Nobody wants trouble. I can understand your helping them out, seeing them on their way, not wanting to make any enemies among the people they may be involved with. But we can help you if you're scared or—"

"I say I'm scared?"

"Not in words. Your eyes, though—"

"Lyndell, who is it?"

She came out of the guest room, stumbled down the hallway, using the wall as a brace. How could he chastise her? She wore only one sock, her robe wrapped tight. She gripped his shoulder hard, staring at the two visitors with empty eyes. "Is there something wrong?"

The two seemed shaken, put off their game. Ireton said, "We're tracking two walkers who came over the mountain last night, Mrs. Desmond."

She looked into her husband's eyes with infinite regret. "Did you tell them?"

He swallowed. It felt like a child's fist in his throat. "I did not."

She glanced back at the strangers at her door. "These two young ones, a boy and a girl, they came by a little after dawn. The girl, she was cut up pretty bad. A wildcat got to her along the pass down the mountain, tore her arm up pretty good. The boy got bit by a tarantula. And he had a pistol. He asked for food and water and a ride to a pickup spot north of Sierra Vista. We're pretty isolated out here. My husband, he fears for me. We couldn't tell what might happen if we put up a fight. Most likely, it wouldn't end too good. So we fed them, gave them a couple bottles of water, looked to their wounds best we could and then my husband here drove them to the spot they wanted. He can tell you better than me where that was."

All eyes turned to Lyndell, none more pleading than hers. His mind froze up—say something, he thought, Christ say anything, it doesn't matter, but his tongue was locked up. "I'm not sure I want to say," he managed finally. "Like you said, the people these folks get tangled up with nowadays, I want no part of them."

"No one needs to know you told us," Ireton said.

"Funny how they always find out though, ain't it."

"They're probably long gone by now, regardless," Audrey said.

"I think we'd still like to know," Ireton said.

It would be the only way to get rid of them, Lyndell realized. "You know the old Rogers place, about a mile beyond the Bisbee slag pond? There's an outbuilding behind the house. That's where I dropped them. About eight this morning, it was. I'm sorry. I know it wasn't right. But you gotta understand what we're dealing with here."

He looked at them pleadingly, his need a truth embedded in his lies. Both men stared back, then Lattimore said, "We're grateful for your time."

Lyndell nodded and watched them turn away, sidle down the walk, then closed the door and said nothing to Audrey—he felt relieved but angry, the anger oddly stronger now that they were gone and that confused him—helping her back to the guest room. The girl was awake, looking weak but stable. The boy held her hand, his chair pulled up close beside the bed.

"I don't think it would be wise for you two to stay here much longer," he told the boy. "Call your aunt, tell her to get to Tucson as fast as she can, any way she can. We can put you up in a motel there until she arrives."

"I can't ask you to do that," Roque said.

"It ain't a favor," Lyndell said.

THEY WAITED UNTIL THE BOY CALLED HIS AUNT AGAIN, MADE ARRANGEMENTS for her to come quick, then the girl tried some broth. It seemed to muster some color. She was strong in spirit, stubborn, you could see that in her eyes once she had her bearings, and she said it was not a problem, she would go whenever and however it was best. Audrey gave her a fresh shirt, something better for the cold than the things she'd brought along in her sad little bag. The boy helped her to her feet and she bit her lip but fixed her eyes on where she had to step and they made their way down the hall, a bump here, a stagger there, then through the kitchen to the garage.

"We'll use the wagon, not the truck," Lyndell said, and the boy helped her into the backseat, let her lie down, covered her with a Hudson blanket Lyndell brought from inside the house. "You go ahead and get yourself situated, I just want to check in on Audrey before we head out."

She was already back in bed, inspecting the tall chrome carriage holding her morphine, a curious look on her face, half grim, half tranquil. His heart sank. He knocked gently on the doorframe and it broke the spell. She glanced up.

"I guess we're heading out."

"Come here, please."

He approached the bed and she opened her arms, he leaned down for what he thought would be a hug but she took his face in her hands, kissed him drily, tenderly on the lips. "I have loved you with all my heart, Lyndell, but never so much as today."

It felt like she'd stabbed him with a knife. "You're not gonna do something foolish."

"Not foolish, no."

"Audrey, please."

"You do love me, don't you, Lyndell."

He was trembling all over. His voice left him, then came back, a whisper. "Good God, woman."

She put her fingers to his lips. "Go do what you need to. You know I'd come with you if I could. I'll be here when you get back, don't fear that, all right?"

"Promise me."

"Lyndell, one of these days and soon, too, you're going to have to say—"

"No. Promise me."

"I love you, Lyndell. You are the best man I have ever known.

That day, you remember? Easter Sunday, over at the Murrays' place—my God, you were so damn good-looking. So humble, so shy, so rough. Luckiest day of my life."

"Don't talk like this."

"I'll talk as I please, mister. I've earned that much."

"I can't leave you here, not like this."

"You have to leave me here. And yes, just like this. Now go."

"Promise me."

"I promise. Go."

He didn't dare search her eyes, fearing the lie he would find there. But she was stronger than him and he knew the only thing talk would accomplish would be the wasting of more time. He needed to spare her conscience. He needed to get those two kids somewhere far away.

"I'll be back soon as I'm able."

"You come back as soon as it's right."

He leaned down, kissed her again, lingered—she closed her eyes, the lids webbed with thin blue veins—then left hurriedly, not looking back. Out in the garage he pulled open the roll-up door and squinted against the light, then eased behind the wheel of the station wagon. "My brother-in-law runs this motel near the airfield in Tucson." He cranked the ignition, tugged the gearshift into drive. "You'll be safe there till your aunt comes."

"TOLD YOU," IRETON SAID, TAPPING HIS PEN AGAINST THE STEERING wheel. His other hand held the binoculars. "And it didn't take long."

They were hidden from view, parked on a rise, nestled in a shallow red-rock gulley scruffed with mesquite and cholla. Lattimore watched as the station wagon clipped past on the two-lane road below, heading north toward Tucson.

"Someone in the passenger seat too," Ireton said, "not the

wife. A man or boy. Plus a third person, lying down in back. Learn more when we pull them over."

Lattimore tracked the path of the car, thinking: a boy. Most likely the kid brother, Roque. Somehow he'd survived, made it over. With a girl in tow.

They'd found Happy's body yesterday outside Naco, sprawled below a scarp of rock, like somebody'd shot him out of the sky. The coyotes didn't improve things. Lattimore had tried to keep a handle on himself, project a stern remove as the Mexican forensics crew waved off the flies, probing the corpse for its secrets, but he remembered the edgy young man who couldn't get down even a mouthful of soup in the Vietnamese restaurant that rainy day. Probably the worst CI ever, he thought, which was a kind of testament, snitches being what they are. He thought as well of the woman, Élida—Lucha, her family called her, tough old bird, had to admire that. Just a few days ago, she'd had a family. Now, maybe, she had a nephew. And his fate was hardly enviable.

As for the girl, she was a singer, or so McIlvaine said, one last tip, surprisingly low-key. He seemed rankled by the ungodly spin the Mexicans were putting on Samir's death—terrorist my ass, words to that effect—but like the bureau, he and the Banneret group, whoever the hell they were, saw no percentage in exposing the sideshow for what it was. Let it go, he told himself, walk away, everyone involved in this mess had an angle. The world as it is. The things you don't know about what happened the past few weeks would no doubt fill a very fat book.

Exhibit A: Andy McIlvaine. He'd predictably gone cagey as to where or how he'd come across his info on the girl but she was some sort of tribute from the Salvadoran *mareros* to Don Pato, the gangster who ran this stretch of the Arizona line. Which meant Roque was a marked man. Killers are sentimental. They remember the gifts they've been promised, none more so than the ones that never show up.

There was just one last thing to take care of then. Lattimore wished he could find some way to feel better about it.

They'd done a net-worth analysis on all the agents out of the Douglas Station. Ireton's ex-wife had inexplicably come into some very valuable property around Lake Havasu. Interesting thing about ex-wives, even the ones still friendly. Forced into a corner, they tended to talk.

Ireton put the binoculars down. "Let's wrap this up." He reached for the gearshift.

Lattimore, getting there first, lodged it in place. "Tell you the truth," he said, "I'm a lot more interested in this call you got from across the border than I am in following that wagon."

THEY RODE IN SILENCE, NOTHING BUT THE RUMBLE OF THE MOTOR AND the hum of the tires against the pavement, the crush of the desert wind. Lyndell's eye traveled from the road to the speedometer to his mirrors, making sure he did nothing to encourage a restless cop hoping for a pull-over. Occasionally the boy, Roque, glanced over his shoulder at the girl and a couple times he reached out his hand, she took it, and they rode like that for a while, no words between them.

Sometimes, out of the corner of his eye, Lyndell caught the boy's expression and saw such devotion there, he felt humbled. His mother, his uncle, his cousin the badass, his brother the war hero—the boy had lost them all. And yet look at him. Maybe that was the key. Was there a way to know love, he wondered, before you understood death? So much of life seemed like a rush to get elsewhere. He felt small—only now, with Audrey so near the end, did he really get it. How much time did I waste, he wondered, because I thought there was a way out?

Out of nowhere, the boy said, "Your wife, she reminds me of my aunt." He sat with that a second, studying the desert. "I owe her, my aunt I mean. Same way I owe you and your wife."

Lyndell spotted a red-tailed hawk soaring low over the sunlit bluffs. A feeling like envy came over him: to be free like that, to fly. "Forget about owing us anything."

"I won't forget." Again, he reached back for the girl's hand. "I'm not just saying that."

AT THE MOTEL IN TUCSON, LYNDELL SPOKE BRIEFLY WITH CHET, Audrey's sister's husband. The place was timeworn but clean, a pre-freeway relic used mostly now by families visiting someone at the air force base. Chet had inherited the motel from his mother's people. He was a soft pale man with an ample face ruined by drink then reclaimed by Jesus. He'd already gotten a call from Audrey, knew the situation. "Don't know what's gotten into you two." He said it in a whisper though no one was there to overhear, handing over the room key. "But if somebody's gonna call the law, ain't gonna be me. Too damn old to find new kin."

"They won't be trouble," Lyndell said. "They'll stay in the room till the aunt shows up, should be late tomorrow. I'd stick around myself, make sure it all goes okay, but I want to get back." He had a hard time getting that last bit out. He breathed in deep, then added, "You know."

Chet shook his head, his eyes a sorrow in themselves. "I can't hardly imagine."

"Yeah. Well." Lyndell coughed into his fist. "The girl out there in the car, she's not in too good shape, neither."

"What if she needs doctoring?"

Lyndell shook his head. "She should be okay. If not, it's not your problem, go ahead and call 911. Only so much you can do."

Chet glanced up at the TV perched over the reception desk. "Roger that."

Lyndell returned to the car, helped the boy get the girl up and out of the backseat, let them into their room. The door was pitted from years of windblown sand. Inside, the raw ammonia smell hung like a pall. The girl walked as though the pain was holding her up and plowed straight for the bed, collapsed onto the edge, then shamefacedly refused to lie down, sitting there, panting, eyes closed. Proud. The boy stood there, waiting for her to say something, tell him what she needed. Look at us, Lyndell thought, two men, a lifetime between us, both so damn helpless.

He stirred himself into motion. "Lie low till your aunt gets here," he told Roque, turning on the bedside lamp, fussing the curtains closed. "You'll get no trouble from Chet." He found it hard to look at the girl, too much like looking at Audrey. "There's a market just up the road, get yourself some food or drinks. But I'd stay inside as much as possible, I were you." He stood there a moment, feeling weighed down, then: "I need to get back."

The boy walked him out to the car. Lyndell had nothing more to say and hoped the boy didn't, either. You don't need to repay me damn it, he wanted to say, but why be rude?

Finally the boy cleared his throat and started in again on how he'd never forget their kindness, Lyndell only half listening. It felt like his whole insides were tangled up in nettles. A sixteen-wheeler rumbled past and screamed to a hissing stop at the traffic signal but the boy just raised his voice and kept on talking and despite a kind of weary grace what Lyndell saw in his eyes was fear. To love is to be afraid, he thought, then suddenly the boy was pumping his hand and he turned back and disappeared inside the room, at which point Lyndell found himself just standing there, his mind as blank as a wall of chalk.

He slipped behind the station wagon's wheel, then couldn't bring himself to start the motor. He thought about what she'd said, so humble so shy so rough, luckiest day of her life. I have loved you with all my heart but never so much as today. He knew what was waiting for him back at the house, he'd been secretly picturing it the entire time while trying to think of anything but. He wished with all his heart there was some other way home.

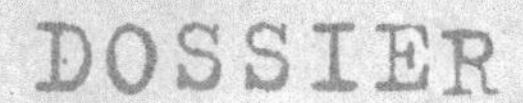

Do They Know I'm Running?

DAVID CORBETT

GOING HUMBLY

An Ear for Tone

I grew up in central Ohio, a fairly provincial and racially segregated backwater at the time, despite the presence of the statehouse and one of the country's largest universities, Ohio State. Before I left, this was changing; African Americans were gaining ground politically, economically and socially, the university's international draw in both students and faculty was quite literally changing the face of the local community, and Columbus was growing into the major metropolis it has become. But I saw firsthand, at times within my own home, the sometimes subtle and other times quite blatant transformation of small-town rectitude and middle-American conformity into racist fear and anger and contempt.

The word "nigger" was a constant drumbeat among the working-class white guys I hung out with, so much so that by the time I made my first black friend—his name was Adrian Bennett, we were both fourteen, working together as volunteers at the Center for Science and Industry—I was startled by how "normal," how like myself, he was.

I felt embarrassed by this reaction and still do. Although I was not paralyzed by white guilt, I realized I was by no means innocent. I bore the emotional and conceptual baggage of my place and time and no amount of feel-good hipness could cure me completely.

In a way racism is not unlike alcoholism. The tendency cannot be escaped, merely controlled, and the control requires insight, honesty and discipline. Put differently, it requires one to become more fully human. And like an alcoholic, I very much wish I did not have the thoughts and feelings and impulses I still sometimes observe within myself. I wish I was color-blind, race-blind. Instead, I have tried to become insightful and conscientious, I've learned to question and control my impulses, I've learned to listen and observe.

Much has changed. I now live in a very mixed community in a California neighborhood so diverse I once reflected, during our yearly Nationwide Night Out get-together, that I and my neighbors looked like we'd been transplanted from a Jonathan Demme movie—white, blacks, Latinos, Filipinos, all intermingling effortlessly with genuine warmth and fondness. We look out for one another and involve ourselves in one another's lives.

It's the twenty-first century. All is well, no?

When I first came to California in the mid-seventies, I worked briefly at a Los Angeles restaurant with a largely Mexican staff. I was supervised by a waiter named Ramon, who asked me to help him learn French, in return for his help in teaching me Spanish. But Ramon was not merely generous and curious. He was also proud, world-wise and reserved. He knew that I, as an Anglo, might easily replace him as head waiter if the Caucasian owners saw fit or if customers groused. The other Mexican waiters also treated me with a mix of helpfulness and detachment; one actually picked a fight with me in the dressing room. And though none of the other waiters who were there came to my defense, none of them jumped in to help my adversary either. The fight was between me and him; we could fend for ourselves.

What is strange to me upon reflection of these incidents is how different in character my feelings were at the time than the racism I'd known growing up. There were clearly tensions between us—and those tensions were the result of our being of different color and class and culture—but there was also an awareness of one another as human. I'd known no Latinos in central Ohio; the Great Brown Threat had yet to register on our radar. I had not been indoctrinated in community-wide resentment and fear. Latin Americans were not the Other, to be feared and mistrusted, controlled and repelled. Not yet, anyway.

But I remain very much attuned to tone. I have a pretty good radar for bigotry, due to my own struggles with it. It's for that reason that I've grown increasingly disturbed at the poisonous distortions that too often overwhelm the immigration debate. I detect in the shrillness that old familiar fear and guilt and anger, with its gloss of righteous indignation and "common sense" and its rhetoric of protection—defense of our borders, our laws, our culture, our way of life.

One of the most frequent things one hears is the epithet "illegal immigrant," with the underlying insinuation that the undocumented are intrinsically criminals, since their very existence in this country is testimony to their violating our immigration statutes. And criminals deserve no compassion, no respect, no "amnesty."

I see the situation somewhat differently. When my wife was dying of cancer, she was once in such extreme pain that, as I drove her to the emergency room, I ran two stop signs and a red light, driving over eighty miles per hour in twenty-five-miles-per-hour zones. She later thanked me, even though what I did was clearly against the law. I would do it again.

The "crime" attributed to undocumented immigrants in crossing the border is analogous—and much less dangerous to everyone but themselves. They do what they must for the sake of the well-being of their loved ones. If this is the moral outrage immigration opponents make it out to be, show me the innocent. Are we to champion as virtuous the heartless, the indifferent, the scared, the ones willing to just sit there and watch their families suffer under the oppressive weight of corruption, poverty and crime that increasingly characterize Mexico and Central America—conditions for which the United States, though not entirely at fault, is nonetheless far from blameless?

The Latino Patriots

Something else was happening while the anti-immigrant backlash was building: Latinos were joining the military in unprecedented numbers. Not just that—their casualties in the Iraq war were disproportionately higher than their representation in the armed services as a whole (11% compared to 9%).

Interestingly, the reasons Latino recruits gave for enlisting was not just the expedited path to full citizenship put into effect by Congress at the request of the Bush administration, though that did frequently remain a motivating factor. A Rand National Defense Research Institute study revealed that in post-enlistment surveys Latino recruits listed "patriotism" and "service to country" as the top two reasons for joining the service, followed by "duty" and "honor." Many soldiers noted that their families were proud of them, even if they disagreed with the Iraq war.

Despite this, legislation was drafted in the House of Representatives that would make being an undocumented immigrant a felony, forever barring a path to citizenship or even legal status. And attempts to provide a means to citizenship for the children of undocumented workers, many of whom arrived as infants and know no other country than the U.S., were sabotaged by the anti-immigrant bloc in Congress.

To paraphrase the father of a Latino U.S. marine killed in Iraq: On the one hand they're recruiting the young men to fight and die, while on the other they're kicking the parents and children out of the country.

Outrage is a luxury. Writers write, and I felt a particular need to contribute something, to bark back at the distorting invective. I felt it particularly important that Anglos chime in on the side of Latinos out of a sense of justice and simple decency. Silence was not an option.

But I'm a novelist, not a pundit. And what right does an American mutt like me, a white boy from the very heart of Middle America, have to depict in fiction the life of a Latino family?

The old arguments against white authors imagining the lives of people of color addressed power, maintaining that the servant always understood the master, if only out of bald necessity and naked survival, but the master was intrinsically self-deluded about the servant. Such reasoning, with its colonial baggage, elevated the term "insensitivity" to a cultural death sentence. The damning reception inflicted on William Styron's *The Confessions of Nat Turner,* in which the author tried to mine the inner lives of African slaves, would be hard to replicate today, and that's a good thing. No work of art deserves to be strangled in its crib. But that doesn't mean we've all somehow become sensitive.

I studied math and music, both arguably universal languages. And though I came to Latino culture first through fiction—Borges, Amado, Cortazar—I gained my greatest appreciation of it through music, perhaps its most accessible art form. Also, being raised Catholic, I felt a special fascination with the manner in which religion took hold in the southerly Americas, both Gothic and primitive, awake to suffering, fiercely immediate. From where I sat, Latin culture in general and its music in particular possessed a vibrancy, a passion, a sense of both the tragic and the absurd I found mesmerizing and too often lacking in what I saw and heard around me here in the States. Steely Dan was a hip act but Santana could blister your soul. And Santana led me to Tito Puente, who led me to Ray Barretto, who led me to Poncho Sanchez and on and on: Willie Bobo to Eric Bobo to Los Lobos to Celso Piña to Control Machete to Julieta Venegas to Ana Gabriel to Pescozada . . . The chain hasn't stopped in thirty years. I pray to God it never does.

Admiring a culture, though, doesn't grant me a right to depict it in my own work. Artists steal from one another at will, musicians especially; it's almost lazy not to. But can fiction writers get away with it?

All artists are outsiders to the extent they observe more than they participate, but everyone joins in to some degree, just as we all reflect. Rather, the crucial question seems to be at what point does observation fail us, i.e., when do we begin to imagine, and why?

I began with my third novel, *Blood of Paradise,* because I felt a need to address the current state of affairs in El Salvador, a country whose current political, social and economic life was significantly affected by U.S. policy, and which I saw being alarmingly misrepresented by those who wished to propose a "Salvador Option" in Iraq. I also had Salvadoran friends who introduced me to their country, and felt an obligation to portray it as they saw it.

Do They Know I'm Running? was simply a continuation of that trajectory, an attempt to depict, as best I could, the effect on Latino families of current immigration policy; the predation on migrants by organized crime and street gangs who now control the underground railroad that transports not just drugs and guns but human beings into the U.S.; and the various ills befalling Mexico and Central America. I was moved because I see these effects all around me in people I know and interact with daily or have met in my travels, some of whom are not just acquaintances but colleagues, neighbors, friends—people for whom in many cases I feel not just fondness but admiration, and whose lives I felt deserved a more fair and honest representation than they were too often getting in the media.

Roque was partially inspired by a number of young Latino

musicians I have met and befriended during performances at various Bay Area venues, some of whom reminded me of my own musical career with its hopes and hardship, the disillusion, the resilience.

Godo was partially conceived after reading accounts of real Latino servicemen who returned from Iraq, with further inspiration provided by my encounters with Latino-American men and women in uniform at the U.S. Southern Command and the Western Hemisphere Institute for Security Cooperation.

Tía Lucha was based on a number of Salvadoran immigrants I have met, including a single divorcee I know who lost her job as office manager for a German construction firm in San Salvador after the 2002 earthquake and was forced to emigrate to find work, leaving her aging mother behind with the hope of building a better future for her children here in the States.

Happy came to me as a patchwork, pieced together from traits observed in various young men I know, one a photographer who supports himself by managing the best taco wagon in my home town, another who works as a paramedic, tending the injured and saving lives while constantly worrying about being deported.

Tío Faustino was a fusion of my own father, who drove a truck to put himself through college and sometimes dreamed of running his own trucking firm; a handful of port truck drivers to whom I was introduced by Ron Carver of the International Brotherhood of Teamsters; and some of the interviewees of documentary filmmaker Don North, who returned to Guazapa Volcano after twenty years to talk to the survivors of the civil war offensive that took place there.

The gang members depicted in the book were modeled after real young men (and their families and friends) whom I met in my travels to Central America or while working as a private investigator, in the latter case when I was entrusted with protecting their rights, their freedom, sometimes even their lives.

But in all these cases I blended the true with the imagined, what I knew with what I felt the story required. And taking that additional step, that leap of imagination, is an act of presumption, yes, but also an act of love. In a way we imagine one another every day. So simple an act as reading a facial expression, whether that of a stranger or an old friend, requires innumerable acts of interpretation we make unconsciously—"interpretation" being the guise imagination assumes to appear more reliable. And as we imagine others, so they imagine us. Are we to believe we never really know the difference, cannot know the difference, between when we're loved and when we're misunderstood—or worse, getting used?

John Coltrane once remarked that when there is something we do not understand we must go humbly to it. That humility is the test of our honesty. Our art will demonstrate not just our understanding—our *sensitivity,* or lack thereof—but how honest we allow ourselves to be, not just about our subject matter, but ourselves.

If we sense sloppiness or laziness or sentimentality, or even a bigoted indifference disguised as a well-meaning advocacy, we can justifiably criticize the result, regardless of who the artist is or what the work portrays. This is a question not just of execution, however, but of motive, and all such inquiries are slippery. We can hardly accuse an artist of botching something he doesn't understand by attributing to him motives we cannot possibly know. The inner life of the artist is no less inscrutable than the soul of the *vato.*

But if the era of identity politics is coming to a close, the craving for authenticity is as strong as ever—thus the popularity of so-called reality programming on TV. Everybody wants the real dope, even the person who wouldn't recognize it if it sat on his head. But the authentic is an illusion, we never possess the truth, we approach it—not just with our eyes but our imaginations. And, if we are wise like Coltrane, we do so humbly. We do so in a spirit of love, not empowerment. And if we are honest with ourselves, we know the difference.

ACKNOWLEDGMENTS

The author owes a profound debt of thanks to the following individuals, without whom this book would not exist: Jane von Mehren and Mark Tavani and Kelli Fillingim and everyone at Random House/Mortalis for their devotion and detailed attention to the project, with special appreciation for Sean Mills, Karla Eoff and Vanessa López for their painstaking review of the manuscript, without which it would be a far inferior book; Laurie Fox for her continuing belief in my work; Leslie Schwerin for her careful slog through and editorial critique of an early draft, as well as her knowledgeable remarks concerning Mexico; Jay Pirouznia for playing wheelman during our field trip to the Arizona border and so much else; Lorenzo Fernandez and Ron Carver for their assistance in understanding the plight of port truck drivers; Joe & Mary Anne DeYoung for their help in connecting with members of the U.S. Marine Corps, including Capt. Joshua Bates, USMC, who in turn referred me to Annette Amerman, lead researcher in the reference branch at the USMC History Division, The National Marine Corps Museum, and Alicia Whitley, head archivist at the Gray Research Center, Marine Corps University; Maryellen Dament, who introduced me to her son, Troy, whose recollections of his training at Camp Pendleton and his service with the 1st LAR in Iraq were invaluable; Ana Ramirez, who as always helped keep me up-to-date regarding events large and small in El Salvador; Don North for providing transcripts of his interviews with survivors of the forced *guinda* off Guazapa Volcano during the Salvadoran civil war, especially the accounts of Dimas Rojas and Chepe Murillo; Ed & Cristina Hyland at Casa Azul in San Marcos on Lake Atitlán, for their generous help in finding assistance and information on present-day life in Guatemala, including but not limited to their roles in introducing me to Evi & Erik, my Guatemalan *guias*; Major Barbara Fick, US Southern Command, for her assistance in finding a liaison at the US embassy in Guatemala City; former Ambassador James M. Derham, and Scott E. Smith, Public Information Officer, U.S. Embassy, Guatemala, for taking time from their demanding schedules to discuss the current situation in Guatemala; Special Agent George Fong, FBI, for his contributions on understanding bureau procedure and methodology, as well as a law enforcement perspective on Mara Salvatrucha; Eugene Rodiguez and Lucina Rodriguez of Los Cenzontles Mexican Arts Center for their tutelage on Mexican music and art; Bob Bausch and Joyce Maynard, both remarkable writers and exemplary teachers, for their review of parts of the manuscript and general encouragement; and the superb authors Luis Alberto Urrea, Francisco Goldman and Horacio Castellanos Moya, for anchoring a gringo author's imaginings in something resembling real life and providing moral support they probably hadn't the faintest clue they were offering. These knowledgeable individuals were exceedingly generous with their time and expertise; any errors, omissions or misrepresentations in the text are entirely the fault of the author.

DAVID CORBETT is the author of three critically acclaimed novels: *The Devil's Redhead*, *Done for a Dime* (a *New York Times* Notable Book), and *Blood of Paradise*—nominated for numerous awards, including the Edgar, and named one of the Top Ten Mysteries and Thrillers of 2007 by the *Washington Post* and a *San Francisco Chronicle* Notable Book. His short fiction and essays have appeared in numerous periodicals and anthologies, and his story "Pretty Little Parasite," from *Las Vegas Noir*, was selected for inclusion in *Best American Mystery Stories 2009*. For more, go to www.davidcorbett.com.